PARADISOS

A NOVEL

BILL KOKKARIS

*The greatest of blessings come to us through madness
when it is sent as a gift of the gods.*

—Plato, Phaedrus *244a*

PART 1
TRANSIT, MAY 2015

CHAPTER 1
The *Grand Duchess*

The ever-triumphant Emilio Politis sat at the helm of the *Grand Duchess* as she glided down the sun-drenched coast of Phaedros. The late afternoon Aegean Sea lay silky smooth, a vast sheet of sapphire stretching to the horizon. A tumbler of whisky in hand, he let out a deep sigh before tasting the amber elixir. Satisfied, he sank into the bucket seat, filling his lungs with the warm spring air. For a rare moment, his frenzied world had paused, or so it seemed. Perhaps it was the sea. He loved the sea: the infinite blue; its deep, hidden possibilities. Or perhaps it was the thought that, at thirty-two, he stood on the verge of becoming Greece's most celebrated hotelier.

The past week drifted across his memory like warm honey. Paradisos II, his recently opened boutique resort, had just hosted the Thirty-Fourth European Antiquity Conference, drawing academics and dignitaries from across the globe. The island had buzzed with life—tavernas spilling into the streets, craftsmen working all hours, tour companies invading every archaeological site. It was the height of summer in the midst of spring. The success of the conference affirmed Emilio's importance—to himself, his family and the island's fragile economy. For Phaedros, it was a renaissance; for Emilio, a vindication. The little boy who once hid beneath his father's shop in Sydney to escape the noise of a forced migration had become the island's future.

And yet, even amid the fanfare, he could not escape the whispers surrounding his broken engagement to Eva Galanos—local lawyer, valiant beauty, and once the other half of the island's power couple. Their separation had deprived the community of a long-anticipated wedding, a spectacle to distract from its economic misery.

The invitation to the overnight cruise came at the last minute. Andrew Bekiaris, captain of the luxury yacht, contacted Emilio after two guests cancelled. Four years older and brimming with Californian charm, Andrew had become both friend and business partner. His charter company now serviced the resort's exclusive sea tours. A man raised on boats, he'd inherited the *Grand Duchess* from his grandfather, who ran cruises along the Californian coast. But Andrew decided to relocate to be close to his estranged Greek father on the island of Samos and grow his business in the Aegean. From their first meeting two years earlier, Emilio had admired his confidence, golden looks, optimism and humour—and perhaps most of all, the unspoken kinship between two men who, by different routes, had come to call Greece home.

For one night, Emilio was willing to set work aside and delegate command to his managers. But Eva was another matter. Though no longer engaged, they still met in secret; weekend getaways in foreign cities, passionate encounters to remind them of their youth. Both, however, were unwilling to offer their families or the island any false hope of reconciliation.

After the conference, he promised her a trip. She wanted Paris; he preferred something less romantic. Andrew, attuned to the vague, unspoken terms of their relationship, had assured him their privacy would be safe among strangers at sea. He texted Andrew: *See you at the port at 4 p.m. Eva will join us.* He sent the message without hesitation, ignoring a niggling reminder that impulsive decisions were fraught with cracks.

***

Andrew leaned into the microphone, announcing in a Southern drawl laid on thick, 'Dolphins! Starboard side. On your left!'

Six grey bottlenose dolphins threaded the surface of the water, eager to race. The Texan guests clambered to the side with their cameras and phones.

Embracing his competitive spirit, Andrew pushed on the throttle. 'They love it if you wave and shout out "S'agapo",' he teased over the PA, winking at Emilio.

Eva, stretched out in her deckchair, twisted her slender neck and lowered her sunglasses down her nose to give him a dry look before joining the others.

'My fellow Americans are so easily amused,' Andrew said after cutting the mic. 'I can make up stories about Poseidon and Odysseus and have them eating out of my hand.'

Emilio barely heard him. His eyes were fixed on the coastline, imagining a new resort—its access, its theme, its capacity. Expansion had never seriously crossed his mind, yet now it seemed plausible, maybe not straightaway, but once the crisis had passed and austerity lifted. His train of thought was suddenly interrupted by one of the dolphins vaulting from the water, its sleek skin flashing a glint of sunlight into his eyes. Could he ever be so free? Content with the simplest of things—eating, breathing, breeding, revelling in the sea with no enemy in sight?

When he finally turned back to Andrew, he asked, 'And what do you tell your Greek guests?'

'Politics,' Andrew grinned. 'Last week, I told a group of posh Athenians: "Tsipras, mas tripas tis tsepes."'

Emilio laughed. The jab about the prime minister putting holes in people's pockets was timely. Like many, he had voted for Alexis Tsipras, hoping Greece might rise from the ridicule of the 'Greek Crisis'. For now, though, he was content to let the *Grand Duchess* hold him and Andrew aloft like trophy figurines—Andrew in his white polo and camel shorts, and Emilio looking equally dashing in white linen pants, a powder pink shirt and blue loafers. In a climate of austerity, running a luxury business required a degree of pretence. Like the new political leader, both men sensed a new era. Imparting that hope to tourists bolstered their confidence.

***

The dolphins had run their course and disappeared into the sea. Guests returned to their deckchairs while Eva remained standing, hands clasping the railings, gazing out at the sea. She resembled a ship's figurehead, her sheer aqua dress draped elegantly over her slender frame, fluttering in the breeze. For a moment, Emilio imagined the goddess Artemis in all her vengeance. Was a bow and arrow about to be drawn?

'Is Eva cool?' Andrew asked.

Emilio looked away, sidestepping his friend's concern. He hated it when Eva withdrew into herself like that. It usually meant she was either sulking or scheming, probably because he wasn't beside her or for ignoring her preference for Paris. Even now, though they were no longer together, her silence remained just as effective.

'Perfect cruising conditions,' Emilio cheered with some effort. 'Thank you for inviting us.'

***

Later, after Emilio's recommendation, the itinerary shifted. Instead of Thea Beach, they would head to the secluded Butterfly Cove. The guests cheered at the prospect of an exclusive detour to a promised oasis. Eva remained silent during the announcement. She slid her sunglasses back over her eyes and returned to her book. She hadn't swum yet, so Emilio assumed she'd jump at the opportunity. After all, he had proposed to her there.

Butterfly Cove lay to the south—the greener part of the island— just beyond the next peninsular. More breathtaking than Thea

Beach, the remote sanctuary was protected by a narrow, rocky entrance. A cavern at the base of a twenty-metre cliff provided access to a small emerald lagoon known as Artemis's Bath. Ancient tablets described how deer and peacocks gathered around the edges to watch the goddess bathe before she chased them into the forest.

As the yacht approached the cove, Emilio called out to Eva on his way to their cabin. She waved him away without looking up from her book. He was surprised if not irritated by her flippant gesture, expecting some speck of enthusiasm. After changing into his swimmers, he took a swig of whisky from the minibar and felt the heat rise along the back of his neck.

The *Grand Duchess* manoeuvred through the narrow headlands into a hidden aquatic amphitheatre. Cliffs and trees circled the mirrored water; wisteria and poplars painted ripples of colour on the still surface. A sudden scent of daphne filled the pristine air. As the yacht came to anchor, a school of bream gathered close before vanishing into the depths.

Emilio took the lead and climbed onto the diving board at the stern. Toned and tanned in his striped trunks, he stood tall—182 centimetres of effortless confidence—looking like a member of the Greek water polo team. Diving in, he sliced clean through the crystal-clear water and felt the cool relief wash over his elevated body heat.

One by one, the guests followed. Only Eva remained aboard.

'Come on, Eva! It's beautiful!' someone called.

'I know it's beautiful,' she replied assertively. 'I'll give it a miss.'

Emilio was a little surprised to see Eva and Andrew standing so close to each other. When she first met him at the resort's opening, she had found him vain and full of himself. Now, he was pouring her champagne, looking like a young Robert Redford, and she like a faded beauty queen. Emilio's jaw tightened as he ducked back underwater.

When he resurfaced, one of the female guests latched onto his shoulders.

'Caught you!' she laughed.

Emilio guessed she was a yoga instructor—high cheekbones, tight hair, bronze complexion and a long neck.

'Don't think so,' he replied, swimming away, unwilling to yield to anyone.

Leading the guests towards the shadow of a cliff, he paused just short of the entrance to the cave. A slight breeze had picked up, carrying the scent of the large oriental sweetgum that jutted awkwardly from the limestone above. As a teenager, he imagined it as a horse's head, which he'd climb and leap from into the water below. For now, the ancient tree was the signpost to Artemis's Bath.

Once the guests had gathered before him, he whispered, 'Look up.'

Emilio's sudden clap reverberated around them, startling an older woman into a small yelp. Thousands of brown and orange patterned butterflies lifted from the rock face, littering the sky like confetti. Putting a finger to his lips, Emilio signalled for everyone to stay quiet, allowing the butterflies to settle back onto the cliff face. Once the sky had cleared, Emilio said in a dulcet tone, 'And that's why it's called Butterfly Cove.'

One guest, unable to contain himself, clapped again. The butterflies startled back into the air.

'Please, no more clapping,' Emilio snapped. 'You're disturbing their habitat!'

The culprit apologised after his wife slapped him across the shoulder. Although Emilio recognised his hypocrisy, he felt a sense of entitlement; after all, this was his island, and the only reason they were here was because of his goodwill.

As the butterflies resettled, Emilio beckoned the party into the cave, shouting out with a half-teasing grin, 'Watch out for bats!' While only a few metres from the cave's exit, it was dark enough to warrant a few jitters. They all followed, spellbound and compliant.

Once they emerged into the light, they found themselves in a turquoise lagoon lined with golden sand. In the background, the jungle-like foliage muffled the sound of partridges rummaging behind the thick green canopy of vines and trees. But the tranquil moment was suddenly broken by a scream. Floating near the shore was a bright orange mass. The guests recoiled with mutterings of sea monsters. Undeterred, Emilio swam closer, heart hammering, contemplating a washed-up giant octopus or jellyfish. Treading closer, he soon realised that it was a cluster of life jackets, held together by seaweed that trailed like tentacles.

'What is it?' someone from the group called out.

'Discarded life jackets,' he replied, holding them up as he tried to determine their origin. 'Perhaps from another boat.'

'Could belong to a smuggler's boat from Turkey,' someone else suggested.

'Turkey is too far,' Emilio responded. 'We don't get refugee boats out here.'

Still, a chill seized him. He thought of his mother's stories of refugees from the nearby island of Chios fleeing during the War of Independence. She always reminded him that he was descended from refugees, his ancestor Irini Vlahos among them escaping with her only surviving daughter, Mary. It was said that the old woman was a witch, and her arrival had tainted the island with a curse that could never be lifted. As a boy, Emilio lost interest at that point, still reeling from being uprooted from his beloved corner shop in Sydney. The only memory that plagued his childhood was his mother's promise of a life in paradise.

CHAPTER 2
Refugee camp, South Türkiye

Maryam Hamoud sat cross-legged in her tent reading one of her favourite texts on chemistry. It was the only book she'd taken the day they fled. Though no longer blessed with their beloved pharmacy, the book anchored her to the person she had once been: a mind that measured, configured, analysed and tested. In its pages she recalled the quiet alchemy of her craft, the transformation of powders and liquids into hope. Placing a vial in a customer's hand and hearing their gratitude had filled her with a joy that no exile could erase.

It was early afternoon, and rain lightly tapped like grains of rice on the roof of the tent. Her young daughter, Maya, rested beside her, wrapped in her blanket on the foam mattress. The recent influx of almost 300 refugees had worsened the camp's already chaotic situation. Everyone was trying to adjust, overwhelmed by their new reality. Some wandered aimlessly; others rushed about as if under threat. Wait times for the communal kitchen and bathrooms grew longer, as did the queues for food rations. The stench of smoke, sewage and stale rubbish thickened in the air. At night, the cries of babies broke the howls of jackals echoing from the mountains surrounding the tent city.

Bassel, being the man he was, helped where he could, pitching tents, repairing fences and stocking shelves with supplies. Each evening he played his oud to lull Maya, their two-year-old, to sleep.

Maryam spent most of the day alone in the tent with their spirited toddler. When not reading or tending to her, she embroidered. With no cotton to spare, she would finish one piece, then undo it and start over. The young couple tried to make a home of their tent, decorating it with the few items they brought from Aleppo—two small silk rugs and a framed photo of themselves outside their pharmacy. It was taken the day Maryam learned she was pregnant. Bassel's white teeth beamed behind his dark beard; his eyes sparkled. She vanished into him as his broad frame enveloped hers.

When Mr Pepsi showed up at their tent that afternoon waving documents, it was as if they had won the lottery. There was always some fanfare when he prowled the camp, but this time the people smuggler appeared rushed and slightly agitated. Maryam noticed the sweat darkening the underarms and sides of his shirt, making the gold he wore glint more than usual. Maryam didn't like the lanky Turk, who strutted about in oversized suits and bulky American joggers. Using a stupid name like Mr Pepsi infuriated her.

'It's a name given to me by my American colleague,' he had giggled when Bassel first quizzed him about it. 'Isn't it obvious? My dark complexion and fuzzy blond hair.'

Though he thought otherwise, Maryam felt his dyed hair made him look ridiculous. But they were so desperate to leave the camp that she put up with his annoying presence. Smugglers swaggered and schemed around them; most behaved far worse than Mr Pepsi. Bassel found him silly but trustworthy, recalling how he successfully arranged his cousin's travel to Germany six months earlier. Patrizio, the security guard, reassured them that Mr Pepsi was one of the better smugglers—just a small cog in a larger network that exploited his demeanour to lure new clients. Maryam trusted Patrizio. The rugged middle-aged Italian with a thundery chuckle had become a daily comfort, stopping by to entertain Maya with his juggling tricks. He would never put Maya in a dangerous situation.

Clinging to that belief, Maryam tolerated all that unsettled her about Mr Pepsi.

***

The Hamouds had been living in the refugee camp for nearly two years. Their sixteen-square-metre tent stood among thousands of others lined along narrow paths. Recent rains had turned these dusty paths into muddy trails, making it impossible to keep their living quarters clean. The small silk rugs once laid at the entrance were quickly rolled away and replaced with old towels picked up from the clothing bin. As months went by, the pride of making the tent homely dwindled. The ban on indoor cooking—imposed after a fire from a gas stove—further alienated Maryam from her domestic setting. Cooked meals now had to be prepared in the communal kitchen. Since giving birth and fleeing Aleppo, Maryam had lost her desire to socialise and avoided the communal areas.

Before escaping, Bassel and Maryam had stocked up on medicines. Packed in old biscuit tins were what they considered essentials: antidepressants, cold and flu tablets, ibuprofen, antidiarrheals, antibiotics and antiseptics. While she managed to keep her depression at bay, supplies were soon exhausted. The camp pharmacy offered a limited range and was always running out of stock. At times, she turned to her mother's herbal cures, whose knowledge inspired Maryam to pursue a career in pharmacy. The communal garden, however, only had oregano, parsley and mint, and, like the medications, they were always in short supply.

Thinking of her mother, Maryam felt a sense of relief knowing that she died from natural causes rather than the violence of a bomb, gun or knife. She only wished her mother could have lived long enough to meet her grandchild, a gorgeous little girl with sparkly brown eyes and cherubic cheeks. Her straight, thick hair was so heavy that tying it back was like lifting a wet mop. Maya would have brought comfort to her Jameela, who spent the last decade of her life grieving: first her cherished son in a traffic accident, and then her much-admired husband, a cardiologist who died, ironically, from a heart attack soon after. At least she departed with the Aleppo she loved intact, a city of colour, bustling souks and stunning architecture.

At the community garden, Maryam made friends with an older woman named Renee, also from Aleppo. She was a Christian and had known Maryam's paternal grandfather, who was a renowned chanter at the church during his lifetime. Renee visited their tent and talked about God, religion, the war and how surprised she was by Maryam's conversion to Islam. Bassel didn't think much of her. It wasn't so much her religious beliefs that bothered him as her conversations about fortune-telling.

'That old woman is cunning. She looks at me spitefully from a distance but laughs and flirts with me when I am with you.'

'She has no one,' Maryam said in her defence. 'I remember her when I was a child, and I used to think she was so sophisticated, impeccably dressed in the most beautiful hats. Now she has no hats and no family.'

'They say that she has Satan in her,' Bassel responded.

'Men, of course, would say that. She is harmless, my love. It's all fun she creates with the cards to pass the time, to give her some meaning.'

'Maybe. But many believe what she tells them.'

'Perhaps those who've lost faith in themselves, or their God.'

One afternoon, while Bassel was at the mosque, Maryam succumbed to Renee's pressure and agreed to a reading. Maya was asleep, and Maryam felt particularly vulnerable. She had argued with Bassel that morning about Mr Pepsi, and it left her full of remorse.

Maryam asked when they would leave the camp. Flipping over the Six of Swords, Renee smiled and glanced up at her. The card depicted a man on a small boat looking out to sea. Renee announced in her gravelly voice that travel and better times lay ahead for the Hamoud family. But then the Death card was drawn after Maryam asked about her family's safety. Despite Renee's attempts to reassure her it wasn't a bad card, Maryam couldn't continue. She didn't want to withhold information from her husband, having until that moment shared everything with him: her fears, her concerns, her aspirations. Yet this time, she would tell him nothing, not wanting to disappoint him. She cursed herself for allowing magic to cloud her rational mind. Renee stopped coming to the tent, and Maryam isolated herself further from the community.

***

'The news is very exciting, my friends,' Mr Pepsi said as he sat on the cushion on the floor, huffing and puffing.

'Some tea?' Maryam offered.

'No time.'

'What's the good news?' Bassel asked as he sat opposite him, alert and fidgety, strumming his amber tasbih between his fingers.

'You're leaving tonight!'

'Tonight?' Maryam repeated.

'Yes, yes, tonight is the night you get to leave this hell and continue with your blessed lives.'

'Alhamdulillah!' Bassel erupted.

'Praise be to God,' Maryam repeated. She picked up Maya, who was clinging to her knees, and squeezed her tight. Gazing into her daughter's eyes, she couldn't contain her tears. The moment had come. Maya looked confused.

'Your mother is happy, that's all,' Bassel said, taking Maya in his arms, kissing her on each cheek before tossing her in the air.

'Not too high, Bassel!' Maryam called out, reminding him of the tent's low ceiling as Maya squealed with laughter. Maryam pulled a tissue from under her sleeve and wiped her tears. Mr Pepsi's news had rekindled the fear from the reading. She hadn't said anything to Bassel about Renee's visit and couldn't now ruin his excitement with something so blasphemous.

'You're going on a very big adventure,' Mr Pepsi said as he pulled a lollipop from his shirt pocket. He peeled the wrapping and offered it to the little girl.

Maya's black eyes lit up and her button nose twitched.

'What do you say?' Bassel prompted.

'Thank you.'

'Bravo! You're very welcome. Now, your parents need to sign some documents, and then they can start packing.'

The plan followed the same route as Bassel's cousin: a boat to Greece, a short stay in Germany, and then on to Canada where Bassel's parents fled in 2012. They had been determined to get their youngest son out, no matter the cost, but Maryam's pregnancy had made travel impossible.

The 'safe passage' to Germany was 3000 euros per person—no concessions or discounts considered. Even Maya would be charged the same. The ticket covered all transportation to the Greek island of Lesbos, where Mr Pepsi's representative would issue permits and tickets to Germany. But first they must walk to the outskirts of Altınözü, where an overnight coach would take them to the west coast near Ayvalik.

'It's a secret route that avoids any security patrols. It's an easy three-hour walk from here,' he explained, clearing his throat.

'And to Greece? How do we cross over?' Maryam asked.

'With a ferry, of course. A large ferry with the comforts of a cruise ship. It will be safe and relaxing for you. These ferries are quite fast, so you will be in Lesbos in approximately ninety minutes.'

'I have never travelled on a large boat before,' Bassel added.

'Don't worry, I will throw in some seasickness pills as part of your ticket. But rest assured, the waters of the Aegean are calm all year round. You'll thoroughly enjoy the experience.'

'Will you provide a cart to take our luggage?' asked Bassel.

Mr Pepsi looked him up and down with disdain. Beads of perspiration dripped from his leathery forehead. 'Sorry, sir, this is not possible. Bring only what you need.' He shoved the official papers in front of Bassel. 'Please sign here.'

Bassel scanned the document. At the top of the page was a logo with the words 'Official Anatolian Immigration Services'. At the bottom was a blue crest with a line for signatures.

Mr Pepsi hovered over them, scrutinising their every movement. 'Please, you must hurry. I have another dozen people to see, and I must be out of the camp within the hour. The money, please.'

Bassel and Maryam glanced at each other, nodded and signed the documents. Within seconds, the mobile transfer of the required amount was done. Maryam looked at the photo of the pharmacy that hung above their blow-up bed. She couldn't bear the thought of leaving it behind, but the textbook she would take.

CHAPTER 3
The *Grand Duchess*

It was 7.15 p.m. and the sun was slipping quickly behind the rocky terrain. Vibrant twilight colours began to fill the sky accompanied by a cool evening breeze. A deckhand secured the rails for casting off, while other staff served hors d'oeuvres and champagne to returning guests.

'Where's Eva?' Emilio asked Andrew, patting himself dry.

'She said she was going to get ready for dinner.'

'I see.' Emilio popped a scallop in his mouth and downed his champagne. 'See you all soon' he called out. Everyone thanked him for the side trip to Artemis's Bath.

'Maybe one day you can show me too,' Andrew said.

Emilio turned quickly, a glare in his eye; suspicious he'd made a move on Eva in his absence? Or was it the other way around? He stepped closer. 'If I can't, Eva will show you, seeing she can't bear to swim with me,' he muttered under his breath.

Andrew's blue eyes clouded over, a twitch in his mouth, his cheeks flushing. 'Is something wrong?' he asked.

'With me? No.' Emilio wiped his face. 'You should focus on getting this old battleaxe out of here before she smashes against the headland. Tides can rise quickly at this hour.' He shoved the wet towel onto Andrew's chest and turned to leave.

'Yes, of course!' Andrew replied, tossing the wet towel back at Emilio. 'Wet towels go in the basket at the rear of the boat,' he reminded everyone as he walked towards the helm.

***

Emilio showered and dressed for dinner, choosing black jeans and a cream silk shirt. Eva was already finished, watching him from the mirror as she applied a deep crimson lipstick. The cabin was tiny, barely room for a queen bed, wardrobe and corner shower. She brushed her long, wavy chestnut hair to the side, exposing the left side of her neck. The open back of her green chiffon dress cascaded into soft folds above her waist.

'Nice dress. New?' he asked.

'I bought it in Athens last time we were there.'

'Oh yes. Of course.' Emilio struggled to remember.

The scent of French perfume felt intense. In her hand, a necklace sparkled—a birthday gift from his sister, an 'Aphrodite' original.

'I thought you would have destroyed this already,' he said, taking it from her hand.

She paused. 'I tried to, but it's beautiful. Besides, I try not to hold grudges.'

Emilio rolled his eyes. *Who is she kidding?*

Catching the gesture in the mirror, Eva swung around, snatched the necklace, and threw it against the wall. Crystal blue beads flew everywhere. 'It *was* beautiful,' her face contorting to mask her fury. 'Shall we go up for dinner then?'

Emilio stepped back, watching the beads gather at his feet. He couldn't be bothered defending himself, and she made it easy by suggesting they go to dinner. She snatched her clutch bag from the dressing table and stormed out. When it came to holding grudges, they were evenly matched.

***

The crew had prepared tables for the five couples on the open deck, dressing them in white tablecloths and silver cutlery. Along the deck's handrails, fairy lights flickered to smooth jazz classics. Stars to the east were twinkling as Emilio and Eva gazed upwards, searching for a conversation starter, only to be distracted by chatter from the neighbouring table. It was the yoga woman—Gabriella—and her husband, Simon. They were on their honeymoon—both their second marriage. Gabriella, a historian specialising in the Hellenistic period, praised Emilio for sponsoring the new Artemis Gallery. Emilio blushed, too embarrassed to admit he had yet to see it.

The boat docked for dinner on the other side of the island, 300 metres from shore. Perched opposite was the village of Melissani, its white houses resembling sugar cubes on the incline of Mount Dillinos. The imposing Church of Saint Constantine, the island's patron saint, with its blue rotunda and illuminating white cross, stood at the apex. The village was home to his sister, the renowned artist Aphrodite Politis.

The first course arrived: oysters on a bed of spinach and pine nuts.

'Does she know we're here?' Eva asked, breaking the silence.

'Who?' Emilio replied, knowing exactly whom she meant.

'Your sister.'

He glanced toward Melissani. 'Of course not.' Every time his sister was mentioned, an argument followed. The two women had been close, but it was their public showdown in Melissani that led to Emilio calling off the wedding. He was away in Milan for a few days following their argument over postponing the wedding date a second time. She suspected an affair and went to confide in Aphrodite, who took offence. Surely Eva wasn't now gearing up for another public showdown?

'You gave away our secret place,' she said, voicing the anger festering for hours.

'I figured that's why you're annoyed.'

'You once called it our Garden of Eden.'

'I remember.'

'Do you also remember saying how lucky we are?'

'Yes, I do.'

Her fingers traced the glass, eyes glistening. 'At the time, I thought: How perfect are we? I feel so stupid to have believed it. You've dirtied our special place.'

'I've done nothing of the sort.'

'You took strangers to a place I thought was sacred between us.'

'It's not really ours, though, is it?'

'The point is you initiated it. You wanted it. That's the difference.'

'I was excited to be there.'

Her hand fell flat on the table. Leaning in, she said, 'And I was excited to be somewhere other than Phaedros. This was to be our getaway. Remember?'

Emilio reached across to hold her hand. Her finger—the one that had worn his engagement ring—looked thin and sallow.

'We'll never be what we imagined…Sorry, what *I* imagined,' she said, withdrawing.

***

'How were the oysters?' Andrew asked as he approached their table.

'So good!' Eva replied.

'Delicious,' Emilio agreed.

'Join us,' Eva invited, flicking back her hair.

Andrew hesitated, looking at Emilio, who smiled. The incident with the necklace, the chat with Gabriella and the frank discussion with Eva had softened his stance towards Andrew.

'Please,' Emilio said, gesturing for him to sit.

'So what's for the main, captain?' Eva asked as Andrew pulled up a chair between them.

'Barbounia. Hopefully they won't be too dry.'

Striped mullet was a local specialty, and the island's restaurants competed each year for the best barbounia award.

'Might be your year,' Eva said.

'Unfortunately, this old *battleaxe* doesn't qualify as a restaurant.'

Emilio swallowed his regret. He had overstepped the mark earlier and knew it. While he hadn't completely forgiven Andrew for whatever might have occurred, he was also grateful that his friend didn't hold grudges. Despite their numerous disagreements, they respected each other enough to accept defeat when necessary.

'Did Eva mention our discussion?' Andrew asked.

'Discussion?'

Eva shrugged and cocked her head. 'I haven't had the chance yet.'

'While you were out there acting Aquaman, I asked Eva if she could help me with some legal stuff.'

'You in trouble?'

'I'm very close to making a deal with a new resort in Naxos.'

'Which one?' Emilio asked.

'Elona Palace. It's a little further away from my hub here on the eastern Aegean, but the deal is too good to let go. I have a catamaran and a skipper ready to go.'

'I love Naxos,' Eva said. 'Now that's an island I could live on.'

Emilio sensed she was toying with him, recalling how, during an argument when they were still engaged, she had expressed her wish to one day leave Phaedros.

'Eva agreed to look over the contracts for me.'

'I highly recommend her,' Emilo said in a tone verging on patronising.

Eva gave him a sideways glance.

A sudden commotion from the stern of the boat silenced everyone. Both Andrew and a deckhand sprinted across the deck as one of the male guests, drunk, stumbled towards the dining area.

'Wyatt!' screamed a woman sitting alone at the table. 'What the hell are you doing?'

Wyatt was returning from the bathroom wearing a life jacket. 'I just want to check if these things work.'

After blowing the whistle on the cord, he handed it over to Andrew. 'I don't want one of those cheap, rubbish life jackets we found today at the lagoon.'

'That's enough, Wyatt!' his wife yelled at him, helping him back to his seat. 'I am so sorry, everyone.'

'Life jackets?' Eva asked Emilio.

'Yes, at Artemis's Bath.'

'Why didn't you say anything?'

'Sorry. I haven't had the chance yet,' he said facetiously, recalling her earlier remark. 'They were in bad shape. Not sure how long they've been there.'

Andrew returned, apologetic.

'I was just telling Eva we found some discarded life jackets in the lagoon, all tangled up and ripped. Have you come across smuggler boats recently?'

'Not in these parts, but plenty in Lesbos.'

'You should have brought them back with you,' Eva said to Emilio, annoyed. 'They could be evidence of some sort.'

Emilio had overlooked her professional interest in the current migration situation, having provided legal assistance on the Moria refugee camp in Lesbos.

'I will notify the port police,' she said, 'just in case.'

'Don't worry, I can do that for you,' Andrew offered.

'Such a tragic situation. I can't see how this will end,' Eva said, clasping his forearm. 'Thank you.'

'Luckily, we are a somewhat removed from it, that's all I can say,' Emilio responded, noticing the gesture.

'That's so empathetic, Emilio!' Eva hissed, removing her hand and taking a gulp of her wine.

***

After dinner, Andrew spun around in his seat and jived over to the bar, slipping into his alter ego, DJ Andy—hat cocked, shirt untucked. After a few taps on the console, fairy lights strobed as Donna Summer pulsed from the hidden speakers.

Eva rose almost instantly. After three glasses of wine, all that had angered her dissipated. She now wanted her body to do all the talking. Emilio, however, couldn't shed the weight pressing on him since she smashed his sister's necklace. He sat to the side with his wine, lit a cigarette and tried to distract himself with thoughts of upcoming events: a farewell party for waiter Celine Larson; a British travel show arriving soon to cover a story on the resort; a Beauty and Wellness Expo in October; and rooms booked out until November. The busy year ahead now filled him with a flicker of joy.

Emilio checked emails on his phone. None required immediate action. He accepted Celine Larson's friend request, a small gesture he normally wouldn't make for staff. But as she was leaving, he clicked the blue Confirm tab. A photo memory popped up: his baby brother, Dimitri, aged five and dressed as a scarecrow and Emilio, then eighteen, in a long purple warlock cloak and matching hat. It was Apokries, carnival day, the start of Lent. That little scarecrow was now taller than him, wearing army greens and serving his conscription in northern Greece. Emilio felt his heart sink. Their relationship had not been great over the years.

Finishing the rest of his wine, he pocketed his phone, butted out his cigarette and headed to the packed dance floor. Everyone was dancing, including the crew. Champagne flowed, and the music soon changed to Greek. The floor opened up, leaving Eva at the centre, swinging both hands and waving them above her head. Unclipping her hair, she flicked it from side to side, extending her arms into the Zeibekiko pose, an improvised dance for men broken by love. Eyes half-closed, she seemed entranced. Andrew dropped to his knees in front of her, clapping to the beat, encouraging her. Her skin shimmered as she twirled and swayed, her eyes acknowledging the captain's enthusiasm. A single tear slipped down her cheek, determined to finish the dance.

Emilio watched with guilt. It should have been him on his knees, clapping for her. But the realisation that their arrangement was no longer tenable seized him with brutal force. The guests erupted in applause when Eva finished. She was glowing, and her beauty caught Emilio's eye. She quenched her thirst with champagne then lifted the empty glass as if it were a trophy. Gathering her heels at the edge of the dance floor, she bowed to her fans and headed over to Emilio.

'I'm going to bed. You stay.'

'What about dessert?'

'I'm done. Goodnight.' She kissed him on the cheek and disappeared down the stairs, waving as guests cried for more, but she was already gone.

***

The hours slipped away. Emilio didn't want to go to bed. The tension had lifted and he was finally enjoying himself. A middle-aged couple sat beside him, spinning tales of their winter chalet in Aspen. The man's great-grandparents were Greek, entitling him to comment on the crisis. Emilio soon tired of the barrel-chested Texan—the man who had earlier clapped at the butterflies. Politics was the last thing he wanted to discuss. The wife, however, intrigued him: thin, flowing auburn hair, with a crooked nose reminiscent of an actress from an Almodóvar movie. A film editor by trade, she brought up Emilio's favourite movie—Luc Besson's *The Big Blue*. She hadn't stopped thinking about *The Big Blue* since the afternoon swim.

By four in the morning, guests and crew had retired, leaving Emilio alone on deck. At some point he would return to his cabin, but for now, he just wanted to recline in his deckchair and rest under a still night. He thought about the sea and *The Big Blue*. The dead quiet of the sea was magical. Beneath the surface, another world thrived—marine creatures eating, swimming, mating. The stillness transcended logic.

Just when he thought he had the deck to himself, the squeak of the metal stairs interrupted the quiet. He panicked, thinking it was Eva.

'Good morning!'

Andrew's appearance surprised him. His friend's lean frame seemed stiffer than usual. In his hands was a bottle of port and two crystal tumblers. He took a seat on the padded leather bench across from Emilio.

'Can't sleep?' Emilio quizzed.

'My bed is occupied…Eva.'

'Oh.'

'Nothing happened. She's fast asleep. I took one of the benches inside the galley, but it was too uncomfortable.'

Andrew poured the port into the glasses. Emilio took a swig and fell back into his chair as the sweet liquid warmed his throat. In the far distance, fishing trawlers were setting off for the day's catch.

'How lucky are we to live in one of the most beautiful places in the world.'

'It certainly is,' Andrew said, swirling his glass before taking a sip.

'But those life jackets…' Emilio's voice darkened. 'If refugees spill onto this island, we'll be finished.'

'That's extreme,' Andrew challenged. 'Those people are drowning out there. They're people like us, without privilege, trying to survive.'

'I don't need your moral high ground right now,' Emilio snapped. 'I have enough crap to deal with.'

'Don't we all,' Andrew pressed.

'Sometimes you just need perspective. The world's full of bullshit. While we need tree- and refugee-huggers, we also need visionaries to perfect this imperfect world.'

'Sorry, but that's fucked up, Emilio. What's perfection if it lacks humanity?'

'Survival.'

'You've become quite the barbarian, haven't you?'

'Says the "friend" who set this whole charade up to steal his friend's fiancée.'

Andrew froze. 'You know that's not true. Come on, man! What are you implying?' Andrew's crystal blue eyes glassed over. He got up, placed his hands behind his head and moved to the railing. Emilio had hit a raw nerve. After a long silence he returned, stopping just before Emilio's knees. Expecting the towering Californian to pull him up by the collar, he sat back down instead.

'Fiancée? Seriously? She is your ex-fiancée, just to remind you. You couldn't even dance with her tonight. What sort of relationship is that?'

'One of convenience.'

Andrew's jaw dropped in disbelief. 'Jesus, Emilio.'

Emilio felt some remorse but wanted to cut to the chase. 'Calm down!'

'What the fuck, man! For your island to survive, it's going to require more than the cold, callous, self-centred dick you've become.'

'She likes you,' Emilio said, rapping Andrew on the knee.

Andrew reclined and gave a deep sigh. 'I like her too,' he eventually admitted.

But Emilio stayed still and quiet, gazing up at the sky just as a shooting star fell. He made a wish—hoping his friendship with Andrew would survive. Over the years, he'd lost many friends—some had left the island, others were offended by his ambition. Being Emilio Politis often felt like holding a poisoned chalice.

'You two looked great on the dance floor. You're meant to be together.'

Andrew looked at Emilio, confused.

'I'm serious. I'd rather she go to someone I trust.'

'She's not a commodity you gift to someone.'

'You know what I mean.'

'You guys have history. You can't give it up like that.'

'If I dwelled on my past I'd have achieved nothing. It's better to let go, swallow the bitter pill and seek new opportunities.'

'But you must love her, surely.'

'Of course I do, but I can't let the love of one person define me.'

'But it's not "one person". We're talking about a life partner.'

Emilio didn't respond. Andrew's words stung, leaving him questioning his capacity to truly love. He tried to imagine whether he would ever grow old beside a wife—the mother of his children—reminiscing through all the fleeting years. Would he have children at all? He assumed he would, but he had never longed for them. Had he become so selfish? Was he subconsciously building a retreat within himself?

'Where to from here, my friend?' Andrew asked.

'I'm happy to stay here for the rest of my life. When I was a child, my mother said I would love it here. I am still holding onto her promise.'

'So there's no new opportunity?'

'What do you mean?'

'Another woman!'

'Huh! No, not this time. I need a good, long break. Right now, I want to wallow in the anguish of a man whose ego has been crushed.'

'The last thing I wanted to do was hurt you.'

'I will be fine. Trust me. Probably do me good.'

Andrew got up, finished his port, grabbed a blanket and lay down opposite Emilio on a deckchair. 'If you don't mind, I might join you.'

'Be my guest, my captain.'

The men drifted into sleep. A silver-crested crane swooped in and landed on the deck. Once satisfied that there was nothing to scavenge, it took to the air and disappeared into the dawning light.

CHAPTER 4
Ayvalik, Türkiye

It was late afternoon, and the warm air hung heavy with diesel fumes and stale sweat. Three days had passed since they were herded, like sheep, into a dilapidated shed five kilometres south of Ayvalık. The journey from the Altınözü camp had taken its toll. Over two days, they had travelled more than a thousand kilometres across Turkey. By the time they reached the holding station, everyone was exhausted. Families were given mattresses on the laminate floor, while those on their own made do with camping mats or tattered armchairs. The boarded-up windows offered little relief from the constant roar of motorbikes and trucks. Dim lighting barely concealed the skittering of rodents and insects.

The shed sat in a gully just off the highway. Once a petrol station, it was now overgrown with weeds and thistles. A collection of gutted, rust-riddled cars lay dumped beside the building. Fifty metres further back of the property, an outhouse enclosed toilets for men and women, four washbasins, and a smaller room where one could wash using a plastic bucket. The stench of the sewer drove many to the scrubland behind the outhouse, littered with toilet paper.

In a few hours, a minibus would transport the two dozen passengers to the coast, where a ferry would take them to the Greek island of Lesbos. Maryam hoped for a short ferry ride, recalling Mr Pepsi's words. She prayed there would be no more false promises. This was the third time they had been instructed to get ready in the past forty-eight hours. They couldn't remain another night. Food was running low and tempers were frayed. That morning, an elderly woman had to be carried out screaming after soiling herself, shouting that she would kill herself. Maryam tried to console the grandchildren while their parents tended to the stricken grandmother.

Maryam covered Maya's head with her dark brown scarf, hoping she might sleep a little longer. Her small hands clasped the pink velvet baby blanket that went everywhere with her. She whispered a prayer of thanks that her daughter had something to comfort her, a simple object that went beyond her parents' love, offering immediate, unconditional calm.

Bassel's head rested against Maryam's shoulder, quietly sleeping, his long lashes fluttering. Was he dreaming of their new home? An end to this nightmare? A new pharmacy filled with the scent of soap and colognes? A kind, loving community? She prayed for him too, longing for his dream of a large family to come true.

Bassel was emotionally drained. His grasp of basic Turkish had made him the group's spokesperson. Not that he resisted; he was always the first to rush to anyone's aid. But after days of carrying complaints between the two parties, even he ran out of patience. Often he bore the brunt of people's frustration, their disappointment heavy in his chest. Maryam had witnessed it many times: him throwing himself into projects or friendships with so much enthusiasm, only to be let down. Yet he always found a way to bounce back, energy renewed and spirit revived.

At the start of this journey, his optimism had been contagious. At a rest stop, only hours after they left the camp on foot, he unpacked his oud and played a Syrian folk tune beneath an olive tree. Maryam watched with pride as her husband brought reprieve to the travellers and joy to the children. An Afghan youth named Kurush found a twig, mimicked a flute and fingered a rhythm to

Bassel's tune. The children got up to dance as he led them around the neighbouring trees, moving energetically despite a limp. Maya squealed with delight when Kurush swooped her up in his arms. She proudly called out, 'Abu! Abu!' as her small arms reached for her father. Hearing children laugh and play in nature was a new experience for her. Bassel had created a joyous moment of distraction. Even the two Turkish guides lowered their masks of authority and clapped along. No one knew their names. Mr Pepsi introduced them simply as their guides to Aljana—to paradise.

Maryam adored her husband; he was her pillar of strength. At times she closed her eyes and focused on his sonorous voice: 'Everything will be alright,' a phrase that always soothed her. His charm attracted many of their customers: singing while compounding pharmaceuticals, poking his head around a corner to startle them deliberately. Maryam had to pull him into line a few times, his playful nature not always attuned to people's moods. She suspected he had ADHD, but he refused to address it, insisting his impulsiveness came from a desire to make the most of life.

But it all seemed like another life—one that had vanished long ago. Now they were homeless, jobless and hungry. Each day, Maryam tried to focus on what she still had: a good husband and a beautiful daughter. In her darkest moments, she'd close her eyes, take deep breaths and imagine Bassel, Maya and herself in the courtyard of their new home on the outskirts of a European city. Bassel would sing as he watered tomato plants while Maya played with her dolls. She would be stitching a new piece of embroidery for her daughter's dowry. This image had become her Arcadia—a pause from a desperate life, a hopeful glimpse of a brighter future.

***

Since giving birth, Maryam had become a terrible sleeper, not because of an unsettled baby but because of the thunder of explosions or the crash of shattering windows clawing through her dreams. Her body would spring up with such intensity that it took hours to fall back asleep. Sleeping pills once helped, but these days, meditation and deep breathing were her only options. Trying to slow her racing heart and mind often proved impossible.

Maya was born just weeks before civil war unleashed its fury on Aleppo. Fear and anxiety had driven thousands to evacuate the city. At thirty-nine weeks, escape was no longer an option. Maryam's waters broke five days after her due date, and the stress of the delay had taken its toll. She clung to the delusion that some divine force was keeping her baby safe within her womb. Turning to the Quran, she sought solace through prayer, with Bassel by her side guiding her through the thin, transparent pages. He did what he could to support her: buying her favourite chocolates, watching Turkish TV dramas together, massaging her shoulders.

While in labour at the hospital, a bomb detonated in a nearby Alawite neighbourhood, killing eleven people. Every window shattered in an instant. The sound of debris showering around her and the smell of smoke seeping through vents etched themselves into her memory. Sirens blared; nurses, doctors and visitors frantically raced along the corridors, wheeling trolleys and patients in wheelchairs. Bassel embraced his wife tightly, whispering reassurance as she gripped his hand, overwhelmed with guilt and dread. *What sort of world am I bringing our child into?*

The anticipation of holding his first child eclipsed Bassel's fear. With high spirits and stamina he tried to calm her, steadying her, breathing with her. But Maryam was gripped with embarrassment, ashamed of having lost control. *This isn't the woman he married.* The lone midwife administered gas to calm her. For six hours she drifted in and out of consciousness, battling the urge to sleep as excruciating pain hit in waves. When Maya finally arrived, the world seemed to explode. Maryam called on Allah to take her, but her baby's cry cut through the chaos, giving her the strength to open her eyes and find that sound.

Bassel appeared in front of her with their newborn in his arms. 'A beautiful girl!' he whispered as tears streamed down his cheeks. Their baby's tiny hands stretched upwards, brushing her fingers against his coarse beard. Full of love, he showered their baby's forehead with gentle kisses. Maryam reached for him, wanting to be part of it. He squeezed her hand tightly. They were all connected, bound by a force no horror outside the hospital wall could break.

The call to prayer now drifted through the gully on a crackling microphone. Bassel unrolled his mat, joining others in prayer, while Maya whimpered, restless with molars breaking through. Maryam took a tube of gel from her medicine bag, squeezed some onto her finger and rubbed it over her daughter's inflamed gums. A pasteli bar soon followed, a treat that always soothed her.

Rummaging in her backpack, Maryam took stock: pistachios, almonds, jars of baby food, Tetra Paks of milk and juices, enough food for at least three days. The bag was heavy and impractical to manage alongside a pram. The previous day, she had thrown it to the ground in frustration. Bassel was already loaded with two mid-size suitcases and a backpack from which hung his oud. All their clothes and a few of their valuables were with him, including a photo album, the chemistry textbook, and two tubes containing their pharmacy testamurs. Before fleeing their beloved city, they sold most of their jewellery following warnings that robbery was likely at refugee camps. The only pieces they kept were their wedding bands.

Once prayers had finished, Bassel leaned over and kissed his little girl. She soaked up his affection, patting his thick black beard. Maryam discreetly caressed the back of his head. She gently took his hand and whispered, 'I love you, my husband. Allah is great.'

The stomping of feet outside broke the tender moment. The door burst open and two guards barged in, their voices cutting through the air like gunfire. The room froze. Eyes darted, children whimpered and Maryam's stomach plunged. The guards instructed

Bassel to tell everyone to pack and get ready. A bus to the coast was parked on the main road, waiting for them. Tonight, at 10:30 p.m., they would make the crossing to Lesbos.

CHAPTER 5
Paradisos II resort

Celine Larson hadn't expected Emilio to appear at her farewell party. The guilt of not telling him in person about her resignation gnawed at her. Their chance meeting at the beach the week before had been pleasant but also awkward as she'd assumed her flamboyant supervisor, Chef Alfonzo, had already broken the news. But Chef's comment the previous day that Emilio had gone to Milan 'on business' had caught her by surprise. Confused and too timid to press further, she couldn't help feeling disappointed.

That night on the beach stuck in her memory. Emilio had asked her to join him, but she'd already been for a swim. Twenty-year-old Celine blushed as he stripped down to his blue-and-white swim trunks. His muscular legs, defined chest and tapered back revealed his commitment to fitness. While taking a swim, his phone, lying face up on his towel, lit up. Eva's name and face flashed across the screen. She had heard so much from Chef about the enigmatic Eva, and rumours were circulating that they were back together. When Emilio returned from his swim, he mentioned a short cruise—a quick getaway to unwind from the conference. Listening to him reminded her of Nicolai Cleve Broch, the Norwegian actor she had always adored.

The intimate party being held in her honour at the resort's Lighthouse Bar felt hollow. The man hosting it was missing. With only two days before leaving the island, she wanted to thank

Emilio personally. Always generous and encouraging, he had even promoted her to head waiter during the conference, drawing her into his trusted circle. She had worked at the resort for just over a year, and Paradisos II had become her home, its staff her family. Her familiarity with Emilio, though recent, had further entrenched her. She couldn't leave without saying goodbye—not when her cousin Jorgen Larson, Emilio's good friend and the resort's architect, had secured her the job. Without him, she'd still be in Oslo stacking shelves at a suburban supermarket, saving for her travels.

She sipped her sparkling wine with apprehension. Normally she would have escaped such a crowd, but this was her night. Her colleagues, forever encouraging, fussed about her borrowed red cocktail dress. The plunging neckline and thin straps accentuated her swimmer's body; her long, platinum hair fell sleekly down her exposed back. She hardly recognised herself in the glances and whistles she drew.

Close to midnight, the atmosphere shifted. The music faltered, the lights flickered and murmurs swelled into applause. Emilio had arrived, alone. Celine had imagined that if he did appear, it would be alongside Eva, confirming the rumours of their reunion. A wave of relief washed over her.

He moved through the room with effortless command, his dark eyes widening at her transformation. Wrapping his arms around her waist, he pulled her close and kissed her on both cheeks, his voice brushing her ear: 'I'm going to miss you.' As he slipped away, the weight in her chest eased.

When Emilio called her forward from the front of the bar, she adjusted her dress and moved through the corridor to the sound of rapturous claps and whistles. Taking her hand, he drew her to his side, his other hand clasping her hip. His spiced cologne was fresh in the humid air. Above them, smoke hung motionless in the spotlight, catching the glint of the gold chain around his neck.

Emilio's speech was heartfelt and inspiring, his hand now resting at the small of her back, steadying her. He wished her well in her studies and assured her she would always be welcomed back. Describing her as hardworking and professional, it was the word 'beautiful' that made her lips quiver and cheeks flush. From behind the bar, the barman handed Emilio a small gift-wrapped box. For a wild moment she imagined him dropping to one knee and laughed at her own absurdity. Coming to her senses, she unwrapped the box to reveal a stunning Aphrodite aqua bead bracelet. Emilio immediately lifted it from its satin bed and fastened it around her wrist, claiming her. The room erupted in applause. And then a hug—a warm, firm hug that she wished would linger longer.

Outside, a flash of lightning suddenly knifed open the midnight sky. Everyone turned towards the floor-to-ceiling windows as thunder boomed across the harbour, rattling the glassware at the bar. Emilio, unruffled, made his way to the PA console, turned up the music, dimmed the lights and drew the curtains with a remote, sealing the room from the storm.

***

At two-thirty in the morning, Chef, Celine and Emilio were still at the bar, with Celine seated between them. Outside, the storm wreaked havoc. Chef glanced at his phone and saw a news alert about a significant weather system moving across the Aegean. Warnings of cyclonic winds and perilous seas filled the screen. They were calling it a medicane.

'What's a medicane?' Celine asked.

'I'll google it,' Chef replied.

'It's just a big storm,' Emilio said. 'They're rare.'

'Here we go,' Chef said, holding up his phone. 'Medicanes, or "Mediterranean hurricanes", are rare tropical-like cyclones that form quickly, often within twenty-four hours.'

'That sounds frightening,' Celine said nervously.

'We had something similar about seven years ago,' Emilio said, trying to calm her. 'A couple of roofs blew off some of the older homes. We're safe here. It will pass. Don't worry.'

Emilio excused himself to go to the bathroom.

'Do you want me to walk you back to your room?' Chef asked, ever-protective of his junior staff.

'I'm fine. Really. Thank you so much for tonight. And for everything.' She hugged him tightly. The stocky, middle-aged, gay Spaniard had become somewhat of a guardian to her. He had worked at the restaurant since it opened and was a notorious flirt.

'Oh, chica! You are so welcome.'

'I don't want to leave,' she whispered as tears welled. Chef grabbed some napkins from the onyx-lustred bar. She wiped at her eyes quickly, not wanting Emilio to see. She needed to get out quickly before it was too late—stop mid-fall before she crash-landed. At least she had kept her word to Jorgen not to become some local's summer fling, as he once had during his own visits to Phaedros. But Emilio wasn't just some 'local'; he was Emilio Politis, entrepreneur and hotel visionary. Now, with a few drinks behind her, she was open to throwing the rules out the window. After all, one reckless adventure before the constraints of university didn't seem so terrible.

When Emilio returned, Chef rose awkwardly, wanting to make himself scarce. He hugged his boss firmly and wished him goodnight.

'Don't worry about Celine,' Emilio said, lightly patting him on the back. 'I'll make sure she gets to bed.'

As Chef shuffled away, he turned and winked at them before disappearing down the spiral stairs.

'I am so going to miss him,' Celine said.

'I hope you'll miss me too.'

'Of course,' she replied. 'I have had the most amazing time here.'

He moved closer, towering over her.

'I didn't ask you about your cruise,' she said.

'My cruise?' he said, tilting his head, somewhat surprised.

'Yes, that night on the beach—you mentioned you were going on a cruise.'

'Oh yes, of course. The cruise was fine but too short, so I took an impromptu trip to Milan.'

'Milan?'

'One of my favourite cities. A place that makes me feel inconspicuous.'

The word 'Milan' felt dirty, but she didn't care. It gave her more reason to distance herself emotionally. 'I didn't think you were going to turn up tonight,' she said, looking down at her glass.

'Why would you think that?'

'For not telling you in person that I was leaving. I should have said something on the beach that night. I'm so embarrassed.'

'Don't be.'

'I didn't want to ruin your mood,' she said as she turned to face him. 'The conference had finished, and you seemed so relaxed and happy.'

'I was…and still am. You'll come back next year,' he said, as if it was a given.

Celine laughed. 'As a student, I doubt I can afford it.'

'For you, I will make an exception.'

He leaned down and kissed her—a sensual, heartfelt kiss. She could taste the alcohol on his lips. Her thoughts drifted to Eva. *How could she have let him slip away?* Suddenly, a determination to find out struck her. If she was going to sleep with him, it had to be with a clear conscience.

'What about Eva?'

'Eva?' he recoiled.

'Sorry, I'm not trying to pry, but there are rumours that you two are back together.'

'Is that so?'

For a moment, Celine felt she had gone too far, that he would simply tell her to mind her own business. Taking a step back, she thought he was going to leave, but instead he propped up his collar, brushed his hair back with his fingers, then sat down next to her.

'Eva and I are not getting back together. What we had is no longer possible.'

'People were saying you two were Phaedros's version of David and Victoria Beckham.'

Emilio laughed. 'That may have been the case, but *this* got in the way.'

'The resort?'

He nodded. 'I had returned from my studies in Milan to build this, and she had returned from London after her divorce. We were high-school sweethearts. Destiny had brought us back to the island, but our goals didn't coincide. Since breaking off the engagement after the resort's opening, we just slipped into a painful arrangement. It's now over.'

Celine moved her hand across to his.

'Shall I make sure you get to bed?' he asked, taking her hand and squeezing it. 'It's pretty bad out there.'

Celine had become oblivious to the storm. She left the warmth of his arms and walked over to the large window, hoping he'd follow. His honesty had made her feel better, more confident. Pulling back the curtain, a flash of lightning streaked across the sky revealing a violent, roiling sea. Thunder cracked; a gasp escaped her mouth as heavy rain lashed against the glass.

'I don't think I've ever seen a storm this bad on the island.'

'It will pass. Don't be frightened,' Emilio said, moving behind her, kissing her on the neck. 'Come on, let's go,' he murmured, his hand gently clasping her neck.

***

The storm was wild. Rain pelted them as they ran, arm in arm, into the half-sheltered courtyard. Emilio grabbed a plastic chair from the outdoor café and used it as a makeshift umbrella as they swiftly took the path to his apartment. The rain was so heavy that even the garden lights struggled to illuminate. Before the night began, it had been a calm, warm spring evening—now it was cyclonic.

By the time they ascended the two flights of stairs to his top-floor apartment, they were drenched. Inside, he called the kitchen and the concierge from the landline, instructing them to delay any room service until the storm eased. Celine was frightened. Even if she wanted to escape him, the chaos outside had trapped her.

'You okay?' he asked, wrapping his arms around her.

It was so weird, she thought. Even with wet clothes, he was desirable. His fervent kissing left her breathless. Water trailed behind them on the marble floor as he led her to the bathroom. Inside the oversized shower, hot water soon cascaded over them. As steam clouded around them, Emilio eagerly helped her slip off her dress. Between giggles and laughter at how difficult it was to remove wet clothes, they kissed again. She felt him hard against her belly. A fierce desire to please him swept through her.

Afterwards, as she lay in bed next to him, she listened to his heartbeat slow as he drifted into a deep sleep. She thought of leaving, but her clothes were still wet. Outside, the rain lashed and the wind continued its eerie howl. Then it came—a scream, sharp and jarring. The clock glowed 5.10 a.m. *Maybe a rooster*, she thought. Making her way to the toilet, she heard another scream, distant but chilling. A sudden panic seized her as she imagined Eva rallying the locals to arrest her. Reluctantly, she slipped back into bed after collecting the condom box from the floor and returning it to the drawer, hiding any trace. More than anything, she wanted to wake up with Emilio, start a new morning together. If she left, he might forget their night altogether.

The screaming outside grew louder. Car horns blared. Something was happening. She buried herself into Emilio's side, his naked torso warm and safe. He was dead to the world. Pulling a pillow over her head, she tried to muffle the noise. She just needed to sleep, then everything would be fine.

CHAPTER 6
Kamiros Beach

Shouting and banging doors convinced Emilio he was having a nightmare. His name echoed again and again—one voice deep and manic in the distance, another high and trembling nearby. As he emerged from his deep sleep, he had no idea where he was. His head throbbed as if his heart had climbed into it. Through half-opened eyes, flashes of light streamed through the window louvres—a blur of dreams, fear and confusion. He fumbled for the lamp on the bedside table and switched it on. A young, frightened girl sat next to him, clutching the sheet to her chin, shaking. The bedside clock read *5:30 a.m., 15 May 2015*.

Emilio jolted upright with such ferocity it felt almost superhuman. 'Something's happened,' he gasped, dazed.

'Emilio! Wake up!' bellowed the frantic male voice behind the front door.

'Coming!' he yelled, pulling on a pair of pants from the wardrobe. His mind raced through scenarios: had a guest died? His parents? Had a building collapsed?

'I think it's Chef,' the girl whispered before darting into the bathroom, taking the bedsheet with her.

He switched on the outdoor light and flung open the door. Alfonzo was pacing, out of breath, struggling to hold a resort umbrella steady over his head. Wearing a bright green rain jacket, he looked pale and was shaking all over.

'What's happened?'

'They're drowning. Come quick!' he screamed, grabbing Emilio's arm.

'Who's drowning?'

'I don't know. I couldn't sleep. The storm passed, and I went for a walk. I can't swim, otherwise, I…I…It's so rough out there. Mierda!' His words broke into panic. 'I called your mobile, but it went to message bank. Where's Celine?'

'Celine?' As the name registered, her body beneath his flashed across his mind. 'Shit!'

'She okay? Where is she?'

'She's fine,' Emilio snapped. He ran back inside, yanked on a T-shirt and sneakers from under the bed. 'Celine! I'll be back soon,' he yelled at the bathroom door.

'Don't worry about me. I'm okay,' she replied, her voice unsteady.

Grabbing a windbreaker from the coat stand, Emilio slammed the door behind him and followed Alfonzo down the concrete stairs to the slippery path below. The lights in his parents' ground-floor apartment were on. They'd be calling him, worrying. Guests were up, freaking out. He reached for his phone to call the night manager but had rushed out without it.

They bolted through the side gate of the main building and dashed across the road to Kamiros Beach. The wind was fierce and cold. Flashing lights darted everywhere, silhouettes of people running frantically as dogs barked.

'Rudi!' Emilio called out, recognising his dog's hoarse yelp. 'How the fuck did he get out?' In between his panic, more flashbacks: the party; Celine; the sex. Then a bloodcurdling scream pierced through the rain. A woman's scream, amplified and distorted by the howling wind. Suddenly, a beam from of a torch captured him.

'Emilio!'

His father, Mihalis Politis, grappled with Rudi, who was lunging wildly towards him. Dressed in overalls and a resort cap, the sixty-five-year-old still had the energy of a lion.

'A tourist boat must have capsized,' his father called out.

Emilio thought of Andrew. Was it the *Grand Duchess*? Eva? If only he had his phone, he'd call her or Andrew. Rudi, his large alsatian and kelpie mix, broke free and leaped on him, all but knocking him to the ground. Even his dog's eyes were wild with fear. Emilio gave Rudi a quick rub before pushing him back to his father.

Again, the same scream, high-pitched and terrifying. Emilio grabbed his father's high-powered torch and scanned the waves, but there was nothing but a shifting, murky greyness. Turning the beam towards the back of the beach, he looked for his aluminium dinghy. Months had passed since he had taken it out. Usually he left it near the concrete stairs, but the area was empty. Flicking the torch beam further along the beach, he eventually spotted it, wedged between two large rocks.

'Quick, help me,' he yelled to Alfonzo and his father as he ran towards the dinghy. Vangelis's old wooden rowboat, usually anchored further down the beach, was also missing.

'Hope Vangelis isn't out there,' Mihalis said. 'That old thing would have been shredded to pieces.'

Vangelis Papaioannou's dinghy was an eyesore, but one he stubbornly refused to remove. The bitterness between the neighbours stretched back centuries, resurfacing in the early 1990s when the original Paradisos hotel was being built. Mihalis Politis had offered to buy him out but Vangelis refused, sneering that he didn't trade with anyone associated with that devil-witch Irini Vlahos. He clung to the belief that his great-grandfather Giorgos Papaioannou had been cursed by Emilio's ancestor and that 'such things are never forgotten'.

Together, the men yanked Emilio's dinghy out and flipped it over. The smashed motor dangled on its bracket. With a mighty kick, Emilio snapped it off. While the side of the hull was slightly dented, the oars remained strapped tight in the boat's rowlocks.

By now the winds were subsiding, as were the waves. Repeatedly, a woman screamed something in a foreign language, her voice disjointed and despairing. The strange light, the wailing, the churn of the sea—all created a deep sense of foreboding.

They pushed the dinghy across the wet pebbles and launched it into the water. Rudi pranced about, eager to jump in, as Mihalis tried to push him away. Alfonzo grabbed the dog's loose lead, stammering apologies for not going out with them. 'I can't swim …but I can make food for survivors!' Two local fishermen came running with ropes, life jackets and torches, followed by the sound of a foghorn as old Manolis, the octogenarian fisherman, manoeuvred his ancient fishing trawler away from the jetty at the southern end of the harbour.

'Emilio! Look after your father!' cried his mother, Margarita, who suddenly appeared in a long, purple velvet robe. She thrust two blankets into Mihalis's hands. 'Be careful!' she said as she stepped back, clutching the robe tight around her. She reminded Emilio of Medusa, her shoulder-length grey hair flicking wildly like hundreds of snakes across her stoic face.

As they cast off, Emilio glanced back at the beach where rows of people—local and tourists—had assembled along the boardwalk. Splintered thatched umbrellas and twisted beach chairs lay strewn in front of them. In the distance, the bells of Saint Constantine tolled. The air smelled different—thick with salt and something sour.

As they headed towards the northern heads, debris surfaced in the grey water—a single shoe, plastic water bottles, clothing—barely two hundred metres into their journey.

'I think I can see her!' Mihalis shouted, pointing to something thrashing nearby. Emilio rowed harder, his muscles burning, his breathing loud and laboured. Noticing the light on him, the man in the water shouted something undecipherable—his voice like screeching metal as he waved frantically. As he swam vigorously towards the boat, Emilio handed the oars to his father and leaned over the side.

'Grab my hand!' Emilio shouted.

The man turned to look over his shoulder as he grabbed Emilio's hand. 'Woman!' he shouted. Mihalis dropped the oars to help haul him aboard. He was young, maybe still in his teens, thin and olive-skinned, possibly Middle Eastern or Asian. 'There! You see?' he spluttered. 'Woman still alive!' Snatching the torch from Mihalis, he shone it further to the right of where they were heading.

At first, Emilio thought it was spilled cargo—orange-coloured bags, possibly fruit, crates and coconuts. 'She scratch and hit me. She wants to drown,' the man said. His dark eyes were blood-red from the salt. 'Bad men!' he gasped, struggling to piece his words together. 'They kill my friend. They kill everyone!'

'Anyone alive?' Emilio asked.

'I don't know. I cannot find my cousin.'

Barefoot and wearing long trousers and a dark T-shirt, the young man murmured something that sounded like Arabic, possibly a prayer. His voice faltered, rose in pitch, escalated in rhythm, breaking into anger. He screamed, cursing at someone or something before collapsing to his knees, sobbing uncontrollably.

Emilio and Mihalis rowed through the debris. Bodies and luggage drifted everywhere. They were now past the pier, with the headland to the right. What Emilio had mistaken for coconuts were human heads. Plastic bottles bobbed among shoes and clothes and children's toys. The orange plastic bags were not bags at all but deflated life jackets.

'Syrians!' Emilio blurted, recalling the two recent boat tragedies off Lesbos where dozens had drowned. But boats in Phaedros were unheard of. *How the fuck did such a small boat drift out so far?* He looked at his father and saw his eyes welling with tears.

'Are you alright?' he asked.

'There are children out there.'

Emilio felt like his heart would collapse. Picking up speed with his rowing, the boat halted suddenly after a few metres, causing them all to fling forward. The oar had snagged on the remains of the deflated rubber boat. Handing the oars to his father, Emilio jumped into the cold water to clear it away. The smell of diesel and excrement was suffocating.

'There! There she is!' Mihalis called out, shining the torch towards the woman. Emilio followed the beam to the right, pushing through the debris, swimming hard and fast until his arm struck something. Instinctively, he grabbed and lifted it, but it was heavy. The body of a man rolled over; eyes half open, pupils rolled back and skin the colour of slate. Emilio released him, shoved the body to the side and swam towards the woman. Only her head and shoulders were visible. Around her neck, a half-deflated life jacket cradled her head.

He placed his arm around her waist, trying to keep her head out of the water, but there was something attached to her chest, perhaps a backpack that seemed to hold her buoyant. His fingers dug in for a better grip. Untying the rope connecting her to the deflated rubber boat, he dragged her towards the approaching dinghy. Only when they had hauled her in did they discover that her 'backpack' was the body of a little girl, strapped tightly to her mother by a red elastic hook rope. Dressed in a pink raincoat, her thin arms hung loose, her head limp and lifeless.

'It's Maya. Her little girl,' the young man cried.

Emilio immediately unhooked the elastic rope as his father slowly peeled the body away. She had been dead for some time.

Beneath the mop of wet hair, her face was blue and swollen. Mihalis tried to close her eyelids, but it was too late—rigor mortis had set in. With shaking hands, Mihalis gently pushed the wet hair to the sides of the child's temples, then buried her deep into his chest.

Emilio climbed over the woman's waist and began CPR, clamping his mouth over her cold, blue lips, his palms pumping her chest. The currents underneath made it difficult to keep steady as he worked hard to maintain a regular rhythm. Her large, almond-shaped eyes were half-shut; water seeped from her nostrils. He laboured for about two minutes until a gurgling noise suddenly rose from her throat. A cough then jolted her body upright, prompting Emilio to turn her to the side as seawater poured from her mouth.

Emilio nudged the young man and pointed to the oars. 'Can you take control of the oars?'

He nodded, drained of any emotion.

'What is your name?' Mihalis asked.

'I am Kurush,' he said, grabbing the oars at Mihalis's feet.

'Are you Syrian?' Emilio asked.

'I am from Afghanistan, sir.'

The woman regained her breath and called out, 'Maya!' As more life returned, her anguish intensified. 'Maya! Maya! Maya!'

Emilio propped her up and sat her against the side of the hull. 'You are on the island of Phaedros, in Greece,' he yelled at her, hoping his words would penetrate through the wind and sea spray. 'My name is Emilio.'

She was delirious. Tears streamed down her face, her voice raw and broken. 'Maya! Maya!'

Emilio looked at his father. No words were needed. Gently opening the flap of his jacket, Mihalis withdrew the toddler from the warmth of his body. Emilio hoped that by some miracle, his father had been able to restore life, but what he presented was a little girl who was well and truly dead. Holding the woman by her shoulders, Emilio tried to stabilise her as Mihalis gently laid her daughter into her arms. As the weight of her daughter rested on her belly, the woman looked down to face what she already knew. A convulsion seized her; her mouth flung open as if her insides were being ripped from her. And when completely emptied, she dropped her head to kiss her daughter's lifeless cheeks, sobbing, rocking back and forth, keening as she cradled her dead child's head against her heart.

Taking the blankets, Mihalis covered the mother and child and sat beside them. His shoulders sagged, his face hollow with defeat. Witnessing the scene churned Emilio's stomach. He got up, jumped back in the water and threw up.

More local boats were now heading their way, and the recovery of bodies had begun. Emilio was desperate to find someone alive, someone else he could give life to. Noticing the body of a man close by, he grabbed it and brought it to the boat, turning the head around so Kurush could see the face.

'Is this her husband? Does she have a husband?'

'Yes, of course,' Kurush said. 'His name is Bassel. But this is not him.'

'Can you help me find him?' Emilio asked.

Without hesitation, Kurush dropped the oars and dived into the water. Emilio released the body as if it were worthless. Kurush described a heavily built man with a dark beard. Having become desensitised to the harrowing expressions of the dead, Emilio's focus was on finding Bassel and giving this woman something to alleviate her pain.

'Here!' Kurush called out. 'Bassel!'

Emilio swam between two bodies to reach Kurush. With all his strength, Emilio hooked his arm around the man and, with Kurush's help, dragged him back and hauled him into the boat. The commotion diverted the woman's attention away from her dead child. When she saw the body, a bloodcurdling scream pierced the sky. 'Jawzi! Jawzi! My husband!' With her child still in her arms, she lay across her husband, wailing, 'Allah Yarhamha. Allah Yarhamha!'

Emilio took control of the oars and steered the dinghy back to shore, intent on delivering this family back to the safety of land. Another boat had retrieved three bodies. Villagers rushed forward, their stunned faces stricken with horror as they laid the dead on the pebbly shore. Margarita approached and gently escorted the wailing woman onto a sun lounge, her child still locked in her arms. After placing her husband next to the other bodies, Emilio, Mihalis and Kurush returned to the sea. Kurush said that there were over twenty people on the boat, his cousin among those still missing. The sun had yet to break through the wall of black cloud on the horizon. The icy-grey light that seeped through painted a seascape that would haunt the islanders for generations.

PART 2
PROVIDENCE

CHAPTER 7
Revolution

In 1822, while Theodore Kolokotronis led the revolution to free the Hellenes from the Ottomans, Phaedrian rebels secretly constructed a fireship in a remote inlet. From there they sailed their fire-laden vessel to the island of Chios and set it ablaze; it was their contribution to the Greek cause. The pasha, meanwhile, remained oblivious to his subjects' activities, preoccupied with drinking mastika and lounging in a state of inebriation at his palatial villa in Meliz. In retaliation, Ottomans on the mainland committed a brutal massacre. Nearly 120,000 Chians were slaughtered or enslaved, while another 20,000 escaped to neighbouring islands such as Phaedros and Samos.

Caïques carrying refugees from the ravaged island arrived at Butterfly Cove, where local Phaedrians guided them through a cave into Artemis's Bath. This secret location, unknown to the pasha, was the nearest and most protected destination for those fleeing. Doctor Haralambos Kaligeros, the pasha's physician, had set up a makeshift examination station to assist with their arrival. The tall, handsome Greek from Smyrna secretly aided the resistance by dosing the pasha's raki with crushed poppies. The pasha's vices conveniently allowed the islanders to liberate themselves from the Ottomans, whose focus was on more commercially significant territories like Chios.

A few days into the rescue operation, the doctor observed an older, statuesque woman gather her black skirt and move to a clearing at the edge of the lagoon. Sitting on the pebbles, she removed her wet shawl and laid it before her, placing her golden bangles and rings on top. She then murmured arcane words as she pressed her hands down on the jewellery. Suddenly, as if the items had become too hot to touch, she lifted her hands to inspect the imprints on her palms. Intrigued by the intensity of her stare, he concluded that she must be a priestess.

Accompanying her was a younger woman, an otherworldly creature, no more than sixteen. As she sang, her body swayed from side to side like a cornstalk in the wind. Her voice was angelic, the melodious tones echoing off the rocks behind them. Dressed in a light brown tunic with an embroidered apron, she tapped her bare feet backwards and forwards. Gold chains glistened across her long neck, and her thick, black hair spilled down to her waist.

Father Spiro, a short, round-bellied man, blessed each refugee after the doctor's examination. Once approved physically and religiously, the locals transported the refugees to their villages, offering them a bed and work. None, however, approached the strange woman and her even stranger daughter. Even the priest kept his distance, waving his cross at them from afar while reciting a lengthy prayer.

While assessing the woman, the doctor noted her angular face and good bearing. The greys in her hair revealed where the reddish henna had grown out. Her cheeks were hollow beneath high cheekbones, and the pupils of her chestnut-coloured eyes were constricted. He immediately suspected medication.

She introduced herself as Irini Vlahos, nearing sixty and the surviving matriarch of a long line of mastic exporters. Accompanying her was her fifteen-year-old daughter, Mary. Without prompting, Irini described Mary as compassionate and respectful, adding that while beauty might not be in her favour, she possessed the rarer gift of being able to 'touch one's soul'.

The girl's eyes were equally intriguing and constricted like her mother's, but hers were the colour of forest green. When asked if they had consumed opium or laudanum, the old woman reached for her embroidered satchel and pulled out an amber-coloured vial, explaining that she was a herbal healer. The elixir contained extracts of coca, opium and mastic, which together formed an effective treatment for melancholy.

Irini and her daughter maintained a serene composure while others wept and lamented the loss of their men and homes. Irini accepted the doctor's offer to accommodate them. They were happy to have survived and grateful for his attention. Mary twirled with an ethereal demeanour, her voice trilling like a lark.

***

After a month in his modest house, the doctor made a proposal to the women over lunch. 'I have come to an arrangement with my previous employer, the pasha.'

'I thought the fat fool had left!' Irini said before placing a spoonful of stew into her mouth.

'He and his entourage should be in Smyrna by now,' the doctor replied, having facilitated the pasha's exit the previous day. The genocide at Chios and the escalation of the Greek resistance had made it dangerous for him to remain on the island.

'If there is a God, may he be struck down at sea by an almighty storm.'

'Mother, there's no need to be so vindictive.' Mary gently clasped her mother's hand.

'Because of those Turks, we not only lost our home but your father and brothers. *Remember that!*'

'May they rest in peace,' Mary replied, dabbing her eyes with her sleeve. 'But we should be seeking God's help in finding our way, not damning the enemy.'

The doctor was struck by the young woman's eloquence and calm demeanour.

'I thought you might have wanted to return with him,' Irini told the doctor, ignoring her daughter's altruism. 'I have been to Smyrna. It's a beautiful city. I'm surprised he let you stay.'

'I told him I was dying from an incurable disease and wished to live my remaining days on the island. He left me his villa in gratitude. I thought you might move in with me. Establish yourselves here in Meliz—no, sorry, Melissani, its Greek name. You would manage the household, tend to the pasha's peacocks and the garden. I'll open my clinic at the front of the villa; the small mosque at the back can be for your elixirs. Share them with me if someone is beyond traditional therapies.'

Irini Vlahos lifted her chin. 'My therapies rely on more than elixirs alone. During my examinations, I find the right chant to stimulate their effectiveness.'

Over the past weeks, the doctor had come to understand that she was harmless, a woman genuinely devoted to healing.

'My brand of medicine,' she continued, 'though scorned in public, is secretly yearned for. I have treated babies with severe diarrhoea with a drink of honey, dill, and carob. Their mothers burn frankincense and recite a special chant, crafted by my ancestors from the ancients.'

'But we no longer have the book, Mother,' Mary said.

'What book?' the doctor asked.

'The book of recipes and incantations. I couldn't retrieve it— likely burnt by the barbarians. If we come and live with you, could you spare some paper for Mary to scribe the recipes and chants I still have in my head?'

'Of course. That's easily arranged.'
'Then we will stay with you.'

***

The pasha's whitewashed two-storey villa featured an enclosed courtyard with a magnificent maple tree that provided shade for the upstairs balcony and privacy. Located opposite the village square, it was also in the most spacious area of the neighbourhood. The rest of the village was maze of narrow cobbled alleys that branched out from the square. Inside the villa, Persian tiles adorned the main entrance, while intricate plasterwork framed the tall wooden ceilings. At the villa's rear stood a small mosque with a red dome and blue mosaic flooring. The doctor kept most of the pasha's furnishings along with the exquisite silk rugs that decorated each room. He also maintained the pet peacocks that roamed freely within the enclosed garden, which gradually became a sanctuary for various bird species.

The doctor never ventured into the converted mosque nor questioned Irini's treatments. He did, however, consult with her, and she with him, over the kitchen table. Referrals became more common as the two 'opposing' practices continued to operate in tandem.

A few months later, as winter settled over the island, the doctor finally asked about their first encounter at Artemis's Bath. 'What were you doing with the jewellery that day at the lagoon? I can't stop thinking about it.'

The question did not surprise her—she had been waiting for it. The priest and the locals had witnessed her ritual, and word had spread that the physician was harbouring witches. Not that it troubled him. Being respected and depended upon by all on the island had granted him the security and freedom to do whatever he wanted.

'I cannot reveal this therapy,' she answered, taking his hand and squeezing it firmly. 'If I told you, I could never cure you of a broken heart.'

The doctor scoffed at the suggestion. A man of science, he considered himself immune to such human frailties. Yet matters of the heart soon prevailed. When Mary fell ill with influenza, he realised the intensity of his emotions. As he cooled her burning forehead with a damp cloth, he asked her to be his wife. The announcement of their engagement caused a public uproar. Beautiful, single women, who dreamed of marrying Doctor Kaligeros, were inconsolable, questioning how such a handsome and outgoing man could love someone so 'hideous' and 'unsociable'. Only black magic could explain it.

Mary bore him three daughters—Evridiki, Myrto and Polixeni—radiant little girls with vibrant personalities. Of the three, it was Myrto, the middle child, who inherited her grandmother's yearning to heal. Practising her potions on her sisters, Irini soon agreed to mentor her to prevent any harm. Mary, still scarred by the villagers' cruelty, had renounced her mother's craft, wanting no part in her neighbours' health and wellbeing. The manuscript she was meant to scribe for Irini fell by the wayside.

In 1836, during the birth of their fourth child, tragedy struck. Complications arose, and their little boy was stillborn. As Irini cradled the lifeless baby, the doctor attended to Mary, but neither medical procedure nor witchcraft could save her. Irini clung tightly to her grandson, refusing to let his soul leave her protection. Had the doctor not stopped for a drink of mastika in a neighbouring village, he would have been home when Mary's waters broke. Following three straightforward births, a similar delivery was expected for the fourth. But now, because of his misguided assumption, he lost not just his only son but also the woman he loved and cherished.

Immediately after their funeral, the doctor locked himself in his clinic and stupefied himself with ether. The smell of death seeped through every wall of the villa. He was so distraught and emotionally paralysed that he couldn't face anyone, let alone himself. Irini begged and pleaded for him to come out, promising to heal his broken heart. For the treatment, she needed his jewellery. He would hear nothing of it. Not even the tears and screams of his daughters would bring him out.

On the second evening of his self-imposed incarceration, the doctor sneaked out of the villa shortly after midnight and made the hour-long walk to Kamiros. Reaching the beach, he stripped off his clothes, relishing the fresh breeze and breathing in the sea air. It was a cool autumn night, with the only sound an owl hooting in the distance. The full moon hovered above the horizon like a lantern, its light shimmering across the water as if laying a trail for him. For the first time in days, he felt invigorated. Folding his clothes, he placed them on a rock at the edge of the beach. On top, he put his tortoiseshell glasses and the jewellery Irini had gifted him at his wedding—a gold chain and cross, and a ruby ring. Naked, he walked to the shoreline, stepped into the moonlit trail and entered the sea.

His folded clothes and jewellery bore silent witness to his suicide. Giorgos Papaioannou, a local fisherman, found them the next morning and promptly handed the doctor's belongings to Irini—all but the jewellery. His battered wife, outraged by her husband's sinful act, confessed the theft to Irini, who cursed him with severe gastritis. After his death, the wife returned the jewellery, left her children with her sister, and moved to the island of Patmos to spend the rest of her days in the nunnery of Evangelismos.

***

Irini struggled to raise her three granddaughters alone. Though the islanders rallied around her out of respect for the late doctor, their suspicion of her as a witch only deepened, especially after the Papaioannou incident. Inheriting the doctor's grand villa only inflamed their resentment, yet there was nothing they could do. They wanted no part in provoking her wrath should it ever be unleashed. Moreover, since the doctor's death, the island had been left without a physician, and in times of need, they could at least appeal to Irini Vlahos.

In time, Irini's momentum faded. Failing to cure the doctor's heartache had broken her. She had lost her husband and sons in Chios; now another man—her saviour—was gone. He had given her and her daughter a new life, bringing her to Melissani and allowing her to practise her craft. Without him, she felt unmoored once more.

The doctor left enough property and assets for Irini to raise his daughters, yet only Myrto continued to be schooled. Determined to preserve her grandmother's knowledge, Myrto recorded her recipes, spells and chants in elegant script. A talented illustrator, she meticulously filled the margins with delicate icons and sigils, classifying each page by ailment.

Three years later, cholera swept across the island, claiming half its population. To this day, that disaster remains vivid in local memory. Some say it was Irini's vengeance for the cruelty shown to her family. Among the old folks, a song still drifts around kitchen tables and tavernas:

> My doctor, my witch
> Let death take you
> The poor folks of Phaedros
> The black curse claims them
> Weep for their bodies, weep for their souls
> May Christ grant them mercy
> Love or death
> The pain poisons us
> The unnamed child took it all.

CHAPTER 8
Sydenham, Australia, August 1990

Margarita Politis knew she had to be straightforward with her seven-year-old son. This was no time for soft talk. The future of the family business was a serious matter that required adult foresight. But it wasn't just about the shop; it was about their lives. Not that Emilio would see it that way. The Citizens Corner Shop was his world—nothing else mattered.

The family had just returned from her father's six-month memorial service. It was a cool winter morning with the promise of sunshine. Margarita wanted her Sunday to be like any other Sunday—low-key and family-focused. It was their only day together away from the shop.

A small tray of koliva, the sweetened puffed-wheat dish served at the end of memorials, sat half-eaten on the orange laminate kitchen bench. Mihalis and the children picked at it while Margarita put the Sunday roast in the oven. She lit a small candle at the iconostasis above the range hood; the saints' faces glowed, and baby Jesus nestled in his mother's arms.

She had changed out of her mourning clothes into her favourite jeans and knitted top patterned with flowers. A purple scrunchie tied back her shoulder-length hair. She had inherited her father's height and, without heels, stood a centimetre shorter than her husband. One of the shop's regulars called her 'Nana', after Nana Mouskouri, because of her straight, dark hair and thick-rimmed glasses.

Catching her husband's attention, Margarita nodded, giving him the sign. Still in his formal church clothes, Mihalis loosened his tie. She liked seeing him in a suit, being accustomed to the long white apron that he wore most days in the shop. He still had his good looks: brown eyes like chocolate, a prominent dimple, and a gap between his front teeth that enhanced his brooding charm. He pulled up the stool next to Emilio's and rapped his thick fingers on the laminate, checking the neighbours weren't peering in. As he was about to speak, he stopped to scoop a tablespoon of koliva into his son's cup.

'No more koliva!' Margarita snapped.

'More, more, more!' shrieked two-year-old Aphrodite, banging her empty foam cup on the highchair tray.

'The last little bit for my boy!' Mihalis insisted, rubbing Emilio's back.

Margarita picked up the tray of remaining koliva, tossed it in the sink, yanked Aphrodite from her highchair and stormed out. Mihalis had blown it.

'Do it!' Margarita hissed from the adjoining room, leaving him to make the announcement on his own.

Mihalis shifted closer to Emilio and stretched out his hand to caress his son's rosy cheek. From the mirror in the next room, Margarita watched the scene unfolding. Aphrodite had become preoccupied with a box of crayons and paper.

'What's wrong with Mama?'

'She is a little sad. Pappou's service brought up many memories for her.'

He took hold of Emilio's sugar-coated hand. 'I have some exciting news to tell you. It will change our lives for the better.'

The boy looked at his father. Hyper from the sugar, he kicked the kitchen bench repeatedly.

'We are going to Greece!' His voice was broken and croaky, and so he tried again, clearing first the mucus that had gathered at the back of his throat. 'We are going to Greece!'

'For a holiday?'

'No. To live.'

The kicking stopped. Emilio's eyes widened and his ears pricked up. 'To live? We won't come back?'

'That's right. We'll live on your mother's island, Phaedros. It will be exciting. You'll have your cousin nearby, your grandmother.'

Margarita felt a sense of relief as she watched the scene unfold while trying to look impressed by Aphrodite's messy drawing. But Emilio slid off the stool and huffed towards the middle of the kitchen. His untucked white cotton shirt looked tight on him, his long woollen pants finishing just above his ankles. A sudden growth spurt in the last few weeks was accompanied by a more brazen attitude. 'What do you mean live on Mum's island? This is where we live!'

'We had to sell the shop and house to the government,' Mihalis said softly.

'You're an idiot!' Emilio screamed at the top of his voice.

Mihalis's calm broke. 'What did you call me?'

'An idiot!'

'Don't speak to your father like that!' Margarita yelled as she skidded around the corner, lunging at her son and forcefully putting him back on the stool.

'Leave me alone!' Emilio screamed.

'Half of Sydenham will be bulldozed,' Mihalis shouted. 'They're building a new runway for the airport. No one can live here because of the noise.'

'We're going to take over Pappou's café,' Margarita said gently, trying to adjust her approach.

'You're lying!' he screamed, pounding his clenched fists on the bench. Margarita jumped back. She had never seen him so aggressive. Long black curls flapped around as he shook his head. Mihalis tried to grab his hand, but he retracted it with a look of disgust, his little body shaking with rage.

'It's the truth. I wouldn't lie about something like this,' his father explained.

Margarita crouched beside him and cautiously wrapped her arms around his torso. Her bosom pressed against his shoulder. She wasn't usually a touchy-feely type of mother, and Emilio wasn't a child that craved affection, but she sensed it was needed.

Emilio elbowed her away. 'Get away from me!'

A large plane flew directly over. The room vibrated, and the fine crockery rattled loudly in the glass cabinet.

'You hear how bad it is now?' Mihalis hollered. 'It will get much worse. The government wants us out of here!'

'When?'

'In six weeks or so,' Margarita answered.

'You can all go, but I'm staying.'

'You can't stay here, my darling,' Margarita said apologetically, daring to rub his sweaty back.

'What are you going to do? Kidnap me?'

'If necessary, yes!' Mihalis yelled, slamming his hand on the bench.

'Enough!' Margarita cut in. She flicked her head to the right, motioning Mihalis to leave them. Although her husband was the calmer of the two, his anger was frightening when he lost his patience.

'I hate you!' Emilio screamed as he jumped from the stool and ran outside, slamming the back screen door.

Mihalis started after him, but Margarita held him back.

'Leave him for a bit. He needs to calm down.'

Mihalis looked at her, confused and hurt. 'That didn't go well. Sorry.'

Feeling bad for him, she leaned into his chest and kissed him on the cheek; his heart was pounding. Twenty successful years of marriage were only tested by children. She needed to reassure him that everything would be okay. After all, this was her doing.

***

When Emilio first came into the world, Margarita called him a miracle. After many miscarriages, she was convinced they would never have children. Mihalis, on the other hand, joked to customers that he was overcooked, arriving thirteen years late.

Soon after the birth, Mihalis and Margarita bought the large Federation house next door to their shop. A mansion in comparison to the flat at the back of the shop, with a large backyard and a garage off a rear lane. Emilio assumed he would live there forever. But it was in the shop where Emilio spent the first few years of his life, hanging from Margarita's waist or sitting in a highchair observing every interaction between his parents and their customers.

When he started school, he was furious, believing his parents were sending him away on purpose because the customers liked him best. He forgave them once he realised that school was a place where one learns about money. After school, he'd race to his room, change out of his uniform and enter the shop wearing his white apron. A stool allowed him to talk to customers and watch the cash register. His goals were to make a milkshake on his own then one day take over the business.

Margarita encouraged her son to learn the piano and join the local soccer team, but he wouldn't hear of it. As far as he was concerned, the shop was the only extracurricular activity he was interested in—obsessed with. His enthusiasm and charisma brought a beautiful spirit to the shop. It made up for Margarita's more reserved personality.

'You're just like your Pappou Kosta,' Margarita often told him.

The comparison to his grandfather had become more frequent since his recent passing. Margarita was devastated that they would never meet—something she had dreamed of since Emilio's birth.

***

The smell of chicken, oregano and lemon permeated the house. Lunch would soon be ready. The formal dining table had been set, and Emilio's favourite dessert, custard and jelly, was in the fridge. Mihalis distracted himself by building a Lego house with Aphrodite but ended up fighting with her because she insisted on red bricks only.

Over an hour had passed and Emilio still hadn't returned. Margarita's high-pitched whistle from the back door calling him in for lunch fell on deaf ears. Mihalis nervously watched as she put on her cardigan and walked down the concrete path towards the back of the yard. Emilio's small cubby house, made of old fence palings and a rusty corrugated iron sheet, was squeezed between the garage wall and the side fence. It infuriated Margarita whenever he went back there—it was dark, mouldy and overgrown with weeds. The rear lane was also a drug haunt. Once Emilio brought a used needle into the house. It was during the height of HIV/AIDS, and Margarita was hysterical. 'This would never happen on my island,' she cried.

There was no sign of Emilio. Although boisterous and confident, he wasn't adventurous—unless Margarita was around. She doubted he'd run away. Mihalis waited at the back door, hoping for some sign from his wife. After peering through the garage window, she shrugged and shook her head. Agitated, Mihalis disappeared back inside the house before reappearing with Aphrodite in his arms, racing towards Margarita and shouting, 'Emilio! Emilio!'

Margarita kept calm and poked her head over the fence to check if he was next door. The shop's yard was a mess. Empty blue milk crates were scattered around along with cardboard boxes. They had neglected the lawn and garden, spending whatever free time they had in the yard of the house instead. She unlocked the padlock to the gate they had installed between the two properties and walked through as pigeons scattered.

Mihalis, with toddler in arm, followed. Aphrodite was in better spirits—if art didn't work, picking her up usually did the trick.

'He has to be here somewhere,' Margarita said, approaching the shop's back door.

'It's locked, so he can't be inside.'

'Emilio! Where are you?' Margarita called out.

'Emi arr yoo?' Aphrodite repeated.

Mihalis unlocked the door and went in, searching every corner, cupboard and fridge.

'Nothing,' he said as he stepped back outside. He knew it would have been impossible to break in. Since the robbery three years earlier, the shop had been heavily secured with bars across the windows, double deadlocks and an alarm. 'Where the *fuck* could he be?'

'Mihalis!' Margarita yelled back at him. She hated it when he swore, especially when holding their impressionable daughter.

'Fuck, fuck!' repeated Aphrodite.

'That's naughty!' Margarita shouted back as she gave her a slight whack on her hand and a bigger whack across her husband's shoulder. Aphrodite burst into tears. Margarita had no choice but to take her from Mihalis. Within seconds, Aphrodite stopped.

Mihalis went back inside to turn the alarm back on. As he was turning the key to double deadlock, he heard a scraping sound coming from underneath the floor.

'The crawlspace!' he called out.

'The *what?*' Margarita quizzed.

'The space under the shop!'

'It's filthy under there!

Next to the back doorstep, a small, hinged hatch led to the space under the shop's flooring. Shallow, cramped and pitch black, the underground space deepened to about a metre at the building's centre.

Margarita passed Aphrodite back to her husband and lifted the wooden door. 'Emilio! Are you in there?'

'Go away!' Emilio's frightened voice bellowed from the darkness.

'Emilio!' Mihalis screamed.

'Shush with your shouting!' Margarita scolded her husband.

Aphrodite mimicked her father's shouting. Margarita shushed her as well, which infuriated her. Mihalis tried to put her down, but she grabbed his shirt collar and refused to let go, squealing and carrying on. By now, his anxiety was peaking, his heart racing, and sweat dripped down his face.

'Shut up!' he yelled at his little girl, startling even Margarita. Shocked, Aphrodite ceased her crying as her bottom lip started to quiver. She let go of his collar and pushed him away. Mihalis plonked her on the ground where she collapsed on the lawn, head down, and fell into a full-blown tantrum.

Another jumbo flew overhead. The air was permeated with the smell of jet fuel.

Margarita propped open the hatch while Mihalis got on all fours and poked his head in. 'I can't see anything but darkness. It's filthy! Emilio!' The echo of his voice boomed back at him. Threats of police, the bogeyman, bats and rats eating him alive didn't faze him in the slightest.

'I am going to stay here and die!' he screamed at them.

'Then we will die too!' Margarita screamed back, finally losing her calm. She tugged at her husband's leg to move away. She wanted to handle the negotiations.

'You've got Aphrodite,' Emilio said through tears and a snotty nose. 'You don't need me anymore! How can you do this? What about my teacher? My friends? Billy is going to cry so much!'

'We're going to have a new shop,' Margarita called out as she got on her knees, taking over from her husband. 'Pappou's café, Kafenio Paradisos, is ours now!'

'I don't want Paradisos. I want Citizens Corner. That's my shop.'

'We will fix it up and make it new again. It will be just like our shop but bigger and better. It's so beautiful there. We will live near the beach and it will be so quiet. No aeroplanes!'

'How could you do this to me?' he sobbed. Margarita felt like her heart would break. She had been trying to hold herself together throughout the memorial, but now she couldn't stop the tears. Mihalis sat beside her and held her hand.

Minutes later, the crying from under the shop stopped.

'Will the shop have a milkshake maker?' Emilio asked. His tone was more frightened than angry now.

'We'll take ours with us,' she answered. 'And guess what?'

'What?'

'When you grow up, it will be yours. All yours, Emilio!'

'The milkshake maker?'

'No, silly, the shop. All yours!' Margarita exclaimed.

There was a longer silence. Emilio may have been digesting it all, but the cold and dampness of the confined space shifted his attitude.

'Mum, I'm scared!' he shouted. 'My knees are shaking, and my heart is rattling really badly. And, and…there are spiderwebs all over me! Mum!'

'It's okay, my darling; nothing will happen to you. Just come towards the light. Can you see me?' she said, poking her head further in.

'I'm coming. Don't leave me!'

'I am not going anywhere. I promise.'

Margarita could see him approaching slowly, until suddenly he stopped.

'Mum, something's grabbed me.'

She watched as he struggled, pulling away from whatever it was, ripping the jumper off his back. 'Mum!' he screamed. 'The bogeyman!'

He was now in a panic, as was Mihalis, who was shouting, 'What's happened?'

Margarita kicked her husband as he tried to squeeze in beside her.

'He's got me and won't let go,' Emilio squealed. 'Something with eyes is blinking at me.'

'It's probably a bat or rat!' Mihalis yelled.

Margarita's instinct told her to go after her son, but then his hand came into view, as did his dirty, wet face. He latched onto Margarita, and she gently escorted him out. Burying his head into her neck, he sobbed so hard that it scared Mihalis, who had by now turned pale and run back into the house, grabbing Aphrodite along the way.

'Where's Baba gone?' Emilio asked.

Margarita had been expecting her husband's anxiety to give way sooner or later. 'He got scared that his poo would come out.'

'That happens to me all the time,' Emilio said. 'I hope he makes it.'

'Are you okay, my baby?'

'Mum, he grabbed me and wouldn't let go. The bogeyman, just like Baba said.'

'There's no such thing, Emilio.'

'He ruined my jumper!'

'You got it caught on something, my sweetheart.'

'But I saw its eyes.'

'Maybe a bat, like your father said. We get lots of bats here. You may have disturbed its sleep.'

'Mum, they're bleeding,' Emilio said, pointing to his knees. The material of his trousers had ripped, exposing the wounds.

'It's okay. A little Dettol and they will be fine. And guess what? I made you custard and jelly for dessert.'

He hugged and kissed her over and over; his need for affection broke her heart. 'Please don't make me stay in Greece.'

'We must go, Emilio. All this will be gone soon—the house, the shop, the garage. Now that Pappou Kosta is dead, I must go back and look after Yiayia. And one day, you'll care for me, won't you?'

'Of course, Mama.'

'And your cousin Christopher needs you. He's been so lonely since his brother died. He is desperate to have his little cousin around. You will make him so happy.'

'But I don't know him, Mama. I don't know how to make him happy.'

'Of course you do! Look at all the smiling faces leaving the shop. It's all because of you.'

'But I can't even speak Greek properly.'

'Once you're there, you'll learn it so quickly. You'll love it there. You'll be happy. I promise. It's one of the most beautiful places in the world.'

'How do you know, Mama? You haven't seen the rest of the world. Have you been to Africa? China? America? My teacher said that Bali is like paradise. Can't we go to Bali?'

'Phaedros *is* paradise,' she said, squeezing him tighter.

CHAPTER 9
Constructing Paradisos

The Kafenio

Kosta Kanarakis, a descendant of Irini Vlahos, built his fortune by taking a gamble. As the Second World War intensified and rumours of an Italian invasion loomed, residents of the harbour town of Kamiros fled to the mountains. Reckless yet resourceful, Kosta seized the opportunity of plummeting property values to buy the kafenio in the centre of the harbour. The property came with an abandoned warehouse at the edge of a large, weedy field not far from the pier. With an entrepreneurial mindset, Kosta reasoned that if the enemy came, it was best to sway them with food and hospitality. With his wife's blessing, he traded the olive groves he received as a dowry for the three hectares of prime coastal land. Dimitra had vowed to follow her husband to the edge of the world, even if it meant abandoning the best house in Melissani. In the end, despite people's initial misgivings, the gamble paid off.

Following the Italian occupation in the summer of 1941, Kamiros transformed from a shabby seaside village into a bustling commercial port town. What the Italians had done for Rhodes began to unfold on Phaedros. A new military clinic was constructed, and Kosta's warehouse was refurbished as a rehabilitation facility. The pier was extended, and roads leading to a new town square were widened. Kosta's kafenio, Paradisos, was at the heart of this development, servicing the rehab facility and clinic. While the enemy grew to love Kosta and Dimitra, the locals in the surrounding villages branded them as traitors.

In 1944, tragedy struck when Dimitra died while pregnant with their first child, just as the war was turning against the Italians. Within a year of their retreat, Kosta remarried. His second wife, Freda Poulos, was the priest's eldest daughter, who defied her father by marrying a Kanarakis, a name associated with black magic and unorthodox cures. But Freda was robust and determined, having proven her worth through hard work. If anyone could rescue Kosta from the family curse it was her.

The priest relented, giving his new son-in-law a dowry of land adjoining the area behind the café. Many saw Kosta's selection of a new wife as a strategic move based on his ambition to build an empire.

Following the war's end, the town of Kamiros filled again with former residents who returned to the coast to open tourist rooms. Word had spread about a hidden paradise between the islands of Chios and Mytilene. Kosta and Freda capitalised on the demand for accommodation by converting three rooms at the back of their house into guestrooms. They also leased the warehouse to the archdiocese (with the help of Freda's father), turning it into a hostel for pilgrims visiting the monastery of Saint Sophia on the opposite headland. The larger pier, built by the Italians, welcomed larger ferries from the mainland.

By 1950, Kosta and Freda had three children: Apostoli, Margarita and Salome. Growing up in the kafenio and interacting with travellers from all over the world helped them refine their exceptional hospitality skills. Upon reaching adulthood, Kosta subdivided his coastal properties into two portions—the southern half towards the town square went to Toli, while the northern half, which housed the kafenio and warehouse, went to Margarita. Salome, the youngest and more rebellious, inherited two hectares of olive grove near Ancient Tallos and the house in Melissani. The old pasha's villa had lain in disarray since Kosta's move to Kamiros, but Salome had no interest in it. Like many, she believed it was haunted. Years later, with no children to bequeath it to, she sold it to her brother for his retirement.

After Kosta passed away in the winter of 1990, Freda, undeterred by age or grief, continued to run Paradisos with the help of Desar Deevish, a newly arrived Albanian. He was the youngest of three brothers who took advantage of the recent liberalisation measures in Albania allowing its citizens the freedom to travel. Freda couldn't rely on her children. Margarita had been in Australia since migrating in 1970; Toli was struggling following the recent death of his son, Kostaki, to leukemia; and Salome and her husband were the last people she would trust. She considered her youngest daughter too flighty and conceited, and Vasilis, a farmer, preferred the company of crops and animals to humans.

Freda pledged that Paradisos would remain open until she could hand over the business to Margarita. At eighty-two, she was as sharp as a fresh blade of grass. Her piercing blue eyes and snow-white hair, immaculately tied back in a bun, made her look younger than her years. But beneath that composed nature was a feisty woman who didn't tolerate raucous behaviour. If the kafenio got too rowdy, she'd pick up the goat bell from under the counter and give it a shake, just as she had done when her late husband often blurred the lines between business and pleasure.

The Hotel Restaurant

Within eighteen months of relocating to the island, Margarita and her family built a two-storey mansion on the parcel of land between the kafenio and the warehouse. The farmyard, which had housed chickens, rabbits, a vegetable garden and twenty orange trees, was transformed into the Politis villa. The house, featuring expensive German appliances, Swedish double-glazed windows, and a wraparound marble verandah, epitomised every returned migrant's dream home. Yiayia Freda was provided with her own living quarters. Desar, the Albanian worker, was not forgotten and moved into a small studio next to the garage.

Once the family settled in, the old house behind the kafenio was demolished. This freed up space to expand the kafenio into a larger café-restaurant with a courtyard and outdoor clay oven. A facelift at the front included new floor-to-ceiling windows and bi-fold doors, all framed in cedar, letting in light and views of the harbour. The name Paradisos was retained to honour the late Kosta Kanarakis. Being so close to the pier, Paradisos was the first stop for travellers stepping off the ferry, lured by the aroma of coffee and freshly baked cheese pastries. 'Such a contrast to our shop in Sydenham!' Mihalis boasted. 'No more noise from the traffic and those planes,' Margarita replied with relief.

Now, the sound of seagulls and the toot of boats served as the long-play soundtrack. Emilio was elated, weaving through the new tables and chairs as if he was Maria skipping through the hills of the Swiss Alps.

'Look behind the bar, Emilio,' Mihalis called. 'There's something there for you.'

Expecting a bike or maybe a scooter, the boy raced to the back of the bar only to find the space empty.

'What is it, Baba?'

'Lift up the blue towel from the shelf!'

Tossing the towel into the air, he stood back, stunned. 'Our milkshake maker! You brought it with us.' Emilio ran and hugged his parents. 'Can I make us a milkshake? Please?'

'Of course!' Margarita said, having already organised fresh cow's milk instead of the canned evaporated variety they'd become used to since their arrival.

Yiayia Freda sat in the corner, watching in silence. 'Do you like the new Paradisos, Mother?' Mihalis asked.

'If you like it, then I like it more!' she grinned.

***

At the time, Kamiros had two small hotels and numerous guesthouses. But the recent discoveries at Ancient Tallos had garnered considerable publicity, attracting archaeologists, professionals, and middle-aged tourists to the island. People were also looking for alternatives to the crowds of Mykonos and Santorini. Consequently, demand for accommodation surged. While the café-restaurant was being expanded and modernised, the warehouse was converted into twenty Cycladic-style studio apartments across three floors. This was all part of the grand plan to grow a business for the children to inherit.

Hotel Paradisos opened in 1992 boasting a pool, terraced garden and cabana. A bamboo-lined path connected the hotel to the café, running behind the Politis villa in the middle. Hotel Paradisos came under Margarita's management, while Mihalis—with Emilio's assistance—took control of the café-restaurant.

After the first year, Margarita stopped spruiking for business at the wharf. Pre-booking by phone was the only way a visitor could secure a room. The family's work ethic had redefined hospitality and changed the social dynamics of the port town.

To keep up with the restaurant's demands, Mihalis installed a large outdoor barbecue in the courtyard next to the clay oven. Staff were employed to make bread in the morning and prepare pita and souvlakia for lunch and dinner. Margarita, ever inventive when it came to cooking, introduced her first pizza topped with local feta, cherry tomatoes, olives and oregano. 'Because "Margarita" was already taken,' she joked, 'I have decided to call it Politis Pizza.' Islanders came from afar to dine on the new taste sensation.

All who came and stayed were drawn to the little boy fluent in English with an Australian accent. The older regulars saw in him echoes of Kosta Kanarakis—his gestures and gift for conversation. As Emilio's Greek improved, he became the town's unofficial interpreter, sometimes even assisting local men to chat up younger tourists. When Margarita caught wind of what was happening, she quickly grabbed her mother's goat bell, rang it in their ears and reprimanded them. Once Emilio was old enough to understand the intent behind his mother's embarrassing behaviour, he was able to manage the situation on his own.

In another expansionist venture, Mihalis secured a twenty-year exclusive catering lease for Kamiros Beach. Sixteen thatched umbrellas and thirty-two daybeds were installed, and a small beach kiosk was erected to serve the summer crowds.

The third Politis child, Dimitri, arrived on 14 April 1996. The unplanned pregnancy came when everyone was run off their feet. Fortunately, Margarita had her mother on hand to assist. Unlike Aphrodite, Dimitri was a more placid baby, constantly smiling. His curly honey-blond hair gave him an angelic look, and soon he became the most beloved baby on the island.

Within ten years of opening the hotel, the entire face of the port town had transformed—physically, economically and socially. Tavernas, bars and souvenir shops sprouted along the waterfront. During summer, the nightlife was bustling, and the waft of freshly cooked souvlakia lingered until daybreak every day of the week.

For a while, Mihalis contemplated opening another restaurant but changed his mind after Emilio's godfather, a real estate agent from Australia, visited in 1997. 'The Olympics are coming. Sydney's about to explode,' he bragged, much to Margarita's dismay. 'Whatever you do, don't sell your place in Earlwood! Now is the time to buy more properties.'

Mihalis had bought a house on a large block in Earlwood in the late 1970s. He held onto it in case Greece didn't work out. But as time went on, Greece went better than expected, and business was booming.

Mihalis returned to Australia in January 1998 and purchased three studio apartments in Pyrmont, just before the Sydney property boom. Margarita wasn't happy. Deep down, she understood his intentions. The children should own something in the country of their birth, and if Dimitri wanted to become an Australian as well, surely it wouldn't be that hard. Moreover, there was no guarantee Greece's economy would improve. While it all made sense psychologically, Margarita wanted to cut her ties with Australia. She couldn't bear the thought of losing her children to migration like her parents lost her.

As their property portfolio grew, so did Margarita's anxiety.

The Resort

The idea for the resort first surfaced after Yiayia Freda passed away in 2007. At eighty-eight, she had endured more than her share of life's cruelty. The last two decades had been particularly cruel. Witnessing her son, Toli, collapse under one tragedy after the other had driven the final nail into her coffin. Toli Kanarakis was a man marred by loss: a daughter stillborn, one twin dead from leukaemia at eight, the other, Christopher, to suicide in 1996. While Margarita enjoyed fortune and happiness in marriage, her brother lived its grim opposite.

After his wife, Antigone, died from a stroke in 2004, Toli leased out his car hire business and withdrew to the shack he built on her land behind the hotel. The villa at Melissani, which he purchased from Salome, no longer held any appeal. Instead, he embraced a nomadic lifestyle with his chickens and goats. On Easter Sunday in 2007, eleven-year-old Dimitri found his body in the shack while delivering food and red-dyed eggs.

It took months before Dimitri could bring himself to leave his room. Margarita was beside herself with worry, and Mihalis had to bring in Desar to help run the hotel. Her devastation only deepened when, two months later, Margarita's mother died. With half the family scattered outside Greece, Margarita felt increasingly isolated. Emilio was in Milan pursuing his master's in business, while Aphrodite, a budding artist, lived in Berlin with her young daughter, Rika. Margarita decided that things had to change.

'It's time we re-evaluate our lives,' Margarita told her husband late one night at the dinner table. 'Emilio and Aphrodite may never return. We can't rely on Desar to run the hotel forever—he wants to marry and run his own business. It's time to hand Paradisos to Emilio and let him do what he wants with it. We made him a promise. We should honour it before it's too late.'

'You want me to retire already?' Mihalis asked. 'I still have years ahead of me.'

'You don't need this anymore. You've worked your whole life— what good is wealth without your children? Give Emilio his dream. And now that the children will inherit my brother's properties, the timing is perfect.'

With no children to leave his properties to, Toli left everything to his niece and nephews. The Melissani villa would go to Aphrodite; the olive groves behind the Paradisos to Emilio; and the car-rental business and yard to Dimitri.

'Emilio can double the size of Paradisos now that he owns Antigone's olive grove,' Margarita continued. 'And if Dimitri sells him the car yard, Paradisos could become a suburb of its own. Aphrodite just might return now that she has the villa in Melissani and our granddaughter can grow up close to us.'

'Your stressed brain is trying to cope by coming up with grand illusions.'

'These aren't illusions! I know this is right.'

'Build their future on tainted land?'

'What are you talking about?'

He turned his head away from her. 'I feel uneasy.'

'Don't be ridiculous!'

'You know I'm not superstitious, but it will always dig at me… that we capitalised on your brother's tragic life.'

'It's what he wanted. I can't believe that you're thinking like that.'

'I can't believe you're not!' he yelled, turning to face her again. 'It's in your blood to think like that.'

Margarita stared at him, dumbfounded. 'So no other family has bad luck? Have you joined the ranks of the Phaedrians? Stooped to the ridiculous mentality that keeps them in the Dark Ages?'

'I just don't want any more suffering.'

'The future of this island lies with us. We need to give Emilio the responsibility of moving this family forward. We need to consolidate all our resources and help him!'

Mihalis shuffled in his chair and glared at her. A fork holding a piece of galaktoboureko dangled in mid-air before he dropped it onto his plate. He got up and retreated to the bedroom. Margarita knew he would eventually come around.

***

'They've offered me a full-time role as deputy customer service manager,' Emilio announced over lunch on his first day back on the island. It was July 2007 and he was on two weeks' leave from his employment at the renowned Golden Rafael Hotel in Milan.

'What did you tell them?' Mihalis asked.

'Yes, of course. It's not every day one gets offered such an opportunity, especially before even graduating.'

'Congratulations,' Margarita forced herself to say.

'Baba?'

'Yes, yes. Congratulations. If that is what you want.'

'Well, of course it's what I want. It's what I've been working towards. This is an exclusive international hotel!'

'Well…that's good then,' Mihalis responded, conscious of his wife's stare.

'Is everything alright? You both look a little confused.'

Words tangled in Mihalis's throat. He shifted restlessly, then rose and walked across to the window. Outside, the haze of the heat blanketed the headland opposite, blurring the monastery of

Saint Sophia. Margarita cleared her throat and sipped from her glass of water.

'What is going on? Has something happened to Dimitri? Aphrodite? Rika?'

'Everyone is fine,' his mother answered.

'Where's Dimitri?'

'In his room with a migraine.'

'Of course he is. A quick hello would have been nice.'

Before the mood deteriorated, Mihalis cut in, his voice raised. 'We understand that…you need to make some decisions about… your future.'

'My future?'

Mihalis walked back to the table and sat down.

'Remember what we told you back at our old house in Sydney?' Margarita interrupted. 'When we dragged you out from under the shop? Well, your father and I believe the time has come.'

'What are you both going on about?'

'We're giving you Paradisos,' Mihalis blurted out.

Emilio blinked, his thick eyebrows raised. 'What?'

'The business will be yours!' Margarita said, taking his hand. 'Your father and I aren't getting any younger.'

'Now?'

'We need to make the necessary arrangements first,' Mihalis replied. 'Now that you have inherited land from your uncle, God rest his soul, you can grow this place to be whatever you want it to be. If we clear the land, you can expand the hotel.'

'Expand?'

'Yes, expand to the back, to the side, to the top.'

'What side? That's Dimitri's land!'

'He has no interest in a car hire business. He'll be happy to sell it to you.'

Stunned, Emilio rose and paced the room. 'Well, this is a surprise. I just need a minute.'

'I will sell the properties in Australia,' Mihalis declared. 'You can build the Taj Mahal if you want.'

'You're going to sell up?'

'Your mother and I don't have any plans to return to Australia, and I don't think any of my children do. Do you?'

'Well, no. Not if I have my own resort.'

Margarita jumped in. 'If you want the business to continue, we must put everything into it. It must be something special, something magnificent!'

'You've dropped a huge bombshell here. I appreciate the offer, don't get me wrong, but I must consider the Golden Rafael. I mean, we are talking Milan here. This is Phaedros…you know what I mean? I would be an idiot to give up such an opportunity.'

'But Emilio!' Margarita protested. 'What better opportunity than owning your own hotel?'

'Let's be realistic; we are a mere speck in the sea. Beyond ancient relics and nice beaches, there's little commercial future here.'

'What do you mean?' Mihalis snapped. 'How can you say that considering all we have done?'

'I will need to borrow money from the bank, you realise,' Emilio pointed out, knowing his father hated anyone in his family being in debt. 'And lots of it.'

'Maybe not, depending on the sale of our properties in Australia,' Mihalis stressed.

'Perhaps, but let's be clear: I will be making all the decisions.'

'Well, yes, Emilio, it will be yours,' his mother assured him.

'Baba, are you in agreement?'

Mihalis shot Margarita an angry glance, simmering at the quiet power play his son was exerting. 'As we said, it will be yours.'

'But I don't want to fight you whenever a decision needs to be made. I want complete control of this project, otherwise I can't accept your offer.'

'Of course!' Mihalis barked. 'How much clearer do we need to be?'

'You know Jorgen is here?' Margarita said, jumping in to avert an escalating argument.

'Yes, he messaged me to check if I was coming.'

'He's an architect; maybe you can talk with him,' Mihalis suggested.

'Yes, I know he's an architect, Baba.'

'Okay, okay, I'm just trying to be helpful.'

'When will Aphrodite and Rika get here?' Emilio asked his mother.

'Next week.'

'I'll talk to Aphrodite about some art for the new resort.'

Emilio got up, squeezed between his parents, clasped his arms around their shoulders and drew them in towards his face. 'Thank you,' he said as he kissed them each on the cheek before disappearing into his room.

***

Jorgen presented his drawings to the family the following Sunday before lunch. The formal living room had been opened for the occasion, and the stone-coloured leather lounge given a quick wipe down. Aphrodite had arrived that morning for the summer holidays. The flamboyant artist entered the large ornate room in her Jackie Onassis sunglasses, jingling bangles and matching neck beads. Three-year-old Rika trailed shyly behind her. Mihalis was glad his daughter could make it. Her laughter and vibrant energy were always welcome, lighting up the family dynamics whenever there was a threat of collapse.

'I can't believe you've cut your hair!' Aphrodite teased Jorgen, whom she hadn't seen in a few years. His blond hair, once past his shoulders and always tied in a ponytail, was now cropped above the ear with a long fringe combed to the side. 'It brings out your beautiful blue eyes. Look at you! What are you, eighteen?'

'Always the flirt, Aphrodite. Twenty-seven.'

'How's Astrid?' Mihalis asked Jorgen.

'She's in Jordan on an expedition.'

'Unfortunately, we won't see Astrid this year,' Margarita lamented.

'She said I'm old enough now to travel to Phaedros on my own.'

Jorgen and his mother, Astrid, were among the first guests to stay at Paradisos when it opened in 1992. Back then, Jorgen was a shy, straggly twelve-year-old who clung to his mother like a scared puppy. Their bond with the Politis family had grown from that first difficult trip, taken after Astrid's separation from Jorgen's father. For years afterwards, they returned every summer.

Jorgen's proposal for the resort was based on a twenty-four-hour guest experience. After checking in at the antiquity-inspired reception—the current café-restaurant—guests would be transported by golf buggies to 'The Village', a cluster of thirty-three luxury suites built on Aunt Antigone's olive groves. A mix of single and two-storey buildings, with one three-storey villa at the back, would give the effect of a Cycladic-hillside village. The infinity pool at the front would provide uninterrupted views of the harbour, with a breakfast bar beside it. For lunch, guests could stroll down the tree-lined path to the courtyard restaurant behind reception. If they wanted a facial, massage or a workout, a short walk south would lead them to the wellness centre, converted from Uncle Toli's car rental business. In place of the old car yard, a twenty-five-metre infinity pool would stretch towards the main reception. Dinner options ranged from al fresco dining at the Pool Café to à la carte dining in the new restaurant on the reception's first floor. Late night cocktails would be served at the rooftop bar, boasting a 360-degree view of the island. The existing hotel would be refurbished to match the aesthetic of The Village. The family home would gain two new floors for offices, a media centre, a staff tearoom and a penthouse studio apartment for Emilio, Aphrodite and Dimitri.

'I love it,' Aphrodite yelled at the top of her voice, clapping. 'I think it embodies something unique, intimate and luxurious. How exciting! And yes, you can commission me for some art, Emilio.'

'Can we really build this, Jorgen?' Mihalis asked.

'Of course, Mr Politis. It will be magnificent!'

'What do you think, Dimitri?' Margarita asked.

'It's cool,' he replied aloofly while playing Nintendo with Rika.

Margarita looked at Emilio, waiting for his response, observing that he had remained silent throughout the presentation. 'Emilio?'

'I think it's brilliant!' he said. 'Absolutely brilliant!'

***

The following autumn, Emilio completed his master's degree and resigned from Golden Rafael. Upon his return, he immediately began his mandatory twelve-month military conscription. When he completed his posting in Alexandroupoli in September 2009, he flew to Athens to search for a construction partner. With Greece sliding towards bankruptcy, many engineering companies were seeking projects abroad. Emilio struck a partnership with a leading engineering firm and M-Design, one of the most awarded design firms in the country, known for outfitting luxury hotels for the 2004 Athens Olympics.

The idea of embarking on a significant construction project in 2010 was considered madness by many. Private investment in the country had more or less stopped. But it was a gamble the family was willing to take. Like Kosta Kanarakis who had seized an opportunity seventy years earlier, his grandson, Emilio Politis, now intended to redefine the island once more.

CHAPTER 10
Birmingham and Phaedros, March 2013

'The man's an idiot!' Professor Papadopoulos fretted over the phone. 'I just want to prepare you. He's determined to meet you at the port. God knows what he's organised!'

'I'll be fine,' Doctor Hossein Basra reassured him, sealing the last box of books. 'Meeting Mayor Dimitriadis may help with my assimilation.'

The professor's cavalier tone helped lift the sombre mood that had engulfed Hossein since morning. His final lecture had ended with the expected fanfare and a bouquet of flowers, still wrapped on his desk. Excited as he was about his new appointment, there was no escaping the finality of this chapter of his life. Outside, a branch from the ginkgo tree scraped against his window—the spring foliage would be one more thing he would miss.

Only the exit interview with Human Resources awaited him. All his rehearsed criticisms—poor pay, bullying, missing out on the department head position—now felt irrelevant. Everyone had assumed the position would be his. Yet, by some miraculous alignment, a posting outside academia on the Greek island of Phaedros had fallen into his lap.

When Professor Yiannis Papadopoulos encouraged him to apply for the position at the Museum of Ancient Tallos, his heart skipped a beat. He had spent many summers as an undergraduate on Phaedros, excavating the buried Temple of Artemis Ismene.

Its treasures of murals, ceramics and scribed tablets, and a toppled statue of Artemis, were astonishing. But it was the remains of a human skeleton, Nicephorus, hermetically sealed for more than 2000 years, that made the excavation extraordinary. Nicephorus, the slave, had scribed the details of the city's siege by Demetrius I Poliorcetes before an earthquake in 306 BC destroyed it. The tablets became the foundation of Hossein's PhD and the launch of his academic career.

Deservedly, Hossein impressed the interview panel. His fluency in modern and ancient Greek and his field experience in Phaedros, Lebanon, Turkey and northern Greece were unmatched. The list of his published articles on Ancient Tallos made him the leading expert. The professor's influence with the Ministry of Culture secured his appointment. When the offer came, Hossein felt as though Atlas had finally kicked the world off his shoulders.

Hossein's quick trip to the island in January confirmed what he already suspected: Professor Papadopoulos was a terrible administrator. Since his 1992 posting to Phaedros, he had done little to bring the temple's treasures to the world's attention. Hossein's priority would be securing modernisation funding. If it meant playing politics with the mayor, then he would be a willing player.

***

The long haul to the island on 27 April 2013 was unforgiving. It was Holy Week and the ferry was packed. He wished he had flown to Mytilene and taken the shorter ferry trip from there, but he had a romantic longing to sit in his cabin by a porthole with hours to relax and read. 'Never again,' he said to himself after eighteen hours of rough seas. However, the poor weather wasn't the only thing that marred the trip.

'You Greek?' the skinny, beady-eyed kiosk attendant asked.

'No. Iranian from England,' Hossein answered defensively, picking up the man's dismissive body language.

'Iranian? What is your name?'

'Hossein Basra.'

'Where are you going, *Hossein*?'

'To Phaedros.'

The attendant frowned. 'No mosque in Phaedros.'

Sensing the impending racism, warm blood rushed to Hossein's face. 'Yes, there is. In the capital of Melissani. A small mosque built during the Ottoman occupation. Besides, I don't need a mosque to pray.'

A woman behind him grew impatient. 'Please take the man's order so we can return to our seats.'

'Beer or wine?' the attendant asked facetiously.

'Black coffee and a tiropita, please.'

'No alcohol?'

'I am Muslim. Besides, it's seven in the morning.'

'So, you're Muslim?' He said it as if uncovering a deep secret.

'Yes,' Hossein replied in Greek. 'I follow the teachings of my scriptures. And you—as a Christian—do you follow yours? Which part of Greece are you from? I might know it, having spent years unearthing your ancestors.'

The man's jaw dropped. Stroking his bushy moustache, he uttered, 'Kalamata.'

'"Friendship or enmity is everywhere an affair of time and circumstance." Thucydides, *History of the Peloponnesian War*,' Hossein recited in Greek.

Confused at first by the ancient phrase, the man soon offered an embarrassed smile. 'Ime megalos malakas,' the man said as he held out his hand. 'And that's from the ancient text of *Malakismenos*, by Theodoros. Nice to meet you, sir. My name is Theodoros, or Theo to my friends, and I apologise.'

Hossein took his hand and shook it. 'My name is Doctor Hossein Basra.' He found the comeback humorous, adding that he would make a point of reading Theo's 'ancient text' of 'Wankers' sometime soon.

The racism was not an isolated encounter, and normally Hossein would restrain himself, but the professor's warning echoed in his head: 'You either stand your ground or be willing to get stomped into it. If you are to lead a museum, you need to embrace authority.' The professor was right. Hossein's 'passive nature', according to the interview feedback, was why he didn't get the position at the university. But he didn't care about that anymore. Phaedros was where he wanted to be. With that certainty came the responsibility of being accountable, showing leadership and being ruthless when needed.

As Hossein stepped onto the pier at Kamiros harbour on that cool spring morning, a short, stocky man with leathery skin grabbed his hand and shook it vigorously, not wanting to let go. 'Welcome, welcome, Doctor Basra,' said the man in English.

'Good morning,' Hossein politely responded, towering over him. At 190 centimetres, he felt intimidating beside the shorter man.

'Doctor Hossein! I am Mayor Dimitriadis.'

'Nice to meet you,' Hossein said, continuing the conversation in English.

'I recognised you from your photo on the university website. Welcome to our beautiful island—our Phaedros,' he said as he huffed and puffed while still shaking his hand. 'You remind me of Poseidon.'

'Maybe the long beard,' Hossein replied as he stroked his beard.

'The beard, your height, dark tan...'

'But no trident!' Hossein joked.

The mayor froze, unsure.

Hossein raised a fist. 'Triana.'

'Yes, of course, of course, triana!' Clearly, he didn't know the Greek word either. The mayor released his grip. 'With your expertise, we will shine a light on the island's most significant treasures.'

'Let's hope so.'

'He is now one of ours!' the mayor called out to a thin younger man with a camera around his neck. 'May I introduce you to Pandelis Milopitakis, editor-photographer-journalist for *Island News*.'

'Welcome, Doctor Basra. Can I take a few photos?'

'Yes, of course!'

No older than twenty-five, the photographer looked more like a Mormon missionary than a Greek newspaper editor. He had mousy blond hair, crew-cut style, and wore a white short-sleeved shirt that fitted loosely over his slight build. A name badge—Pandelis Milopitakis, Chief Editor, *Island News*—was pinned to his shirt pocket.

The professor had warned Hossein that the mayor wanted his arrival to be front-page news, seizing any opportunity for a good news story. Manoeuvring next to Hossein, the height difference became more obvious, calling for a more distant shot. And then—just when the pose could not have been more contrived—the mayor pulled out a small statue of Artemis from his pocket.

'A picture can tell a thousand words,' he announced, holding the statue like it was an Oscar.

Pandelis shared a private giggle with Hossein. They were all doing their jobs—the mayor hunting headlines, Pandelis selling his newspaper and Hossein marketing the museum. But more was at stake for Hossein: he wanted acceptance by the community. Even with perfect Greek he was still a Muslim, an outsider. The tension in Syria was worsening and infiltrating everyone's consciousness. But he was not a refugee—he was there because they chose him, they wanted him. On command, he put on his best smile for the camera.

'We must go for a coffee,' the mayor insisted as he passed the statue to Pandelis, a prop to be reused again.

Despite his eagerness to reach his Melissani home, collect the car and visit the museum, Hossein recognised the need for patience.

'It's just a short walk. Kyra Margarita's galaktoboureko is like eating heaven,' the mayor proclaimed, gripping Hossein's arm to ensure he didn't escape.

'Yes, of course,' Hossein answered, noticing the mayor's impressive belly, wondering how many trays of galaktoboureko he'd consumed over a lifetime. He was himself a fan of Greece's famous sweet, but for now, swallowing thick, gelatinous milk was the last thing his ferry-tossed stomach could tolerate.

The pier buzzed with a flurry of activity—fishing boats unloading the day's catch, mopeds and cars driving off the ferry ramp, and tourists being accosted by boisterous spruikers. An elderly lottery vendor approached only to be shooed away by the mayor. Several stray dogs lifted their heads to check out the commotion. The mayor hissed at them, but they merely shifted a few metres away and resumed their sprawled positions on the asphalt.

'Big problem. Too many strays, and they think they own the place.'

Crossing the road, Hossein knew exactly where they were headed—the new resort, Paradisos II. He remembered it in the mid-nineties as a small hotel with a popular restaurant and having never managed to get a table. The professor had stressed the importance of the Politis family. He hadn't expected the introduction to happen so quickly.

The large white neoclassical building rose before them with two Ionic columns framing the entrance. A shallow, U-shaped driveway lined with young pencil pines led to the newspaper-covered glass doors. Inside a radio blared, while in the distance a power saw screeched through marble.

'Kalimera pedia!' the mayor called out to the painters, who stopped in their tracks, confused by the visitors.

The smell of fresh paint was overpowering. A sepia-coloured relief of ancient scenes thirty centimetres high ran along the length of the wall.

'Welcome!' echoed a voice from the marble staircase. A tall man descended dressed in designer jeans and a black polo. 'I am so sorry. I hope you haven't been waiting too long. We are just putting some final touches to the restaurant upstairs.'

'Kalimera, Emilio,' the mayor boomed.

'Kalimera sas, and welcome.' Emilio extended an enthusiastic hand to Hossein. 'Doctor Basra—so good to meet you. Emilio Politis.'

'Please, call me Hossein.'

'Welcome, Hossein, to Phaedros and to Paradisos II. Excuse the mess. We're running way behind schedule. Easter's just around the corner and we're all desperately trying to catch up before Jesus's resurrection. At least the heating is working. March can be bitter here.'

'I'm fine, thanks,' Hossein said, loosening his scarf. 'I'll acclimatise soon.'

'Pandelis, take some photos,' the mayor ordered.

'Of course. If I can get you to stand…perhaps here,' he said, pointing to a freshly painted wall.

'Allow me,' Emilio interrupted, turning his back to Pandelis. Gently guiding Hossein by the elbow, he led him towards a relief near the marble stairs. 'Much better, don't you think?'

'Of course,' Pandelis replied, accepting his place in the world. He raised the black Nikon to his red face and started shooting. Hossein understood that no one challenges this hotelier.

'You as well!' Emilio called to the mayor waiting eagerly at the side. He wedged himself between the men as if negotiating a truce between two warring giants.

Then, by complete surprise, Emilio pulled an envelope from his back pocket. 'A small gift for the museum. You come with extremely high regard. The professor assured me the museum hired the best of the best.'

Inside was a cheque for 5000 euros. Hossein was speechless. Another round of clicks immortalised his surprise.

'This is very, very generous. I don't know what to say.'

'Renovations are awful,' Emilio said. 'Anything you need—information, tradesmen—please let me know. I enjoy sponsoring worthwhile projects.'

'I will. Thank you!'

Hossein hadn't expected this donation, though now it made sense. It was all carefully orchestrated—news-making, subtle marketing and grooming.

Emilio ran a hand through his wavy hair then smoothed his eyebrows before giving Pandelis the thumbs up to take photos.

'I understand you speak fluent Greek.'

'Yes, I do. I can speak several languages, but I prefer Greek.'

Hossein noted his disappointment.

'I was a little excited about speaking English with someone of your background.'

'Well, English it is.'

'No. Greek. I insist. But I must warn you, I automatically switch to English when the conversation becomes intellectual. If I start rattling away in Greek, you'll know my emotional intelligence is waning.'

'Well, if you hear Farsi coming out of my mouth, you'll know I'm doing the same.'

The mayor laughed aloud, a little too forced. Emilio winked at Hossein, another jab at the mayor. Hossein was enjoying the banter until Emilio suddenly leaned in towards his ear.

'Your appointment will displease many,' he murmured. 'But they'll get used to it.'

The comment, though startling, didn't surprise Hossein. Even with EU freedoms, his position as a curator would have begrudged many Greek archaeologists, let alone the locals.

'Thank you for that reality check.'

'We have the best, and that's all that matters,' Emilio reiterated, patting him firmly on the back.

'Everything alright?' the mayor asked, a little affronted by his exclusion.

'Everything is perfect. Time for some refreshments,' Emilio announced, pointing to the lift next to the stairs. 'We just had it installed. Fingers crossed we don't get stuck,' he chuckled as they all got in. The tinted glass at the back of the lift overlooked the building rubble which soon fell away to reveal a blue sky and the sea. As the southern coastline came into full view, so did the topographical division of the island—the lush southern forest jutting up to the rocky, arid north, Yin and Yang.

Exiting the elevator, Emilio led Hossein to the floor-to-ceiling windows. 'That's Melissani. Your village!' he said, pointing to Agios Constantinos perched on Mount Dillinos. Then, lowering his voice: 'From here, I can keep an eye on my sister.' Another private exchange, its intent unclear. Was it directed at him? Putting him on notice? Emilio then pointed towards the rear courtyard below to what appeared to be a fountain.

'The statue of Artemis will stand there. She is being replicated on Rhodes—an adaptation of "Artemis in Chase" from the temple. Something my sister, Aphrodite, organised. She is an artist.'

'I know. I have seen some of her work in a catalogue.'

'And?'

'Very commanding and vibrant.'

Following Emilio's finger, Hossein's attention fell on the new development at the foot of the mountain about 200 metres away. 'The courtyard path leads to The Village.'

Fleetingly, he mistook it for an actual village. 'It's beautiful. I see why you've called it The Village.'

'Yes, it will be once it's finished. We're currently waiting for a shipment of furniture. The garden and pool area are being tiled this week. Fingers crossed we will open by the end of summer. Let's go upstairs. It's a little more private.'

Taking a small flight of marble stairs, they entered a circular room.

'The Lighthouse Bar. From here, everything in the harbour is in view. Down there,' he said, pointing south next to the infinity pool, 'will be the health and fitness centre. Would you believe it was once my Uncle Toli's car rental business?'

'God rest his soul,' the mayor said.

'I'm sorry to hear of his passing,' Hossein added.

'It's been a few years now, but thank you. No doubt you'll hear about the tragic life he led and lots of other stories about my family. If you have questions, please come to me. Gossip can be dangerous, especially in a remote community where many people are idle.'

The mayor nodded solemnly. Hossein felt the power dynamic settle, his presence there to remind the other men of their place in Emilio's orbit.

'You've done an amazing job, Emilio,' Hossein said, trying to change the focus.

'Fantastic!' proclaimed the mayor.

A rattle of crockery sounded from the stairwell.

'Kyria Margarita. Good morning!' exclaimed the mayor as an older lady in a navy skirt suit appeared, balancing a silver tray with refreshments. 'He still has you working in the kitchen?' he chuckled.

The woman ignored the mayor. She nodded at Pandelis and turned her attention to Hossein, placing a large silver tray with coffees, glasses of water and pastries on the table.

'Hossein, this is my mother, Margarita.'

Hossein promptly extended his hand. 'Pleased to meet you.'

Margarita gave him a long, piercing look. 'Welcome to Phaedros, Doctor Basra.'

'Please, call me Hossein.'

She was a striking woman, tall with short silver hair, sharing her son's big brown eyes.

'Hossein, I know you will do very well here. If you need anything, my family is here to help.'

'Thank you for your generosity.'

'You are here alone? No family?'

'Just me. Oh, I have my mother in London.'

'Your father?'

'He was killed when I was young, in Iran.'

'I'm so sorry. It's strange to hear someone from Iran speaking Greek so fluently. I hope you will bring your mother to visit one day.'

'I hope so too.'

Her manner, though slightly abrupt, still felt genuinely warm and sincere. Her failure to ask any questions about his marital status surprised him, though. In fact, no one did. Perhaps they already knew? Was 'divorcé' attached to his bio? Maybe his appearance suggested that this man was best left alone.

Her smile reassured him that she approved.

'I would have brought you some galaktoboureko but the oven isn't working yet. I'll bring you a tray when I visit Aphrodite next. She also lives in Melissani.'

'Yes, so I understand. I've heard a lot about her.'

'She runs a café right next to her studio,' Emilio added.

'Your galaktoboureko is like eating heaven!' the mayor said, leaning in closer and nearly knocking over his glass of water. 'That's what I told Doctor Hossein.'

Margarita turned her head towards the mayor, clearly annoyed. She didn't seem to like him very much. She smiled at Pandelis, half-looked at the mayor and nodded. 'Adio sas. Welcome to Phaedros, Hossein,' she said, then gracefully descended the stairs.

The men sat around the table for refreshments. The discussion turned to the economy. There was no doubt what the collective sentiment was. The recent news of public officials collecting government benefits from the deceased had outraged the nation. The bailout from the International Monetary Fund was embarrassing. A glimmer of hope—at least for Phaedros—lay with Paradisos II. The new resort would become the gateway to the island's treasures, beauty and history.

'Like the rest of the country, people here sit pretty on a name, a history, a beautiful landscape,' said Emilio. 'They have this misguided belief of entitlement. This is the *Greek* problem. I'm happy you're here. It's been years since I visited our museum. Do you know why? My last visit left me disheartened. I want our museum to inspire, the way Italy's, Spain's and France's do. Our history needs to be brought back into our everyday life.'

Hossein was a little surprised by Emilio's spiel and had initially assumed the envelope was a bribe. But the sincerity in Emilio's words now gave him some comfort.

Emilio's phone rang. He got up and walked across to the large window. 'Yes, I see your yacht. Sorry, and your name is…Andrew Kappos. That's no problem, Andrew. See you shortly.' He ended the call and returned to the table. 'Excuse my manners but I'm interviewing for a new cruiser company and, unfortunately, I must leave you. He has just docked. An American by the sounds of him.'

The timing was perfect. Hossein felt elated. His stomach had settled, and his introduction to Emilio Politis had gone very well.

Outside the resort, the sky had turned a metallic grey and the forecast was for a rainy afternoon. Hossein checked his watch. 'Time to go, Mayor Dimitriadis. Please take me to my new home.'

'I thought you might visit my office, meet my team.'

'No. Not today,' Hossein replied firmly.

'Of course. You're the boss.'

Am I? Hossein thought, a little surprised. 'Yes,' he said aloud, 'I am. Thank you.'

CHAPTER 11
Melissani, Good Friday 2013

It was nine in the morning, and Melissani was stirring to life. Aphrodite Politis was on her way home after dropping eight-year-old Rika at her friend's house. It was a holy day, and everything felt softer, quieter, enhanced by the light of what promised to be a sunny Easter weekend.

The smell of offal lingered in the air as families prepared kokoretsi and soup. Kid hides dried on exterior walls while their seasoned carcasses rested in cool cellars, waiting for Sunday's spit-roast marathon. Outside St Constantine, the Ladies' Committee arranged chrysanthemums along trestle tables, ready to decorate the Epitaphios. They barely glanced at Aphrodite as she passed. Good Friday was Father Efthimios's biggest service—a guaranteed full house and unrelenting adoration.

Under the shade of the giant platanus, children played hopscotch in the village square. Aphrodite admired their focus and innocence, unaware of why Jesus died or the brutality of his execution. At the kafenio across the pavement, the old men sat with their coffee and worry beads, some in traditional dress of black baggy pants and sash with polished boots, hoping tourists might take their photograph. Their banter ceased, however, as Aphrodite walked by.

Statuesque in red jeans and a fitted white T-shirt, twenty-six-year-old Aphrodite kept walking. Her straight, raven-coloured hair fell loosely down her back, and a pair of fluorescent green sunglasses concealed the loathing in her eyes. The old men ogled her openly, reminiscent of the scene from *Zorba the Greek* where the widow, played by Irene Papas, is silently ravished. But the days of hostility were gone. She had put an end to the behaviour when she moved into the village two years earlier.

Pericles Lacopoulos, the village's most arrogant man, had tested her within her first week. As she stepped out of the bakery next door to the kafenio, he rose from his chair and heckled: 'Go to hell where you belong, you witch!'

Stopping in her stride, surprised but not alarmed, she walked straight towards him. Those around him fidgeted in their seats, while another pulled Pericles back into his. Grabbing his wrinkly hand, she leaned close and whispered: 'From now on, whenever you masturbate with this decrepit hand, a vicious itch will plague your cock. If you want a remedy, come to me and I will lift this spell. But it will cost you.'

Pericles raised his walking stick to strike her, only to be restrained by the waiter. Panting and on the verge of cardiac arrest, he shouted, 'Kakourga! Witch!'

The villagers were furious at her audacity to settle in Melissani. As a descendant of the island's infamous witch, Irini Vlahos, they claimed she had repeated history by seducing one of their most esteemed men, the previous priest, and giving birth to their 'devil child'. In their minds, Father Nicholas had fallen victim to the same Vlahos curse that had doomed Doctor Haralambos Kaligeros two centuries earlier.

The harassment continued that week when a neighbour burst into Aphrodite's courtyard, consumed by jealous rage and accusing her of sleeping with her husband. A little brandy and some logical reasoning soon revealed the real adulteress—the woman's cousin— but also the source of the rumour—Father Efthimios.

Aphrodite knew she had to tread carefully. There was already bad blood between her and the church, and any aggression towards him would only alienate her family further. Instead, she retaliated in the only way she knew—through her art. *The Devil's Advocate* depicted a priest in a red cassock, his naked backside impaled by a devil's horn as he scrambled up a familiar platanus tree. It caused quite a ruckus when exhibited in Munich, although she claimed that any likeness to Father Efthimios was purely coincidental.

***

Years later, when Aphrodite returned from Berlin after her breakup with a prominent German sculptor, her parents begged her not to settle in Melissani. An apartment for her and Rika would soon be ready at the new Paradisos resort. But Aphrodite was unwavering. She had inherited her Uncle Toli's grand villa and nothing would stop her from establishing her independence, home and studio in the most picturesque village on the island.

She transformed the old mosque into her studio and converted the front rooms (once Doctor Haralambos's clinic) into a café and shop for her art. The villa remained largely unchanged apart from a new bathroom, doors and windows. The arched doorways and wooden ceilings remained untouched. She also kept the original two-metre-high boundary wall of the property, replacing the old wooden gate with a tall Gaudi-inspired wrought-iron gate.

During the renovation, Aphrodite came across Irini Vlahos's book of therapies wedged between two leather-bound anatomy volumes in the doctor's clinic. She knew of the book but assumed it had been destroyed. Margarita urged her to burn it. Aphrodite refused, calling it a beautiful heirloom to be treasured. Margarita remained unconvinced; she wanted nothing to do with the book or the remedies and black magic associated with it.

Defiantly, Aphrodite claimed the book. Not only did she follow the recipes to prepare her own elixirs but she replicated the book's motifs onto the glass beads of her signature necklaces and bracelets.

She encased the book in a glass box on the sideboard at the entrance to the villa, its leather cover gleaming with gold-leaf lettering:

> Remedies from my grandmother, Irini Vlahos
> Illustrations by Myrto Kaligeros
> In loving memory of my parents, Mary and
> Haralambos Kaligeros
> 1836

As Aphrodite approached her gate that morning, three tourists—two women and a man—emerged from Yianoula's Guest House adjacent to the villa. They had their heads buried in maps, figuring out names of the alleys that ran throughout the village.

'Good morning' she interrupted. 'Where would you like to go?'

'Oh hello!' a conservative-looking middle-aged woman responded, looking relieved. They all appeared to be in their fifties if not older. 'We would like to go to the Monastery of the Transfiguration.'

'Is it worth the hike?' another asked.

'Of course,' Aphrodite responded, noting their Australian accent. 'From the viewing platform you can see Turkey to the east, Chios to the south, Lesbos to the north and, in the distant west, Skyros, the Island of the Magnetes. If the wind picks up, you may feel as though you'll float away.'

'Ooh, that sounds nice,' the man said. He looked a little more upbeat, sporting a beret and round spectacles.

Aphrodite pointed out the route on their map—seven hundred metres up the ridge behind them.

'Kalo Pascha,' a shorter woman said, looking proud of herself. Aphrodite noticed the crosses hanging from her neck.

'Kalo Pascha,' Aphrodite said as they waddled off. 'Oh and don't go too close to the edge of the viewing platform. Some people have fallen to their deaths.'

'We won't,' one of them called back.

After her cousin, Christopher Kanarakis jumped to his death in 1996, the council finally fenced off the viewing platform. While the chicken wire kept chickens away, it did little to deter people from jumping. With austerity, suicides had increased across Greece. The rocky ledge below stopped victims from plunging deeper into the chasm. Being close to God's house gave the troubled a misguided sense of divine guardianship.

Aphrodite hadn't visited in years. She couldn't bring herself to take Rika. Christopher's suicide had left a black stain on the family, especially Emilio, who was still deeply wounded by the tragic loss of their cousin.

She was about to step through her gate when she heard footsteps. It was the man in the beret.

'Excuse me,' he said. 'I hope you don't mind me asking but are you Aphrodite Politis, the artist?'

Slightly taken aback, she nodded. 'Yes, that's correct.'

'I just wanted to say I am a great admirer of your work. My wife not so much, I'm afraid.'

'Oh, that's okay, no offence taken.'

'I read about your visit to Mount Athos. I am not meaning to pry—just curious. I used to be a priest in Melbourne and I have visited the Holy Mountain many times.'

It wasn't uncommon for tourists to ask Aphrodite about her audacious trespass in 2012. Her capture and expulsion made international headlines. Only one other woman, Aliki Diplarakou, Miss Europe 1930, had ever dared to enter the Holy Mountain. While the community, and her family, were initially outraged and disgusted, tempers soon wavered. The media coverage and subsequent fame did wonders for tourism and Aphrodite's art. The villagers understood she was a necessary asset—even if she was a 'witch'.

'So you were a priest?' she asked.

One of the women, possibly his wife, was calling out to him. 'Leave the young woman alone!'

'Coming!' he yelled back. 'Yes, a priest, but I've strayed from the dogmas of orthodoxy.'

'Are you now an axe murderer?' Aphrodite joked, still unsure of his intentions.

'No, no, I am a poet now,' he laughed. 'Sorry for taking up so much of your time. I am intrigued by human behaviour in all its contradictions,' he rattled off, looking as though he was trying to impress her—chest puffed out and waving his hand as if conducting a one-man orchestra. 'Kalo Pascha,' he said as he turned to leave.

She stopped him. 'You wanted to know why I went to Mount Athos. Do you have children?'

'We have one son, but unfortunately our relationship is somewhat strained.'

'Who hates who?' Aphrodite challenged.

'Sorry?'

'Who hates who?' she pressed.

'It's not as simple as that.'

'Of course it is. Human interaction is always about hating or liking someone.'

Aphrodite felt herself firing up as a hot flush washed through her. The man was hardly threatening, but he had hit a nerve.

'I went to find the father of my daughter, which I did, as the media reported,' her voice now faltering. 'A man of the cloth is still a man. A man's responsibility to his child should never be forsaken.'

'What's going on?' one of the women called out, picking up on the tension in Aphrodite's voice.

'It okay,' he called, waving back at her. 'I'm sorry if I caused you any distress.'

She stared at him, stepping back. 'Go look to your son,' she snapped, 'instead of old relics and fading icons!'

The man nodded and walked away.

'Who was that?' came a voice behind her. It was Peris, her café manager. In his hands was the sign: *Aphrodite's Café, Now Open.* 'What happened? Did he say something to upset you?'

'Just a tourist looking for salvation. I'm afraid I lost my temper.'

'Sweetheart…' he said, concerned.

'I don't know what's wrong with me this morning. I feel so out of sorts.'

'You didn't cross paths with my grandfather?'

'No. I watched the children playing in the square just now. For some reason it upset me, their grandparents on either side. I worry they'll become like them.'

'Well, I certainly won't,' Peris said, winking and giggling.

Peris was Pericles Lacopoulos's twenty-one-year-old grandson—gay, out and proud.

'That's true,' she said.

'I just worry about Rika, and I wonder if I made the right decision about settling here.'

'Rika is having a great time, just as I did when I was her age.'

'I think I just need to dose up on some remedies, consult with the book, try to shake off this negativity.'

'Nothing like a bit of witchcraft to start your day,' he said as he placed the A-frame sign on the pavement.

Although most shops closed for Good Friday, Aphrodite opened hers. If the men's kafenio could open, so could hers. Besides, she had work to do—a two-metre-square painting for the resort's new restaurant, saints and gods enjoying a summer's day at Kamiros Beach: Jesus on a jet ski, Saint Luke reclining on a deckchair, Saint Sophia playing beach volleyball with her three daughters, Faith, Hope and Love, and Artemis on lifeguard duty. It would be a playful echo of her National Art Prize winner, *The Last Suppression*.

Before entering the café that morning, Aphrodite picked a few stems of the wild poppies in the courtyard.

'They're pretty!' Peris said.

'My contribution to commemorating the blood of Christ. It is His day, after all.'

'That's very honourable of you.'

'You don't hate me for asking you to work today? I wanted to make a point to the old fools in this village.'

'As long as you are paying me, it's no problem at all!'

In a time when work was scarce, one took what one could get. Peris was one of her most devoted staff, a budding artist and in awe of Aphrodite. Rumours circulated that Aphrodite, unable to seduce the flamboyant young man, turned him gay as revenge against his grandfather.

'Anyone of interest I should pull up my chair next to?' she asked, peering inside the café. Occasionally, she would mingle among café guests.

'A couple of boring English tourists, some noisy Canadians and one distinguished-looking gentleman.'

'On his own?'

'He certainly is.'

Aphrodite noticed the dark gentleman sitting alone at the corner table by the window.

'He's the new museum curator,' Peris whispered.

'Ah! My aunt's new boss, *the* Doctor Hossein Basra,' she said. Aunt Salome had been managing the souvenir shop at the Museum of Ancient Tallos for years. 'A major improvement on the old hunchback professor!' she had declared on the phone.

Aphrodite flicked her hair and adjusted her top. She recalled the feature story in the recent edition of *Island News* and the silly photo of him with the mayor.

'Shall I introduce you?' asked Peris.

'No, that's okay. I'll introduce myself. I'm sure he's heard everything about me.'

For the first time since her breakup, something inside her stirred—like that thrill when she first met Father Nicholas. But she was no longer a schoolgirl. She was now an established artist who had lived in Berlin.

Perhaps this Good Friday would lead to her resurrection.

CHAPTER 12
The opening, September 2013

The grand opening of Paradisos II coincided with the festivities of Saint Sophia, the patron saint of Kamiros. Her 400-year-old monastery, carved into the side of a large cliff, stood proudly on the rugged peninsula opposite the resort. Through its red wooden door one is greeted by a large, cracked icon of the saint. Beneath her astute smile lay the agony of the horrific torture and beheading of her three young daughters: Faith, Hope and Love. A two-kilometre boardwalk led visitors from the port to the solitary stoicism of a mother enduring the price of her Christian devotion.

It was Paniyiri, the festive week preceding her martyrdom day, 17 September. Hundreds of pilgrims from neighbouring islands flooded Kamiros to pay their respects. As practised for decades, the main road filled with pop-up stands selling souvenirs, food, clothes and toys. The smell of freshly grilled souvlakia wafted through the air. The nights were still warm, and the light from the full harvest moon enticed crowds to wander, play and pray. The Paniyiri also marked the official end of the tourist season, the last festivity before Christmas in the port town.

Emilio had intended to open the resort in June 2012 in time for the summer, but the economic crisis had upended everything. As the country sank deeper into recession, the Politis family persevered through many moments of anguish—especially Emilio. For a time, Mihalis was plagued with regret for ever returning. It wasn't only the pressure from within the family—the whole island had pinned its hopes on the resort to lift it from economic ruin.

***

Mihalis sat on the white leather lounges in the new lobby, catching his breath. Sleep had eluded him for nights, and he'd lost his appetite. Butterflies stormed in his stomach as sweat trickled down his temples. His promise to young Emilio, made years earlier in Australia, had been realised—alongside his fear of becoming redundant.

Being in charge was in Mihalis's DNA, a trait forged by generations of hardship and self-determination. His great-great-grandfather, Emilianos Nikolaou Politis, a Corfiot, was a revolutionary fighter during the War of Independence; his father, Emilianos Evangelou Politis, had risen as a leading communist rebel in the Civil War. And now, his son, Emilio Mihalis Politis, would continue the legacy of the Emilianos before him.

He glanced at the gold Rolex watch his family recently gifted him for his sixty-fifth birthday. Only a few minutes remained before the diamond-encrusted hour hand reached 8 p.m. when the doors would open to the public. He wasn't one for extravagant jewellery; a wedding band and a gold chain were more than enough. However, this watch was special, and it was a special night, and he wore it with pride. At long last he surrendered the old Omega he bought before leaving Sydney.

Mihalis missed Australia: the pace, the anonymity of urban life. He hadn't been ready to give it up and often felt short-changed. Running a small business had become a routine—easy, reliable, secure. Yet despite their success, he missed out on discovering his new country. Twenty years of residency had confined him to a ten-kilometre radius, trapping him in the prison of Citizens Corner Shop.

'What's the matter?' Margarita sat beside him, eyes narrowing.

'Nothing.'

'You're sweating.'

Mihalis pulled out his handkerchief. She took it and started dabbing at his face. He snatched it back. 'I can do it!'

She gave him a stern look before resuming his grooming—dusting down his jacket, straightening his tie and slicking down the stray hairs above his right ear. Annoyed but accepting that he lacked his wife's finesse, he kept quiet. She looked good, he thought, noticing how her black lacy dress rose above her knee. Her legs always appeared shapely when she wore high heels. Her silver bob however, side parted and sleek, made her face too severe.

'You look nice,' he said awkwardly.

Her small smile revealed how long it had been since he'd paid her a compliment. Strong, capable, patient—without her, they would never have come this far. But he missed her softness. The stress of the business, health and children had hardened them both.

A few months earlier, sensing the depth of his sadness after a heated argument with Emilio over courtyard furniture, Margarita curled up beside him as he lay silently in bed. All it took was her touch and he fell apart like shattered glass. Placing her arm across his chest, she stroked the grey hairs and kissed him gently. It had been years since they had been intimate; he had forgotten what it felt like to be loved.

The sound of heels on the marble floor signalled Aphrodite's arrival. Her entrances were always grand, amplified by her theatrical gestures and clothes.

'Kalispera,' she said, swooping in to kiss her parents.

'Kalos tin,' Mihalis replied. 'Where's Rika?'

'Running around somewhere,' she said as she scanned the room. 'So, this is nice! Very nice indeed!'

A sudden squeal came from the top of the stairs. It was Rika.

'Shh!' Margarita hissed, jumping up from her seat. 'Come downstairs at once!'

'No!' Rika shouted back.

Aphrodite rolled her eyes at Mihalis and walked away.

'Come and say hello to your pappou,' Margarita beckoned, gesturing with her hand.

Rika ran down the stairs, dodged her grandmother and fell into Mihalis's arms.

'How's my little girl?' he asked, hugging her.

'Good, Pappou,' she said, stepping back to get a better look. 'You look so different.'

'I hope I look nice?'

'I think so.'

'What do you mean you *think* so?' he teased, lunging forward to tickle her, making her squeal louder.

'Shh!' Margarita hissed again, gently slapping her husband across his arm. 'You both look very nice!'

'Bye, Yiayia.' Rika giggled cheekily and ran up the stairs.

'What is she wearing?' Margarita said, catching sight of Aphrodite's attire.

'It's very colourful,' Mihalis replied, unfazed by his daughter's dress sense.

'A pantsuit? She looks like a genie!'

But she wouldn't dare say that to Aphrodite face; mother and daughter knew exactly when to back off.

Mihalis watched as Aphrodite swanned across the floor to inspect the position of her painting. *In Glory*, lit by a spotlight, showed Artemis (looking very much like Aphrodite) charging on a white horse, bare-breasted, her long, thick hair tangled in the tailwind. Mihalis hadn't liked it at first, describing it as too dramatic and provocative for a reception area. But seeing the two-by-two-metre painting hung behind the reception desk changed his mind. Now he couldn't stop looking at it.

Dimitri sat like a bored clerk, his head barely visible above the reception desk, slouched over his mobile phone, headphones in, playing video games. Aphrodite snuck behind him and kissed his neck. Startled, suspecting his mother, he got up and gave her a hug, his demeanour a little brighter. Mihalis knew he didn't want to come to the opening and agreed on the condition that no one would tell him what to wear. Dressed in jeans and a patterned shirt with his long, unruly golden hair and goatee stubble, he looked like a child from the sixties.

The elevator doors suddenly opened and Emilio emerged with Eva, hand in hand. They had been having a private drink in the Lighthouse Bar.

'Ola kala?' he called to his parents.

'All good, pedi mou,' Margarita said as he kissed her cheek.

Mihalis got up to shake his son's hand. They hadn't seen each other in the last forty-eight hours. Margarita subtly pulled Eva away to discuss dresses and how beautiful everyone looked.

'You look very handsome, son.'

Emilio clasped his father's shoulder, looked him over and smiled. 'Thank you. *Ke esi, levendis.*'

The term—man of honour and bravery—was bittersweet. While the coldness between them might thaw for the night, Mihalis remained wary. Still, he reminded himself that this was Emilio's night, who appeared as if he was on cloud nine; his handsome face relaxed, his shoulders lowered, head held high. He'd worked so hard, and for that he was incredibly proud of him.

'Good idea, Baba, about the opening. I just hope they turn up,' Emilio said.

Surprisingly, Emilio agreed to Mihalis's public relations strategy of hosting an opening party for the locals during the Paniyiri. 'Give them a sneak peek and something to talk about,' Mihalis had said. 'It's not as if they can ever afford to stay here.'

The success of Paradisos Hotel had shielded Mihalis from the toxic social undercurrents, but he was aware of the islanders' envy. Ironically, it was Margarita's ancestry, not the family's wealth and status, that set tongues wagging. Aphrodite's short-lived liaison with the handsome priest reignited the island's old fervour for witchcraft. Dimitri's reclusiveness, and the rumours around it only fuelled the gossip. Even Mihalis, the patriarch, was a target, a shepherd's son from the Peloponnese who had married the daughter of one of the island's wealthiest families. Only Emilio escaped any adverse judgement. He was the son everyone wanted.

Now that wealth had finally afforded Mihalis power, the opening of Paradisos II offered him the perfect chance to rub the locals' noses in it.

'Oh they'll come,' Mihalis said. 'Once Father Efthimios makes his entrance, you watch them swarm in. Rumour has it that he's organised a bus excursion to the monastery for the Melissians followed by refreshments here.'

Mihalis noticed a worried look on his son's face. 'What's wrong?'

'I'm sorry, Baba.'

'What for?' Mihalis asked.

'For being such an arrogant shit. For cutting you out.'

'I am proud of what you've done for yourself.'

'This is for all of us,' Emilio added. 'Did you see the photo?'

'Photo?'

Emilio grabbed his father by the hand and led him to small alcove beside the marble stairs. On the wall hung a large plaque with the family portrait printed on it. It was the image used to promote the original Paradisos Hotel in brochures and websites: Mihalis in his fisherman's hat, Margarita at his side, Emilio and Aphrodite peering out from behind them, toddler Dimitri tugging at his mother's colourful apron. That family image had become the face of Paradisos, and now it was set in stone in its new home.

Overwhelmed, Mihalis pulled out his handkerchief. Across the room, he noticed Margarita's watchful eyes flicker across, nervously monitoring their exchange. Emilio, visibly upset, excused himself and ran to the bathroom.

'What's happened?' Margarita said as she rushed over.

'Is everything alright?' Eva asked.

'Yes, yes. All is fine,' he said as he proudly looked back at the plaque.

***

By midnight, the resort had emptied except for family and close friends. Most of the locals left with Father Efthimios around 11 p.m. It was quite the spectacle watching his congregation follow him out, fearing that without his spiritual protection they'd fall victim to 'the curse'. Before leaving, he doused holy water throughout the foyer using a large bunch of basil, under the watchful eye of Aphrodite, who stood guard over her painting.

The night was also dedicated to Jorgen Larson, who was the special guest, having arrived on the island for the opening. Before the priest's blessing, Emilio delivered a speech celebrating Jorgen's architectural accomplishments and presented him with a gold-inscribed Paradisos II keyring.

After the formalities, the party spilled into the courtyard, where local band The Asteria played the usual folk and popular classics. Margarita gripped her husband as he whirled her around the small dance floor near the outdoor bar. He was a little tipsy and had removed his tie and jacket. The night remained warm and comfortable, scented with lavender from the garden.

The opening had gone to plan. People turned up, clapped, ate and drank, and the remaining few now danced alongside them. The only serious hiccup was Salome, Margarita's sister. As expected, she unfurled her good-looks charms on the younger men—this time Andrew Kappos. Her husband, Vasilis, long accustomed to her flirtations, drowned his anger in drink. Stocky, bald and barrel-chested, he looked more like a retired wrestler than a farmer. Mihalis noticed his agitation rising as Salome, in a tight-fitting dress with her fourth cocktail in hand, barraged Andrew with questions. Andrew, newly hired as a tour provider, was meeting her for the first time. After coaxing him into a tsifteteli dance, Vasilis finally snapped. Grabbing her by the arm, he dragged her away as she admonished him for being jealous.

'Has she no decorum? Her boss is here,' Margarita hissed, referring to Doctor Hossein Basra who watched curiously. 'Can't she control herself just for one night!'

Whenever Margarita tried to intervene, her younger sister's behaviour worsened. Eleven years separated them, and the generation friction often flared publicly—something she avoided at all costs. Mihalis pulled his sister-in-law to the side at one point after pressure from both Emilio and Margarita asking her to slow down with her drinking.

As expected, she cocked up her head, hand on her hip, finger wagging. 'Tell my sister that I can look after myself, thank you very much.' Her words slurred. 'Just because she can big-note herself with her many children—whom I adore, don't get me wrong, I adore those three like they were mine—but that doesn't give her the right.'

Her infertility had long been a source of tension between sisters. Vasilis carried her guilt heavily; smitten by her beauty and still deeply in love with her, he tried to appease her by giving her independence.

'A tango and a waltz, please!' Mihalis shouted to the musicians as he swirled Margarita towards the violinist. 'Nothing like a romantic dance to end a party,' he whispered.

'I'm done. My feet are killing me,' she said, clutching onto him.

Throughout the night, Jorgen Larson joined the musicians, borrowing their violin to play the various Greek songs he learned during his teenage holidays on the island. At one point he led the dancers in a line dance through the bar and along the garden pathways.

Rika laid curled asleep on a beanbag while Aphrodite sat at the bar chatting with Jorgen and Doctor Basra. Much to her parents' irritation, Aphrodite had put on quite a show and was exhausted from dancing. Even Doctor Basra had partnered her on the dance floor and surprised everyone with his smooth, soulful moves. Mihalis hoped she hadn't worn him out, though he seemed to be enjoying himself. Margarita remarked on their surprising connection.

'He's certainly loosened up since the first time I met him,' she whispered.

'Quite the dancer. They seem to be getting on,' Mihalis replied.

'I haven't seen Aphrodite this happy in a long time,' Margarita added.

The archaeologist was also in high spirits after the successful joint grant submission with the resort. A new Artemis Gallery had been announced earlier in the evening. Emilio, elated, immediately offered Doctor Basra use of the restaurant for a fundraising event. Mihalis knew of their submission but, amid the ongoing economic crisis, hadn't believed it stood a chance. Still, it was inspiring seeing someone so new to the island be so driven—he reminded him of himself when he first arrived.

Dimitri had disappeared earlier. Mihalis noticed him laughing and chatting with Pandelis from *Island News*, which was unusual. *Perhaps they shared an interest in computer games,* he thought. It made him happy to see him like that. Unlike his siblings, Dimitri preferred his own company. Mihalis blamed Margarita and his mother-in-law for spoiling him. With national service looming, Mihalis believed conscription would be a cure for his aimlessness. University was also an option, but he had no desire to study. Mihalis often wondered whether things would have been different had Emilio not left for Athens after high school. Dimitri was four at the time and inconsolable.

As Mihalis spun past the table where Emilio, Eva, Andrew and Eva's mother, Fotini, sat, he called out cheerfully, 'What's wrong with you? You young people should be dancing!'

'No more for me, I'm afraid!' Eva shouted back.

'Too old-fashioned, Baba,' Emilio joked.

'Rubbish!' Mihalis bellowed, twirling Margarita dramatically.

'That's enough now!' Margarita laughed, slapping him across the shoulder.

Andrew rose and offered his chair to Margarita.

'Thank you, Andrew.'

'I would ask you to dance, Mrs Politis, but I think I know the answer.'

'Sorry, Andrew, my feet can't take another step.'

'I'm down for that, ma'am.'

Mihalis silently chuckled at Andrew's accent. The Californian had once struck him as a potential catch for Aphrodite, but the night didn't seem to go that way. Besides, the little he knew of him convinced him that Aphrodite would tire of him quickly. Decent, courteous and respectful, Andrew's focus was on making money and building his cruising empire.

'Emilio, why don't you dance with your mother-in-law?' Mihalis called out.

Before Emilio could answer, Fotini cut in. 'First of all, I am not yet a mother-in-law. And secondly, I don't dance European.'

'Mother, you can be such a snob!' Eva growled.

Fotini Galanos was a bitter old woman. A widow whose lawyer husband had been killed during a confrontation with an Iraqi refugee—later acquitted on grounds of self-defence—she had, from that moment on, nursed nothing but hatred for all Muslims. Claiming Thessaloniki had been overrun by the 'criminals of the Gulf War', she relocated to her matriarchal home of Phaedros, despite the fierce resistance from her fifteen-year-old daughter, Eva.

Mihalis was surprised that Fotini had stayed for so long at the party. She didn't like the family, especially after Emilio and Eva's breakup after high school. As much as Mihalis adored Eva, he worried about his son's wellbeing with a mother-in-law like Fotini.

'Cheer up, Fotini,' Mihalis blurted out, unable to resist. For a moment he saw the forlorn expression of Saint Sophia in her face, her skin grey and weathered with eyes clouded with bitterness. Only the veil was missing. 'We have a wedding coming up. Our children's!'

'A toast!' Andrew announced. 'To the soon-to-be newlyweds!'

'To Paradisos!' Emilio added.

PART 3
SALVATION

CHAPTER 13
Kamiros Beach

Mihalis and Kurush hauled the body of an elderly woman into the dinghy as Emilio pushed her up from the water. Her shawl was entangled around her neck, ensnared in the straps of a deflated life jacket he couldn't free. Small and fragile, her fingers were blue and rigid like twigs; her legs drifted behind her like tentacles. After handing her over to the others, Emilio turned without hesitation and plunged back into the churning water.

Fishing trawlers and hobby boats joined the rescue. Their crews moved like shadows, working in stunned silence, dipping nets into the dark waters for debris and the dead. Torches jittered across the surface, capturing images of devastation.

Above him, light rain shimmered over the dawning sky. The weather was clearing rapidly. Around him floated the remnants of lives—children's shoes, a baby pacifier, backpacks, drink bottles, a book, scraps of clothing. Pushing aside the debris, he hoped for a body. It had become a compulsion: the more bodies he could find, the better he would feel about himself. The woman, her dead baby and husband had thrown him into a desperate drive he no longer controlled.

Something scraped against his naked ankle. Kicking it free, he dove after it. In just his underwear and T-shirt he felt lighter, more streamlined. But all he could latch onto was a frayed rope attached to an old anchor. No sign of a body or a person sinking to their death. He resurfaced and took in a fresh supply of air. The dinghy had caught up to his location; his father slowly steered as the Afghan hung over the side, checking the debris. The colour of the sky was now transitioning to a lighter purple. The sun was on its way. Desperate to retrieve at least one more body, he ducked back under as his father screamed: 'That's enough, Emilio!'

The water remained murky, though the emerging light of daybreak was helping. They were perhaps three hundred metres from shore, though he wasn't sure how deep the water was. As a child he never feared these waters. One time he swam across to the opposite headland and explored the shallow caves beneath Saint Sophia. He stopped going after stepping on a sea urchin and then having to swim back in excruciating pain.

Grabbing the algae-covered rope from the anchor, he pulled himself deeper. The slippery surface, however, was making it difficult to make much headway. A shadow brushed past him. He flinched, wondering what a manta ray was doing in the Aegean. The shape soon sharpened into an older boy, his black raincoat ballooned around him and fastened at the throat by a drawstring. Emilio felt the rush of adrenaline as he darted towards him, tugging the garment free. The boy's mouth gaped and the white of his eyes glowed like small beacons in the greenish dark. Another deflated life jacket hung like a noose. Emilio successfully ripped it away.

Hooking an arm around the boy's neck, Emilio kicked furiously for the surface, focusing on the wavering net of light stretched across the ceiling of the sea. His mind drifted. He was Enzo in the *The Big Blue*, dragging a diver from a shipwreck. As he pushed further up, his thoughts turned to his ancestor, Doctor Haralambos Kaligeros, bones lost to the same sea. And as his mind spun, he caught glimpses of his cousin Christopher jumping to his death, Uncle Toli collapsing from grief, Eva spinning in her green dress. And then his mother's controlled voice, beckoning him out from the crawl space under the shop, cobwebs tightened around him.

And in a final assault, before giving in to the gravity of his mind and body, he forced his legs to push once more. Breaking through the surface, he felt the air smack his face hard. Gasping for air, he felt the blood slowly drain from his head.

Towing the body towards the dinghy, Kurush screamed: 'Nasir! Nasir!' before leaping from the boat to help Emilio. 'My cousin! It's my cousin Nasir,' he cried as he surfaced.

'I'm sorry,' Emilio said. 'I couldn't save him.'

Kurush's face tightened with horror as he whimpered indecipherable words.

'Help me get him on the boat,' Emilio urged, trying to break him free from the grief that paralysed him. Mihalis leaned over the edge and grabbed the boy's collar as Kurush scrambled back on board and helped haul him in, gently laying his cousin next to the old woman. He then collapsed over him, sobbing.

'We need to turn back,' Mihalis said firmly. 'There's no room for others. The police can do the rest. Get back in the boat, Emilio.'

In the distance, the sound of engines rumbled closer. Petrol fumes stung Emilio's nose. It was the *Grand Duchess* coming in from behind the dinghy, Andrew at the helm with Police Superintendent Harry Drivas beside him. The scene wavered with a sense of déjà vu, a memory from a world he didn't remember living—then darkness overcame him.

***

As Emilio regained consciousness, Andrew's wet face stared down at him, golden hair plastered across his forehead. The creaking of the floor beneath him and the squelching of soggy shoes signalled someone approaching. Lifting his head, Emilio was struck by a wave of dizziness and fell back as Policeman Harry loomed into view, his bulging eyes blinking constantly. Harry was his mother's second cousin. He was closer in age to his father and twice as big, burly with a silver beard, bushy eyebrows and pockmarked face.

A violent urge to cough overtook him. Emilio quickly rolled to his side, spewing seawater onto the deck. Only then did he realise he was on the *Grand Duchess*.

'You alright, Emilio?' Andrew asked, rubbing his shoulders. 'You passed out buddy.'

'Why am I here?' Emilio asked.

'Your friend went in after you,' Harry replied, pointing to Andrew.

'Emilio!' his father shouted in the distance.

'He's okay, Mr Politis,' Andrew called back.

Emilio lay flat looking at the clouds dispersing. Hints of blue sky gave promise to a new day. Things could only get better, he reassured himself.

'You did well, buddy, very well,' Andrew said.

Emilio stared long and hard into Andrew's eyes as he tried to come to terms with his surroundings, his exhaustion. And then a flashback to the week before where he danced and drank on this very deck. Shame tightened around Emilio's throat. 'I am so sorry. What I said to you last week was fucking stupid. I was an idiot.'

'Take it easy, buddy. It's all good,' Andrew said as he gave him a gentle slap across his face. 'You know me, I take nothing personal.'

'Thanks for saving me.'

'It's what I do.'

'Not dickheads like me.'

His father suddenly appeared in front of him, his face panicked.

'I'm alright, Baba.'

Harry and his father helped Emilio into a deckchair as Andrew grabbed a few towels. Emilio was cold and in shock, but his mind itched to return to the water.

'I need to get back out there,' he insisted, trying to stand.

'No chance!' Harry snapped. 'You have done more than enough.'

'But I am fine. Honestly!' Emilio fought back.

'Enough!' his father roared.

Emilio was taken aback by his father's rage, his face turning a deep purple, eyes red and watery.

'Where's the Afghan?' Emilio asked.

'He is on the dinghy with the bodies,' his father answered.

'We will continue with the recovery, and you are going back to shore,' Harry said, raising his voice as he pointed to land with his thick hand. 'I won't risk more lives. You take your father home, get cleaned up and drop by the station later. There's nothing more you can do here.'

'But what about the bodies?'

'I have spoken to the superintendent in Lesbos. They see this all the time. They will be buried tomorrow.'

'This is a fucking disaster!' Emilio said. 'How the fuck can this happen?'

'They left Turkey at the worst time. No one knew the storm would develop so quickly,' Andrew said as he helped him to his feet.

'But to reach here? How is that possible? And those fucking life vests. Who the hell gave them such defects? They were murdered!' Emilio was now yelling as he slowly stood up.

'We will be making enquiries with the Turkish authorities,' Harry responded. 'Just leave it with us.'

'Are the coastguards coming?' Emilio asked.

'No. They are swamped in Lesbos and Chios. This is happening three, four times a day over there. We're going to deal with this by ourselves.'

'By leaving them out there? Letting the traffickers get away with murder?'

'This is my problem. Not yours!' Harry said, raising his voice. The islanders loved Harry, but he was no pushover. When he got mad, people kept their distance.

'We have also collected five,' Andrew interrupted as he gestured with his head to the line of bodies on the deck a few metres away. Emilio hadn't noticed them until now. They were covered in towels, bodies in all shape and sizes.

Emilio felt his stomach churn and rushed to the side of the boat and vomited. The taste of the sea burned his throat.

His father followed him and rubbed his back, waiting in silence till he recovered.

'Come, Emilio. Your mother will be worried sick,' Mihalis said as he reached for his son's hand 'We'll take the Afghan to the clinic. You've done your part. I am so proud of you.'

Emilio allowed the words to penetrate. He felt pathetic and useless. Tightening his grip on his father's hand, he was grateful he was with him and that they were both alive.

CHAPTER 14
Melissani

Hossein gave up on sleep and climbed out of bed at 5.30 a.m. The thunder, rattling shutters and torrential rain had kept him awake through most of the night. Stumbling into the kitchen to make tea, he stepped into a large puddle of water on the linoleum, saturating his slippers.

Looking up for traces of a leak in the ceiling, all he noticed was paint flaking. Like the professor, Hossein had paid little attention to the décor and condition of the house that had come bundled with his post. He checked the fridge, confirming it was humming normally and opened the freezer to confirm the contents were still frozen.

Only then did it register.

Switching on the outdoor light, he opened the metal door to find the courtyard resembling a shallow swamp. The air smelt of dampness and salt as rain continued to fall. From what he could tell, the sky looked packed with black clouds. A chill seized his bones. In the two years he had lived there, rainwater had never entered the house.

After mopping up, he sealed the bottom of the door with towels and then prepared for morning prayer, not worrying about his tea. As he laid out the prayer mat, the phone rang. *Mother?* he thought. She had a habit of calling him whenever she wanted to chat, no matter the time.

'Mr Hossein!' The mayor's voice crackled through the line. 'We have a problem. Please come to the port. Refugees have drowned. Syrians. Like in Lesbos and Chios. Can you help us? Please come quick to Kamiros Beach!'

The line went dead. A wave of hot blood flushed his face, and his legs buckled. A memory of crawling out of a semitrailer truck with hundreds of others, gasping for fresh air, struck him. He frantically searched for the TV remote under a pile of newspapers on the dining table. Rarely did he watch TV, preferring the radio for news and weather updates. As he switched it on, the cawing of crows pierced through the wind. Their proximity was unsettling.

The black screen flickered to life with disjointed images and noise. People spoke over one another, shouting. Shaky footage of uprooted trees, crushed cars and damaged roofs flashed across the screen. The windswept newsreader reported that the eastern Aegean and Turkish coastlines were hit hardest. Izmir and Chios were mentioned, but not Phaedros. Even the BBC covered the event, referring to the storm as a 'medicane'—a Mediterranean hurricane—a term he'd never heard of before. Dumbfounded, he switched off the television, wondering how he could have stayed in bed for all those hours. Casting his eyes on the old, oval clock on the dining room wall, he watched the seconds tick by. It was 6.10 a.m. and dawn was breaking. Ephorus, the cat, rubbed against Hossein's leg. Picking him up, Hossein held him tight to his chest, allowing the tabby's warmth and purring to calm him.

'This is going to be a horrible day, my friend.'

Ephorus brushed his head against his beard, miaowing.

The old cat had come with the house. When Hossein asked about him, the professor claimed no knowledge of any animal. Hossein named him Ephorus after the ancient historian, imagining the secrets the old cat might reveal if he possessed speech. After filling Ephorus's bowl with dry biscuits, he began texting Salome to let her know he'd be in late. But before he could finish, the phone vibrated. It was her. 'There are bodies everywhere, Hossein. I don't think we should open the museum today. It's a disaster. I have just been speaking to my sister. You need to go quickly. They need someone who speaks Arabic. It's so awful, Hossein.'

It seemed his name had been bandied around the island's communication networks. Having Salome instruct him on what he should do infuriated him.

'Please ring the tour operator and let him know what's going on,' he said before ending the call.

There was no time for morning prayers. Hossein needed to get ready and leave. He scrolled through his contacts for Aphrodite's number. He wanted to hear her voice. She always sounded so composed and assured, at least with him. But he didn't want to wake her. Time was slipping by and people were waiting for him. He got dressed and grabbed a dusty umbrella from on top of the wardrobe and a raincoat from inside the laundry.

And then another thought hit him—the museum and the ancient city. He imagined columns toppled over, Artemis's Tablet split into pieces and the makeshift roof over the temple torn away like paper, exposing the chamber to the elements. All the accolades he had received at the antiquity conference completely wasted. Taking deep breaths, he reminded himself that the ancient city had endured centuries of severe weather and was still intact.

The professor's raincoat was tight on him, but it would have to do. As he left through the front door, debris of leaves and dust flew by under the glow of the streetlight. The intense wind howled through the narrow alleys as he tried to stop the umbrella from turning in on itself. He gave up, folded it and ran. Although it was normally a five-minute stroll to the car park at the entry to the village, it felt like forever.

Once inside his Toyota Yaris, he took several deep breaths and switched his thoughts to positive memories: the charming village square, the aroma of fresh bread wafting from the nearby bakery and the tolling of church bells. This technique, coupled with deep breathing, had been taught to him by his ex-wife, Audrey, who had also been his counsellor. Although their marriage lasted only a few years, he emerged with the strength and resilience to manage his anxiety and ultimately leave her. His mother called Audrey's therapy 'control dressed as empathy'. Over time, her words lodged in him like splinters.

Since moving to the island he felt his mental health improve. He cherished living in Melissani; the views, solitude and tranquillity were qualities he came to value. Most importantly, he was surprised by how welcomed he felt in the community. People invited him to christenings and weddings and often stopped him on the street to ask about the museum. He had never experienced such a sense of belonging.

Hossein pulled out a pocket-sized copy of the Quran from the glove box; it was gifted to him by his mother when he left Birmingham. Wrapped in a green silk cloth and tied with fine decorative twill, she had placed it on his bed with a card: *May your Allah always be with you, my son.* It was an unexpected gift.

***

Salma was not religious—in fact, she was agnostic. Religion had killed her husband, and she had rejected it ever since. Not that she expressed disappointment when Hossein rediscovered his faith during his marriage to Audrey; her concern was more focused on his safety. Islamophobia had ripped through the heart of Birmingham following the 11 September attacks. He was sixteen at the time.

The following morning after the attack, thick red paint with MUSLIMS DIE was sprawled across the brick face of their building. His mother's hand, cold and shaking, double deadlocked the door and drew the curtains. Horrified and frightened, he turned against Islam. Not only was it a front to keep his school friends on side but a surrender to his mother's subtle pressure to abandon all religious thoughts. He changed his looks, got a piercing in his ear, a buzz cut and dyed his hair blond. For a short while he even participated in anti-Islamic marches and graffitied racist slogans on public buildings. But when a family friend, a local mufti, was killed in a targeted home invasion a few years later, he abandoned his rebellion. He had also started university and discovered ancient history.

When he met Audrey at a university social function, he found her to be the most non-racist person he had ever met. Slowly, the psychology student began to unravel him, picking apart his trauma and making him take ownership of the childhood he rejected. And as part of that process she encouraged him to embrace Islam as 'it was at the very core of his psyche'.

Salma was excited about his posting to Greece. Not that she wanted him to leave but she had seen him lose his self-confidence and joy since his marriage. She would miss him terribly, but she was happy for him because, for a long time, he had been anything but.

'At least you speak Greek,' she told him, after he expressed some concern about assimilating. When they arrived in the UK as refugees in 1985, Salma had found it shameful that she was illiterate in English. As a lecturer in political history in Tehran, she was accustomed to the confidence and pride that comes with language proficiency.

'Fluency in Farsi and Arabic means nothing in a city like Birmingham,' she told twelve-year-old Hossein. 'They only push you further into poverty, and we are not going there!' Within weeks of settling into their new home, they enrolled in the free English classes for refugees.

***

Flicking through the thin, sheer pages of the Quran, Hossein searched for prayers related to funerals. His hands shook as he folded the corner of what he thought was the relevant page. A wave of nausea teased him. Returning the Quran back to the glove box, he turned on the ignition and slowly manoeuvred from the packed car park speaking Arabic to himself. Other than the prayers he recited daily, it had been ages since he'd spoken it, let alone his native tongue of Farsi.

As a distraction, he practised breaking the news about his relationship with Aphrodite to his mother in Farsi: 'Mother, I have met someone. She is so lovely, funny, smart and very creative. Alhamdulillah.'

As he repeated the phrase, the mobile vibrated. It was Aphrodite. 'Hossein. Are you going to the port?'

'Yes. I'm just leaving the car park now,' he replied calmly, happy to hear her voice.

'I'd come with you but Rika is still sleeping. I don't want to scare her. Those poor people. Mum said they were trying to contact you.'

Before he could answer, a large black shape materialised in the middle of the road. For a split second he thought it was a bear, but then noticed the glint of a large gold cross. It was Father Efthimios, backlit by dawning light. A large umbrella over his head swayed from side to side.

'Father Efthimios is waving me down,' Hossein told Aphrodite.

Hossein pulled over to let the elderly priest in. Adjusting his bulk into the seat of the small car, he turned to Hossein, unimpressed.

'The mayor told me you were on your way. What took you so long? I've been waiting fifteen minutes.'

'He mentioned nothing about picking you up. If I had known…'

'My car is at the mechanics, otherwise I'd have driven myself. Do you know how to perform funeral rites for your people? Most are dead!'

'I'll call you back,' Hossein said to Aphrodite and hung up. 'I am an archaeologist, not a mufti,' Hossein answered sharply.

'I have arranged for you to speak to a mufti in Mytilene. He will guide you. Come to the beach once you have finished at the hospital.'

'Hospital?'

'Yes, they have just taken the two survivors, a woman and a young man, to the hospital. They are in shock. Find out who they are and what happened.'

'I hope we speak the same language.'

'You speak Arabic, don't you?'

'Of course, but—'

'Then you can interpret for the police.'

Hossein sensed the priest looking at him. There was something grotesque about him, definitely a fitting subject for Aphrodite's paintings—the pointy, patchy beard, the bent nose and thick neck. He was the sort of person who'd stare you down while waiting for a response.

'Yes, I can interpret,' Hossein finally said, not bothering to educate him on the variants of the Arabic language.

'Who was that on the phone?'

He answered too quickly, blurting out, 'Aphrodite.'

'Aphrodite Politis?'

Hossein had forgotten the hour of the day. He turned his head to the window and mouthed, 'Fuck!' His relationship with Aphrodite was still private.

'Be careful of that one,' the priest warned. 'There was some hope that when Kosta Kanarakis married the priest's daughter, the witchcraft would have been bred out, but not with that one! Now she lives in a house with the spirits that plague her family.'

'Any damage to the church?' Hossein quickly asked, bringing the conversation back to the storm. He knew exactly who Freda and Kosta were. Aphrodite never shied away from talking about her grandparents or her family's 'dark' history. As for ghosts, even if they were around, they never bothered Aphrodite. 'I had some flooding in the kitchen.'

'In the altar, of all places. Matina is there now mopping up the water.'

'I think the storms impacted the coastal towns more.'

'This situation with the refugees is a big problem. Of all the places they could go to, why Greece? We are barely surviving ourselves.'

'I don't think they have a choice.'

'Of course they have a choice! Haven't there been enough deaths to stop one from taking such journeys? And with this weather? Who in their right mind would even consider it? Seriously, are people so stupid?'

Hossein knew the priest was provoking him. He felt his gaze again, hanging on every breath for a rebuttal. Hossein kept his composure.

As they drove down the mountain, the priest called the mayor with an update on Hossein's movements. 'They are still retrieving bodies,' Father Efthimios reported. 'They are laying them on the pebbles. There is a plot of land near Saint Sophia—we must bury them there. One of the survivors is a young man. Speak to him and find out how many were in the boat.'

'The other survivor?'

'She is in poor condition and is heavily sedated. Her daughter and husband drowned. Their bodies have been recovered.'

As they rounded the bend towards Kamiros, Hossein noticed the dark clouds in the rearview mirror retreating towards the mountain. In front of him, sunlight started to fill the harbour, illuminating the tufts of sea foam on the choppy water. Small boats bobbed up and down, and to the left, a large fishing trawler manoeuvred slowly.

At the fork in the road at the bottom of Mount Dillinos, he saw the sign for the clinic and turned right. He had only visited it once, during his field trip days in the 1990s, after slicing his palm on the edge of a ceramic pot. The neoclassical building now appeared depressingly run-down. Emilio had expressed his frustration with council's refusal to give the clinic a fresh coat of paint, who argued that beautifying the town was not a priority in the current financial climate.

'Stop!' the priest suddenly called out. 'Let me out here. I am going straight to the beach.'

'I can drive you.'

'It's not far, and the rain has stopped. You go in,' said the priest as he climbed out of the car.

'Don't you want to come with me?' Hossein called after him.

'I have things to do on the beach,' he turned around and shouted. 'I may need to carry out last rites of some sort. Call the mayor when you find out how many are out there. We can't spend all day searching. We need to get things back to normal as soon as possible.'

Hossein watched the priest from the rearview mirror as he waddled away, holding his black robe above his ankles. There was mud everywhere. After parking the car in front of the building, he grabbed the Quran from the glove box, took deep breaths and rushed into the clinic through heavy swing doors.

CHAPTER 15
Aphrodite's villa

Aphrodite ended the call with Hossein, her gut churning. She'd been up for hours, experiencing an existential response to the chaos outside. Since meeting Hossein and witnessing the depth of his devotion, she sometimes felt bereft of spirituality. He had recently introduced her to mindfulness, and while cynical at first, she eventually understood its significance. Now, before beginning a new painting, she would take a few moments to focus on her breath, scan her body for sensations and visualise a beach, forest or some imagined masterpiece. But that morning, the clamour outside interrupted her efforts to enter that zone. Fear had settled in. Weather events rarely fazed her, but this felt distinctly ominous. Rain hammered the villa and the winds rose in a ghostlike howl— her ancestors, she thought, echoing a warning. In the early hours of the morning, she went to Rika's room at the back of the villa and quietly slid under the sheet beside her. At least Rika had slept through it all.

The phone vibrating beside her pillow jolted her awake. It was her mother. She tiptoed out of the room to answer. Her heart raced. As her mother spoke, Aphrodite recognised the strained, deliberate voice she used when concealing her emotions. Her mind leapt to Dimitri, away on military duty in northern Greece. But the news was closer to home, and she felt a fleeting, guilty relief that her little brother was out of the picture. But the news that Emilio and her father were out in the harbour caused her to shudder.

Frustrated that her call to Hossein had been cut short, she took comfort in knowing he had his faith to lean on. Taking a moment to pray, she asked God to protect her men. These reflexive gestures—praying, making the sign of the cross—reminded her how deeply Orthodox dogma still shaped her. She wondered whether such instincts would ever take root in Rika. Would the child of a priest inspire her peers towards any kind of spiritual awakenings? She doubted it.

A text message from Rika's teacher startled her: the school would be closed for the day. Aphrodite sought distractions. Bake a cake? Make some herbal medicines? Finish a painting? No. Her energy felt wrong; it had to be something new—a blank canvas into which she could disappear. A painting of Hossein? She had yet to paint a portrait of her lover, her tall, intelligent, philosophical companion. The English gentleman marked by the colours of the East and shaped by another theology altogether.

On her way to the studio, she picked up Irini's book. Leafing through its illustrated pages often centred her. From the kitchen drawer she retrieved a small vial labelled *Iremia*—an elixir for serenity. It contained sweet basil, St John's wort, bergamot and lavender. Using the eyedropper, she placed three drops on her tongue. Closing her eyes, she recited the corresponding passage Myrto had inscribed: 'Intrepid may the mind go, fearless and strong, anathema the heart and all its failings.'

It had been months since she had felt a need for an elixir. Life had been good lately. She had been productive, buoyed by new patrons after the antiquity conference. And she had fallen in love.

'Mama! I'm up,' Rika called, her voice ringing from her bedroom. Gone were the mornings when Aphrodite had to coax her awake. Now she rose like clockwork – 7 a.m. sharp. Hossein's portrait would have to wait. After breakfast they would head to the resort. There was now a sense of urgency to reach her family.

She kissed Rika on the neck as she stretched out her long, thin arms. With eyes half-closed, Rika hummed 'Steal My Girl' by One Direction. It was her latest obsession, and, for once it didn't annoy Aphrodite. 'Good morning, sweetheart.'

'Why were you in my bed?'

'Your bed?' Aphrodite noticed her pillow still tucked beside her. 'Because I felt like it. Is that okay?'

'Did I have nightmares or something?'

'No, not this time.'

Rika's night terrors had eased over the past year. They'd been quite frightening—at times almost demonic. Margarita had urged her to move out of the house, insisting it was full of bad spirits, but Aphrodite refused. The night terrors persisted even during stays at the resort with her grandparents. She turned to Irini's manuscript, testing elixirs until one—*Ekvoli*—made a remarkable difference. A mix of valerian root, chamomile, sage and dandelion root, its bitterness sweetened with chocolate milk and taken before bed. Within days, Aphrodite was able to enjoy a full night's sleep.

'There is no school today, Rika.'

'Why not?'

'A boat sank in the harbour near the resort. People drowned.' Aphrodite was not one to whitewash information for Rika. 'Everything will be closed today so the community can help.'

Rika looked at her mother, confused, unsure if she was being serious. 'What kind of boat, Mama?'

'I don't know, koukla. Your uncle and pappou are there. Hossein has gone down as well. We should help too, don't you think?'

Aphrodite cuddled her little girl, then pulled her out of bed and pushed her towards the bathroom. 'Okay, go to the toilet, wash your face, get dressed and I'll meet you in the kitchen. We have a lot to do today.'

Rika looked back with her solemn, angelic eyes. 'Mama, I hope I don't cry today.'

'There is nothing wrong with crying, my sweetheart. Crying washes away the sadness.'

After breakfast, Aphrodite got to work on Rika's hair. She had her tools ready: a bottle of spray-on detangler, a wide-toothed comb and a scrunchie to hold back her abundant curls. As she brushed, something unusual caught her eye. She put on her glasses and leaned closer: a single red curl behind Rika's left ear, bright against the dark waves. She brushed Rika's hair every morning, usually in a rush, but this was not something she would have overlooked. She thought of Nicholas's dark brown hair and then recalled a conversation—Nicholas describing his mother as a quiet, timid woman whose hair was the colour of clay. Aphrodite's heart sank; the poor woman still knew nothing of her granddaughter.

When she finished, a wave of sentiment washed over her. You know I love you very, very much,' she said, pulling her daughter onto the lounge and wrapping her in her arms. 'Sometimes I do and say crazy things, but you're my number one. Don't ever forget it.'

'Yes, Mama, I know. You don't have to keep telling me. I'm not stupid!'

'Before we leave for the resort, I want to talk to you about your father.'

'My father? Why?'

'I just need to.'

Rika fell silent as Aphrodite held her close.

'Remember how I told you that your father was a priest? How young I was? How interesting he was to talk to—how handsome?'

'Our priest isn't handsome. He looks like a hippopotamus.'

'True, but your father was very handsome—and deeply in love with Jesus. For him, Jesus was his number one. That's why he went to a monastery.'

Aphrodite had always been open about Nicholas, and despite their many talks, she could not shield Rika from the gossip and rumours. Thankfully, no one dared speak badly about Aphrodite in front of Rika, fearing her mother's vengeance.

'But when will I see him? Is he still at the monastery?'

'Yes, I think so.'

'He has been there for so long now.'

'I went looking for him once, to tell him about his beautiful little girl.'

'What did he say?'

'He was very sad because he didn't know. I gave him a photo of you so he can see how beautiful you are.'

'But why doesn't he come and visit me?'

***

Aphrodite first met Father Nicholas Yiakoulis in 2003, the day he joined her family for lunch only weeks into his new post. At sixteen, Aphrodite was a vision: tall and curvaceous, with long hair and a tomboy edge. She was taken by surprise by the handsome young priest and found herself at a loss for words.

The twenty-five-year-old priest was eloquent, charming, and gifted with a melodious baritone voice. He was about her height, with broad shoulders and green eyes, defying the mould of the Orthodox priest she was accustomed to.

Once shyness subsided, her curiosity surged. Setting down her fork, she fired questions at him, determined to understand how someone so young could preach. 'Have you ever lived in a refugee camp? Been to Africa? Were you an orphan? Were you ever abused as a child?'

Mortified, Margarita tried to silence her, while Mihalis threatened to kick her out of the room. Dimitri, only seven, sat giggling, revelling in his sister's command of the situation. Emilio was in Athens, studying.

Father Nicholas wiped his mouth with a napkin, stroked his beard and answered patiently. He hadn't suffered hardship, but as a priest's son, he spent some time in an orphanage reading the Bible to the children, telling them stories of saints and disciples.

Aphrodite suddenly sprang from her seat. 'Wait, I need to show you something,' she said as she ran out of the room, returning moments later with a large sketchbook clutched to her chest.

'Aphrodite!' her mother snapped.

'Your drawings can wait!' hollered her father.

'No, it's fine,' Father Nicholas insisted. 'I have finished. Lunch was delicious.'

Pushing aside Father Nicholas's empty plate, she laid down her sketchbook. Staring up at the priest was the Virgin Mary carrying Jesus in a pouch alongside an angry dog. Turning over the page, Saint Sophia appeared in a tank top with a sleeve tattoo, a lit cigarette dangling from her lips.

While confronted, Father Nicholas acknowledged her exceptional drawing talent. He then suggested she visit him after school or on a weekend so they might talk about the traditional Byzantine representation of saints. Her parents exchanged panicked glances, but it was too late; Father Nicholas insisted, and Aphrodite enthusiastically accepted. The aspiring artist had found a mentor. That he was handsome only fuelled her enthusiasm.

By the second visit, the mentorship had crossed the line. It happened in the cramped office behind the candle stand near the church entrance. He had been speaking about the icon of Saint George, describing the saint's muscular legs and armoured torso, the horse's flaring nostrils. His voice—masterful, warm and hypnotic—pushed her over the edge. She lunged at him, overwhelmed by the desire to feel his hands on her breast, his beard against her neck, the urgent compulsion to disrobe him.

The affair continued for a few weeks, on weekends or after school. She'd ride Emilio's moped up the mountain to his small apartment behind the church, condoms hidden in her bag. One afternoon, Father Nicholas tearfully announced he would leave the church and marry her. Aphrodite was taken by surprise. She reiterated she had no interest in being in a relationship with anyone until she finished her studies, lived in France or Germany and established herself as an artist.

Old Matina, the church cleaner and notorious gossip, must have overheard their argument while watering the garden bed. Within minutes she had rallied the mayor from the kafenio and a handful of his cronies, who soon barged into Nicholas's apartment, catching them half-undressed.

Mihalis and Margarita were outraged and humiliated. Emilio phoned from Athens to berate her for dragging the family's name through the mud. Aunt Salome offered her niece refuge in her home on the outskirts of Melissani while tempers cooled.

Within a week, clerics from Athens removed Nicholas from the island. Until his last hour, he begged Aphrodite to marry him. She stood firm.

Returning home from Aunt Salome's, she quietly announced that she had missed her period. Margarita howled for hours before insisting they immediately go to a clinic in Athens 'to fix everything'. Appalled by the suggestion, Aphrodite argued that the pregnancy was destined. Learning for the first time that her mother herself had had a baby before marriage changed nothing. Though shocked and distressed, Aphrodite refused to be swayed; if anything, she felt even more determined to proceed.

Meanwhile, Mihalis frantically tried to contact the church and track down Nicholas, but the clergy refused any dealings with Aphrodite or her family.

For the final two trimesters, Aphrodite moved to Athens to live with Emilio, returning after the birth to her parents' home in Kamiros, baby in hand and eager to complete her schooling.

Eight years later, Aphrodite Politis successfully tracked down Nicholas.

She learned of his whereabouts by accident. Construction delays at the resort in 2011 allowed her father and brothers to take their pilgrimage to Mount Athos. While dining at the Monastery of Stavronikita, Mihalis spotted Nicholas, although Dimitri was unsure, having met him only once. Nicholas was barely recognisable, having aged and appearing seemingly lost to another world. They subsequently moved to a different monastery and insisted his sons never tell Aphrodite. However, after an argument with his father upon their return to Phaedros, Dimitri told Aphrodite.

The day after a friend's wedding in Halkidiki in August 2012, Aphrodite took the bus to Ouranoupoli. She checked into a hotel behind the port, shut the curtains, and spent the night putting together a version of herself no one would recognise. By dawn, an overweight, devout zealot checked out of the hotel: long beard, wiry grey eyebrows, oversized dark trousers and a baggy shirt. A wide elastic band flattened her breasts; an old cushion gave the impression of a pot belly, and around her neck hung a large wooden crucifix she'd picked up from a souvenir shop. With forged documents prepared using Photoshop, she received a permit from the office near the port, no questions asked.

The Monastery of Stavronikita, one of the smallest monasteries on Mount Athos, had limited electricity and relied on candles and oil lamps for lighting. On approach, it resembled a medieval castle built on the edge of a cliff. A wooden cantilever balcony jutted from one of the towers, evoking the scene where Juliet declared her love to Romeo.

When the bells tolled for dinner at around 5 p.m., Aphrodite followed the men into the refectory and sat in silence at a long table. Frescoes by Theophanes the Cretan wrapped the walls in faded hues of burnt umber and yellow ochre. She wanted to take photos of the saints staring back at her disguise, but it was strictly forbidden.

When a monk chimed a small bell, thirty monks entered in orderly formation and took their places at the designated tables. The pilgrims waited in silence for permission to eat. Aphrodite didn't realise how hungry she was until the smell of dill and garlic rose with the steam from her plate of stuffed green capsicums and baked potatoes. Carafes of red wine were dispersed along the length of the table. Once prayers had finished, another chime signalled it was time to eat. They had ten minutes.

The monks all looked so alike in their movements and gestures, dressed in long brown habits with their hair pulled back in a bun. Suddenly, a flicker caught her eye, triggering the memory of Nicholas's tic—the abrupt, sporadic jolt of his head. It was him, the third monk from the far end of the table opposite her. He looked older and thinner, yet she recognised him instantly; his perfectly straight back, even while eating, gave him away. She watched him study the frescoes around him. Was he contemplating his former lover's reimagining of Gabriel? Or was he so brainwashed that he no longer thought of her at all?

A monk chimed the bell. Dinner was over. Wooden chairs screeched across the slate floor as everybody filed out in order, table by table. She watched Nicholas and three other monks stroll across the courtyard towards a room at the end of a stony corridor. Aphrodite gathered up her slipping pants, tightened her belt and followed.

The monks entered the library, a restricted area reserved for study and solitude. Aphrodite had no idea how events would unfold but trusted her instincts. Despite the heat of August, a chill overtook her as she moved through the dark medieval corridor. The old stone walls, flickering lanterns and musty air gave the impression she had slipped through a crack in time.

Checking her pot belly, beard and eyebrows were still in place, she turned the metal handle and pushed open the large wooden door. Her silhouette filled the thick doorway as rays of sunlight streamed in, partially illuminating the chamber. The monks sat at a table piled with large books, their faces aglow from the lantern. A Caravaggio painting gazed back at her.

'The library is not open to pilgrims,' one of them called out.

Aphrodite remained silent and took a few nervous steps into the room. Again, they asked her to leave. Her silence prompted them to rise in unison and shuffle towards her, murmuring anxiously. Once she identified Nicholas, she half-fainted into his arms.

'Sorry, I got lost. I am not feeling very well,' she said in a deep, breathless tone. 'Would you take me outside for some fresh air?'

Nicholas immediately obliged and told the others to continue their studies. His hand rested lightly on her padded waist as he guided her out of the room towards an archway overlooking the sea. Aphrodite noted the ten-metre drop to the rocks below, where small waves lapped at the tower's base.

'Are you feeling better?' he asked, gripping her shoulders. 'Should I call Monk Paolos? He is a trained nurse.'

Aphrodite turned to face him. 'That's not necessary, *Nicholas.*'

His hand slipped away as he stepped back. 'My name is Monahos Ayisilagos,' he said, struggling to get the words out. 'I no longer use that name. Do I know you?'

Aphrodite composed herself and then, with one swift motion, peeled off the beard and eyebrows. Her hair spilled down past her shoulders.

He staggered further back, his face empty of all expression. Tears welled in his eyes; his lips quivered and he shook all over. A mixture of fear and rage soon surfaced as he crossed himself repeatedly.

'Yes, it's me. Aphrodite.'

'How did you get in here? This is illegal. You cannot be here!'

When he turned to run, she grabbed his cloak and pulled him back.

'Help! Help!' he yelled. 'Amartia! Sin!'

Aphrodite only had a few seconds left with him. She could hear wooden chairs screeching and then the patter of feet as the other monks ran towards them.

'Listen to me. You have a daughter. Her name is Rika.'

'Lies. You are the Devil!'

'Nicholas, listen to me. She is seven years old. When they took you away, I didn't know I was pregnant. She is your child—born on 9 October 2004. I want you to meet her one day. I want her to know she has a father!'

By then, the other monks had gathered around her screaming, reluctant to touch her, each frantically crossing himself.

Aphrodite reached into her jacket for a photo.

'She has a gun,' one of the other monks called out. Their screams echoed through the six-hundred-year-old building as panic took hold. The monks fled, shouting, 'Help! Help!'

Aphrodite flashed the photo before Nicholas and tucked it into the large pocket of his tunic. On the back she had written Rika's birthday, their address and her mobile number.

'I am sorry for what I did to you,' she said. 'I was young, arrogant and disrespectful. But I don't regret our child…Now, please get me out of here.'

The head monk escorted her down to the jetty and surrendered her to the port authorities. The archdiocese tried to contain the scandal, but photographs and video footage of her arrest were leaked. Fortunately, the court overturned her prison sentence provided she paid a fine and refrained from speaking to the Greek press. Not one to be silenced, she spoke instead to the German press, with whom she already had a connection through her art.

***

'Wait here, I want to show you something,' Aphrodite said to her daughter as she ran upstairs to her bedroom, returning with a photo of Nicholas.

'Here he is. That's your father, Nicholas Yiakoulis.'

Rika studied the image, a candid shot of her father laughing. It was Aphrodite's favourite photo of him, one she had never shared before. She remembered the moment clearly, chasing him around the table, trying to tickle him as he protested. Straddling him on the floor, she pulled the camera from her backpack and took the shot. One day, she planned to recreate that image in a painting for Rika.

'You have his eyes, you know—big, beautiful green eyes.'

'Thank God I don't have his beard!' Rika squealed.

Aphrodite loved her daughter's humour and couldn't resist digging her fingers into her ribs. Rika soon escaped squealing as Aphrodite chased her, mobile in hand, and tackled her to the floor. Pinning her down as she had done with Nicholas, she took a photo, then collapsed on top of her.

'Mama, you're going to suffocate me!'

'Don't grow up too quickly, my sweetheart.'

'Well, that depends on whether you let me live.'

Aphrodite kissed her cheek and rolled off her. 'I'm so proud of you.'

'Can I keep the photo of my father?'

'Of course you can.'

'Don't worry, I'll look after it.'

'I know you will. Can I tell you something else, Rika?'

'Yes.'

'I really like Hossein. Really, really like him. He makes me feel special. When you meet someone who makes you feel special, you look at the world differently. Every time you see that person, your heart races; you feel like jumping out of your own skin.'

'No, thanks, I don't want to die,' Rika replied with a deadpan expression, head flat against the floorboards.

'You won't die, silly; in fact, you feel more alive than you ever thought possible. And then you realise—only that person can make you feel that way.'

'Mama, are you saying you're in love with Hossein?'

Aphrodite thought long and hard before answering. 'Yes, I am, my sweet.'

'Why do you always fall in love with men with black beards?'

'No, I don't.'

'Benn had a beard,' she said, referring to her ex-boyfriend in Berlin.

'Yes, but his beard was ginger.'

Rika examined the photo again. 'I still think Hossein looks like my father,' she said, pushing the photo in front of her mother's face.

It had been years since she looked at it. Rika was right. Although the eyes and nose were different, the soft expression and smile were familiar. For a fleeting moment, she saw Hossein's face transition onto the face of a past lover.

'Well, I think you may be right, sweetheart,' she said as she snuggled up next to her on the floor.

'I hope he doesn't leave the island too, Mama.'

'Do you like my boyfriend?'

'Hmm…If he stays, I will love him forever!'

'Oh wow, that much?'

Her daughter's words landed with unexpected force. Something within her loosened. The fear she had sensed earlier eased its grip. From the window, she could see that the rain had stopped and that the grey of the sky had brightened. Jumping up from the floor, Aphrodite felt charged and ready to face the world again, no matter what tragedy and horrors the day might yet deliver.

CHAPTER 16
The clinic, a week later

The woman looked at peace as she slept in the clinic bed. Margarita gently pushed her hair aside, tucked it behind her ear and whispered, 'Maryam.' A flicker of guilt passed through her, sensing she was intruding on whatever tranquil place the survivor had found. But Maryam needed to eat and take more pills. Three of them sat in a small white cup on the overbed table. Not wanting her to wake up with medication shoved in her face, Margarita nudged the table further down the bed, revealing Maryam's delicate, overlapping hands.

Margarita drew back the curtain beside the bed. Sunlight spilled across the stark white sheets. Outside, it was a beautiful, calm day. The ferry was leaving the harbour, taking tourists home to their loved ones. The sea was smooth. If only Maryam had postponed her travel, she thought. How cruel.

Maryam's jaw twitched. Her cracked lips parted as she drew in air, then stretched into a half-smile.

Maryam was in the Haralambos Kaligeros Clinic, named after Margarita's ancestor, the beloved physician who witnessed Greece's War of Independence. The migration crisis in Lesbos had left the twelve-bed clinic in Kamiros understaffed, and the Phaedrians were up in arms. In the bed beside Maryam, an older woman from one of the island's more remote villages lay in a coma, quietly dying from heart failure. The nurse said she was over 100 years old and had no relatives left. In another room, two elderly male patients complained about the lack of care.

Margarita placed a bag of clothes in the bottom compartment of the bedside cabinet. She neatly stacked sanitary pads in the top drawer and discreetly swapped the Bible for the Quran that Hossein had lent her. Tucked into the corner of the drawer was Maryam's passport and gold wedding band, sealed in a ziplock bag. It was all she had from her former life.

Margarita quietly took out the passport, put on her reading glasses and examined the photo. She noticed that the patient's smooth skin and oval face appeared shadowed and harsh in the image; her lustrous black hair hidden under a hijab, while thick eyeliner narrowed her eyes. The stamps showed trips to Egypt and the UK. Born on 12 April 1987, Maryam Hamoud was the same age as Aphrodite.

A deep, guttural cry suddenly escaped from Maryam's mouth. Margarita returned the passport, took hold of the patient's hand and sat in the chair beside the bed.

A week had passed since the capsizing, and the doctor wanted to discharge her as soon as possible.

'She must face the truth,' he told Margarita, his annoyance evident.

Margarita didn't appreciate his attitude and told him he lacked empathy. The reality was that he was overworked and young. His plea to the community for support hadn't gained much traction. Margarita remembered her first few weeks in Australia, when neighbours brought biscuits and flowers. Here, she felt ashamed. While some locals dropped off food and clothes, none offered to sit with Maryam. Once it became known that she was a Muslim from Syria, a severe case of xenophobia took hold on the island. The flood of refugees in Lesbos had put the fear of God into them.

An article by Fotini Panagoulas, Eva's mother, in the latest edition of *Island News* didn't help. It rambled on about how Islam would soon squeeze out Orthodoxy and deprive Greeks of hospital beds. A day after it appeared, Eva arrived at the hospital with a large bag of clothes. Margarita hadn't seen her since the breakup, and although their initial encounter was awkward, she greeted Eva with a hug and a kiss on each cheek. Eva immediately apologised for her mother's article, clearly embarrassed. She was still living in her apartment at the other end of Kamiros Beach; it was a wonder the women hadn't run into each other. Margarita missed her, but she understood how frustrating life with Emilio must have been. As she pulled out some garments from the bag, Eva acknowledged that her past fashion choices might not be appropriate for a Muslim.

Margarita visited Maryam twice a day, at midday and in the evening, bringing cooked meals and fresh fruit. Feeding her was often a battle, but she could at least brush Maryam's hair and pin it up before covering it with a headscarf. Their talks were in English, but Maryam usually responded with single words, as if speaking more might lead her to open up and break down. Margarita didn't press for information; her aim was to encourage her to eat, take her medicine and drink water. Even so, it felt like pushing against a tide. Antigone, her sister-in-law, had suffered much the same after Christopher's suicide. The surrender to life felt painfully familiar.

Emilio visited daily to check on Maryam. A few times his visits coincided with his mother's, but he always kept his distance at the foot of the bed. Margarita tried to coax him closer, but he simply gestured a hello. He kept thanking her, both in person and over the phone, as if she were doing him a favour. Once or twice she had to tell him to stop because his concern was becoming obsessive, but it seemed to go in one ear and out the other. Since the drownings, she had noticed a change in her son—an uncharacteristic neediness and nervousness. His voice often wavered, lacking its usual boisterousness.

Margarita, meanwhile, had time on her hands. She was a woman who loved to be busy. Since the resort opened, that all changed. Life had become unsettling. For someone who was always on the go from morning until night, the days now dragged, especially since Dimitri started his national service earlier in the year. Old aches and pains crept back, and finding motivation for even the simplest chores became difficult. Idleness not only caused her to gain weight but also increased her worries about her husband and children.

****

Margarita and Aphrodite took charge of Maryam during the burials. The bodies of the refugees were transported in the back of pickup trucks to a designated field near Saint Sophia. Loosely wrapped in sheets, they were laid out in the midday sun like a harvest of corn. Father Efthimios moved among them, inspecting their condition. Nine graves had been prepared. Pandelis, the editor, took photographs for immigration records. With Kurush's help, Pandelis placed marble offcuts inscribed with a number and the deceased's name, if known, at the head of each grave.

Hossein received instructions on preparing the bodies and relayed them to the volunteers. Women washed the bodies of women and children; men tended to the men. A truck delivered a crate of four-litre water bottles, a sight that would have infuriated people like Fotini. Water was scarce on the island, and many would not be pleased to see it used this way. The resort supplied face washers and liquid soap for cleaning the bodies.

While Margarita had experience dressing the deceased—her brother, mother and nephew—it was Aphrodite's first time. She struggled but remained determined. The children proved the most difficult; their small, blue, decaying bodies looked inhuman. A few times, Margarita noticed Aphrodite drinking something from her handbag and suspected it was a concoction from Irini's book.

Emilio soon arrived from the hospital with Maryam. She was heavily sedated but had insisted on attending. Unsteady, she climbed out of the car dressed in one of Margarita's black mourning suits, a brown scarf wrapped around her hair. The sight of the bodies laid out on the ground brought her to her knees; her scream pierced the air. Margarita rushed to help her son, who was struggling to lift her. Together, they escorted her through the tall green grass to where her daughter and husband lay. Maryam's body shook uncontrollably.

'Whose dress is my daughter wearing?' she asked.

'My daughter's,' Aphrodite replied. 'She's too big for it now.'

'She looks beautiful. Thank you.'

Maryam observed her husband's lifeless form, dressed in trousers and a shirt that was too tight across his bloated chest. The old brown leather shoes were peeling at the tips. She dropped beside him, lifted his hand that still bore his wedding ring and kissed it repeatedly.

'My brave husband, I am so sorry I can't be with you. Take care of our baby. I will come to you soon.' She kissed his purple lips, sobbing.

Then, as if guided by her husband's spirit, she stood, composed herself and wiped her face. Adjusting her scarf, she looked up and fixed her gaze on a small cloud, reading it as if it were sending messages. Margarita watched as the widow then scanned the surrounding vegetation and noted the sun's position before asking if the graves were of adequate depth. Father Efthimios assured her that the plots were prepared according to the imam's instructions in Lesbos.

Maryam crouched next to her daughter and asked for a brush. Aphrodite reached into her handbag and pulled out the comb she kept for Rika. Lifting her daughter's head, Maryam attempted to comb back her hair but couldn't get through the knots. It didn't matter; it was more about the gesture—a final act of motherhood. She picked up Maya, held her tightly and then placed her on her husband's chest, insisting they be buried together.

No one dared argue.

Rigor mortis made it difficult to secure them. Removing her cardigan, Margarita used the sleeves to bind Bassel's hands so

Maya would not slip away. Aphrodite assisted, understanding her mother's intent. This crude solution proved effective. Maryam then drew the cardigan over Maya's small upper back, tucking it around her stomach and Bassel's chest.

In life, Maya had been strapped to her mother. In death, to her father.

The image was more than Margarita could bear. She stepped away. Though she may have attended many funerals, none felt quite like this. Burial without a coffin felt barbaric. No one deserved this. She gathered a few sprigs of wild lavender and returned to the graveside, where Maryam lay sprawled across the bodies. After a few minutes, Hossein caught Margarita's eye and nodded. It was time.

'Bury me with them!' Maryam screamed as Margarita and Aphrodite struggled to lift her. Emilio intervened, and Maryam screamed again before her strength gave way and she crumpled into his arms. Aphrodite stood frozen, her eyes puffy and bloodshot, her nose running.

Mihalis and Kurush covered the bodies with the sheet Bassel had been placed on. With assistance from two locals, they gathered the corners of the sheet and lowered father and daughter into the grave. Margarita looked over the opening and scattered lavender over them. Hossein stood at the head of the grave, Quran in hand, receiving instructions from the imam via mobile phone. His voice trembled as he recited the takbirs.

After the burial, Emilio drove Maryam back to the clinic and dropped Margarita off at home on the way. She wanted to prepare lunch before the others arrived. Aphrodite insisted on staying behind to support Hossein, unwilling to leave him alone with the weight of the day.

The events of the past week had distracted Margarita from the sadness she'd felt in recent months. Rika's refusal to spend time with her had been like a dagger to the heart. She had never imagined the impact a grandchild would have on her.

'Give her space, for God's sake!' Aphrodite yelled at her over the phone. 'She wants some independence!'

Margarita sensed the emptiness other grandparents warned her about, when their grandchildren grew tired of them. It felt like a marker in one's life, signalling that it's time to grow old and prepare for death. Maryam's arrival had briefly circumvented that reckoning.

She laid the tablecloth on the kitchen table, smoothing the creases with her palms. The flyscreen door slammed shut and Emilio stood in the doorway, breathless and dishevelled.

'Is she alright?' Margarita asked.

Emilio began pacing back and forth. Margarita got him a glass of water. 'Here. Sit down.'

He drank it in one go, wiped his mouth and continued pacing. 'Sit down, Emilio.'

'I don't want to sit down!' he shouted.

Margarita was stunned by his outburst and didn't respond. She gave him some time. He had come to see her for a purpose—to unload. 'The immigration authorities from Mytilene were on the phone while I was at the clinic. They said that Maryam and Kurush must apply for asylum and stay here, otherwise, they'll be sent back to Turkey. Kurush has an aunt in Norway and that's where he wants to go. Maryam has cousins in Canada but doesn't want to go anywhere. She can't see past the next hour. They gave us her brother-in-law's number in Germany. He went off at her. She was telling us in English that he was blaming her, that it was all her fault! I couldn't believe how he spoke to her. He couldn't give a shit about her. She went crazy, screaming for someone to kill her. We had to pin her down like a wild animal until the doctor was able to sedate her.'

Margarita's heart cramped as Emilio described the scene. She had never seen him so frazzled—not since that time at their old house in Sydenham. Over the years, his bravado had worn thin.

She felt awful for him and responsible. 'It will be okay, Emilio. She'll be fine.'

'I should have let her drown,' he said. 'At least she'd be with her family. But look at her now. No one wants her. And it's my fucking fault!'

'And how would you feel if you had left her?' Margarita tried to reason with him.

He opened the drinks cabinet and pulled out a bottle of tsipouro, poured himself half a glass and drank. Then he poured another.

'Please,' she said. 'It will only make you feel worse!'

'Stop telling me what to do. You promised I would be happy here, that Phaedros is paradise! Is this the happiness you wanted for me, Mum? You've made me a prisoner of this island! A fucking prisoner!'

***

Margarita felt a hand clasp her shoulder. It was Aphrodite.

'How is she?'

'She seems to have more colour today. Don't you think?'

Aphrodite stepped forward for a closer look. 'Yes, I think you're right.'

'Alla madad,' Maryam murmured as she began to open her eyes.

'What's she saying?' Aphrodite asked.

'I wish I knew. Hello, Maryam,' Margarita said, raising her voice. Maryam looked at them, unsure.

'Kalimera!' Aphrodite excitedly called out.

'Hello,' Maryam slowly responded, her voice hoarse. She studied Aphrodite's face and then turned to Margarita. 'You have a beautiful daughter. I can see the resemblance. You are so lucky.' Turning her head to face the wall, she whimpered, 'I am so embarrassed.'

'No, no, please. You don't need to be embarrassed,' Margarita reassured her.

Aphrodite grabbed a few tissues from the side table and handed them to her. 'You must never feel embarrassed with us,' she added.

Maryam rubbed her eyes and then looked at her hands. She leaned over and retrieved her wedding band from the drawer, carefully putting it on and admiring it as if she were wearing it for the first time. 'I must keep the memory of Bassel and Maya alive. They existed! Only I can tell the world that, otherwise…they will become nothing. I must not let them become nothing.'

Margarita took hold of her hand as Aphrodite offered her some water. With shaky fingers, Maryam managed a few sips.

'There is a man. I see him here all the time. The doctor told me this man was the one who saved me. He pulled Maya and Bassel from the water. Took me to the burial.'

'That's my son, Emilio.'

'Your son?'

'He's been very concerned about you.'

'Do you have other children?'

'Dimitri. He is eighteen years old and doing his military service.'

'Alayhi wa-àala āli-hi wa-sallam. Allah be with him. May he return safely.'

'Thank you.'

Margarita reached for the white plastic cup with the pills. 'Your medicine. The doctor said you should take them when you wake up.'

Maryam examined the pills, trying to make out the imprints. 'Could you please pass me the medicine chart?'

Margarita unhooked the chart hanging from the rail at the foot of her bed.

Maryam scrutinised the notes. 'I told him no more fluoxetine.'

'He said it's important that you take them.'

'These are antidepressants. I don't want them.'

'You know about medicines?' asked Aphrodite.

'I am a pharmacist. My husband was also a pharmacist. Our pharmacy was in Aleppo.'

Her mood shifted slightly as she eased herself into a seated position. Margarita's old nightgown hung loosely from her shoulders.

'My ancestor was a traditional herbalist,' Aphrodite said, placing another pillow behind Maryam's head for support. 'I have a book of her recipes at home. She had cures for everything and—'

'Let's put that story aside for now,' Margarita interrupted. 'Maryam needs to eat so she can get her strength back.'

Aphrodite fell quiet. When it came to her family's secrets, she was quick to unearth them. It wasn't that Margarita was ashamed of her roots; she just felt it needed to be told in a particular way—and that's where mother and daughter clashed.

'The doctor told me you'll be ready to leave the clinic soon. We have a room for you. You will be staying at our resort, Paradisos.'

'That's not possible. I cannot pay you.'

'We are not expecting you to pay. You are our guest. Please don't worry about that. The resort has several rooms for staff—complete with a kitchenette and bathroom.'

A faint smile returned. Taking Margarita's and Aphrodite's hands, she kissed them. 'Thank you. I am so grateful. One day, I will repay my debt.'

'This is not a debt,' Aphrodite said.

'Emilio insists on you staying there,' Margarita added.

'Your son?'

'Yes, he's the owner. He made it very clear that you would stay at Paradisos until you were back on your feet.'

Maryam peered across to the old woman in the next bed. 'I don't see anyone coming to visit her.'

Aphrodite crossed over to check on her, having forgotten she was there.

'Sadly, she has outlived all her children,' Margarita said.

'I hope her dreaming is filled with joy,' Maryam said, bringing her clasped hands to her heart and drawing in a deep breath. 'God help her.'

Margarita unpacked a Tupperware container from her bag. The three women then sat together on the bed as Maryam picked at Margarita's spinach and cheese pie.

'My mother used to make a similar pie,' Maryam said. It's delicious.'

'Your mother. Where is she?' Aphrodite asked.

'She died of cancer a few years ago. All my family have passed on. All of them.'

'I am so sorry,' Margarita said. 'What kind of cancer took your mother?'

'Pancreatic.'

'God rest her soul,' Aphrodite commiserated.

Margarita thought of her own cancer. It had taken her breast. She was in remission now, but the fear of its return never loosened its hold. It hung over her, constant and tightening. Still, she had her husband, her children, her grandchild. Her life, despite its heartache, was rich—a jackpot beside this young woman's. She had come to see that the tragedies of others—her brother Tolly, and now Maryam's—threw light into the darkness that sometimes engulfed her.

The young nurse came in to take Maryam's blood pressure. She was improving. She even took her pills and ate more than she had the previous day. Margarita sensed they had made progress. For the first time in a long while she felt useful and almost unbearably happy.

CHAPTER 17
Paradisos II resort

It was 8 a.m. and Mihalis was already feeling the heat. The morning radio program predicted thirty-eight degrees Celsius, which was unusual for June. Fortunately, shade blanketed the alcove between the resort's kitchen and laundry during the morning hours. Sitting on a blue drinks crate, Mihalis withdrew a jar half-filled with cigarette butts from behind the drainpipe. Boxwood hedges, growing against the corners of the diagonal walls, concealed the secluded space from passers-by.

Unfolding the newspaper, he licked his finger and flicked through the pages. He shook his head and tutted. All the headlines were about the migrant crisis: 'Three more drownings'; 'Syrians arriving by the hour'; 'Mytilene overtaken'. He let out a deep sigh. It was starting to feel like an invasion.

Getting up, he peered around the corner across to the harbour to check whether a boat was sinking. The harbour had become everyone's centre of attention. What used to be a serene body of water now stirred up panic. Fear of more boats arriving, or that Phaedros would become the overspill for Mytilene's asylum seekers, was playing on people's minds. The worst-case scenario was that tourists would stop coming. Without tourism, the island was dead.

'Are you okay, Mihalis?' asked Anna Ivanaj, a staff member. Placing his frappé and water on a small wooden stool, she looked him up and down. 'You seem pale.'

'Just hot. I didn't sleep well,' he responded matter-of-factly.

Anna walked away but then glanced back. 'Are you sure?'

'I'm fine…Wait!'

She turned, pleased he'd changed his mind.

'Can I ask you a question without overstepping my boundaries?'

'Of course.'

'How's the new girl—Maryam?'

'Umm, endaxi, okay. Still learning,' she replied diplomatically.

He had a soft spot for Anna, as she did for him. He hated to see good people leave. A devoted staff member for eight years, she was retiring at the end of the summer to care for her mother back home in Albania. He dreaded the thought of not having that short, full-bodied woman, with permed, bleach-blonde hair and ridiculously long fingernails, swanning around the place. Her humour and insightful nature would be dearly missed.

'So you think she's a good fit?'

'Did you think I was a good fit when I started?'

'I can't remember…I think so.'

'Well, I remember, and you wouldn't talk to me for months.'

'I employed you, didn't I?'

'Your wife did. I started in the laundry.'

'I was very busy.'

'Too busy to say hello?'

'Well, you know we love you.'

'Now you do, yes.'

'Well, if you want to keep it that way, go before I cancel your resignation!'

'You're no longer my boss. Your son is.'

Mihalis couldn't help but smile.

'I love you too, old man. If I didn't admire your wife so much, I would have kidnapped you a long time ago.'

'Get out of here.'

Anna winked at him before disappearing around the corner.

Mihalis sipped his frappé and lit a cigarette. He was now down to three a day, still aiming to quit. Since Margarita's cancer he no longer smoked in front of her. From his pocket he took out two little red pills for his blood pressure and swallowed them with cold water. He folded the newspaper, not wanting to know any more about the refugee situation.

Mihalis didn't agree with Emilio's decision to employ Maryam. No one knew her background. As far as he was concerned, she could be an ISIS spy. While Hossein and the doctor believed she was a pharmacist, Mihalis wanted written proof. Five weeks had passed since the drownings, and it just didn't sit right with him that she should be working. She had lost everything—her husband and child. How anyone could resume working after that was beyond him.

He recalled his first few months in Australia. He had made a choice to be there; she hadn't. He had a spouse; she had no one. He went to a place where they wanted him; she was in a place where no one knew what to do with her. To him, it seemed implausible for her to be working in an exclusive resort.

Even Kurush managed to find employment. Vasilis Kapakis, Salome's husband, hired him as a casual farm worker. Mihalis thought Margarita had arranged it, but it was actually old Katina Drivas, Policeman Harry's mother, who had taken the young refugee in as a guest. Last week, Kurush visited the resort with Harry while on his way to the port police station to obtain his temporary visa. They stopped by only because Kurush wanted to thank Mihalis and Emilio again for saving his life. Harry reminded Emilio that Maryam should address her visa situation in case of any job opportunities.

'She will work at Paradisos,' Emilio quickly responded. 'It's all arranged, and she has agreed. My mother will take her to the station for the appropriate permit.'

Mihalis was taken aback, hearing this for the first time. While he had agreed to provide Maryam with a place to stay, there was no mention of employment. Local young people were waiting desperately for jobs at the resort. This would get everyone's noses out of joint. What the hell was Emilio thinking?

An argument broke out between Mihalis and Margarita that night.

'Haven't you noticed he is suffering severe stress because of the drownings?'

'Of course I have!' he shouted back. 'But he can't just start creating jobs for them.'

'It's not "them". It's one person.'

'And what's everyone on the island going to think?'

'That we are doing a good thing!'

'Where do you think you're living? This isn't Australia. People here are desperate for work. This country is being strangled with refugees, and here we are offering them careers and luxury living.'

'It's for Emilio's benefit. Having Maryam work here will help him.'

'Help him with what?'

'His sanity! You might not see it, but it's me he's coming to—crying, throwing things around. I didn't tell you that one day I found him in his office, drunk, in the middle of the afternoon!'

'She's getting free accommodation. Isn't that enough?'

'No, it's not!'

Mihalis realised that since the drownings, Emilio had changed. Witnessing his son's actions that awful morning would have crushed anyone's spirit. He also noticed that Emilio was avoiding him. Neither had spoken to the other about that event. There existed a silent agreement that the less said about the incident, the better the memory would remain adrift.

It wasn't just the newspaper headlines that troubled Mihalis that morning. He had woken at four in the morning with a sense of foreboding, shaken by a nightmare. It was Christmas back in Australia, and all three children were in the old shop in Sydenham. But the shop was different—it was an antique shop. He was dressed as Santa Claus, and snow was falling outside. The children were barefoot and scantily dressed, and he desperately tried to find clothes and shoes for them so they could play outside. Dimitri cried, inconsolable. Aphrodite clung to his leg, begging him to hurry. Emilio, frantic, jumped on the counter and threw old crockery from the shelf. As Mihalis pounced on Emilio to stop him, he woke up.

The dream was so vivid that even thinking about it sent a shiver down his spine. He wondered why Margarita wasn't in the dream—had she left him with their children?

The chirping of sparrows on the ledge of the kitchen roof distracted him. He wished he had breadcrumbs to offer, but they soon flew off, disappearing behind the overgrown bougainvillea creeping over the roofline. It needed trimming, something he would attend to promptly. The two colours looked magnificent against the blue sky: cherry and burnt orange, the resort's signature colour combination. At first he had ridiculed the colour scheme and questioned Emilio's choice of landscape gardener. Watching these colours now unfold in the morning sun, he recognised he was wrong. Not that he would ever admit it to Emilio.

A shadow suddenly appeared on the opposite wall. Footsteps behind him came to a stop.

'Kalimera.'

It was Emilio.

Mihalis was startled. 'Good morning. What are you doing here?' Evidence that he had been smoking lingered in the air and in the jar at his feet.

Emilio looked a little uneasy. Beads of sweat rolled down his temples; his gait was tense, almost mechanical.

'You're up early,' Mihalis noted nervously, sensing that something was wrong.

'What happened?' Emilio asked, moving closer to his father with an iPad in his hand.

'What do you mean?'

'Read this.'

Mihalis took the device in his hands and looked at the screen. It was a TripAdvisor page. Emilio expanded the screen size with his fingers to make it more legible.

Mihalis noticed a three-star rating and started to read:

A beautiful resort in a stunning setting with glorious views of the sea, the port and the mountain. The rooms were lovely and clean. The food is exceptional. Unfortunately, the creepy hands of Mihalis, the gardener, wandered a little too far during the 'gimmicky' souvenir photo shoot by the fountain. Gross!! Watch out for the unexpected kiss and pat on the backside. Gross!!!

He put the tablet down on his lap, dumbfounded.

'How am I supposed to respond to a review like that?' Emilio shouted. 'Are you completely crazy? Why would you do something like that? What do I tell Mum? This is so fucking embarrassing!'

Mihalis sensed his blood pressure surge. He stood and shoved the iPad back into Emilio's hands. 'Who wrote that?'

'Susan Cornish—the Englishwoman—the marketing manager for the bloody Cannes Film Festival!'

The penny dropped. 'Her! It was her girlfriend. That Isabel is a bitch! I knew she'd cause trouble. I did not touch her girlfriend's bum!'

Recently, Mihalis had become the resort's poster boy. A photo of him with his moustache, worry beads and fisherman's hat had become a parting gift for guests. The statue of Artemis at the fountain, with The Village behind it, served as the backdrop. The gimmicky image, reminiscent of tourists propping up the Leaning

Tower of Pisa, was captured countless times. Mihalis would stand to the side of the fountain, positioned so Artemis's finger appeared to beckon her animals to attack him. He smiled, and the tourists screamed on cue for the shot by the resident photographer, usually, Theodore, the gardener. Mihalis didn't mind posing, especially as his popularity gave him some hold over his son.

He remembered the incident clearly. Before they took their places, Isabel said, 'When I say "now", give her a kiss on the cheek.' Feeling uncomfortable, Mihalis hesitated, but the taller woman kept egging him on. Theodore raised the camera phone at Isabel's instruction, waiting for her signal. Mihalis sensed Isabel's hand behind him. At her command, he kissed Susan's cheek—just as Theodore clicked away—just as Isabel pinched her girlfriend's backside.

Susan screamed, slapped Mihalis on the shoulder, recoiled and then called him a creep. Isabel snatched her phone from Theodore and the women stormed off. Theodore pulled Mihalis back from going after them, not wanting to create a scene, though not before Mihalis regrettably shouted, 'Bitch!' He never mentioned the incident to Emilio but now wished he had.

'That cow set it up to make it look like I squeezed her girlfriend's bum! Boutana!'

'I think it's best you take some time off, Baba. You can't be here right now.'

'I live here!'

'Just stay in the house then!' Emilio yelled back and walked off.

Mihalis stood alone, paralysed, his legs shaking. Picking up the milk crate, he hurled it against the wall with such force that it split in two. With a savage kick, he sent the jar of cigarette butts against the opposite wall. The frappé and glass of water followed. Shards of glass, butts, and crockery littered the lane. If he could, Mihalis would have torn down the surrounding walls with his bare hands. 'How dare he speak to me like that!' he screamed to himself.

Anna came running around the corner. 'What's happened?' she yelled.

By then, Mihalis was slumped against the wall, his head cradled in his arms.

'Mihalis, what's the matter? Speak to me!'

He took a few deep breaths.

'I had a fight with Emilio. I'm okay.' He felt bad for Anna. It wasn't the first time she had dealt with the aftermath of one of their fights.

'Go home, Mihalis. I will clean up here.'

'Home? I don't want to go home. My home has turned on me. If only I'd kept one in Sydney then I'd have somewhere to go.'

'Stop it, Mihalis. Everything will work out.'

'I might join you in Albania.'

'My door is always open.'

'People love me, Anna. I am a good man. I made this place.' Mihalis was tearing up as he started to leave. He called back to her, 'I will be so sorry to lose you, Anna.'

At sixty-seven, Mihalis understood he needed to pull back. What infuriated him now was that something so ridiculous, so mean and unfair, had become the pivotal factor. As he exited the alcove, a guest jogged by.

'Morning,' Mihalis called out.

There was no response. He wondered if the jogger had already read the review. He felt his heart pounding. Gripping the railing along the walkway, he drew several deep breaths and closed his eyes. Too many things had fallen out of place lately: Anna's decision to leave, his youngest son's conscription, the drownings. The security of his surroundings no longer felt guaranteed. Everything he had built, nurtured, and loved was under threat, and an overwhelming fear came over him that he was about to lose everything.

A guest hurried over and asked if he was okay. Looking at the old man, probably in his eighties and in great shape, Mihalis couldn't help but wonder whether he would ever reach that age. The guest's wife was soon beside him, equally charming, asking if everything was alright. Thanking them, he blamed the heat and advised them to stay hydrated as a heatwave was expected over the next few days. The old man offered to walk him to reception, but he politely declined.

A little later, Mihalis climbed the marble steps of his home. The scent of basil was strong, and Toula, their yellow canary, burst into song.

'Mihalis, is that you?' Margarita called out from the kitchen.

'Yes, it is,' he shouted over Toula's shrills. 'Kalimera to you too, my beautiful Toula,' he affectionately cooed to the canary. Her singing grew louder as she tilted her head back and shrilled at a deafening pitch. Mihalis chuckled. It was nice to know that someone was excited to see him. Then Rudi came charging out the front door through the coloured plastic strips that kept the flies out. Jumping on Mihalis, he dropped to the ground, demanding a tummy rub.

'Okay, okay, kalimera to you too.'

Mihalis stayed outside. He wasn't ready to go in just yet. He needed time to calm down before talking to Margarita about what had happened.

He knew the truth about those women would come out. Theodore would defend him; he would talk sense to Emilio. Still, it was hard to lie to his wife. He had been unfaithful, many years ago with a tourist. Margarita successfully extracted the truth from him. After thirty-five years of marriage, she could always sense when he was hiding something. It was a stupid mistake that nearly cost him his marriage, family and business. Recalling that event, and having survived it, gave him hope that this latest crisis would pass.

The sun bore down on his thinning hair. Instead of his Paradisos II staff cap, he grabbed a doily from the patio and draped it over his head. Lying on the table was a pile of junk mail, ready for him to put in the resort's recycling bin. A glossy travel brochure for Hungary and the Czech Republic caught his eye. A yearning to leave the island now poked at him. A long time had passed since he and Margarita travelled together. After her cancer, she lost interest in going anywhere. With much deliberation, Aphrodite convinced her to try some of the ancestor's folk magic, promising her she'd feel better. Mihalis had no idea what she took, but whatever it was, he noticed a difference: better sleep, increased appetite, more mingling with the hotel guests. It wouldn't surprise him if Margarita was brewing the stuff herself. Perhaps she could make him something strong enough to dilute his bitterness.

It was the year of their forty-fifth anniversary—surely they should celebrate. A trip to Australia? He desperately wanted to take her to Surfers Paradise and the Great Barrier Reef, all those places they never managed to see when they lived there. But he already knew her answer. She'd been asking him to take her to France and Italy for years. Mihalis didn't care where he went. He just needed to leave, even for a few weeks. Emilio would have to find another sidekick for the stupid photo gimmick.

CHAPTER 18
Ancient Tallos Archaeological Museum

Hossein sank into his office chair, unbuttoned his collar, and closed his eyes. His brain shifted like a volcano preparing to erupt. All day he had been juggling between security and taking tours. Since the security manager's unexpected death last week, he had no choice but to take on the extra workload. It was 6 p.m. and he had half an hour before Poppy, the cleaner, would barge into his office expecting it to be vacated.

The day's clientele had been Chinese; the next day, the Russians were coming. For a country that was falling apart, tourism was flourishing.

Outside, it was a scorching hot July day. Hossein got up, stretched until his spine cracked, bent to touch his toes and drank a full glass from the water dispenser. He loved his office. Small but functional, it was his private retreat. Behind the closed venetian blinds, a large window overlooked the agora and the marble path that led to the fortress gate. The furniture, though dated, served its purpose. His pride was the antique cedar bookshelf which housed his journals, ethnographies, site reports and his doctorate. It was the one piece of furniture he expected Poppy to polish at least once a week.

Following afternoon prayer, Hosseini rolled up his mat and, as he often did, reached for the museum's first catalogue. He leafed through the yellow-edged pages to remind himself of the museum's state before he took over. It was a ritual of reflection, and vanity. He stopped at Professor Papadopoulos's preface:

> *In one's career as an archaeologist, one occasionally stumbles across an artefact that immediately connects with you. It whispers a key to an extraordinary discovery. In this instance, the artefact was a lead scroll, no bigger than a cigar, unearthed just outside the fortress gates of this magnificent city. As I slowly unrolled the lead, a poem revealed itself: a woman laments the death of her unborn son and longs to reunite with him in the afterworld. She finds refuge and solace in the forest sanctuary of Artemis. A few weeks later, two metres from where the scroll was found, we uncovered a path leading to the buried temple. That temple and its remnants have gifted us with the incredible story of a city under siege, echoing the dying light of the Hellenistic world.*

Flicking through the catalogue, Hossein paused at the page showing the stolen kouros he had helped excavate during his 1995 field trip. The statue vanished in 2012, six months before he took office. Weighing forty-six kilos, it was among the region's finest antiquities—far too heavy to simply disappear.

It took something disastrous, such as the disappearance of the kouros, to make the world notice: artefacts across Greece were being stolen. The collapsing economy was turning people into looters, poaching artefacts to sell on the black market. Fortunately, Hossein had successfully tapped into a UNESCO fund that enabled him to install a new CCTV security system. Now he just needed the appropriate manpower so he could focus on his proper role as a curator.

The Artemis Gallery was an extraordinary achievement for Hossein. Following an elaborate application in partnership with Paradisos II to the Global Antiquity Foundation, the museum secured a substantial grant of 130,000 euros to create an interactive exhibition dedicated to the Temple of Artemis Ismene. Completed in time for the conference, it has since become the museum's main attraction.

At its entrance, a haunting recording of the Katara Tablet—the large stone tablet set into the city gate's arch—serves as the soundtrack to a widescreen video of Artemis running across the entrance wall, stopping at the door, daring visitors to enter. Inside, the stunning interior of the Temple of Artemis Ismene is recreated, displaying frescoes on each wall with translated excerpts from clay tablets shown on digital screens. A fifty-centimetre-wide glass canal runs along the periphery of the floor, highlighting artefacts illuminated by sensor lights. At the centre stands 'Artemis in Chase', the statue of the temple's deity. At just under three metres tall, she is missing the right arm from below the elbow and the left foot above the toes. A resin rod secures her to the podium. Despite these defects, she remains remarkably intact considering she toppled over during the 306 BC earthquake.

Hossein had become something of a celebrity. Documentaries on Ancient Tallos featured him as narrator, universities invited him to give guest lectures, and *Island News* had recently published a series of his short articles on the temple's treasures. His integration into the community had been warmly received, with invitations to every public and religious event. But that momentum had cooled after Father Efthimios spread the word of his romance with Aphrodite. Silent outrage soon surfaced across several channels, including a series of anonymous letters written in an Ancient Greek script and signed 'Artemis, the Goddess', warning him that the curse of 'Aphrodite, the Witch' was more powerful than hers.

'Kyrie Hossein! Kyrie Hossein!' Salome's voice carried down the corridor.

He didn't bother responding. She knew where he was, and her habit of calling out grated on him. She loved the sound of her own voice, especially when it echoed. Hearing her arrive at his door, he called out: 'Come in, Salome,' before she could knock.

Emilio's aunt waltzed into the office, her tone brisk. 'We need to order more stock—the catalogue, postcards and tea towels.' Rummaging through her beige Prada bag, she pulled out her small diary, opening to a list. 'Oh, and we are also running short on the scarves.'

Hossein placed his hands on his hips, taking a moment before responding. 'The new security guard starts in a fortnight. I'll review stock and approve purchase orders then.'

'Finally! Who got the job?' she asked as she manoeuvred past him and made herself comfortable on his settee. She helped herself to water from the dispenser in the corner of the room. 'I keep forgetting to drink. Given my age and time of life, I need to drink at least two litres a day.'

Despite being a woman in her mid-fifties, Salome embodied the vibrancy of someone younger. Her strict diet and yoga routine were common topics of conversation. Terms like 'savasana', 'chakras' and 'prana' often rolled off her tongue. Small in stature compared to Margarita, she was also the more extroverted of the two and very vain. There was a hint of Jane Fonda about her, with long layered, hair dyed blond and a busty cleavage, which she proudly exhibited in tight dresses.

Putting the empty glass down, she leaned back on the settee as if planning on staying a while. 'So tell me, who is the new security officer?'

'Pavlos Economides, an ex-policeman from the village of Mystra. He will report to Manos, who I have promoted to security manager.'

'Do you think he's ready for that?' she asked.

'With a little encouragement, I think he will be fine.'

The current security guard, Manos Savidis, was a gentle giant whose confidence had suffered under the previous security manager.

'And Kurush?' she asked, leaning forward in her seat.

Hossein was taken aback. 'What about Kurush?'

'Vasili mentioned he applied and got an interview.'

'Well, yes, that's right,' he said after a pause. 'I'll put him on casually until the end of the tourist season, cover shifts when the other guards can't be in.'

***

Twenty-four hours after his rescue, the clinic released Kurush and he was escorted to the police station for questioning. Acting as interpreter, Hossein confirmed that Kurush had travelled with his cousin and knew none of the other passengers. They had been piled into the rubber boat on a beach south of Ayvalık. Like many of the others, his cousin drowned because he couldn't swim.

Kurush was born in Kabul in 1996. After the mujahideen executed his father and older brother, his mother fled with him to Iran. For many years she worked as a domestic servant for a wealthy sea merchant, where the owner's son taught Kurush to swim in their pool. He loved swimming and jokingly expressed his desire to compete in the Olympics.

At the age of fourteen, a road accident shattered his dream. A truck ploughed into a group of pedestrians at the local produce market while Kurush was collecting groceries for his mother. He remembered little, only regaining consciousness to find a table full of vegetables collapsed across his ankle. He lost three toes and the sensation in half of his left foot. Despite being left with a pronounced limp, he continued to swim, although his speed never recovered.

During his first days in Phaedros, Kurush stayed with Hossein before moving into Policeman Harry's mother's house, an arrangement that surprised everyone. While delivering freshly baked biscuits to her son at the police station, Kyra Katina overheard the discussion about a refugee needing accommodation.

'I will take him,' she said, cocking her head up.

'Over my dead body,' Harry replied.

The more Harry ridiculed the proposition, the more she dug her heels in. 'I've been on my own for six years. I could do with some company and help around the house.'

'You have two sons! You can always move in with me or Yianni.'

'I also have two daughters-in-law! No, thank you. Besides, I'm not old enough.'

'You're eighty-two!'

'Harry Drivas! I can look after him.'

'He is not a pet needing a home,' Harry argued. 'You don't know anything about him. Besides, he's a Muslim—you know nothing about their religion, the language.'

'Hossein lives nearby. If I need anything, I can ask him. Isn't that right, Hossein?'

It was true. Kyra Katina was only a five-minute walk from his house. 'No problem at all, Kyra Katina!' he said bravely, avoiding eye contact with Harry.

'Don't you dare give him to anyone else!' she yelled at Harry. If there was one person Harry feared, it was his mother.

Kurush had no idea what was happening between the big, burly police officer and the old woman.

'You've struck gold,' Hossein whispered.

'I not understand…"

'Well, I think you just scored a home and a grandmother.'

Although grateful, Kurush later admitted to Hossein that she could be overbearing. Occasionally, he'd escape to Aphrodite's café, introduced to him by Hossein. He liked it there, and one day, Aphrodite convinced him to sit for a portrait. It was there that he also met Angelo, the autistic son of one of Aphrodite's cousins. Angelo, in his forties, lived simply in a shack, caring for his chickens and selling eggs to the locals. The two got on well together, and when Kurush wasn't working and boredom set in, he'd hang out at Angelo's.

***

News of Kurush's casual employment brought a smile to Salome's painted lips.

'I think you did right. That boy is a workhorse and very sweet,' Salome said. 'Can't imagine he'll give Manos any trouble.'

She got up off the settee and pulled out a small envelope from her bag.

'Oh, I almost forgot. Would you mind giving this to Aphrodite? There are some empty vials inside if she could refill them for me, please. It's for my nerves and hot flushes.'

'Of course.'

'And how is my niece?'

'She's well, working on a new painting.'

Salome took a deep breath and released a theatrical sigh.

'Are you alright?'

'I can smell true love, and right now, it smells like the peak of spring.'

Salome was always fishing for news about their relationship.

'When I think of you two, my heart sings a cheerful song,' she said.

'I'll keep an ear out for it,' he replied, resisting the urge to roll his eyes.

'See you tomorrow, boss. I'm going home to soak my feet.'

'Goodnight, Salome.'

She hurried past him, then stopped abruptly and called out, 'Kalos ton! Welcome!'

Hossein turned around to find Emilio standing in the doorway.

'What are you doing here?' Hossein asked, startled. He had never seen Emilio at the museum. Dressed in shorts and a baggy T-shirt, the back of his neck was damp with sweat.

'Yia sou, Thea!' Emilio called out, swooping to kiss his aunt before shaking Hossein's hand.

'Surprise, surprise,' Salome said, stepping back to admire her nephew.

'How did you get in?' Hossein panicked, jumping in front of his computer screen to check the CCTV feed. He had locked up that afternoon as Manos had to leave early.

'I came in through a door at the back of the museum. I knocked, but no one answered. I then turned the handle, and the door opened. I tried to call you, but your phone went to message bank.'

'Hossein, didn't you lock the back door?' Salome jumped in, accusatorially.

'Obviously not!' he replied defensively.

'How's my big sister?' Salome asked Emilio. 'She hasn't called me in weeks!'

'She's packing for Paris. They fly out in two days.'

'I am so glad those two are finally going on a holiday! Ooh la, la! I better call and wish her well.' She kissed him goodbye. 'Don't worry, Hossein, I'll lock the door when I leave.'

'I'll make sure you do,' Hossein said, pointing to the monitor as Salome fluttered her fingers at them as she exited.

'I can't believe I could have forgotten to lock that door.'

'These things happen,' Emilio said, slapping him lightly on the shoulder.

'Thank Allah the new guard starts soon.'

'Aphrodite told me Kurush is part of the team.'

'Yes, but only as a casual when one of the others is sick. Not many applied, and of those who did, only one was appropriate.'

'I'm afraid the talent pool on the island is pretty limited,' Emilio said, standing underneath the air-con vent. 'It's a constant battle.'

'Well, I feel much better that you think the same.'

Hossein's eyes were glued to the screen. 'There she is.' Salome came into focus as she opened the back door. She turned, looked at the camera, waved, smiled and closed the door behind her.

'Yia sou, Thea!' Emilio called out, waving frantically and laughing.

'So have you finally come to see the gallery?'

Emilio looked confused.

'The Artemis Gallery! You haven't seen it yet.'

'Oh, that gallery!'

'You're a sponsor and partner. Remember? You were supposed to give a speech at the opening, but at the last minute you handed it over to Aphrodite.'

'Yes, yes, sorry. I knew Aphrodite could do a better job, you know, with her artistic background and all.'

'So would you like to see it now?'

'Now? No, no. That's not why I am here.'

There was no hiding Hossein's disappointment. Emilio's indifference irritated him more than it should have. He had meant to confront him—Aphrodite had urged him to—but something pulled him back. Emilio looked diminished: eyes sunken, unshaven and a faint stench of alcohol and cigarettes clung to him.

'How are you, Emilio?'

Emilio didn't answer. Instead, he motioned for Hossein to sit on the settee while he sat on Hossein's office chair and rolled across in front of him. 'I need a favour.'

'Of course. I owe you many.'

'You owe me nothing but this.' Emilio hesitated. 'Can you teach me some words in Arabic?'

'You came to the museum for Arabic lessons?'

'It's just between us, okay? I don't want anyone to know.'

'There's nothing wrong with learning Arabic, Emilio. Nothing to be ashamed of.'

'Of course not.' He paused. 'It's Maryam.'

'Maryam? What about her?'

Emilio smiled and looked slightly embarrassed. He leaned back in the chair, gathering his thoughts, his eyes roaming the room as if checking for others in the office. 'I can't stop thinking about her. I really like her, Hossein.'

'Maryam. The survivor?'

'Yes, her.'

Hossein recoiled slightly. The fervour in Emilio's eyes unsettled him. 'You're not serious.'

'Of course I am!' Emilio sprang to his feet and began pacing, annoyed.

'Okay. Sorry. I am just a little surprised.'

The moment felt so surreal—Emilio Politis in his office, revealing something so personal and heartfelt.

'Does Aphrodite know?'

'Just because she's my sister doesn't mean I tell her everything.'

'She won't be thrilled that you told me first.'

'Forget that now.' Emilio dropped back into the chair and rolled closer. 'Please, help me out.'

'Of course, Emilio. But how did it happen? I mean…I don't know what I mean, really, but—'

'Don't overthink it. Everyone thought the same when you and my sister got together. I was so happy when I heard about you two. Be happy for me.'

'I am happy for you. Really happy! But are you two…together?'

'No, not yet.' Emilio's voice wavered. 'I don't want to push her. I mean…she just lost her husband and child.'

'Emilio, are you alright?' Hossein asked, noticing his hands shaking.

Emilio then rolled across to the water dispenser. He helped himself to water, accidentally dropping the plastic cup on the floor.

'Shit!' he yelled, furious at his clumsiness. 'I am so sorry. Have you got some paper towels or something?'

Hossein leaped from the settee and grabbed the box of tissues from his desk. 'It's okay, don't worry.'

'Fucking hell!'

'It's okay. I've got it.'

Emilio walked over to the window and opened the venetians. The western sun blinded him and he quickly shut them.

'I just want to do the right thing by her,' he said hoarsely. 'Give her what she needs so life doesn't feel so fucked up, you know?' Tears ran down his face. He tried to continue but couldn't get any more words out.

'It's okay, Emilo.' He passed him the tissues. 'It can't be that bad.'

'She is such a beautiful person, Hossein. I just want to be able to talk to her and care for her. If we had something in common, she might warm to me. Speaking Arabic might give her some comfort, show her that I mean well.'

'The woman is traumatised, Emilio.'

'Of course I know that, but she can't even look me in the eyes.'

'She needs time.'

'I want to help her. Make her happy.'

'You can't do that.'

'But I think I can, one day.' Emilio looked up, eyes burning. 'It's this feeling I have. Call it a premonition but I believe she'll grow to love me, and our island, despite everything it's taken from her. It's like your work as an archaeologist: you patiently excavate knowing there's something precious, and you're willing to do anything to unearth it. I can't stop thinking about her. She is so remarkable in every sense of the word. So kind—'

'But so broken, Emilio.'

A knock on the door cut through the silence.

'Kyrie Hossein, can I come in?'

It was the cleaner. Panicking, Emilio searched for a place to hide, not wanting to be caught crying by the cleaner. Hossein pointed to the narrow gap between the bookshelf and the wall, then opened the door and stepped outside.

'Hello, Poppy. Don't worry about my office today. I am working late.'

'I won't get in your way, I'll be quick,' she insisted, edging forward.

'I said not today, Poppy,' Hossein said, raising his voice.

'Endaxi. I understand,' she replied, a little shocked, before shuffling down the hall, muttering under her breath.

Hossein closed the door. Emilio emerged from the corner.

The men spent another hour in the office. Hossein found an old exercise book, and Emilio noted down some common Arabic phrases. But Hossein understood that the language lesson was just an excuse. Emilio just needed to tell someone he was falling in love.

PART 4
PANAYIAS

CHAPTER 19
Apollo suite, Paradisos II resort

It was ten in the morning on 15 August, a public holiday in Greece known as Panayias—a day to honour the Virgin Mary. The sun blazed overhead and a silky haze stretched across the sky. In the courtyard of The Village, beneath the shade of an olive tree, Maryam waited for the Villa Apollo guests to leave for breakfast so she could clean their room. Her stainless-steel linen and amenities trolley sat parked on the gravel path nearby.

Reaching into her pocket, Maryam found half a sandwich wrapped in clingwrap, a small reminder to eat. Each morning before her shift, Anna, her colleague, secretly slipped food from the breakfast counter into Maryam's uniform pocket. It was a daily ritual, one she would miss when Anna retired at the end of the summer—another good person soon to disappear from her life.

Maryam ate the sandwich slowly. The tuna and cucumber sandwich was like paste in her mouth. After three small bites, she rewrapped the sandwich and put it back in her pocket. Her white uniform felt loose on her; a month ago, it had been snug. That morning, she also noticed the dark shadows under her eyes. Anna had given her some skincare products, but it all seemed so irrelevant. There was a time when she took pride in preparing her face each morning, carefully applying moisturiser, foundation, eyeliner and her favourite shade of lipstick. Her mother always praised her on her beautiful olive skin and how pretty she looked, but those words now seemed meant for someone else. These days, she could barely look at herself in the mirror.

Still, after this shift, she knew she would have to make an effort. The Politis family had invited her for lunch to celebrate the Virgin Mary's death and assumption into heaven.

Although she was grateful to have a job to occupy her mind, waiting for guests to leave their rooms was starting to frustrate her. Staying busy no longer came easily. Idleness felt like sinking into quicksand, and the more she remembered, the deeper she sank. At least she was assigned to The Village, the adults-only quarters of the resort. Watching children play would have been torture.

'Kalimera,' came a voice from her side.

Maryam was caught off guard and became flustered. It was one of the guests. Had she seen her eating? How unprofessional. 'Kalimera, madam,' she quickly responded, bowing her head in shame.

From the corner of her eye, she watched the large woman walk towards the pool. A pool attendant rushed to her side with a towel, laying it on her chosen daybed. Shedding her shimmering, flowing dress, she moved without hesitation towards the edge of the pool and dived in. Observing this woman in a bikini, strutting around publicly without any sense of modesty, reminded Maryam of how out of place she was. The only similarities between Aleppo and Phaedros were that the sun was hot, night fell and morning came.

The resort was quiet. Some guests from The Village were heading out on a day cruise. From where she stood, Maryam could see the luxury boat readying for departure. Further along at the main pier, people queued for the eleven o'clock ferry. The sea looked serene and bright, but her thoughts wandered to the bodies never recovered. Her stomach cramped. She turned away, fixing her gaze on the dry, imposing mountain rising above The Village.

A sudden eruption of cicadas from the tree startled her into a scream. She moved to the other side, but the noise only intensified.

Returning to her original spot, she rolled pieces of tissue from her pocket into two balls and pressed them in her ears. The sound dulled, but it was too late to ease her pounding headache. Maryam took a sip of her lukewarm bottled water.

She was rarely thirsty. Drinking water brought back the sensation of seawater choking her. Sipping had become her only way of hydrating. Strangely, she had taken a liking to the tsipouro Emilio had offered her the previous night. Even though it tasted like poison, it went down easily. It didn't phase her that it was alcoholic.

***

The idea of visiting the Monastery of Saint Sophia was Margarita's. The previous afternoon she had come to Maryam's door and knocked repeatedly until she answered. Her silver hair had been freshly blow-dried, her navy dress formal and immaculate.

'It will be good for you to visit the monastery—the icon has special powers on the eve of the fifteenth. Will you come with me?'

It was more a directive than an invitation, and Maryam felt compelled to say yes. Their relationship had grown unexpectedly close, and she had missed Margarita while she was away in Italy with her husband. She trusted the Politis matriarch and felt safe in her presence. Giving in to her wishes had become an easy option.

Maryam stood before her wardrobe and surveyed the meagre contents. The funeral dress still hung there. She couldn't bear to look at it, yet she couldn't throw it away—it belonged to Margarita. There were a couple of garments from Aphrodite's donations which had more colour, but she had little choice. She settled on a paisley patterned frock, too heavy for the summer, but modest, its hem falling below the knees.

When Maryam entered the Politis family home for a cool drink before they set off, she was surprised to find Emilio inside. There had been no mention that he would be joining them. Margarita remarked on how lovely the paisley dress looked on her, but the compliment barely registered. Maryam was acutely aware that Emilio was seeing her in his sister's dress.

He approached, uneasy, and extended his hand. He too was formally dressed, his manner stiff, so unlike his hurried ease at the resort. When their paths crossed, he greeted her in Arabic, always with an awkward handshake; more often he would wave from a distance. Now, even returning a smile felt beyond her.

On three occasions he invited her to his office for coffee, but she kept putting it off. When she finally accepted, she brought Anna along. It was an uncomfortable twenty minutes of impromptu small talk, during which Anna did most of the talking. At one point Anna reminded him that Maryam spoke perfect English, and that she understood everything. His enthusiasm completely diminished. Maryam felt awful—the last thing she wanted was to come across as ungrateful.

Anna later told her that he liked her, saying she could tell by his voice. The comment infuriated Maryam, and for the next few days she avoided Anna. Anna apologised, said she felt awful and promised to be more sensitive in the future. The fact that Maryam was making people feel bad only deepened her isolation.

'Here's to the peak of summer and the Virgin Mary,' Emilio toasted, insisting on a drink before leaving. 'We celebrate death by drinking, eating and partying!'

Margarita slapped him on the shoulder. 'Stop it!'

'Oh my God, I am so sorry, Maryam!'

Maryam didn't pick up on how his words could be taken the wrong way.

'He's not usually this insensitive,' Margarita said sharply.

'That's alright,' Maryam replied.

'I just wasn't thinking. I just meant that we celebrate the death of saints in…non-religious ways, if you know what I mean.' Emilio stammered. 'This heatwave is really getting to me. You'd think after so many years on this island I'd get used to it, but the older I get, the less I tolerate it.'

The temperatures reached forty degrees Celsius that day, which Margarita said was typical for that time of year. Emilio kept apologising, but Maryam wasn't offended. If anything she found it endearing, watching him being scolded by his mother, who also got angry at him for offering Maryam tsipouro rather than a juice. But Maryam quickly defended him by saying that she was not partial to sweet drinks. Watching the exchange between mother and son made her feel unexpectedly at ease. Her anxiety stemmed more from being seen in public with the boss. Still, she was going to go through with it, push herself to please them so they did not feel responsible for her misery.

She owed so much to these people, especially Emilio. His attention and concern, though annoying at first, were now needed. She had come to forgive him for rescuing her and recognised that he, too, was suffering. Margarita shared her worries about his recent erratic behaviour. Maryam suggested medications, which made her feel hypocritical, having been reluctant to use them herself.

She tried not to think about him, but it was impossible. Emilio was everywhere—if not in person then in conversation. Yet she could not dissociate his face from that morning. How could she forget those red, sea-drenched eyes? In that moment, she thought him a jinn, wanting her alive to possess her. But there were tears on his face. In her moment of disorientation, she'd thought of her presentation. Where was her hijab? She needed to cover her head. She was outside, and the sun was rising. In her arms lay her baby girl, lifeless. Her husband's body was sprawled across the floor of the boat, his black T-shirt torn at the shoulder. *This is the price of freedom.* Emilio was the last person she saw before she blacked out.

The church bells tolled in the distance. Emilio and his mother rose. It was time to leave. Maryam followed them out the door, taking the boardwalk along the coast. Around them, people watched as she walked in between mother and son, their stares filled with mistrust and confusion.

Once they arrived at the monastery, Maryam lit the candle and placed it in the small sandpit beside the icon. The scent of incense was strong. Two elderly women inside the chapel stood up to leave, nodding their veiled heads as they walked past. The icon of the Virgin Mary stood beside the entrance to the nave. A wooden trellis, where parishioners added tributes of flowers, supported the large icon. Next to the Virgin Mary was the larger icon Saint Sophia. Below her, three slain daughters stared out into the world.

Maryam returned her focus to the Virgin Mary only to feel judged, perhaps scorned. But then she saw the serenity in Mary's eyes as she cradled her baby boy, dressed in a pale green tunic. *Why so sad when you have a beautiful baby in your arms?* Maryam looked away, unable to bear the pity she imagined would soon fill Mary's eyes.

The scent of incense carried her to Aleppo—to narrow alleys where she and her best friend, Sasha, used to play hopscotch. The recent bombing at Sahat Al Hatab Square had damaged the nearby Greek Church of the Dormition. The images on TV were unbearable, and she was certain that she recognised her pharmacy's sign among the rubble. Where was Sasha now? The other children of all faiths and colours? A harmonious community, obliterated. A playground in ruins.

She had heard much about this miraculous icon. Stolen many times over the centuries, it always mysteriously returned. The painted lips of women who came before her had marked the glass. Maryam stooped down and did the same. It had been a while since she had kissed anyone. The last time was at the burial of her daughter and husband, when she convinced herself that if she kissed them enough, they would come back to life. Their bodies lay buried only a few hundred metres away.

She touched the wooden frame of the icon, hoping for a transfer of serenity. But her mind kept turning to her god, Allah. She felt his presence stir within her, asking, 'What are you doing here?'

They returned to Margarita's house and sat on the veranda for chamomile tea. It was hot, airless, and she was acutely uncomfortable. Not only because of the dress but under the weight of so much attention. Even Mihalis had joined them.

Emilio placed a mobile phone in her hand. It was hers now, another gift that she felt obliged to accept. He explained it was an old phone but one with plenty of life in it. She tried to refuse it, abandoning the effort when Margarita insisted.

Seated beside Emilio, she listened as he guided her through the applications, entered the family's contact details and helped her set up an email.

'Whenever you need anything, call me,' he said as he showed her the home screen where a shortcut displayed his name.

'Thank you. I will,' she replied, slipping the phone into her bag before excusing herself. 'I have an early start in the morning.'

Even though it was only eight o'clock, her head was spinning and her nerves were beginning to fray. Sweat trickled down her neck as she hastily bid them good night and thanked them for a pleasant evening. Although her room was only a short walk, she could not make her feet move fast enough.

*****

Maryam looked at her watch. It was past ten and there were still no signs of the Villa Apollo guests. She started to worry about being delayed. At two o'clock, at the end of her shift, Margarita was expecting her for lunch. Already queasy with nerves, she now regretted eating anything at all.

'It's also your name day, and I want you to come for lunch. Everyone is coming. I don't want you to be alone on your name day.'

Maryam loved Margarita. She couldn't imagine how she would have survived without her. While she was comfortable visiting her at home, the upcoming lunch made her anxious. Anna's teasing didn't help: 'Aren't you the lucky one? An invite to the palace to eat with the Queen!'

The last thing she wanted was to sit there among them and cry. She hadn't met Dimitri yet. He would be arriving on the ferry in the next hour. What was he going to think of her? What could she offer in conversation? And what if it all backflipped and her pent-up resentment of being alive surfaced? Or the jealousy—that they should all be together. Yet they had all treated her so kindly. Even Mihalis had become more receptive of late. The other day he gave her a jar of his marinated olives. He was nothing like her father—a reserved man with no time for his children other than to feed and educate them.

A door closing snapped her from her thoughts. A woman hand in hand with a tall man descended the stairs towards the breakfast area at the far end of the pool. A wide-brimmed red hat flopped on her head, her face covered by the biggest sunglasses she had ever seen. They both wore oversized white linen shirts, he with matching pants.

Maryam looked at her notes to recall their names: Mr James Herman and Ms Greta Greeves. They had arrived the previous night. He was a Hollywood actor, though she had never heard of him. Hollywood held no place in her thoughts. It was Anna who kept her abreast of the glamour and superficiality of her new world. Anna was obsessed with celebrities. Working at Paradisos allowed her not only to meet them but also to fold their underwear, wipe their hair from the basin and, when the mood struck, roll about on their beds. Maryam was continually astonished by what the fifty-five-year-old confessed to, and by her own growing tolerance of Anna's crudeness.

On entering the villa, Maryam caught the fragrance of an expensive perfume, sweet and floral. She'd always possessed a keen sense of smell; she could predict rain, detect pheromones and identify the components of various medications. However, the perfume, combined with the scent of the yellow roses on the side table, made her feel queasy. Pulling back the red velvet curtains near the bed, she opened the shutters and window for the air to escape. As natural light flooded the room, she noticed a large Louis Vuitton suitcase on the floor. Empty except for a pair of high-heeled shoes and several cosmetic bags, she wondered why they hadn't placed it on the luggage holder. Two white bathrobes and a bra were tossed over the lounge chair while wallets, passports, papers, socks and tissues lay scattered across the table. After scanning the room, she couldn't help but think of the Hollywood couple as selfish and lazy.

As she stripped the crumpled white sheets from the bed, a pink packet of medication on the bedside table caught her eye. She froze and lost focus; her knees started to shake. The perfume, the hot air and now the sight of the little pink box were enough to suck the wind out of her. She fell onto the bed. That one glimpse was the straw that broke the camel's back, another horrible reminder of the broken, childless, widowed refugee she had become. The pillow muffled her sobs and screams as she punched the mattress with all her might. She was angry because she couldn't forget, furious that a packet of antibiotics had the power to cripple her. Time and again, something would trigger her—a bird, a fragrance, a colour—and tear her down.

Maryam took deep breaths and eventually pulled herself up from the bed. Her head was heavy and hot as she dragged herself to the bathroom and turned on the cold shower. Adjusting the shower head from rain-shower to jet, she thrust her head beneath the cold stream and let it pierce her scalp. The pain felt good, jolting her from her self-loathing. Grabbing the used towel off the floor, she dried her hair and wiped the tears and water from her face. Staring at the mirror, she repeated, 'I will live for them.' It had become a mantra for those who mattered.

Her mind turned to Emilio. Their visit to the monastery had briefly eased her misery, her affliction momentarily distracted. How could she permit even the faintest thought of another man? Bassel, her devoted and loving husband, had taken everything from her to his grave. Her love belonged solely to him. How she missed his touch, the soft caress of his fingers on her neck as they sat together each evening. She missed him so deeply that it felt as though she had lost her soul. In another life, in another week, they would have been celebrating their fifth wedding anniversary.

If anyone could save her from herself it was the man who had saved her from the sea.

CHAPTER 20
Emilio's apartment

Emilio woke up happy and optimistic. He couldn't remember the last time he'd enjoyed six consecutive hours of sleep. Even the taste in his mouth was different—fresh and minty—his nasal passages clear. He attributed it to nicotine withdrawal, deciding to quit the previous night during his visit to the monastery. Never overtly religious, he now felt open to embracing it. For the first time, he wore the cross and chain that once belonged to Doctor Kaligeros. It was a gift inherited from Uncle Toli. Surely the Virgin Mary would take notice and help him.

The bedroom was still in complete darkness. Only the chirping of sparrows and roosters crowing in the distance suggested the sun was up. And then there was his cock, semi-erect, adding another surprise to his morning. Usually a nightmare would shake him awake, leaving him sweaty and gasping for breath.

He had been actively trying to manage the panic attacks that followed the drownings. A collection of vials sat in the bedside drawer, potions his mother had prepared from the witch's book. Since Aphrodite's success in converting her she had been pressuring him to drink the stuff, swearing it would help. He tried it once but it did nothing, so he stuck to sleeping pills instead. Alongside the drugs, an anxiety self-help website offered late-night research, quizzes and breathing exercises that sometimes helped, other times not. But that morning, he felt different—calmer, unexpectedly amorous. He masturbated before drifting back to sleep.

An hour later, the vibrating phone under his pillow woke him. It was Aphrodite.

'Hello,' he said.

'Are you still in bed?'

'Yep!'

There was a long silence. 'You sick?'

'No. Just trying to sleep in.'

'Oh, sorry, do you have company?'

'No!'

'Okay. Have you been taking those remedies?'

'Tried it once, did nothing.'

'You can't give up after one dose. Did you read the chants?'

'No, I didn't.'

'Emilio! We told you to read them first.'

'Oh my god, listen to yourself.'

'Honestly, Emilio, if you just tried to cooperate.'

'I'm not into that voodoo stuff!'

'They're therapies from your ancestors. Look how it helped Mum after her operation, Rika with her nightmares.'

'Okay, okay, I will!'

After a short pause, Aphrodite asked: 'You're coming to lunch, right?'

'Yes.'

'Just checking. Hossein's coming too.'

'Cool, so is Maryam.'

'Really?' She hesitated. 'That's so good…Rika's super-excited to see Dimitri. I just spoke to him. He's about to board the ferry at Mytilene.'

'How did he sound?'

'The same as always…Doesn't give anything away.'

'You don't think Maryam will change her mind, do you?'

'I don't think so. Of course she'll come.'

Emilio sensed relief. He trusted his sister's intuition, even though she sounded a little guarded.

'See you there, Golector!' she said, ending the call.

Emilio chuckled. She hadn't called him that in years. The nickname, a combination of the Greek word 'bum' and the English word 'collector', had been given to him by their mother shortly after they arrived from Australia. This was the time when Emilio began bringing stray animals to the house. Despite her protests, his father defended him.

'You need to put aside your hygiene concerns for Emilio's wellbeing,' he heard his father argue through their bedroom door.

'The animals are keeping him from spending time with his cousin. He needs to be out there meeting other children, not animals,' she replied.

'We need to make him happy first!'

For a time, Emilio became Phaedros's equivalent to Corfu's Gerald Durrell. But Emilio's compassion towards strays ended abruptly after Christopher's suicide five years later. That event profoundly altered his perspective towards the vulnerable and weak. As far as he was concerned, effort only led to devastation. Even Sydney, a rescue puppy, was neglected, leaving Mihalis to raise the pup and release the other animals back into the wild.

Before getting up, he scrolled through the emails and recent TripAdvisor reviews. Since last month's fiasco with his father, he monitored them closely. One post had sparked a backlash: outrage at the reviewer, praise for his father. Furious that the review page had become a sexual harassment forum, Emilio contacted the administrator, who promptly removed the posts. Though Emilio apologised to his father for 'sacking' him, he remained convinced it was the right decision. Despite everyone rallying behind his father, Emilio doubted his complete innocence. Over the years, he had noticed subtle gestures and remarks that annoyed him, which he justified by blaming his father's generation and the industry they worked in. The temptation for affairs was common, and in past years, Emilio himself hadn't abstained from the occasional fling with a guest or two. But now, as CEO, his priority was professionalism.

Paradisos II had reclaimed its number-one ranking among boutique resorts in the Aegean. It was recently a runner-up in a travel award, but more exciting news had arrived in the mail a few days earlier: he was a finalist for the 2016 European Boutique Hotelier of the Year. The lucrative award ceremony was taking place in Brussels the following spring. He would announce the news to the family at lunch, and to his managers in the next day or so, before the nominations went public.

The business was flourishing. Bookings were at capacity for the next eighteen months, even through winter. He had recently expanded the ground staff to ease workloads. His senior managers, all of whom had been recruited from outside Greece, now rented homes in Kamiros, reserving staff accommodation for domestic employees.

The only disappointment that morning was Maryam's silence. He had expected a text—something to test the phone he'd given her, something to acknowledge him. Last night had been wonderful. For weeks he'd tried to engineer time alone with her—perhaps a coffee after work, a meeting in his office, always under the guise of business. But she constantly looked confused and uncomfortable. When she finally visited she brought Anna along, who corrected his assumption about Maryam's English. Until the previous night, she had hardly said more than a few words. Besides, the Arabic phrases he'd learned from Hossein were already forgotten.

It was Margarita's idea to visit the monastery.

'I was thinking of taking Maryam to light a candle,' she said over the phone. 'Would you like to join us?'

'Yes, I would,' he replied immediately. 'But I doubt she'll go if I'm coming. She fears me, Mum. I don't know how to fix that.'

He hadn't meant to reveal so much. Margarita always sensed when he was vulnerable and peeled him open like an orange; if only he were more self-contained, more like Aphrodite.

'Maryam is having a difficult week,' she told him.

'But all her weeks are difficult!'

'Next week would have been her wedding anniversary.'

'Oh, right. I see. I feel so bad.'

'I told her about the icon and its special powers, urging her to visit the monastery.'

'She needs a mosque, Mum, not an Orthodox church.'

'A place of worship is for everyone, not just Greeks!'

'Agreed, but she'll panic if I turn up.'

'Just come along. Maryam will be fine.'

When it came to women, Emilio was used to being pursued. His looks, wealth and charm turned heads, captivating many but leaving most wounded. Over the past few months, the faces of those he'd hurt haunted his dreams. During the day he recalled their scent, their laughter and their frustration, acknowledging the guilt he had once ignored.

Grabbing his journal and pen from the drawer of his bedside table, he turned to a fresh page. Of all the tools he learned online to fight anxiety, journalling was his favourite: *Put your thoughts down on paper and free them from your mind.* Feeling contemplative, he desperately wanted to redeem himself with those he had hurt.

Eva

I remember Eva's first day in class, looking as though she'd stepped straight off the set of Happy Days. *Her mousy blond hair was tied in a high ponytail, and she wore a purple satin bomber jacket and black tights. She was from Thessaloniki, but she didn't look Greek to me—pale and freckled, her body was lean and fit. She was fifteen, pretty, and a bit stand-offish, but by the end of the week we had our first kiss.*

We went our separate ways after high school with no hard feelings. I moved to Athens to study marketing and business, and she returned to Thessaloniki to study law. We promised to remain friends and called each other, usually on our birthdays. When she separated from her English husband, she rang me. I was surprised by how calm she seemed, perhaps calling to better understand my situation. It didn't take long for us to reconnect once we returned to Phaedros. We were twenty-six, single, educated and connected by geography and history. She visited as soon as I finished military service. I remember how grown-up she seemed and thinking her London residency had refined her speech and gestures. Looking back, we got together at the worst possible time. I was consumed by the construction of the resort, the greatest challenge of my life; ending our relationship became the second.

Now, seeing her with Andrew, I feel no resentment. Recently, I had dinner with them on the boat. It was surreal sitting there in good humour when only months ago the Grand Duchess *had borne witness to our final undoing. Eva was gracious and attentive, never once revelling in the fact that she had run off with my friend.*

Ursula

Ursula from Berlin had been a regular guest of the hotel since the late nineties. Just before meeting Eva, at the age of sixteen, the thirty-something German had become my sexual fantasy. Each time she walked by—her voluptuous body wrapped in revealing summer dresses—I'd have to dart around the corner to conceal my excitement. Ursula was a divorcée, an actor and the author of half a dozen adult novels.

The following summer she returned to the island, and one afternoon I was summoned to her room to move the bed closer to the window. I remember the room smelling of roses, while Arethra Franklin's 'Chain of Fools' played in the background. As she thanked me, she caressed my cheeks, a gesture that both unsettled and invigorated me. I read it as an invitation for sex, and, astonishingly, she didn't refuse. It was my first time, and the experience was extraordinary.

Of course, I felt guilty about Eva, but that relationship meandered along on a different plane, innocent and adolescent. We never pushed the high-school romance beyond kissing, hugging and holding hands. With Ursula, I had transgressed into another realm—one that belonged to adults.

Not only did I enjoy the casualness and secrecy of our summer relationship but I also enjoyed her company. I was inspired by the quiet confidence with which she inhabited her life and by her independence. She could spend an evening reciting monologues from the plays she acted in or passages from her forthcoming novel. Our relationship was easy, with no sense of obligation or commitment.

But it was never only the sex with Ursula. In retrospect, it was she who drew me back into world. After Christopher's suicide, I had lost the will to excel at anything. I abandoned the stray animals I cared for, my soccer and my commitment to friendships. But through the retelling of her life, she taught me the importance of rebuilding oneself, 'because only then can one die in one's own palace'.

Ursula's final trip to the island was in 2005. I had just returned from Athens for the semester break when she told me she had ovarian cancer. I returned to Athens completely devastated. Five months later, I flew to Berlin for her funeral, where hundreds gathered to party and celebrate the life of a queen who remained radiant even in death.

Eliana

I met Eliana within a week of settling in Athens. I was eighteen and ecstatic to have finally left the island. It was the year Greece abandoned the drachma for the euro. Our integration into Europe suddenly appeared more real than ever, and I started dreaming of a postgraduate life in the UK, France or Italy.

Eliana and I were co-workers at Melina's Bar; she was the owner's daughter. There was an instant attraction although she was a few years older, but that was nothing new for me. She was lively, tall, a mousy blond with a thin frame, a whisky drinker who also smoked a packet of cigarettes each day. She was very much like her idol, the activist, actress and politician Melina Mercouri. Eliana's politics leaned firmly to the left, and her passion was the environment. Being an Athenian, she grew up with the taste of pollution on her tongue. With her, I felt like I had finally arrived in the industrial age.

Eventually, she moved into my apartment in Neapolis, near Athens University. It was just after Aphrodite had returned home following the birth of my niece. Our parents had bought the apartment for the family's use whenever we had business in the capital. During our period of living together, our politics drove us apart. Our drunken fights often lasted until morning, and a few times complaints were relayed back to my parents. In the end, it was unsustainable, though she believed otherwise.

Only later did I recognise the worth of her magnetism and conviction. Without realising it, Eliana was teaching me resilience and how to embrace my own beliefs. I heard recently that she was running for office in Corinth.

Jorgen

I feel awful about Jorgen, my friend and architect. Like Ursula, I met him at Paradisos during its pre-resort phase. I was ten years old at the time. All I knew about him was that he was Norwegian, two years older than me and holidaying with his mother. He returned each summer and soon revealed himself to be not only a talented violinist but also a brilliant draughtsman. Sitting in the restaurant bar, he'd sketch the landscape and create detailed drawings of the hotel and surrounding architecture. Jorgen's mother always sat at a distance, quietly observing and admiring him. I was shattered when he told me about his father. I couldn't believe how anyone could commit violence against such beautiful, gentle people.

After Christopher's suicide in 1996, I gravitated towards him. Being an outsider made it easier to hang out with him rather than my school friends who couldn't stop talking about my cousin. I envied Jorgen's mellow ease, how unaffected he seemed by everything. He and his mum suggested I come to Norway for a short break. At first I was keen, desperate to get off the island, but in the end it didn't feel right. Dimitri was just a few months old. With Mum stuck at home, I needed to be more useful.

Aphrodite took a liking to him when she was barely in her teens, curious about his drawings, but he found her annoying, as did I, of course. We often went on long hikes or night walks to the beach to get away from her.

When I was nineteen, I returned for the summer after my first year at university. Sitting at the bar one evening, Jorgen approached me and confessed his feelings for me. I was shocked as I had no idea. I tried to be gentle as I told him I was straight, reminding him of Eva, my current relationship with Eliana, and Ursula—whom he had no idea about. He simply nodded and said, 'I hope we can still be friends.' Afterwards, it felt less like a proposition than something he simply needed to express.

Looking back, I put it down to the emotional intelligence of northern Europeans—Ursula included. They seem to accept the ways of the world far better than we southern Europeans. If the earth opened up in front of them, they'd shrug and say, 'Oh, well,' while the Greeks, well, they'd throw every profanity at it.

In him I see a version of myself, waiting at the kerbside, hoping the bus will stop and take him to the destination he longs to reach.

Sabine

Sabine, a fellow student I met in Milan, was undeniably the most magnetic woman in our class. Her Chinese-Italian heritage gave her an exotic flair. Her waist-length black hair, always in a ponytail, swung across her back like a metronome, always to the same rhythm, exuding control. She also lived two floors above me where she ran her escort business, information disclosed by the landlady before I signed the lease.

One morning, she surprised me by tapping my shoulder during a lecture. She said she'd seen me on the landing and wanted to introduce herself. Afterwards, we'd greet each other in the stairwell and occasionally sit together. I found her manner slightly confronting though never threatening. At the time, I had also started dating another girl from class, but that fizzled out as my association with Sabine became more familiar. Our relationship developed after we began an internship together at the Diana Hotel as part of our master's program.

On our way home one night, she invited me in for a glass of wine. Her casual remark about her work was so blasé it was as if she were telling me she worked at the local pet shop.

Her father was a hotelier in Abu Dhabi, and she grew up living in penthouses. After informing her of my background in the hotel industry, she shared her dream of opening a high-class brothel in Milan with themed rooms—Berlin cabaret, Roman court, Japanese bathhouse, and, for the penthouse, a Middle Eastern palace.

I was intrigued—not only by our shared hotel interests but also because I had never been with a prostitute. When she refused payment, I realised I had misread the situation entirely. After much deliberation, she agreed that the sex between us would be transactional and always at her workplace to avoid any confusion. After that, we never walked home together from work.

Sabine was the woman I flew to when things got heated with Eva—like the time I asked her to reschedule the wedding. At least I had the sense to take my dirty business offshore. We spent twenty-four hours together in the 'Japanese' quarters. It was an act of malice, and I feel ashamed.

Celine

What happened with Celine was both thoughtless and cruel. Yes, the timing was disastrous, but I can't excuse my complete disconnection from her. To abandon Jorgen's cousin like that was unforgivable. After the sunset cruise debacle, my mood shifted to anger. Attending Celine's farewell turned me into an arrogant, selfish predator. Her resignation from work gave me the green light to take advantage of her. She was no longer staff, and I used that as a licence to behave disgracefully. A Scandinavian beauty unravelled that night and I became obsessed. Fuelled by alcohol, my furious self-pity and her own complicity, it was inevitable we'd end up in bed together.

I feel awful that I couldn't give her a proper, heartfelt goodbye. She came to see me just before her ferry departed and asked if

I wanted her to stay, but I could hardly see through the fog of adrenaline and exhaustion. I am ashamed that I couldn't even get up to hug her, thank her or wish her well.

A month later, I emailed to apologise for dismissing her, explaining that I had been badly affected by the drownings. I lied by saying I loved our time together; in truth, I didn't remember much. I invited her to come back anytime but then deleted that line, not wanting to set her up for more hurt. She was too good a person and deserved better.

Celine immediately emailed back. She was in Thailand but was really missing Phaedros.

I didn't follow up with another email.

Maryam

There's so much I want to journal about Maryam. Unlike the others, I sense she's here with me, watching. I imagine her floating in from the kitchen, delivering a tray of coffee and baklava. Her scent of oud filling the room. What I feel for Maryam is something different. The word 'desire' keeps circling in my mind, like a silk cloth wiping away the remnants of a past life. It has little to do with physical attraction. Yes, I have the urge to touch her skin, kiss her lips and stroke her hair, but more than anything, I want her to feel safe and comfortable beside me.

I want to peer into those big dark eyes and sense her hidden warmth and generosity. I've never felt so helpless or shy. Is this what I put others through? Did they feel the same weight inside them, dragging their heart deeper into the pit of their bowels? I've never felt such loneliness or such inadequacy in love. If my father was able to find that kind of love then surely I too deserve a taste of that apple.

Last night's visit to the monastery felt like progress. For the first time, she seemed to speak without anguish in her voice. When she shook my hand to say goodnight, it felt like I had touched something holy, not because she is a saint but because with her I sense the potential of becoming better. I want to be worthy of the love I seek.

***

Opening the wooden shutters, Emilio was temporarily blinded by the morning sun reflecting off the blue sea. Fishing boats brought in the day's catch. Seagulls circling above. A sudden urge to look for orange life jackets and waving hands broke the tranquil scene. He closed his eyes and remembered the online instructions for managing anxiety: deep breaths, long and slow exhale; palm of the hand on one's chest, feet firmly pressed on the floor. When he opened his eyes again, Emilio's vision was washed with a blue light, the sea dissolving into the sky.

A lone figure bobbed in the water, waving happily. It was his great-great-grandfather, the renowned Doctor Kaligeros swimming towards the shore while locals gathered at the beach, cheering him on. At the water's edge, the doctor shook their hands triumphantly as if he'd won a race. Had he changed his mind about ending his life?

As the doctor climbed the pathway towards his apartment, Emilio noticed he wore the same beige linen suit as in the portrait hanging in his parents' lounge room. When he stopped at Emilio's window, he looked younger and more athletic, his wet hair tossed across his face and his round spectacles magnifying his deep blue eyes. Emilio could smell the sea, as if the doctor had filled his pockets with fish.

In a deep, whispery tone, the doctor spoke: 'The hands of God reach out to you.' Emilio felt compelled to cross himself and bow.

Emilio sensed that maybe he died and now stood before an angel. When he lifted his head to greet his ancestor, he had vanished. Fearlessly swinging around to check if the doctor had come inside, Emilio was disappointed to find the room empty. Only the smell of the sea lingered. There was no fear, no sense of intrusion, just a quiet overwhelming feeling of joy.

Emilio hopped into the shower. After a coffee he would head to his gym. It had been months since his last visit. A family lunch was only hours away, and his brother would arrive soon. They hadn't spoken since the tragedy. While Emilio acknowledged the restrictions of army life, Dimitri could have easily called. Phlegm thickened at the back of his throat, making him gag. After a few attempts, he coughed it up and watched the slime wash away down the drain, visualising all his negative thoughts sealed in the yellow membrane.

Emilio dried himself and felt clean and fresh. He reached for the gel from the vanity drawer and massaged a generous dollop through his long, wavy hair. He was well overdue for a haircut. Once his grooming had been meticulous: thick eyebrows kept even, skin moisturised and expensive cologne splashed across his freshly shaven face. Since the tragedy, the discipline had waned. His eyebrows were coming together, his nostril hairs jutted out and his skin looked patchy and rough. An unruly beard had started to grow and a few greys caught the morning light. It had been a long time since Emilio had studied his appearance.

Returning to his bed, he opened the drawer and pulled out a ziplock bag. Inside were several vials and a small note containing the accompanying chant his mother had written for him. He read the passage out loud, drank the clear liquid from one of the vials, kissed his cross as an apology to the Virgin Mary, then lit a cigarette and called his brother.

CHAPTER 21
Blue Star Aeyios, eastern Aegean

Dimitri pulled the vibrating phone from his jacket pocket and saw Emilio's face flashing. He let it ring for a bit. His brother's calls unnerved him.

'Hi…I'm okay. You?…The ferry just left Mytilene and is running about an hour late. I've already called Mum…I'm tired. Is something wrong?…Oh, okay. That's good. I just thought someone was sick or something…Yes, the boat's packed…They gave me a week's leave…Okay. See you soon…Yeah, looking forward to seeing you too.'

Dimitri moved to the far end of the ship where other smokers had gathered. He lit up and savoured the nicotine in his lungs. The last twenty-four hours had been exhausting, and Emilio's call hadn't improved his mood.

Refugees had delayed the train from Idomeni to Thessaloniki. Families and clusters of young men formed a parallel human train moving in the opposite direction, carrying the delusion that freedom was close. Dimitri pitied them, knowing the disappointment that awaited them. Even at the port of Mytilene, the dark faces of the displaced were everywhere. At one point he unnecessarily felt threatened—heart fluttering, a tremor and pain in the gut that had him desperately rushing to find the nearest toilet. He had left one refugee camp only to fly into another.

A lone seagull hovered above the ferry, its beady eye watching him. Dimitri wanted to stretch out his hand and offer it a place to rest. How lucky to live so simply, to eat and fly wherever the wind took your fancy. The thought of returning to Idomeni—the grey, wet, windy town at the top of Greece—seemed like a curse. His destiny was one of persistent misery.

At the start of his national service in January, authorities assigned Dimitri to Alexandroupoli. After three months of snow and freezing weather, he was transferred to Idomeni in northern Greece to help with border patrol. The last train station in northern Greece had become a human holding pen. Thousands waited to be processed, with tents pitched on the station platform and along the rail track. They were mostly Syrians but also Afghans and Pakistanis. The locals complained that their small town had become unrecognisable yet set up kiosks selling water, food and alcohol at exorbitant prices. Others sold wood for fires to keep people warm at night. Dimitri had never known such cold. They might as well have posted him to Iceland.

Last week's patrol was marked by the discovery of the body of an Afghan man. Dimitri had earlier restrained that same man for allegedly stealing food, shielding him and absorbing punches and an elbow to the face. Bloodied and bruised, Dimitri ended up at the local clinic for stitches above his right eye. Sitting alone in the corridor, with an ice pack on his split lip, he thought of his parents; they had never hit him. No one ever had. The mollycoddled child turned nineteen-year-old spoilt brat, had been thrown into the den of a heinous mob. Never had he felt so defeated, humiliated and frightened. Even now, as he neared home, he couldn't shake the feeling of being on guard. In uniform but unarmed, he kept his eyes constantly on patrol.

Mihalis contacted his cousin at the Ministry of Defence, hoping Dimitri would be reassigned elsewhere. The best he could do was arrange a week's special leave. His mother begged the local doctor to issue a document declaring her son mentally unstable.

'Tell them I'm crazy!' Dimitri cried over the phone.

Aphrodite even did her bit by writing lengthy letters to the local commander. Emilio, however, did nothing.

'He's going through a tough time!' Margarita told him over the phone. 'Don't take it personally.'

How could he not take his brother's silence personally? He knew about Emilio's situation—the drownings and deaths—but it couldn't compare to what he was going through. And at least Emilio was home. As far as he was concerned, his brother hated him. He was the runt of the litter—a weakling homosexual who had tainted the family's reputation.

****

Dimitri was the only Politis child not born in Australia. His father often pointed this out, calling his siblings 'Ta Afstralezakia', the Australians, and Dimitri 'To Ellinaki', the little Greek. Emilio used this distinction to boast about his and his sister's supposed superiority, their 'Aussie blood'. Dimitri remained silent; he was in awe of his big brother and believed whatever he said. Ironically, Dimitri was the smartest of the three—the keen reader, obsessed with graphic novels, with a talent for mathematics. He spent most of his free time gaming online. After high school, he deferred tertiary studies because he couldn't decide on a degree. By doing so, he had no choice but to start military service.

When Dimitri was five, his idol left the island to study in Athens. For months he wandered around like a lost puppy, crying to his mother and demanding that his father force Emilio back to the island where he belonged. As time went on, it became clear that Emilio might never move back. Even when he returned for the summer, Dimitri was never his priority. No sooner had Emilio arrived than he'd be out with friends, chasing after a girl or telling his parents how to run the hotel. As puberty hit, Dimitri used physical pain to hide his feelings. When facial hair started to appear, he began plucking it, often leaving bare patches across his face. To avoid his parents' questions, he went to places where the patches weren't visible.

By the time Emilio resettled on the island, it was too late. Dimitri's feelings had hardened, and he had no desire to try anymore. At least he had his sister and a niece, whom he loved and enjoyed. They were enough.

***

A PA announcement stated the kiosk would close in half an hour. The two-hour cruise from Mytilene had been smooth, but the strait between Phaedros's northern tip and the tiny, uninhabited Metopos Island often produced unpredictable currents. During this stretch, the kiosk shut. Ancient writings called the strait Poseidon's resting place. If the barbarians from Asia Minor dared come near, the sea god would unleash his wrath with tidal waves, smashing ships against Metopos's rocks. When news spread of a refugee boat capsizing in Kamiros Harbour, Dimitri's thoughts immediately turned to Poseidon.

Blue Star Aeyios was a large ferry, transporting cars and up to 1300 passengers. Its route covered the north Aegean: Lesbos, then Phaedros, Chios and Rhodes. The big blue-and-white ferry had mesmerised Dimitri since childhood. When it entered the harbour every morning to the sound of a booming foghorn, Margarita would pick him up, run towards the front of the hotel and wave wildly as it manoeuvred alongside the pier. It was the island's most exciting hour. Shopkeepers in Kamiros put their chalkboard signs out on the pavement, the smell of pork souvlakia filled the air, and spruikers for accommodation charged towards the steel gates at the pier to capture disembarking guests.

The mobile vibrated again. This time it was Pandelis. 'Hi...We'll be entering the strait soon...Tired. I just want to sleep...Tonight?'

The thought of leaving his bedroom after finally reaching it filled him with dread. Dimitri and Pandelis Milopitakis's sporadic relationship had spanned two years. They first met at the opening of Paradisos II when Dimitri was seventeen. Although a little older, the island's good-looking news editor was charming and intelligent. Dimitri couldn't understand Pandelis's attraction to him. While both shared a passion for ancient Greek history, that's where their similarities ended. Dimitri often felt smothered and hated when he turned journalist on him, barraging him with questions to get him to open up more.

While the family was aware of the relationship, only Aphrodite was happy about it. Margarita thought it was a phase that would pass. Emilio refrained from saying anything but raised his eyebrow whenever Pandelis's name was mentioned. His father clung to the illusion that conscription would 'cure' Dimitri. But nothing could have been further from the truth; Dimitri had never been so sexually active, especially in the bigger city of Alexandroupoli. Anonymity had spurred a series of hook-ups as an escape from his usual morose self.

'Sure, but I won't stay long. I'm exhausted.'

Dimitri shuddered when Pandelis said, 'I love you, agori mou. I've missed you.' He swiped the phone off. It annoyed him to no end when Pandelis spoke like that. It fuelled his guilt. He hoped that one day Pandelis would get a job on the mainland, where he'd meet someone decent to settle down with, because he could never make Pandelis happy.

'Excuse me,' called out a young sun-bleached blond girl sitting nearby. 'Would you mind taking a photo of me and my friends?'

Dimitri peered around and saw four more girls. 'Sure.'

'Thanks so much.'

The thin girls scrunched up together into a tangled mess. For a moment, he forgot which one had given him the camera. They all looked alike in shorts, midriff tops and long hair.

Dimitri snapped away and then handed the camera back to its owner.

'Thank you so much.'

'You're welcome.'

As Dimitri turned to leave, the same girl called out, 'Wait, wait!'

For a moment, he thought he had dropped something.

'Would you mind…being in the photo with us?'

'We're from Melbourne,' another girl called out.

'Are you going to Chios?' shouted another.

'No, Phaedros,' he replied.

'Are you a soldier?'

Dimitri removed his sunglasses, exposing the yellow bruising and stitches below his eyebrow. Until then, his Wayfarers had concealed the damage. 'A soldier in training.'

'Nice uniform,' the girl with the camera said.

'It's forbidden. Excuse me. Enjoy your holiday.'

Dimitri turned his back to them and walked away. He refused to be a part of their Greek island memory. Swiftly taking himself downstairs, he ordered a coffee from the kiosk. Stepping aside to wait for his order, he took a tissue from the counter to wipe his Wayfarers clean of sea salt. Someone tapped him on the shoulder before he could put them back on. Had one of the Australian girls followed him?

'Dimitraki, is that you?'

It was Kyrios Matsis, his old primary school teacher. Dimitri's heart lurched. It had been years since he'd last seen him. The short, balding man with a huge black moustache was now shorter, older and fatter, sporting a wiry white beard and yellow-stained teeth. Dimitri put his glasses back on before he asked questions about his face.

'Hello, sir, how are you?'

Kyrios Matsis rubbed Dimitri's shoulder. He sensed the roughness and malice of his touch through his thick khaki shirt and edged away. He hated the man.

'I didn't recognise you in uniform. It suits you!'

Feeling his fingers squeeze his biceps sent shivers down Dimitri's back.

'You've become a man. So proud of our young conscripts. Bravo. How long have you been away?'

'Since the end of January.'

'Well, you're nearly done then,' he said facetiously.

'I wish,' Dimitri responded.

Balloon Head, as students called him because of his large, round head, was a problem. Dimitri remembered his meaty hand on his thigh during one lesson when he was supposedly explaining a maths problem. As a nine-year-old, Dimitri thought the gesture meant the teacher liked him and wanted to help him succeed. But when Alex, the new boy, joined the class, Balloon Head's gestures stopped. Dimitri felt abandoned once more and tried hard to compete with the more handsome Alex by wearing nicer clothes. By the end of the year, Balloon Head had vanished, along with Alex and his family. Years later, Dimitri heard of Kyrios Matsis's attempt to assault Alex. News spread that he had returned to Phaedros with an Asian wife and opened a bakery in the remote village of Kremasti.

'How's life as a conscript?'

Before Dimitri could respond, Balloon Head answered for him. 'Don't worry, it will soon be over and you can return to your brother's resort. So you'll work there? Your family is one of the lucky ones. The lefties have destroyed the country and the EU is screwing us. At least your family is thriving.'

His voice dripped with sarcasm. Dimitri knew the envy towards his family.

'So where are you posted?'

'Idomeni.'

'Idomeni? Well, you scored well. Make sure you keep pushing those Muslims out. If we're not careful, mosques will replace our churches, God forbid! You obviously heard about the boat that sank in the harbour. Your brother was quite the hero. Don't get me wrong. It was tragic. Unbelievable that a small dinghy made it to our harbour. The Metopos Strait let us down this time. One survivor is now working at the resort, as you probably know. Shame a job like that couldn't have gone to one of our young girls.'

Dimitri had no idea what he was talking about and didn't want any clarification. He just wanted to get out of there.

The bartender shouted Balloon Head's coffee order and placed it on the counter. Picking it up, he turned back to Dimitri. 'Mytilene is a disaster zone,' he continued, his voice more aggressive. 'My sister lives there and can't go anywhere without her husband. They live in fear. I was there for my cousin's funeral and they were pitching tents in the cemetery. I shouted at them to get the fuck out of there—where's their respect?'

Balloon Head drew a breath. Dimitri hoped he would have a cardiac arrest.

'You know Fotini? The mother-in-law your brother never got to have? She lives in my village. A very clever lady who has her heart and head in the right place. She's starting a local branch of the political party Ellas, Yia Mas! She could use your family's support, especially financially. We all need to back her—we can't keep letting this government trade our ethnicity and religion for cheap deals with the EU. We won't be the dumping ground for the dregs of the Middle East. You understand me, right?' Again he answered for Dimitri. His ruddy skin flushed and veins protruded at the side of his neck. 'But you're young; you don't get what's at stake here. Your generation is blind to reality—you're all glued to your phones and the fake world Mr Facebook keeps shoving in your faces every minute of the day.' Balloon Head was shouting.

'Stop harassing this soldier!' shouted a man standing nearby. 'It's a holy day, so keep your bigoted views to yourself and stop polluting the air with your malakies!'

Dimitri didn't recognise the man. He looked to be in his thirties, clean-cut, wearing an Adidas wind jacket, a baseball cap and expensive-looking sunglasses. He spoke with an American accent.

'Keep your nose and ears out of my private conversation,' Balloon Head shouted. 'This is an ex-student of mine. How dare you interrupt our conversation.'

'Conversation? You're a fool!' the man replied.

The surrounding crowd took a step back, anticipating a confrontation. Sensing things were getting out of hand and having done nothing to defend himself, Dimitri shouted, 'Please stop. Enough!'

The bartender intervened: 'Please, we have international guests on the ferry!'

Dimitri decided he didn't want to wait for his coffee. He excused himself and pushed through the waiting passengers to the stairs leading to the deck.

'When you return to Idomeni, remember my words, Dimitraki!' Balloon Head yelled after him.

Up on deck, Dimitri lit another cigarette. 'Fucking malakismeno!' he muttered under his breath. *Could this journey home get any worse?* The boat had slowed as the currents picked up. The sea breeze felt hotter, though maybe Balloon Head had something to do with that. He felt stupid for allowing himself to be spoken to like that. *What a fucking idiot I am.* Tears welled in his eyes. Thank God for his sunglasses.

'You okay?'

It was the man who'd come to his rescue. Dimitri wanted to jump into the sea and disappear.

'I'm good,' he replied, quietly panicking his voice might crack.

'You don't remember me, do you?'

What the fuck! He knows me? Dimitri didn't want to engage but now felt obligated. Having him witness his humiliation only made him feel even worse. The man took off his sunglasses and hat revealing a recent haircut of light brown hair with dyed blond tips. A diamond stud pierced his left ear. Dimitri couldn't identify him, then he recalled the American at the resort's opening. Emilio had brought him over to introduce them. 'You're Emilio's friend,' Dimitri said.

'Andrew Kappos.'

'Sorry, I didn't recognise you. We met at the resort's opening.'

Andrew extended his hand. Dimitri grasped it and sensed a sharp jolt of pain shoot up his arm from the strength of Andrew's grip.

'Well, I'm glad that's why you remember me and not because I'm the evil bastard who took his girl.'

'I'm sorry. I don't understand,' Dimitri replied. 'Which girl?'

'Eva, Eva Galanos.'

'Oh, sorry. Emilio never spoke to me about it. And anyway, I've been away.'

'I can see that. But don't worry, things are good between your brother and me. But your brother's not been doing so well, you know, since the drownings.'

God, another pity-seeking story about my brother. Was Andrew expecting him to ask: 'Why, what's wrong?' Instead, he changed the subject. 'You run charter cruises, don't you?'

'Yes, I do! I've left the *Grand Duchess* docked at Plomari in Lesbos for a few days. I'm taking a few days off to hang out with Eva. I'm stoked to spend some time on solid ground for a change. We'll do a trek on the island, climb Mount Dillinos and camp by Butterfly Cove. Ever checked it out?'

'I've heard of it but never been there.'

'You should get your brother to take you. It's so cool!'

'Maybe one day. How's Eva?' Dimitri felt obliged to ask.

'Yeah, she's doing well. Her mother…that's another story. That old fart down there may be a fucking idiot, but he was damn right about Fotini. She's a maniac. A fucking ma-ni-ac! Eva no longer talks to her, but it really bugs her, you know. Can't understand it when your own mother turns into a fucking witch! Anyway, how are you doing?' Andrew asked.

'I'm fine. Just looking forward to getting home.'

'Nothing like coming back to one's old comforts.'

Dimitri nodded and tried to disengage. Andrew seemed to thrive on his own positivity.

'I didn't mean to make a scene down there but Greeks like that really piss me off. Sure, things are rough right now, but let's not turn into fucking retards. I've had to save a couple of boats myself, you know. Sailing around the Aegean, you can't just let them folks drown out there. That's inhumane…Anyway, I hope you're okay. Just wanted to check on you, that's all.'

'I'm fine. Really, I am.'

'Such a beautiful part of the world,' Andrew said, gazing across to Phaedros. Dimitri nodded. 'You can tell your brother I've applied for a Greek passport. I'm still figuring out what level of conscription I need to undergo at my age, but I hope I can pay my way out. It's not that bad, right?

'I'm the last person you should ask!'

'Okay, I'll leave you to it. Got my stuff downstairs. We should be there in about thirty minutes, I guess. Say hello to your brother and tell him I'll call him.' Andrew put his hand out to shake and Dimitri obliged.

'I will, thanks.'

'See you again,' Andrew said before disappearing down the stairwell.

Dimitri shut his eyes and took deep breaths. He sensed the swell rising beneath him. He imagined Poseidon lying on his back on the seafloor, strumming his fingers across the ferry's hull, deciding whether to flick it or stroke it. Waves started crashing against the boat, and spray soaked the sides of the deck. Someone shouted, followed by a shrill burst of laughter. Dimitri opened his eyes, fearing it was the girls again, but instead saw a young Asian couple holding the rail, letting themselves be showered by sea spray. The boy held the girl tightly as she giggled and jumped around. They looked so connected that even if Poseidon threw a tantrum and their bodies were tossed overboard, they'd still be laughing.

As the boat steered right, the harbour came into view. Dimitri never took for granted how beautiful his island was. Each time he returned, he believed it was the most special place on earth. The sea eased into a smooth glide, and tourists emerged like ants from the galleys to take photos. A shudder came over him. Home was within arm's reach, and his pent-up frustration began to subside. It was his Ithaca—he had made it. Poseidon had been kind. While there was no Penelope, at least his mum would be waiting to hug and kiss him and cook him a feast.

CHAPTER 22
Politis family home

Of all the ancestors, Irini Vlahos chose to remain in the realm of the living. Sometimes her son-in-law, Doctor Haralambos Kaligeros, would appear, his visits always fleeting. He'd rush in through a door or climb through a window and whirl around each of his descendants. After examining them, he'd zoom across to Irini with his opinion, his tone always clinical, factual and devoid of emotion. Never did they reminisce about their lives as mortals; such sentiments, like their bodies, had been discarded at death.

Irini's family sat at the long dining table laden with platters of food. She watched her descendants converse, cough, clap, stare and laugh. At opportune moments, she squeezed in between them to get a better sense of their wellbeing. The ghosts agreed that Aphrodite had thrush, Dimitri was stricken with severe melancholia, Rika's glands were swollen, Salome was going through menopause, Emilio was in psychological distress and Margarita's breast cancer had returned. While others were in the room, Irini and the doctor could only see, hear and examine their kin. Everyone else was a blur of shimmering grey hues.

The dining room was brightly lit by the afternoon sun. It was a spacious, open area with a long settee next to a glass wall cabinet containing heirloom trinkets and crockery. A small painting of the doctor hung on the wall beside it. Dated 1817, it was painted by his brother before he left Smyrna to take up his posting as the Pasha's physician on Phaedros.

All doors and windows were shut. Irini knew it was the feast of the Virgin Mary, so she guessed it was very hot outside. In her time, they wouldn't dare sit inside during the long days of August. A large white box protruding from the wall seemed to offer some comfort. Salome stood beneath it, using a paper fan to cool her hot flushes. Aphrodite pointed at the white box with a small object that looked like a whetstone, pressing her thumb down repeatedly. Irini figured she was sending messages in code.

Irini acknowledged the advances in science and technology but couldn't benefit from them. Over time, she observed how life grew simpler for women: meals cooked inside wall cavities without fire, winter warmth at the press of a button, dishes washed to a shine inside a humming box.

Many descendants had been born since Irini's arrival at Phaedros on that morning in 1822. Since her passing in 1858 at the age of ninety-one, she had woven herself into all their lives in one way or another: Toli (1939–2007) inherited her stubbornness, humour and pride; Aphrodite, the artist, shared her creative passion; Margarita embodied her stoicism and compassion. Over eighty descendants lived in Greece; others were scattered across Turkey, Germany, Canada and Argentina. Distance was never an obstacle for Irini; she could connect with all of them in a single day if needed.

The doctor, on the other hand, could not leave Phaedros. The sea's magnetic force, which claimed his life, would lure him back if he wandered too far. That morning, he appeared in his usual dramatic form before Emilio. This young man was the most difficult for Irini to infiltrate. His vibrant personality, confidence and arrogance were a challenge. The doctor was usually more successful, especially in the last few months, and usually during Emilio's semi-delirious state of awakening. Since he started wearing his chain and cross, that connection had grown stronger.

While Emilio was curious about the doctor, he lacked his sister's commitment and interest in the family's history and legacy. Since his recent traumatic interaction with the sea, his weakened constitution enabled a few windows to open and allow connection. The doctor encouraged Irini to forge ahead with her attempt to infiltrate Emilio's being, believing that her remedies would be very effective for his worsening anxiety.

Irini used the occasion of the religious lunch to make some progress. She hovered over Emilio, darkening like a cloud building up rain, and then shifted down behind him. Bending her frail body, she locked her hunched torso before flipping back her long hair, sending fine debris into the air. With thin arms, she scooped it into her chest before blowing it all over Emilio. Her descendant, feeling a breeze on his back, turned around and inhaled.

Irini's legacy was captured in the manuscript of remedies written by her granddaughter, Myrto. At the top of each page, the girl had drawn small symbols or icons under Irini's guidance to classify the type of remedy. A fever had the symbol of the sun; for a rash, small dots; for heartache, the shape of a heart; for mental strength, an owl; for vision, an eye; for breakages, a stick in two pieces; for inflammation and pain, a line with a bump. Below each recipe, Myrto beautifully illustrated the main herb or featured plant—sage, chamomile or St John's wort, detailed illustrations in colour that had withstood the decay of time.

The page's lower-right corner displayed the unique chant for administering the remedy. The spoken words served as an essential call to the body, encouraging it to accept the healing. It took some time for Margarita to attune herself to the healing powers of the remedies. Like her son Emilio, her self-confidence and resilience acted as a hindrance. Margarita knew the book was in the villa, abandoned on a shelf, much like her father had abandoned the house, until Aphrodite claimed it.

Following Margarita's operation, while feeling mentally and physically weak, she agreed to her daughter's intervention. She applied Aphrodite's prepared solution with a face cloth to the area where her breast once was. Irini took this opportunity to penetrate Margarita's psyche more deeply, capitalising on her vulnerable situation. Whatever those butchers did to her body, her elixirs would soothe her pain and help her recover faster. The desired outcome came to fruition after Margarita acknowledged that the warm, pungent solution had provided some topical relief.

Since discovering the manuscript, Aphrodite had prepared most of the remedies. She devoted a whole cupboard to them and bottled them in small vials. All the botanicals were from plants that grew abundantly on the island or could be bought from the weekly growers' market. She meticulously labelled them as named in the manuscript and included the symbols used to classify each remedy. Irini's aim in death was to keep her remedies alive. How they were used and with whom was up to the dispenser. As long as the remedies were prepared correctly, the rest was up to the conviction of the patient. If they were receptive to it then the therapy would be effective.

Irini's book of remedies, which had lain dormant for years, was coming back to life. In Aphrodite, she had found a new conduit to strengthen her presence. Each remedy this family prepared made her more productive. Today, at the lunch gathering, Margarita had prepared an elixir for rejuvenation. Its ingredients were:

red wine
root of *Ferula moschata*
honey
mastic
cloves

Serving it in small thimble glasses before the main meal, Margarita toasted the Virgin Mary and her ancestors then whispered the associated chant as everyone took their first sip.

Aroma too tharous (Perfume of courage)
Anthos tis psihis (The bloom of the spirit)
Skorpise varos (Begone the burden)
Kala hronia na zis (May you live good years)

Even Emilio, once sceptical, drank it wholeheartedly. Margarita sat down slowly, gripping her chair. The cancer had begun to grow in her other breast.

PART 5
VIOLATION

CHAPTER 23
Rhodes, April–July 1967

On 22 April 1967, seventeen-year-old Margarita Kanarakis first met Mihalis Politis in embarrassing circumstances. She had just left Kyria Eleni's sewing school on Filerimos Street in Rhodes Town. It was lunchtime, and the young ladies of the school were rushing down the stairs of the neoclassical building. Next door, at Nikos's Kafenio, eighteen-year-old conscript Mihalis Politis was drinking ouzo while reading the newspapers, his legs stretched across the footpath. Margarita would have avoided the hazard had she gone straight home, but she'd forgotten to buy bread and turned back. Her timing and Mihalis's focus sent her crashing headfirst into a lamppost.

When she came to, Mihalis's flustered face came into view. His hands were under her armpits, his breath quick and hot against her cheek. Apologising profusely, he splashed water from his glass onto her face.

'I am so sorry, miss. Can you hear me? Hello?'

'I am okay,' Margarita managed to say. Sunlight pierced a crack in the canvas awning and fell across her face. Her mouth felt parched. The heads of other men crowded her vision.

'Don't pick her up in case she's broken something,' someone shouted.

'She's okay. Please, give her air. Return to your tables,' Mihalis ordered.

Feeling his hands adjusting her skirt, bunched above her waist, she pushed them away and pulled it down herself.

'Military?' she finally said, her focus sharpening on the young man's soldier's uniform.

'Are you in any pain?'

She felt no pain, only disorientation and growing irritation at the water being flicked at her. She put her hand up to stop him. 'Military? Here on Rhodes?'

'No, no, in Athens. Here, please sit down.' He helped her to her feet and into a chair. 'Waiter, a glass of water for the lady, please!' As he turned to speak to her he noticed her legs. 'Oh no, your stocking is ripped.'

Margarita peered below her right knee and saw a large tear. She couldn't hide her disappointment. They were her only pair, and she had paid seventy drachmas, the equivalent of four loaves of bread.

'Please, I'll buy you new ones. I don't have much money on me, but I will next week. I'm so sorry.'

'It's okay. Maybe I can mend them.'

The waiter arrived with the water, which she quickly drank.

Mihalis pulled up a chair next to her. 'I can at least buy you a coffee or a lemonade.'

'No, I need to go. I must get bread from the bakery.'

'Well, let me buy the bread for you.'

Before she could say no, he put on his khaki side-cap and ran to the bakery next door. An elderly man at the table beside her leaned over to check if she was okay. She nodded, though she felt silly. Several men watched her intently. She noted plates and glasses on empty tables and cigarette butts littering the concrete floor, a stark contrast to her father's meticulous kafenio. Picking up the newspaper she read the headline: 'Coup d'état: Army seizes power in Athens'. A shiver ran down her spine. Behind her, an argument was brewing between a couple of old men until the owner silenced them. Mihalis reappeared holding a loaf of bread. Taking the newspaper from her, he folded it and tucked it under his armpit.

'Come, let me walk you home. It's not safe. Times are changing. Where do you live?'

'Just down the street, Odos Triantafillou. What's happening?'

'The colonels have taken control of Athens. Tanks are rolling onto the streets. I need to report back to the base.'

'You don't need to walk me home. I'm fine.'

'I will buy you stockings next week… I promise.'

She detected a tremor in his voice and wondered if it came from nerves or the news in Athens. She suddenly had the urge to grab his arm and squeeze it. Until then, she hadn't noticed how handsome he was. His dark eyes, wide eyelids, slicked-back hair and full lips reminded her of Hollywood's Victor Mature.

'Can you believe it? I get a day off to come into town and what happens? A coup, and I almost kill a young lady.'

'Don't worry about me,' said Margarita. 'It's the country I'm more concerned about. I knew there was unrest over the elections but I didn't expect this.'

'You follow politics?'

'Well, yes, I read the paper.'

'Bravo. It's good to take an interest.'

'I think it is our responsibility as citizens, don't you?'

He froze mid-breath. Not wanting to put him off, she quickly introduced herself: 'My name is Margarita Kanarakis.'

'How stupid of me. Mihalis Politis.'

'Politis? There you go. A citizen by name as well.'

He chuckled. 'How old are you? Not that you need to tell me— and excuse me for asking—but you're very…smart.'

'Oh, I thought you were going to say beautiful!'

He needed a moment to catch on. 'That too! And funny! I'm glad you're not angry with me.'

Margarita pulled back on the flirting. 'What does this situation mean for you?'

'I'm not sure. News travels slowly to the islands. By the time we conscripts hear about it, we've already been thrown into the fire. My service here in Rhodes ends in three months.'

'Where are you from?' she asked, trying to sidetrack him.

'A village called Goura, near Corinth.'

'Corinth?'

'Yes. Are you from Rhodes?'

'No, I'm from Phaedros, a small island between Lesbos and Chios.'

'Oh, I've never heard of it.'

'It's tiny but beautiful. I'm here learning to sew and living with my cousin Koula and her husband. I'm also finishing up in a couple of months.'

'I love it here. It's so cosmopolitan, sunny and full of history. It was occupied by the Italians for a while, and all these grand buildings and roads are because of them.'

'Same with Phaedros. My father's kafenio catered for Mussolini's injured soldiers during the war.'

'You have a kafenio?'

'Yes, Paradisos.'

'So you'll go back to your island?'

'I don't want to, but I probably will.'

I think I'll come back and settle here, but first, Australia.'

'Australia?'

'Yes, but only for two years. My older brother recently migrated there. There's plenty of work, and he owns a café right in the middle of Sydney.'

Margarita slowed as they approached her cousin's house, wanting to prolong their walk. 'We've arrived.'

'Already?'

Margarita noticed Tsambiko, Koula's husband, peering through the window. 'I'd better go inside. They're waiting for me to have lunch.'

'Of course, of course. Don't forget your bread,' he said, clumsily handing over the loaf. 'But, please, I…I will see you again? I need to buy you a new pair of stockings. Could you help me out with, umm, size and style? I'm not sure what to ask for.'

He was barely into manhood, and the image of him walking into a hosiery shop to buy stockings made her giggle.

'Maybe I'll come with you. That might be easier.' She had already decided she wanted to see him again and didn't care about the stockings.

'That would be perfect. Is there a phone number I can call you on? I'm not sure when I can take leave again. Maybe in two weeks, depending on how this mess plays out.'

She looked through her bag for her exercise book where a school stamp with a phone number was on the inside cover. She took out her eyeliner. 'Give me your newspaper.'

Mihalis immediately handed it over. Using the eyeliner, she wrote down the number.

'Call the school and leave a message. My parents do the same when they need to contact me.'

Mihalis straightened, almost saluting, then stopped himself. 'Thank you for being so understanding. I will most definitely call.'

Margarita's heart raced. Intuition told her that she had met her husband. She wanted to kiss him but stopped herself as they were in a public place and most probably under the gaze of her cousin's husband. She put out her hand to shake his.

'I promise I will call,' he said, eagerly shaking her hand.

'Hopefully the colonels won't stop you.'

He laughed and walked away with a spring in his step, the laces of his black army boots coming slightly loose. He turned, executing a masterful salute. Margarita played coy and gave him a gentle nod and smile, then pointed at his shoelaces. He quickly retied them, looking a little sheepish, then lit a cigarette, waved and disappeared around the corner.

The scent of basil greeted her as she pushed open the gate to the small whitewashed house. One of the neighbourhood cats ran towards her, rubbing its warm body against her leg. She stooped to stroke its fur, whispering, 'Margarita Politis. Margarita Politis.'

***

Margarita's mother was determined her eldest daughter would not be trapped in the family café. With few options on a small, isolated island like Phaedros, she eagerly agreed to sewing school in Rhodes, a place that had enthralled Margarita at fourteen when she attended her cousin Koula's wedding. The Castle of the Knights, the bustling old town, the tourists and the restaurants made her feel as though she had stepped into Paris.

Three years older, Koula had always been Margarita's role model—independent and strong-willed, with a boisterous laugh. At sixteen she had defied her family by fleeing to Rhodes to work as a domestic at a new resort. There she fell in love with a bootmaker from Mandraki Harbour, and they married six months later.

Koula was excited to have Margarita stay while she learned her trade. In return for accommodation, Margarita helped with housework and babysat Kyriako, their two-year-old. Koula was pregnant again, making the timing ideal, though weeks passed before Kyriako could see Margarita without erupting into a tantrum.

Tsambiko, by contrast, took an immediate liking to Margarita. His wandering eyes often lingered too long, and his winks made her want to spit. She was striking—tall, curvaceous, with long, bleached-blond hair. It was the 1960s, and Aliki Vouyiouklaki, Greece's answer to Brigitte Bardot, had become a national fashion icon. Women brightened their hair to a golden hue and raised their hemlines above the knees. As an aspiring seamstress, Margarita designed her own Vouyiouklaki-inspired outfits.

One evening, Tsambiko approached her while she was finishing the hem of a new dress. He had returned from the kafenio drunk. His loose shirt was untucked, and his dark thinning hair was slicked down to one side. Koula was asleep in the bedroom with Kyriako in her arms. Grumbling that he had no bed, he began shoving furniture around. Margarita ignored him, focusing on the skirt and the location of the scissors nearby.

'How short will you make this dress, pretty lady?'

Margarita sighed, knowing where his question was leading. 'I need to finish this tonight for class tomorrow.'

'That's not my question,' he hissed, coming up behind her and placing his hand on her thigh. 'Will it be this high? Or even higher?' His breath reeked of alcohol and cigarettes.

Margarita jumped from her chair and grabbed the scissors. 'Don't you dare touch me again!'

'Shh! I was just wondering.'

'Try that again and I'll use these!' she said, pointing the scissors at him.

'I open my house to you and this is how you treat me!'

Margarita knew Tsambiko feared his wife and only feigned his bravado when she wasn't around.

'All you've got to do is raise your voice and he'll run and hide like a little boy,' Koula had once told her after she made a complaint.

Margarita often wondered what Koula saw in Tsambiko, let alone why she married him. Was she that desperate not to return to Phaedros? Recalling her cousin's advice, Margarita scolded, 'Go to bed, Tsambiko! You're drunk and you don't know what you're saying.'

He growled at her then shuffled away into the sitting room like a wounded animal. At one point he half turned as if to argue then slumped onto the settee. Margarita watched him fumble with his shoes, his thin frame wavering on edge. He cursed under his breath then stretched out across the sofa and, within minutes, began to snore.

***

Over the next three months, Mihalis and Margarita met whenever he had a day off. If needed, she'd skip class if it clashed with her timetable. If it was a weekend, she told Koula she was going out with her girlfriends. Margarita would have willingly told Koula the truth, but Tsambiko would have questioned, pried and judged. Besides, Koula almost certainly knew and chose to give her space.

Margarita quickly fell in love with Mihalis, helped by periods of absence and longing. She met him at the steps of the sewing school and from there wandered along Mandraki Harbour or through the cobbled streets of the old town. Their favourite spot was a small, secluded rocky inlet next to the harbour, from which they imagined where the mighty Colossus once stood.

Margarita enjoyed his sense of humour. His laugh rolled, always ending on a high note. She loved how he turned something bad or sad into something positive. 'One of the good things about the junta is the return of stupidity. I feel much better about leaving this damned country.'

With Mihalis, she felt safe, free to be candid. Her mother often reprimanded her for it, warning that such a trait limited her options in husbands; not that she paid much attention. Now, having found Mihalis, she briefly lamented that he had arrived too early, not giving her the chance to meet other men. Still, deep down, she believed he was the one. His sense of adventure was infectious, and once he planted the idea of Australia, she could think of nothing else—especially with the coup. Georgios Papadopoulos and his cronies were mapping an oppressive future. Music, art and media were being censored and many artists arrested. The coup had ended the swinging sixties in Greece.

The uncertainty in Greece cast a shadow over their future. She needed to finish school and return to Phaedros while he would go back to his village, pack before sailing to Australia. Facing a two-year separation, she was crushed, but they devised a plan—he would return to marry her. That night, as he kissed her in their special spot on the beach, she unzipped his pants and began to stroke him. She had no idea what she was doing, but it felt right. Her actions had caught him off guard but he didn't resist.

'You don't think badly of me?' she asked afterwards. 'I love you, Mihalis. I want to do whatever I can to make you happy.'

He drew her close, kissing her neck and mouth. He now felt comfortable touching her body, her waist, her padded bra. He grew hard again and moved his body over hers, his legs between hers, his mouth travelling from her neck to her cleavage. But she stopped him.

'Next time,' she said.

'But I want to make you happy as well.'

'We will have something to look forward to. Something special. We can book a hotel.'

He kissed her passionately. 'I love you. We will have beautiful children together.'

'Our own little citizens,' she whispered.

***

By their next meeting, everything had changed. Koula was in hospital with high blood pressure and Kyriako was with his grandparents. Sometime after midnight, the crash of a chair in the kitchen woke Margarita. For a moment she thought Tsambiko had fallen and hurried in wearing only her petticoat. His eyes were fiery and his movements agitated. As he approached, she noticed his left cheek was red and swollen and a slight cut ran across his right eyebrow.

'What happened to you?' she asked, reaching for a cloth to clean his face.

He circled the table, pushing chairs in and out, ranting, 'Bastards! Bastards!'

Margarita wet the cloth under the tap and followed him into the sitting room, where he sat on the settee.

'They think they can badmouth me. I hope Papadopoulos and his colonels squeeze the life out of them. For ten years I have worked to make them rich. The ungrateful bastards!'

Margarita suspected that the landlord of his shoe shop had finally evicted him. He blamed his left-wing views; she suspected it was his sloppiness. As she dabbed the dried blood from his brow, he seized her hand. He didn't want that kind of care. Tears welled in his eyes. He wrapped his arms around her waist, pulling her towards him, burying his face in her belly.

'They will ruin us,' he sobbed. 'The scoundrels!'

His grip tightened as she tried to pull away. 'Stop it, Tsambiko, you're hurting me!'

But the more she resisted, the more determined he became.

'I've seen you and your soldier boy. You and your short skirts. How many army boys have you had?'

'Stop it! Think of your wife in the hospital. Stop it!'

Her words were no match for his uncontrollable rage. He swung her around with brutal force, throwing her onto the settee. She fought back, punching and scratching until his fist plunged into her belly, knocking the wind out of her.

'Poutana!' he screamed. 'See what you've done? You've made me lose my temper.' He grabbed her hair, yanking her face up to his. 'It doesn't need to be this way, but you are so selfish!'

A slap across her face sent her crashing onto the settee, the back of her head hitting the armrest. She felt the burn across her cheek and the pounding in her head.

He pinned her down, stuffing the cloth she still had in her hand into her mouth and tore open her petticoat. His bites and the scrape of his scaly fingers on her bare skin ignited a searing pain. She spat out the cloth and lunged at his neck, biting so hard that it drew blood. Another blow to her temple knocked her unconscious.

When she came to, she immediately gathered up her energy and crawled to the kitchen for a knife. Anger numbed the pain in her groin. Standing up, she clutched the tattered remains of her petticoat around her shoulders and grabbed a knife from the drawer. Noticing the blood all over the settee, she screamed, 'I will kill you, you animal!' as she charged into his bedroom. But the bed was empty. A howl escaped from her mouth as she collapsed on the floor.

***

Three weeks passed before she saw Mihalis again. He had given her the base's central communication number for emergencies. As desperate as she was to talk to him and collapse into his arms, she couldn't bring herself to call. The fear of abandonment held her back. Not that she believed he would, but a faint doubt lingered. Ending the relationship at this stage, when none of their families knew about it, would make things easier.

Initially, she considered saying nothing and returning to Phaedros. But the more she dwelt on it, the more she knew she couldn't. She refused to live a life of regret and self-blame. Tsambiko's vile actions would not dictate her future. She was determined to do whatever it took to protect her cousin and put him behind bars.

The day after the rape, she took herself to the police station. Her wounds were still fresh, and the bruising pronounced. The room smelt of disinfectant, and the policeman's eyes refused to meet hers. It didn't take long to track down Tsambiko who was hiding at his aunt's house in a nearby village. The police wouldn't reveal much information other than to say that he had confessed immediately and was subsequently imprisoned. On hearing the news, Koula picked up the chair next to her hospital bed and threw it across the room. Margarita stood helpless, even guilty, as staff forced her back into bed, screaming. Koula's blood pressure soared and she soon collapsed. Two days later, Koula gave birth to a stillborn boy.

***

Mihalis was waiting at the stairs where they usually met. It was a balmy July evening and tourists were strolling by. Unable to find him at first, she feared he'd learned of the rape and deserted her. But he was there all along; she simply hadn't recognised him out of uniform. When they embraced, she struggled to contain the pain of her bruised ribs. She eased his arms away, took hold of his face, and searched into his big brown eyes for proof he was real. She then drew him in and kissed him passionately, wishing she could let him wrap his arms around her battered body. Mihalis looked confused; they had never kissed like that in public. He looked dashing in his white cotton shirt, navy gabardine trousers and polished shoes. Everything about him infiltrated her senses—his cologne, the gold chain disappearing into his chest hairs, his fresh haircut slicked back with poppy oil.

'I've booked us a hotel. It's not flashy, but it's clean. Can you stay the whole night with me?'

It was to have been the night she would lose her virginity to the man she loved. But that 'virtue' had been forcefully taken, leaving her body broken.

'Let's walk first,' she said. 'I need to smell the sea.'

The fifteen-minute walk to their private corner of the beach felt endless. They exchanged few words. Most of the conversation was Mihalis's recount of the long bus trip from the army base, the bus driver singing Italian cantatas and the mood in the barracks. The thought of being pulled back into the army after his service finished in two weeks worried him. He knew he had to leave the country quickly. Margarita barely spoke, afraid a horrible howl might escape again. Tears filled her eyes as the half-empty moon cast a dark shadow over their corner of the beach. A cool breeze slid through the rocks, and somewhere nearby a bouzouki played from a taverna. Mihalis lit a cigarette, and Margarita asked for one—though she wasn't a smoker, she needed something to help her get the words out.

For the next hour, Mihalis wept, cursed and paced the shoreline. The more he cried and yelled, the more silent she became. He was angry at himself for not protecting her, furious with her for not calling him. She sat in silence as he vented his rage. When he finally sank down beside her, he took her hand, stroked and kissed it.

'I love you, Mihalis. I know in my heart that you also love me. I'm so glad you nearly killed me when we first met, and no, I can't bear to lose you.'

'You're not going to lose me no matter what happened.'

She took his hand and returned the kiss. 'I'll stay longer on Rhodes, help my cousin. I owe her.'

'I will come back for you.'

Heavy tears fell from her eyes. She squeezed his hand tightly and sobbed.

'Everything will be alright, my sweetheart,' he reassured her. 'Trust me.'

'Go to your family and then to Australia.'

'I'm not going to Australia without you. We'll get married and go together.'

'I can't right now, Mihalis.'

'I don't understand.'

'I think I am pregnant.'

For the first time, she wanted him to stop looking at her, unable to bear the sadness in his eyes. Rising, she walked solemnly to the shoreline. Pregnancy terrified her; until now, she had refused to believe it. Her body was changing by the hour. She was at least five days late, and her breasts were sore. Removing her shoes, she dipped her toes into the tepid water, took deep breaths and savoured the sea air. She couldn't bring herself to turn around in case he was not there. But then she heard the soft crunch of pebbles behind her. She felt his arms gently wrap around her waist and did not say a word.

***

Margarita's mother insisted she return to Phaedros, but that was the last thing she wanted. While she had no interest in motherhood yet and doubted her ability to love this child, Koula's tragic pregnancy made her reconsider her plans. It was the least she could do, see the pregnancy through and give her cousin a baby she desperately wanted.

During the pregnancy, Margarita and Mihalis corresponded. The separation had been terrible, but over time they grew accustomed to the distance. All along, she kept him informed about what was going on. His intentions never changed: he would come to Phaedros, marry her and then return to Australia together.

On 27 March 1968, Margarita gave birth to a hefty baby boy and called him Angelo, after Koula's father. After forty days of confinement, Margarita, Koula and their children returned to Phaedros. No one on the island knew of Margarita's pregnancy apart from her parents and siblings. Everyone else believed that Angelo was Koula's.

Koula, Kyriako and baby Angelo settled into a small house in the village of Melissani. Koula's father, who had refused her any inheritance for defying his orders not to go to Rhodes, relented and bought her a house in Melissani. Having that distance helped Margarita forget Angelo, as did her eventual trip to Australia.

Even with the colonels running the government, tourism in Greece continued to grow in the late sixties. The recent excavations at Ancient Tallos had put the island on the map. Margarita found herself captivated by the tales and adventures of young travellers visiting their kafenio. Some had even been to Australia and spoke of the unique animals and beautiful beaches, making her desire to leave even stronger. When Mihalis came for her with a ring in 1970, they married and, within months, left for Australia. On one of their first outings in Sydney, they went to Mark Foy's department store where he bought her a fancy pair of stockings.

CHAPTER 24
Melissani, April 2009

The golden egg Angelo Poulos waited thirty years for arrived on Sunday, 26 April 2009. It was a beautiful, solitary nugget found in a bed of fresh hay. Forty days had passed since he last visited his beloved chicken coop—forty days of mourning since discovering his mother's body. The golden egg was his saviour, a plan hatched by Margarita to rescue her biological son from self-imposed starvation.

Throughout his twenty-eight years as an egg farmer, two incidents stopped Angelo from delivering his eggs to the community of Melissani. The first occurred in 1982, when he was thirteen, and an earthquake caused him and his eggs to land in a neighbour's yard. The tremor convinced him that Melissani might slide down the mountain. Koula comforted him, saying that their village was special and such a thing would never happen. He trusted her completely, believing everything his mother told him.

Years later, two local boys, brothers Jimmy and Alex Mitsos, strung a fishing line across his path to the village square. As he tripped, the basket overturned, causing the eggs to smash all over him. Humiliated, he barricaded himself in the house for a month until the villagers turned up at the front door yelling for eggs. He hated loud noise and came out, holding his mother's hand, to face the brothers, who publicly apologised and gifted Angelo five new chickens. Happiness was restored and, as Father Efthimios put it, Angelo had 'resumed his civil duty'.

Each morning at 7:45, Angelo would arrive at the village square carrying a basket of fresh eggs. 'Fresh eggs! Come and buy your fresh eggs,' he'd call out through his megaphone. His supply was limited, and each household was allowed only two eggs a day. There was no room for negotiation. His dealings with the locals were straightforward, with no time for idle gossip, which he never grasped.

Angelo's approach to his business wasn't always as obsessive and meticulous. At first he was sloppy and heavy-handed, breaking eggs before reaching the basket. When he came into the house, he'd bring manure in on his shoes, and his mother was forever trying to keep the coop clean. One day, when her patience ran dry, she told Angelo that if he took better care of the chickens and eggs, and kept the chicken coop tidy, he would be rewarded with a golden egg. Angelo's eyes lit up, imagining the treasures he could gain from his business. From then on, his routine changed. Each morning he checked for a golden egg, cleaned each egg with a rag before wrapping it in a cloth and placing it in a potato sack-lined basket. And every afternoon, before lunch at the house, he would make sure the coop was clean and tidy, and his shoes spotless.

The chicken coop was located at the back of the family's olive grove, about fifty metres from the house. When Angelo turned eighteen, Uncle Toli built him an enclosed shed beside the chicken coop and furnished it with a sink, a small portable gas stove, a bed, a table and chairs. Later Angelo added a rabbit pen and two kennels for his dogs, Drago and Spiroula, who patrolled the area for foxes. The shed became his retreat and eventual home, sleeping at his mother's house only during winter.

Koula adored Angelo. Over time, her love for him surpassed her feelings for Kyriako, whose aggression swelled in his teens. Tantrums and blasphemous language had become a daily occurrence in the household. Having inherited most of his father's characteristics, she found it hard to show him affection. Sometimes she wished she had left him with her in-laws back on Rhodes, who had been more than happy to take him.

Both boys shared Tsambiko's thick eyebrows and aquiline nose. Like his father, Kyriako was thin and dark-skinned with beady black eyes, while Angelo was a chubby child with plum cheeks and big blue eyes. Kyriako had never questioned why his younger brother looked so different, assuming it was because of his autism.

Kyriako's behaviour worsened after learning he couldn't live with his father on Rhodes. Since his release from jail, Tsambiko had remarried and had three daughters and wanted nothing to do with his sons. When Koula broke the news to him, he was so enraged that he grabbed a saucepan and threw it at her, blaming her for denying him a father. Angelo, who was nine at the time, didn't escape his wrath. He was tossed across the floor so forcefully that he smashed against the doorframe and dislocated his shoulder. With Koula's permission, Policeman Harry detained Kyriako at the police station for a few days, but it did little to dilute his anger.

After completing his military service at nineteen, Kyriako took his anger to the mainland. Rumours circulated that he had mingled with the wrong crowd and become a heroin addict. After several failed attempts to get money from his mother, he vanished. Two years later, he was found dead from an overdose. Despite the relentless bullying, Angelo was inconsolable when he saw his brother's pale, thin, blue body lying in the coffin. The more Koula tried to calm him, the more aggressive he became. Some of the men had to carry him screaming out of the church.

***

When Margarita returned to Greece in 1990, she and Koula deliberated on how to tell Angelo the truth about his biological mother. They agreed it was time; he was twenty-one, after all. Their concern was the level of detail to divulge, given how he processed things. How do you explain such violence to a child who interprets the world so literally?

Koula had lived with a constant fear that Angelo might uncover the truth on his own, and he didn't take being lied to lightly. Years earlier, when Kyriako blurted out that Koula's blond hair wasn't natural, Angelo had hurled a rockmelon at her in a fit of rage. The shock of his actions, the heartbreak in his eyes, had shaken both Koula and Kyriako. Since then, Koula was careful about what she told Angelo and learned to be more honest.

When it came to his father, she never disguised the truth. She told Angelo plainly that the man was evil and should have stayed in jail forever. Having never met him, his father occupied no space in his head. But the golden egg—that lie had been planted a long time ago, before she had learned her lesson.

Angelo hardly knew Margarita, though Koula had spoken of her over the years, describing her as a beautiful aunt who lived far away. So when Margarita arrived for lunch at Koula's soon after returning to the island, Angelo's excitement was immediate and unrestrained. He embraced her and kissed her cheeks again and again.

Margarita was taken aback for a moment. She had seen photos of him over the years, but meeting him, seeing him grown, twenty years later, was overwhelming. Fortunately, he didn't resemble Tsambiko and looked more like a fuller, softer version of Emilio. At one point she excused herself and slipped into the bathroom, gripping the sink as she steadied her breath. She felt no regret, just a mix of sadness for all that had unfolded and happiness that Koula and Angelo loved each other deeply. She returned to Koula and Angelo, composed and cheerful.

Once Angelo had eaten, Margarita and Koula sat on either side of him, each holding their son's hand. Koula spoke first.

'Angelo, my darling son. I want to tell you something about our family.'

'Yes, Mama. Tell me, please,' he said, rocking gently as he always did.

'After Kyriako was born, I couldn't have any more babies.'

Angelo looked at her, confused, then nodded his head from side to side and screwed up his face.

'Your Thia Margarita was so kind that she gave me her baby. That baby was you, Angelo. You were her gift to me!'

'I was a gift?' he asked, rubbing his hands together.

'Yes, you were my baby,' Margarita said. 'You grew in my tummy, and when you came out, I gave you to Koula…your mother.'

Angelo studied Margarita's face, then Koula's, touching their cheeks with gentle, curious fingers. His gaze shifted to their bellies, as though trying to understand how a baby could fit inside. Finally he pointed to Koula and declared, 'Mama!' and then to Margarita, 'Thia!' before bursting into laughter and clapping. When his amusement faded, he asked to go back to his shed for his siesta. Kissing them both, he stood, rubbed his belly, and left. Koula and Margarita exchanged a look of unspoken relief and agreed never to mention the subject again.

Of the three Politis children, only Aphrodite knew the truth about Angelo. When she announced she was pregnant with Father Nicholas's child, Margarita—torn between fear, shame and love—reached for the only leverage she had left. In a moment of crisis, she laid bare the secret she had hidden from her children. But it backfired. Aphrodite reacted with hysteria, fury and disgust at what her mother had endured, yet the revelation only strengthened her resolve to keep the baby. Sympathetic but determined, Aphrodite swore to keep Angelo's origins from her brothers—to protect him from a truth he could never make sense of.

***

Angelo found his mother's body sprawled on the kitchen floor when he got back from his egg run. The night before, he'd celebrated his forty-first birthday with her. At first he thought she had fallen asleep and hurried to fetch a pillow and blanket. He knew something was wrong when he saw her eyes wide open and felt her cold skin. He picked her up in his arms, ran into the village square yelling for help, then collapsed under the platanus tree with Koula in his arms. The villagers tried to pry Koula's body from him, but he wouldn't let her go to anyone but a doctor. When he finally arrived, he confirmed she had been dead for hours. Angelo screamed so loudly that the peacocks and dogs in the village joined in, and all the villagers ran from their homes, fearing an earthquake. Angelo was sedated, taken to the clinic and restrained. When he returned home a few days later, Margarita moved in with him.

For forty days, Angelo refused to eat or leave the house. Margarita was convinced he would die of starvation. He had always loved food, and his appetite was enormous. Within weeks he had lost most of his body fat and became unrecognisable. The doctor had called, concerned about the missed cardiology appointment; Angelo had lived with pericarditis for years. Still he refused to go. The chickens were neglected, and some of the rabbits died. Mihalis threatened to give the animals away if Angelo didn't resume his responsibilities, but Margarita convinced him to wait until after the forty-day memorial service. If Angelo didn't snap out of it, he would need to be committed to a facility in Mytilene.

There was only so much Margarita could do. She wanted to go back to her husband, who was struggling to handle thirteen-year-old Dimitri as well as manage the hotel. At that time, Emilio was away doing his national service and Aphrodite was in Berlin. She was also worried about the lump she had just discovered in her breast. It had been there for about a week, and it wasn't getting any smaller. She didn't want to tell the family until she was back at home.

While collecting eggs one morning, Margarita recalled the golden egg story and Koula's regret for ever mentioning it to Angelo.

'I curse myself every day for saying such a thing! Every evening, he asks why the golden egg hasn't yet arrived. All I can say is that he just needs to be patient. I can't tell him the truth. He'd kill me. Thank goodness Kyriako knew nothing about it, or all hell would have broken out. Angelo is good with secrets. I told him the golden egg is a special secret between us.'

Margarita rang Aphrodite in Berlin and asked if any of her art colleagues could help. Aphrodite quickly arranged for her boyfriend to sculpt a metal egg and cover it with gold-leaf paint. A few days before Koula's memorial service, the golden egg arrived in the post. Once the church service was over, Margarita persuaded Angelo to follow her to the chicken coop.

'I promise you, the most incredible surprise awaits you.'

Once they had entered the coop, she asked him to close his eyes. She eased the golden egg from her pocket, placing it in one of the empty boxes.

'Open your eyes, Angelo. Look what I found this morning while collecting your eggs.'

Angelo recoiled; his mouth flew open, his jaw quivering. Once he realised it was a golden egg, a big, beautiful smile spread across his face. Stepping forward, he carefully picked up the egg, weighed it in his hands, and became very excited.

'Which chicken laid it?' he asked.

'I don't know, I just saw it there, alone in the box.'

'But Mama said the golden egg would appear only if I looked after my chickens. But I haven't. I've been very bad,' he cried.

'This special egg is a reminder from your mother that the chickens need you.'

It was another lie, but Margarita was desperate. 'You must tell no one about the golden egg. Many bad people would love an egg like this. It would make them very rich. You must hide it somewhere in the house where no one will ever find it. This special egg is only for you.'

The plan worked perfectly. Angelo hid the egg in a lockable box under his bed. The key to the lock hung from his mother's gold neck chain, which he proudly wore and never took off. His obsession with the chickens returned, as did his appetite, and he was back on the streets of Melissani selling eggs. Margarita returned to the resort, paid a neighbour to wash his clothes and then travelled to Athens for breast cancer treatment. A few years later, she arranged through Hossein for Kurush to clean the house, shed and chicken coop. The two would become the best of friends, or at least that's what Angelo would tell the villagers.

CHAPTER 25
Aphrodite's villa, September 2015

Emilio entered Aphrodite's courtyard armed with a tray of galaktoboureko. It was early morning, and the place seemed deserted. The amber leaves of the maple tree rustled as a light autumn breeze swept through. It had been a while since his last visit, and he was struck by the scent of wildflowers. The imposing backdrop of Mount Dilinos glowed under the rising sun, its surface textured like cracked leather.

During his last visit, customers spilled out of the café while Aphrodite fielded inquiries about her art. He was proud of his sister. She had done well—not only with her career but also with the villa and her daughter. And now that she and Hossein were together, he noticed a change: quieter in her confidence, less showy, more considerate.

He had timed his visit to avoid Rika, who was on the school bus he'd passed halfway down the mountain. His niece had grown clingier since the capsizing, according to Aphrodite. The last thing he wanted was to scare her. Even if she hadn't seen him, someone would have spotted him walking from the car park to the villa. News would spread quickly.

Emilio had come to tell his sister that Dimitri had attempted to take his life. His mother had taken the call at midnight. Frantic, she pounded on his door, crying. Once he was able to calm her, his father appeared at his doorway looking furious. Emilio shared his feelings only to realise the anger was directed at Dimitri's sergeant rather than his brother.

'I told that malaka not to place him back on his former duties,' his father shouted. 'The fucking moron ignored me!'

'Shut up, Mihalis. That's all too late now. Focus on your son's crisis!' she yelled at him.

Turning to Emilio, she asked him to drive up to Melissani in the morning and tell Aphrodite in person, once Rika left for school.

Aphrodite and Dimitri were very close—closer than Emilio was with either of them. Their brother had become a sore point between the siblings, and the reunion after returning to the island had been far from harmonious. Observing Dimitri's low self-esteem and withdrawal further alienated Emilio, reinforcing his conviction that the women in his family were to blame for his morose disposition.

He just needed to stay calm. The news had thrown him. Lately, everything had been going smoothly. The August heat had eased, as had the crowds. He and Maryam were talking more—sometimes on their own, more often over coffee at his mother's place. The slight downtime had given him room to focus on the upcoming expo, and he'd begun to feel he was getting on top of things. But Dimitri's suffocating sense of victimhood had knocked everything off balance. *If only Dimitri had been at Christopher's funeral he might have thought twice before trying to kill himself.* But Emilio kept having to remind himself that Dimitri had only just been born when Christopher took his life.

When Emilio arrived on the island in 1990, nine-year-old Christopher immediately claimed him. To Christopher, his young Australian cousin was the closest blood tie to his dead twin, Kostaki. On Emilio's first day of school, Christopher marched him through the gates, proudly introducing him to everyone as if he was something precious. Feeling embarrassed and struggling with the language, Emilio felt himself implode. Whatever confidence he had was gone; he had become his cousin's security blanket, if not his prisoner. By the end of the first week at school, Emilio ran home and burst into tears.

Resigned to the fact that he would never return to his corner shop in Sydenham, he locked his bedroom door, flipped his bed upside down and threw his clothes from the wardrobe onto the floor. He refused to talk to his parents banging on the door, screaming at them to leave him alone.

Later that evening, once he had settled, he allowed his grandmother in. Yiayia Freda was an accomplice to his deportation but not a major player like his parents, so he was willing to hear her out. He was also starving, and she had come with a plate of his favourite dish, pasticcio. Frail but still strong, she helped him tidy the room and put his clothes back in place. She didn't come to lecture or console him; he hardly knew her. But when she sat by his bed and sang an old song, something in him loosened. He didn't understand the words, but the intensity of her tone and the tears welling in her eyes struck him so deeply. He reached over and held her wrinkled hand. He still remembered the phrase she said that night: «Εκεί που είσαι, ήμουν· και εκεί που είμαι, θα έρθεις»—*Where you are, I was; and where I am, you will come.*

Seven-year-old Emilio was overwhelmed by the changes forced onto him—not just the new location and culture but the sheer intensity of his relatives' affection. The relentless kisses and hugs from his Uncle Toli and Aunt Freda made him squirm. At times he stared at his mother, silently begging to be rescued. They weren't strangers, but they may as well have been.

Christopher's affection was no easier to escape; he was forever holding Emilio's hand, demanding to know his every move. But after a few weeks, Emilio found himself more at ease and less self-conscious. It was as though a part of him that had long resisted physical closeness had been unlocked.

Tall for his age and athletic, Christopher had long blond hair that reminded Emilio of the Aussie kids who came into Citizens

Corner Shop for lollies. Hyperactive and fast-talking, he often left Emilio scrambling to keep up. Uncle Toli urged him to slow down, but Christopher just laughed, at times mocking his father for being too controlling. Accepting that Emilio was here to stay, his grip on him eased. After a few months, Emilio was in awe of him. Christopher's boisterous nature and comic flair kept Emilio entertained; tears of sadness gave way to tears of hysterics. He even helped with Emilio's new hobby of collecting animals, proudly rescuing a tortoise, a kid, three kittens and a couple of toads.

The guilt of not sharing his brother's cancer had, however, led Christopher down a path of self-destruction. Most days he wore a black armband and occasionally dressed in Kostaki's clothes, which had become too small for him. Fearless and erratic, he kept everyone on edge, lashing out at his parents or climbing dangerously high trees. Once the fire brigade retrieved him from the roof of the school hall. There was some hope that Emilio's presence would calm him, and for a while, it did.

In the spring of 1996, during the paniyiri at the old monastery at Melissani, the boys were playing hide-and-seek. It was Emilio's turn to hide. Under a pew, he waited patiently until he realised Christopher hadn't even tried to look for him. Panicked, Emilio went searching for him. Walking along the track towards the cliffs, he turned the corner to find Christopher standing at the edge of the viewing platform.

'Why didn't you come and find me?' Emilio called out.

But Christopher didn't respond. He just stood there, swaying. 'I've always had this dream that I'm flying,' he finally said, back turned. 'If I flap hard enough, I will lift into the air. I love you, cousin.' He then raised his elbows to the side, vigorously moved them up and down and stepped over the edge.

The image would stay with Emilio forever. The helplessness that seized him had paralysed him. He couldn't scream for help or plead to Christopher to fly back. All he felt was the sensation of his heart falling to the ground. When he finally managed to move, he crawled to the edge, hoping to see Christopher soaring. But there was only emptiness—a void—not even a bird, just the blue horizon where sea blended into sky. Looking down, he saw his cousin's body lying face down, blood oozing from his head.

Emilio clung to the sharp ledge so tightly that it broke skin. When the pain finally registered, a scream burst out, alerting the dogs and the peacocks. Alone and terrified, he stayed there, bawling.

At Christopher's funeral, Emilio was struck by how brave Aphrodite was. She wore a black dress, a colour he wasn't used to seeing her in. It didn't suit her, making her look older. She was only nine at the time and, until then, had been an annoying little sister. But as she gripped his hand and checked on him with those big, sad eyes, he felt an overwhelming responsibility to shield her from the outpouring of grief surrounding them. But he was powerless. Shame overcame him for appearing so weak and pathetic. He focused on her to distract himself from the hysteria. Never had he experienced such public displays of emotion. Only his mother remained calm, surprisingly composed for someone who had given birth only a few weeks earlier.

***

Emilio wandered around the courtyard, imagining it before his grandfather left his tinkering trade to run a kafenio down by the port. Some of the old tools had been repurposed as pots; others cleverly turned into sculptures. Among them stood a water feature crafted from old rusty water cans that drip-fed into each other. He'd never noticed it before or taken the time to congratulate Aphrodite on the villa.

Expecting to find her painting, he tried the studio door at the back of the villa, but it was locked. Through the window he saw three large unfinished canvases. The central one was the most complete, showing a figure in a cream tunic, perhaps a man, looking over his shoulder. A flute was tucked in the pocket against his chest. Emilio wasn't used to seeing solitary figures on such a large scale in his sister's art. It then occurred to him that it resembled Kurush.

Returning to the front of the villa, Emilio looked through the café's glass door, but it was all dark.

'Aphrodite!' he called as he entered the front door. Floorboards creaked upstairs, and then the patter of feet.

'Emilio?' she called out.

'Yes, it's me!'

Entering the kitchen, he placed the galaktoboureko on the bench and sat at the table. He was glad Aphrodite had preserved the old rustic kitchen as it was. It was spacious, the ornate leaded-glass windows filtering coloured light across the dark-wood cabinetry and galley. Two coffee cups rested on the porcelain counter. A smoky arabica lingered in the air. He doubted Aphrodite would serve Rika coffee.

'What are you doing here? What's wrong?' she asked as she entered the kitchen. She wore a crimson satin robe, her hair slightly tousled. Rarely did he see her without make-up.

'Were you still in bed?'

'I was just getting ready. Running a little behind this morning. Hmm, I can smell galaktoboureko.'

'Express delivery.'

'I thought Mum was dropping it off later.' She pulled the chair up opposite him and sat down, looking a little flustered. 'What's with the beard?'

'Nothing, just growing it.'

'Never seen you with a beard this long before.'

'Does it matter?'

'No, but I'm not sure if I like it. You don't look like Emilio.'

'Emilio? Who's that?'

'Hilarious.'

'All prepared for the expo?'

It had been a hectic time, but the expo was fully registered, and accommodation in Kamiros was at capacity. Aphrodite was also hosting a workshop on colour and form as part of the program.

There was a sudden thud followed by more sounds of creaking floorboards.

'Hossein, please come down,' Aphrodite called.

'Hossein?'

'Yes. Hossein's here with me.'

Emilio raised his eyebrows and gave her a cheeky grin. 'Well, well, well!'

A somewhat embarrassed Hossein stumbled into the kitchen and offered his hand to Emilio. He was dressed in last night's clothes, his shirt slightly crumpled. They fumbled a handshake.

'Hi, Hossein.'

'How are you doing, Emilio?'

Emilio still couldn't get over how posh and English he sounded.

'Why are you here, Emilio?' Aphrodite asked. 'Is Mum sick or something? Is that why she can't get here?'

'Dimitri.'

'What about him?'

'Mum received a call last night. He tried to kill himself.'

The chair screeched against the marble floor as Aphrodite shot up. 'Tried, you said?'

'Yes, he's okay. He's in hospital. He cut his wrists, but one of the other soldiers found him in time.'

'Did you speak to him?'

'No, his sergeant spoke to Mum last night.'

'Oh my God! I should go. Unless Mum is, but I don't think that's a good idea. Are you going? Should I go? Baba? Someone needs to go now!'

Emilio cut her short. 'Pandelis is going.'

'Pandelis?'

A few seconds of silence followed. She sat down. Hossein placed his hand on Aphrodite's shoulders, gently massaging her through the satin robe.

'So what happens now? Can I call him? Fucking army! And of all the places to be posted…Idomeni! Shit! I want to call him now. Hossein, could you please grab my mobile?'

Hossein hurried off to the bedroom upstairs.

'Mum's already called him.'

'What about you?' Aphrodite asked.

'What about me?'

'Have you called him yet?

'I thought we could do it together.'

She stared at him, disappointed. He was expecting a scene but was surprised at how still and calm she stayed. A single tear traced down her cheek. He would have preferred if she reached across and choked him. She made him feel like shit.

'He's your brother!'

Hossein rushed back into the kitchen with the phone. She took it and put it in the pocket of her robe.

'Call him. Call him now, Emilio!' Her voice quavered.

'He doesn't want to hear from me. It'll just make him feel worse.'

'That depends on how you talk to him.'

He knew exactly what she meant. Deep down, he just wanted to shout at Dimitri and tell him how angry he was. Apart from the family lunch when he visited in August, the only other time he spoke to him was at Eva's office when they signed the agreement finalising the allocation of Uncle Toli's estate. Dimitri would receive 70,000 euros from Emilio for the car rental land, giving Emilio full ownership of all the resort properties. 'Do you know why he asked Pandelis to go to him?' asked Emilio.

Aphrodite gave him a death stare. 'Probably because he loves him.'

'What's that supposed to mean?'

'Oh, come on, Emilio, stop playing dumb. Your brother is gay, and he has a boyfriend. Stop pussyfooting around. Get off your high horse and call him!' She was yelling now. That was more like her, and he felt better.

Emilio stepped out into the courtyard to make the call. Sparrows flitted below the old olive tree in the corner of the courtyard. Finding a stale muffin under the outdoor wicker chair, he broke it up and threw it towards the birds. He knew he was stalling. When it came to his brother, he always did.

The behavioural similarities between Christopher and Dimitri became more evident to Emilio as Dimitri entered his teens. The vacant stares and long silences were all too familiar. Emilio kept his distance because he couldn't bear to relive another suicide. But something had changed; perhaps his sister's outburst had cracked open some space for compassion to seep in.

'Hi. How are you going?' Emilio spoke gently, using a chirpy tone. 'Are you okay, Dimitri? It's me, Emilio.'

'Hi, Emilio.'

Silence followed, and then the sound of sniffling turning into a torrent of grief.

Emilio sensed a lump forming in his throat and momentarily felt queasy. He sat down on one of the garden chairs and found the strength to say, 'It will be okay, Dimitri. I love you, no matter what.'

Emilio was not used to hearing his brother express anything other than grunts and silence. His outpouring of pain hit Emilio hard.

'I'm sorry, Dimitri. We'll get you home soon. Pandelis is on his way. He's a good man. I like him a lot. Everything will be good again, I promise.'

After he hung up, Emilio pulled a handkerchief from his pocket and wiped his nose. He decided to text Pandelis. Check on him. See if he needed anything. Watching the young journalist work tirelessly through the rescue, preparing the bodies, attending the funerals, writing articles that were sensitive and compassionate, had altered Emilio's view of him. He just never said so until now.

The loud creaking of the iron gate interrupted him. It was Angelo Poulos carrying his basket of eggs, calling out at the top of his voice: 'Aphrodite, your eggs!'

Angelo froze when he saw Emilio standing near the olive tree. The men had hardly seen each other in years.

'Hello, Angelo,' Emilio said as Angelo checked him out from head to toe. 'Yes, it's me, Emilio.'

'Hello, Emilio. You look different. You've got a beard.'

'Yes, that's right. You look the same.'

'I don't like it!' Angelo interrupted. 'You look old.'

'Yes, well, you look fat and ugly!' Emilio replied.

'What the fuck, Emilio?' Aphrodite yelled, overhearing the exchange as she came outside.

Emilio regretted his words. He'd forgotten how sensitive Angelo could be. 'I am so sorry, Angelo. I didn't mean it.'

'What the hell has gotten into you?' she said, trying to calm Angelo, taking his hand and rubbing his shoulder. Angelo started to pant and wanted to leave.

'Angelo, forgive me,' Emilio said as he took some cash from his wallet and placed a fifty-euro note in Angelo's hand before heading towards the gate.

'Where are you going?' his sister called out after him.

'Going to check in on Pandelis,' he replied as he exited the villa. He was so angry with himself and couldn't bear his sister's look of shame any longer.

PART 6
EDEN LOST

CHAPTER 26
Ancient Tallos Archaeological Museum, October 2015

Hossein called Kurush's mobile numerous times, but it kept ringing out. He checked with the rest of the staff, but no one had heard from him. Kurush had taken up casual work at the museum only weeks earlier, filling in after another guard resigned. He had proved to be diligent, punctual and very popular. Because of the expo, he had been rostered on most days. Three days had now passed since he disappeared.

Kyra Katina called again. 'He didn't come home again last night. I've been worried sick. He's been going out at night a lot lately.'

'Did he say where?' Hossein asked.

'To one of the bars at Kamiros. I worry about him drinking and driving that old motorbike.'

'He's a Muslim. I doubt he'd be drinking,' Hossein said.

She hesitated. 'I told Harry, but he said I was being silly, that I am not his mother. That he's out with his friends or a girlfriend.'

As far as Hossein knew, Kurush didn't have many friends other than the museum staff, Aphrodite and Angelo. That morning, Aphrodite asked Angelo about him during his egg run, but he said he hadn't seen him for days.

Dimitri Politis had also offered his services. He had heard from Aphrodite about the museum's staffing issues and said crowd control was his area of training. At least at the museum he wouldn't be dealing with desperate migrants; besides, he had a genuine interest in history. Aphrodite thought it was a good idea, one that might help him regain his footing. Hossein agreed. His first day, the day before, had gone very well, much to Manos's delight.

***

The call from Harry came in just after midday. Hossein immediately sensed something horrible.

'Hossein, kalimera. It's Harry Minas.'

'Harry, hello.'

'We found Kurush's body near the museum on Odos Nymphaion. An old shepherd herding his goats found him. Looks like he's been there for a couple of days.'

'Body?'

'Yes, he's dead. It appears that he was murdered.'

He had expected to hear 'accident'—but murder? 'Why?' he managed. 'Who?'

'We'll let you know as soon as we find out more. Can you please download all CCTV footage from the last few days.'

'Of course.'

'Can you assist with the funeral?'

'Yes, yes…Your mother? Have you told her?'

'Going to see her now. If by chance she calls, don't say anything.' The phone went dead.

Hossein felt sick to the stomach. He began to shake and sat down to consider his next move. Who to tell? Should he close the museum? He called Aphrodite.

'I can't believe anyone would do such a thing,' she said, her voice breaking up as she tried to remain calm for his sake.

'It's so unjust,' he said, unable to control his tears. 'Of all people—to survive all that he's been through, and, finally, when life starts for him again, it's taken away in such a despicable way. Such a fucking waste.'

'Come to the villa, Hossein,' she pleaded.

He wanted nothing more. 'I can't. I need to tell the staff. Coaches are due in a couple of hours.'

'Cancel them.'

'I need to think this through,' he said, then paused. 'What if it's my fault?' he blurted out.

'What do you mean?'

'By giving him a job, by not giving the role to a local. Maybe I'm next.'

'Stop that, Hossein. None of this is your fault. None of it! This community needs you. What you did was honourable, decent and appropriate. You should do it again a million times.'

Hossein took a moment to absorb her words. 'I have to let his mother and sister know. When I offered him the job, he rang them on his mobile in front of me, wanting me to hear their joy. He told them he would soon help them leave Iran. Allah, give me strength!'

There was a knock at the door.

'Someone's here. I've got to go. I'll call you later.'

'I love you, Hossein.'

'I love you too.'

The knocking grew louder. It was Salome, looking frazzled. Her normally coiffured hair lay flat, her usual heavy make-up reduced to a paler shade of pink lipstick.

'Hossein, I'm losing my mind. Have you heard from Kurush?'

'Come in. Sit down.'

'There's only a handful of people in the museum. I've pulled down the shop's shutters. I hope you don't mind. I just don't know what to do.'

'It's okay. I was going to ask you to come in anyway.'

She sat down, pulled a fold-up fan from her sleeve and fanned her flustered face. 'What should we do? This is so out of character!'

'I have some bad news, I'm afraid. Kurush's body was discovered this morning. Someone killed him.'

The fan stopped mid-air. Her jaw dropped, and her eyes welled with tears. She shot up from the chair and screeched, 'Panayia mou! Panayia mou!'

Hossein jumped. Anyone in the museum would certainly have heard her. He snatched the box of tissues from the top of the filing cabinet and tried to console her. Instinctively, he reached for her, but as soon as she felt his touch, she flung his hand away.

'I am not worthy. It's my fault, Hossein. It's my fault he's dead!'

She moved to the opposite corner and sat on the floor, sobbing.

Manos, the security guard, hammered at the door. 'Is everything alright in there, Doctor Hossein?'

Hossein stepped outside into the hallway.

'What's going on?' Manos asked in a panic. 'Did someone attack Salome?'

'Manos, close the museum. Escort the remaining tourists out, call the bus company and tell them that the museum will be closed today. Say it's because of a family emergency.'

'Is it a bomb?'

'No, it's not…It's Kurush.'

'Kurush? Is he alright?' he asked anxiously.

'He's dead. I am sorry to tell you like this, but please, close the museum now! And download all CCTV footage from the last few days for Harry Minas.'

With that order, Manos took off. Hossein, feeling terrible, regretted speaking so sharply to his staff. He returned to his office and slumped into his chair while Salome sobbed, facing the wall like a child sent to the corner.

'Where did they find him?' she asked.

'Not far from here. Near the forest track.'

'Vasili, ti ekanes? Ti ekanes vre ilithie? Skotoses to palikari mou!' Salome yelled, rocking back and forth, before turning to face Hossein. 'Vasilis killed him. The bastard! she shouted. 'Vasilis left the island yesterday. Call Harry!'

Hossein dialled Harry. His hands shook as he tried to hold the phone to his ear, confusion battering his head. The call went to voicemail. 'Harry, call me. Salome Kapakis has some vital information on Kurush.'

'At least my brother, Toli, isn't here to bear my shame. We're cursed, you know. You must protect Aphrodite. She's a wild spirit with a beautiful heart and mind. It's this bloody island that destroys us. Take her away from here.'

Hossein, at a loss for words, just wanted to leave the room. 'I need to help Manos lock up. I'll be back soon.'

***

Once all the tourists were escorted out, Hossein told Manos what Harry Drivas had said on the phone, making no mention of Salome's accusation.

'Why would someone want to kill him? He's just a kid!' Manos said, tears streaking his face.

'The police don't have any details. For now, just go home.'

'But what about Dimitri? He'll be here soon.'

'Please call him and tell him he won't be needed today. I've already cancelled this afternoon's tour. Can you inform the rest of the staff, please, and send them home.'

Hossein ran into one of the storerooms, closed the door behind him and rang his mother.

'Hello, son,' she answered.

'Hi, Mum. Are you okay?'

'Of course I am, Hossein. What's the matter? Why are you calling me in the middle of the day?'

'Sorry, I've had some awful news about one of my staff and I just wanted to call you.'

'Oh, I am so sorry, son.'

He broke down as he told her about Kurush.

'When we first arrived in England, did you believe I was depressed?' he asked.

A long silence followed. 'We both were. We had been through so much.'

'I know, I know, but when we finally settled into Birmingham, were we happy? Kurush seemed so happy. Was I like that?'

'Eventually, yes, I suppose.'

'Did you think it was worth it?'

'You mean us fleeing?'

'Yes.'

'Of course. I can't imagine life had we remained. I give thanks every day.'

'I hope Kurush felt the same way, despite all that's happened.'

'If he worked with you then I guarantee you he would have.'

'But I couldn't protect him.'

She paused. 'I may no longer follow the scriptures, but I do recall something from the Quran: "No bearer of burdens will bear the burden of another." Your grandmother repeated those words to me over and over when your father was taken from us.'

Hossein knew the phrase well, but hearing his mother recite it now felt like a revelation.

'How do I break the news to his mother?'

'Sincerely and to the point. Don't hold back your sadness. Make her understand he was loved.'

Hossein stepped outside for air. The rumbling wheels of a tourist bus dispersed dust into the air as it departed. Looking around at the dry terrain, he saw clouds forming in the distance. He longed for rain to wash away the grime accumulated over the long, dry summer. His phone rang; he thought it was Harry but it was his publisher. Good news—they would publish Hossein's paper on Nicephorus in the new year. He wished he could have been more excited. He thought of the young slave who, at his peak, left a remarkable legacy: storming through the streets as the city burned, seeking refuge in a forest sanctuary only to perish under the rubble of a once beautiful and cosmopolitan society.

***

Hossein sat as a witness during Harry's interview with Salome. What unfolded devastated him. Doubt about his future on the island seized him. Yes, he was panicking, but more so about Aphrodite, the woman he had fallen in love with. How could he possibly leave? Trying hard not to catastrophise the situation, he couldn't help but think of the repercussions such a murder could have for him, the museum and Phaedros.

'Vasilis must have found out about us. In the last week he was making vile comments about Muslim men beheading adulterous wives. One afternoon I came home to the radio blaring Middle Eastern music. That night, he kept changing the TV channel to a Saudi Arabian series. I suspected he knew something, but I never told Kurush.'

Salome launched into a rant about her loneliness, describing her husband of twenty years as a 'lazy, impotent ratbag who couldn't provide her with children'. They hadn't slept together for over ten years. Having left him once, she stupidly returned. 'I adore Kurush. He was more of a man than my husband ever was. He listened to me, loved me and made me feel good about myself!'

Hossein couldn't help but feel that in helping Kurush, he had led him into a predator's mouth.

***

Later that evening, Hossein conducted the funeral over the phone with the mufti in Mytilene. Since Kurush had no family, the burial was not delayed, and he was laid to rest beside his cousin. The only attendees were Salome, Aphrodite and Harry. Kyra Katina was too distressed to go and stayed home. Angelo had not yet been informed.

That night, lying in bed together, Aphrodite and Hossein spoke of Salome, only because they couldn't bear to speak of Kurush.

'She had quite the reputation, and rumours had been floating around for years about her infidelities. None of it was true, though she did have an affair years ago with a plasterer who had worked on the museum renovations. She told me herself. I didn't say anything to my mother, of course—their relationship was strained.'

'What happened? If you don't mind me asking.'

'My mother refused to give her Dimitri.'

'What do you mean?'

'Salome couldn't have children. Dimitri would have been her only chance—her sister's child.'

'That's a big ask.'

'Of course it is, but not without merit. It's not uncommon in these small communities for a family to share children should the circumstances warrant it.'

'That's so sad. How's your mother handling this news?'

'Another obstacle in her life that she'll overcome, no doubt. But she's happy about Dimitri. She said that after his first shift yesterday, he came home a different person.'

'Dimitri has been a godsend.'

'I'm so glad to hear. Emilio, on the other hand, is freaking out.'

'I'm not surprised.'

'He's been in crisis talks with his comms team all night. Pandelis has been briefed by Harry, and by morning, news will be out.'

'When are you going to tell Rika?' Hossein asked

'I couldn't do it tonight. After dropping her off at the resort to attend the burial, I just wasn't in the right state. I will do it tomorrow after she returns from school.'

'Did Emilio ask about Dimitri? I mean, I hope he's fine with it.'

'He did. He thinks it's a great move.'

'I just hope putting Dimitri back in a uniform hasn't stirred anything up.'

'He sounded genuinely happy when I spoke to him last night. He even mentioned enrolling in a history degree. He thinks very highly of you.'

'I'd be happy to mentor him.'

Looking through Aphrodite's bedroom window, Hossein noticed a halo encircling the full moon—a sign of rain, someone once told him. He closed his eyes, desperate for sleep, but all he could think about was the two young men who had recently stepped into his life: one born into abundance, the other denied even the chance to live.

CHAPTER 27
Paradisos II resort, the following day

Maryam loaded her trolley with fresh towels and sheets from the linen room. A sudden sneeze took hold of her. She pressed the back of her hand to her forehead but felt no fever. Perhaps the scent of lavender from the deodoriser, a scent she was no longer partial to. Whatever it was, she didn't feel right.

The past week's Beauty and Wellness Expo had been a major undertaking. A huge success, according to Emilio, but the aftermath was being felt by all those involved. She had hardly seen him, just texts and late-night calls to check on her and apologise for the workload. But the busier she was, the better she felt—except for that morning. She couldn't pinpoint the unease; she just needed to get started. There were still a few minutes before her 7 a.m. start.

She pulled a tissue from her pocket as her mobile vibrated against her hand. A missed call from Emilio flashed on the screen. It was strange that he should call so early. She called back, but it went straight to voicemail. Her stomach fluttered. Out in the corridor, she could hear Anna talking to Lorenzo, the grounds supervisor. Anna's last day had finally arrived, and Maryam suspected that their lively exchange was about her farewell party. Maryam had been dreading this day. They had become such good friends.

'What's going on?' Maryam asked, poking her head out of the door. Lorenzo waved, smiled and walked away. The short, spritely Italian seemed distracted. Usually he'd greet her each morning in

Italian—'Buongiorno, signora'—but this time there was nothing but a wave. Anna looked pale as a ghost.

'What is it?' Maryam called out. Anna remained silent and gently took her by the elbow. 'Where are we going?'

'To the staffroom. There's a special meeting,' Anna replied.

Maryam felt her gut churn as a slight chill brushed against the back of her neck. Autumn had arrived, and the first rain overnight had infused the air with a musty scent. Dark clouds cast a dim light across the resort. The long summer was over. She was still on the island. She was still alive.

'What was Lorenzo saying to you?' she asked Anna.

'It's about the young man who was with you on the boat.'

'Kurush?'

'Yes, that's him.'

'What about him?'

'Apparently he was missing for the last couple of days. They found his body yesterday.'

Maryam jerked her arm back and stopped in her tracks. 'Ya Allah! What happened?'

'Come—we will find out.'

Maryam remembered Kurush as the young man who had dived into the sea to retrieve a stuffed toy belonging to a young boy. It was just as the storm hit, a thunderclap so loud it seemed the sea beneath them might explode. Everyone screamed at him to swim back. They were two hours into their voyage, with no land in sight. Bassel helped Kurush climb back on board, toy in hand.

Kurush visited Maryam just before her discharge from the clinic. He was holding Bassel's oud which he had retrieved from the sea. He remembered her husband playing it for the children that day in the olive field.

'Your husband was very good to me. I tried cleaning it and waited for it to dry. I think you should have it now.'

Maryam took the instrument in her arms and cradled it like a baby, rocking it gently. She thanked him profusely before he quietly slipped away, repeating, 'God be with you, God be with you.'

The television blared loudly as they entered the staffroom. At the centre, a square table was covered with fruit bowls, pastries and magazines—leftovers from the expo. Maryam overheard colleagues murmuring as they gathered in front of the wall-mounted flatscreen. Images of Kurush's passport photo flickered past followed by footage of the museum and an olive grove.

Maryam recognised the journalist addressing the camera—Pandelis, the young man who helped her with the visa permits. He'd wanted to interview her after the rescue, but she couldn't go through with it. On screen, he appeared larger and taller, his face tense as he pushed up his round glasses. He spoke so quickly that she couldn't understand him.

'What's he saying?' she asked Anna.

'He was murdered!'

'Murdered? Ya elahi!' Maryam felt her knees give way. Anna pulled out a chair for her. She now understood why Emilio was trying to call her.

Lorenzo walked in with his usual authoritarian stride followed by three of his garden staff. 'Okay, okay, okay. Can I have everyone's attention, please?'

He grabbed the remote from the table, turned the volume down, hopped onto a chair and cleared his throat as he smoothed down his thick moustache. Maryam noticed sweat glistening on his bald head. She liked Lorenzo but not his management style, preferring Mihalis's more relaxed approach.

'As you now know, Kurush Bassem was found murdered yesterday in an olive grove near the museum,' Lorenzo said. 'Over the next few days, news crews will be returning, while others are still here from the expo. Fortunately, none will be staying at the resort, but they may come here for a drink or to eat. They will be…

how you say? Snooping, si, snooping for information and asking many questions. Please don't say anything. If they insist, just say, "I know nothing." This is very important. Do you all understand? Comprende? The police said that the man who killed Kurush is no longer on Phaedros.'

'Who is it?' called out one of the gardeners.

Lorenzo looked at the screen and turned the volume back up. A photo of the suspect appeared.

'The accused is Kyra Margarita's brother-in-law, Vasilis Kapakis. Emilio's uncle by marriage.'

The room filled with sighs, shuffling feet and muttered disbelief. Maryam stood abruptly, her instinct telling her to run. Her heart sank. *That poor family.* She had met Vasilis at the Politis home for lunch in August, remembering him as quiet and fond of beer.

'As you can understand, this is a difficult time for the family. Do not say anything to the media,' Lorenzo stressed. 'The expo has made many people curious about Phaedros. They will be fishing for any information they can get.'

Maryam couldn't help noticing Lorenzo's eyes pause on her. She and Kurush had become known as the 'survivors', gaining much unwanted media attention for weeks after the capsizing. With the presence of journalists and cameras imminent, she felt certain she would be targeted—that the story would be focused on refugees. The growing hatred towards refugees in Lesbos had turned Greek compassion on its head.

'Are you alright, Maryam?' Anna asked, interrupting her thoughts.

Maryam's eyes filled with tears as she reached for another tissue. A wall of shame closed around her. She sensed everyone's attention shift towards her, as if she were complicit in the murder. Paranoia gripped her; if tourists stopped coming, her colleagues would lose their jobs. And what about Emilio? *Good, decent people, ruined by refugees.*

Unable to contain her tears, she ran out the door and down the corridor to the bathroom, locking herself in a cubicle. Slumped over the toilet, she vomited, then flushed and flushed to drown out her wailing. She wished the toilet would suck her down and expel her into the sea where she belonged. Anna knocked loudly, calling for her to come out. Wiping her face with the saturated apron, Maryam took deep breaths to steady herself. Another knock followed—louder this time. It was Emilio.

'Maryam, please come out. No one else is here but me. I swear. Please! I have sent Anna away.'

Her face flushed with embarrassment. 'Emilio. Please, let me be.'

'I am so sorry. I wanted to tell you myself. Please come out.'

Her boss, her saviour—and now what? She couldn't categorise what he was to her anymore. An admirer? A gentleman friend? Whatever he was, he now stood at the toilet door. Could it get any worse?

'Emilio, please! I need to be alone.'

'Take your time. I'll wait outside until you're ready.'

She knew there was no escaping him. He would wait, no matter how long it took. This had to end. The last thing she wanted was to humiliate him as well.

She got up, unlocked the door, splashed cool water on her face, hoping it would clear away the guilt and paranoia. She dried her face with the air dryer, the echo of the turbulent, hot air filling the white room. Removing her apron, she dried that as well, aware that she was prolonging her exit. She adjusted her headscarf and opened the door.

Emilio immediately hugged her. 'I'm so sorry this is happening,' he whispered in her ear. She was conscious of his hold, especially the fear that someone would see them. He took her hand and led her down the corridor, out of the building to his office next door.

'Emilio, I need to go back to work. My trolley is still in the storeroom.'

'Forget the trolley. I've already told Lorenzo you're not working today.'

Inside his office, he quickly opened the window. The smell of cigarettes hung heavily in the air. Emilio grabbed the crystal ashtray full of cigarette butts from his desk and threw it in the bin. She knew he had been trying to quit and blamed herself for his relapse.

He tapped on his mobile, calling the concierge and the customer service manager to check on communications with the guests. He raised his voice several times, and his intermittent glances at her were unsettling. If only she could disappear forever. When he finished, he sat beside her at the glass table. She could see her legs shaking through the glass.

'Are you okay?' he asked, reaching across to hold her hand.

She turned to him but avoided his eyes. 'Emilio, I had nothing to do with Kurush's murder. That poor boy!'

'Of course you didn't. I know you didn't. Why would you think that?'

A sudden gust of wind billowed the floor-length sheer curtains, making them appear like voluminous ghosts. Maryam felt the urge to get up, but Emilio beat her to it, tying back the fabric with the window sash. Another gust swept through—fiercer—scattering papers from the desk and flinging Maryam's headscarf onto the top of the bookshelf. Emilio retrieved it while she gathered the papers from the floor, securing them on the desk with his used coffee mug.

For the first time since the capsizing, he saw her without the headscarf. He handed it back, but she decided not to put it back on; instead, she stuffed it in the pocket of her uniform and sat down at the table. With trembling hands, she removed the loosened bobby pins, releasing black hair that fell past her shoulders.

'The season of the winds has started,' he said, sitting beside her.

She noticed him watching her hair. In that moment, she felt disconnected from herself, unwilling to return to the woman she had grown to despise. His hand searched for hers and gently clasped it. Maryam's heart was racing.

'Emilio, I don't think I can attend Anna's farewell. I feel so terrible about it. She has been so good to me, and I will miss her with all my heart. But I can't face anyone today. And if I don't go, I know I'll regret it.'

'I'll come with you. I don't want what has happened to ruin her day or yours. In moments like these, we need to focus on the positive. I know she thinks the world of you. So do I. We'll go together.'

She felt herself falling into a deep well. Moving closer towards her, shoulders touching, he gently took her hand, brought it to his mouth and kissed it.

'Everything will be alright. You just need to trust me.'

It was the first time he had been intimate with her. She wondered whether the gesture was sensuous or one filled with pity. She didn't retract her hand. She understood that he was there for her, whether she wanted his help or not. Through a slow, reluctant process, she had eventually become dependent on him for everything.

***

Two weeks earlier, the small village on the island's northern tip had been celebrating its patron saint, Pelagia the Righteous. Aphrodite had called Maryam, insisting she accompany her and Hossein to the paniyiri, arguing that everyone needed a break from the expo preparations. There was no mention of Emilio. Maryam assumed he'd be too busy but held a slight suspicion that he'd be there.

Entering the village square, she saw him sitting alone at a table, scrolling through his phone. Dressed casually in a blue T-shirt and white shorts, he acted surprised when she appeared in front of him. He stood and shook her hand before awkwardly hugging her. His smile was sincere, and there was genuine excitement in his eyes. It had been a long time since she had experienced 'that' feeling—to be the subject of someone's gaze. It was a feeling she believed would never come her way again.

That night reminded Maryam of Eid al-Fitr, the end of Ramadan. Memories of her community celebrating the end of self-restraint and fasting flickered through her mind, but this time without anger, pain or resentment—only brief bursts of happiness. Even as she watched families laughing, dancing and singing, her heart quietly joined them; their fervent joy felt like therapy.

At the end of the night, it was only natural that Emilio drove her home. She had never sat in such a luxurious car before. So many coloured lights, and the black leather seats still had that new smell about them. A komboloi hung from the mirror, its amber beads glinting in the headlights of oncoming traffic. He played soft Western music and spoke about her future.

'Once you get your residency, you can arrange to have your pharmacy qualifications recognised. Maybe one day you can open your own pharmacy—possibly one attached to the resort.'

Maryam listened and politely acknowledged his ideas, though they seemed intangible. The burden of displacement made it impossible to imagine certainty.

She thanked him for the lift as he parked in his designated spot.

'I'm sorry for keeping you out so late,' he said as they exited the car. 'I hope you don't mind me sharing my ideas about your future.'

'No, I don't mind at all. I like hearing what you have to say. It helps clear my head.'

'Would you like me to rearrange your morning shift?'

'No, please don't.'

'I don't know if you'll see me much during the expo. It will be frantic. I hope you don't mind the extra hours. Please let me know if it's too much.'

'I will be fine. Thank you.'

He flicked on the alarm. It chimed a cheerful tune.

'Goodnight.'

'Goodnight, Emilio.'

Maryam looked into his eyes and felt trapped. All she wanted was to slip away quietly, but it was Emilio who turned away first.

***

As Emilio kissed her hand again, he started to shake. She felt so conflicted. Should she cry out? Run? Allow him to caress her? The warmth of his body comforted her. All she wanted right now was for someone else—Allah, Jesus, God or Emilio—to decide what's best for her. Whatever they wanted, she would accept.

He placed his arm around her. He smelled nice; even the trace of cigarettes was soothing. Bassel had been a smoker, much to her dismay, but that familiarity was now welcomed. She felt herself relax.

Forgive me, Bassel; I am lost.

Caressing her shoulder, he leaned his face closer. 'Ever since that awful day…I haven't been able to stop thinking about you.'

Maryam listened. Her heart was breaking. Unable to look at him, she turned her attention to the family photograph on the filing cabinet. Emilio as a child stood between his parents, while Aphrodite was cradled in Margarita's arms. Behind them was a doorway to a shop, and an English sign above reading 'Citizens Corner Shop'.

'I was only a boy when I came to Phaedros,' he said, noticing her gaze. 'For a long time, I cried myself to sleep. I wanted to go home—to our shop in Sydney. I hated it here. All these foreigners with their loud voices and abrupt manners. I was so angry with my father.' Emilio moved back, releasing his hold on her. 'This wasn't his island, yet he never tried to stop my mother from bringing us here. He loved that shop, and deep down, I think he wanted to stay in Australia, but he just followed her. I understand why, but at the time, I blamed him for not resisting her, for not putting me first.' Emilio dropped his head. 'Sometimes there are bigger things that need to be considered rather than one's own selfish desires. He's good like that. I wish I could be more like him, even though I still can't forgive him.'

She felt the urge to comfort him and stroked his back.

'You are lucky to have a father like Mihalis.'

'I know.' Emilio took a few gasps, then slumped forward, cradling his face as he wept. 'I feel so bad about what I did to him. I had no choice.'

'Tell him how you feel. He's a good man. He will understand.'

'He called me this morning, wanting to see how I was. I couldn't answer him.' Emilio's crying intensified. 'After all he's done for me to then treat him like that—to sack him? He made this place, not me.'

'There are many things I wished I had said to my father, but it was too late.'

'I'm so sorry. I feel like such an idiot!'

Emilio walked across to the open window and stared out. His solid frame appeared slightly diminished as his head sank deeper into his shoulders.

'I look at this view and think how lucky I am—lucky to have my family and a successful business, this beautiful island, wealth and respect. Then you arrive, in the most unimaginable circumstances, and everything changes. I think of your husband and daughter, your pharmacy and neighbourhood, and wonder: could that ever happen to me? To have everything you built and loved suddenly ripped away. Sometimes, I feel so bad for saving you, because instead of good, I brought you misery. I can't imagine what life must be like for you. I am so sorry my island has become your hell.'

Maryam moved to his side, threading her arm through his. For the first time, she didn't care who might see them through the window.

'Please don't feel bad, Emilio. Please don't. I can't take on that responsibility as well. What you did was honourable. In God's eyes, you are a saviour—putting your life at risk for others. Never forget that. And as for me, I live for my family; otherwise, they'll be lost forever. I live for them, and I thank you for that. Don't lose hope in me, Emilio.'

'No, no! I would never lose hope in you.' His voice broke. 'You are the most incredible human being. That's why I…I love you, Maryam.'

His gaze held hers—frozen. His words boomed in her head.

Her hand rose to his cheek, thumb tracing his tears. She felt him tremble beneath her touch. A part of her wanted to step back, seek protection in the misery that ruled her. But something inside her loosened, as if her restraints were no longer working.

Maryam reached up and kissed him. His declaration still made no sense, but his vulnerability and sincerity demanded acknowledgement. She felt his tears where their lips met, and then the taste of salt—first flinching back, she pushed through, unwilling to flee again.

She was not in the sea yet drowning all the same.

Her own tears followed, astonished that her eyes were still capable of tears. Immersed in the moment, she rose beyond the life that had broken her. There were no apparitions of Bassel, no shadows pulling her back—only Emilio's overpowering presence. She yielded to the warmth of his embrace and wanted it with all her being, accepting that she had taken a step that could never be undone.

CHAPTER 28
Aphrodite's villa

Angelo's crackling voice over the megaphone was a familiar part of Aphrodite's morning routine. Steady and reliable, his calls from the village square signalled her daughter to leave the house. He would wait patiently for all the children to board the school bus, knowing each of their names by heart. Once the bus recommenced its journey, so did Angelo, always finishing his egg run at Aphrodite's villa. That morning, he would have noticed Rika's absence.

Aphrodite wondered if he had found out about Kurush. Two days had passed since they had discovered his body. He never watched TV and she doubted the neighbours would have said anything. The locals usually refrained from telling him anything that might upset him. No one wanted to deal with his distress.

From her bedroom window, Aphrodite watched her neighbours, old Kaliopi and Polixeni, deep in gossip. They often stood by the pomegranate tree just outside her villa. This time they seemed more lively than usual as they kept crossing themselves, slapping their thighs and cheeks. Aphrodite felt ill, as if their gossip had turned the air acrid. Moments like these made her long for a life in a city.

Since settling in Melissani, Kurush and Angelo had grown close. They were neighbours, and Angelo mentioned Kurush's name daily, referring to him as 'The Musulmano'. Aphrodite occasionally spotted Angelo riding on the back of Kurush's moped (Harry's old motorbike) as they weaved through the village alleyways. Angelo rarely laughed, and those who saw his happiness cheered him on.

When Kurush got his new job at the museum, Angelo helped spread the word, bragging that his friend had become a policeman like Harry. While the uniforms of the two professions were very different, it didn't matter to Angelo. Unlike most, he thought it was fantastic news.

***

When Hossein first introduced Kurush to Aphrodite, she was captivated by his deep-set amber eyes, angular face and gentle manner. She knew immediately she wanted to paint him. Despite Kurush's initial hesitation, Hossein convinced him to sit for her, emphasising the honour of posing for such a celebrated artist. His limp and the story behind it intrigued her. With each sitting, Aphrodite drew personal details, deepening their connection. At the last sitting, Kurush revealed that his greatest wish was to bring his mother and sister to Phaedros.

When the painting was finished, she proudly displayed it in the café until Salome demanded it be removed.

'Kurush isn't happy about the painting. He's very embarrassed.'

Aphrodite was dumbfounded. 'I didn't mean to offend. I just put it in the café temporarily. Hossein never mentioned anything.'

'He's too shy to say anything to Hossein. He's his boss.'

'And yet he told you?'

'Don't tell him I told you,' Salome added sharply. 'He likes you and doesn't want to hurt your feelings.'

Aphrodite immediately removed the painting, feeling stupid for not seeking his permission. Hossein advised her not to bring it up with him as it would embarrass him even further. He was equally surprised that Kurush had told Salome. 'She would be the last person I'd tell. But they do seem to get on.'

***

Rika refused breakfast and sat on the settee, crying. She was still in her pyjamas and bright pink robe. Aphrodite grabbed a velvet throw from the box next to the lounge and draped it over her little girl, having convinced her to stay home from school. Aphrodite had to go and pick her up from school the day before after news of the murder hit the school grounds. Aphrodite felt awful for not having told her herself.

Her daughter's friendship with Kurush started during his first sitting, where she gave him tips on posing, staying comfortable and signalling when he needed a break. Rika, who had modelled for her mother many times, was glad to assist the nervous young refugee. His childlike traits reminded Aphrodite of Jimmy from the children's TV show *HR Pufnstuf*: his build, colouring and way of walking as if he might skip. She pictured Kurush with Freddy the Flute's golden head sticking out his shirt pocket.

Aphrodite thought about calling her café staff to take the day off. Opening the shop didn't feel right as all she wanted was to hide from the world for a day. Still, the baker had already dropped off trays of baklava and kourabiedes, and the resort's tourist bus was scheduled for midday. Having Rika help in the café might take her mind off Kurush. She loved working in the café and chatting to people.

Salome's affair had completely thrown her. There was no doubt in her mind that her aunt had seduced him. Kurush had a naïve sexiness about him. His youthful, high-spirited energy, politeness and beautiful skin would have caught any woman's eye. And her aunt's indiscriminate nature and desperation—along with his willingness to please—would have made him an easy target.

Aphrodite buttered the wheat husks and spread some of her mother's apricot jam.

'Just in case you change your mind.' It was all that Rika would usually eat in the morning, but she wasn't interested. At least she had taken a few sips of chocolate milk containing drops of Iremia, the elixir for serenity.

The sound of the front gate squeaking open put them on alert.

'Yia sou, Aphrodite. Aphrodite, yia sou,' came the cry from the front of the house. It was Angelo.

Rika ran to the door with a bowl for the eggs, her swollen eyes still red from all the crying. They had been waiting for him.

'Yia sou, Rika. Rika, yia sou,' he repeated.

'Kalimera, Thio.'

'Are you not going to school today? You were not at the bus stop, Rika. Why, Rika?'

'Good morning, Angelo,' Aphrodite called out. She noticed he had aged more in the last few months. His hair had greyed at the sides, and his belly had expanded further, partly exposed by buttons that couldn't meet.

'Good morning, Aphrodite. Have you got any rags for me today?'

He'd ask the same question every day, hoping she might have a rag to spare before the scheduled collection day.

'On Friday. Today is Wednesday.'

'Thank you, Aphrodite!' he responded, clapping.

He then carefully unwrapped each egg from its individual rag and placed them into the bowl that Rika held. She paid him the fifty cents her mother had slipped into her pocket.

'Why are your eyes so red, Rika? You missed the school bus. Are you sick? Are you not well?'

'Come in and have a coffee, Angelo,' Aphrodite said, trying to distract him from Rika. She knew Angelo's repetition was a sign of stress.

'Are you sick, Rika mou? Are you not well? Is Rika sick, Aphrodite? She missed the bus.'

'I am too sad,' Rika answered.

'Why are you too sad, Rika?'

Aphrodite squeezed in between her daughter and Angelo. 'Did you see Kyra Katina this morning?' Kyra Katina's house was diagonally across the street from Angelo's, and she was usually his first official customer of the day. Word was out that Kyra Katina was staying at Harry's.

'She wasn't home. I called and called, but no one came out. Kurush went to work because the moped was missing. He looks very handsome in his uniform.'

Rika was tugging on Aphrodite's arm, both realising he didn't know yet.

'Come inside for coffee, Angelo. I think I might have some rags for you to take.' It was a tactic to lure him in; he rarely entered other people's homes.

'Yes, come in, Thio,' Rika repeated.

As they walked down the corridor towards the kitchen, Angelo stopped to look at the painting that leaned against the wall of the adjoining room. It was Kurush's painting. She had left it there after its removal from the café.

'Kurush!'

Mother and daughter looked at each other.

'Angelo, I have some very sad news,' Aphrodite uttered as they all sat at the kitchen table.

Angelo's focus was still on the painting. 'It's not a very nice painting. He looks sad, Aphrodite.'

'Angelo, Kurush is dead,' Aphrodite said, taking hold of his hand. She felt it twitch before a strong jolt hit his body, his gaze still fixed on the painting. 'They say that Vasilis Kapakis killed him. He was buried yesterday evening.'

Angelo stayed silent as he tried to process the information, moving his head from side to side, glancing at the painting, then at Rika and Aphrodite. He found it hard to settle into a comfortable position. The crockery rattled as his knee shook against the leg of the table. Suddenly, he sprang up with such force that he knocked his chair over. Pacing back and forth, he started waving his arms about, muttering Kurush's name.

'It's okay, Thio Angelo, Kurush has gone to heaven. God will look after him,' Rika called out.

He then grabbed at his crotch and started to run on the spot. 'Toilet!' he yelled.

Aphrodite took his hand and led him to the bathroom down the corridor. As soon as he saw the toilet, he rushed in and slammed the door shut. A loud wailing echoed, frightening Rika.

'Mama, he sounds like he's in pain!'

Aphrodite held her daughter tight. 'He'll be fine, my darling. Just give him time.'

Angelo remained in the toilet for a long time, his wailing eventually subsiding to a whimper, then silence. Meanwhile, Aphrodite and Rika set about making rags for him out of old clothes they salvaged from their wardrobes. A sudden thud in the bathroom interrupted them, sending a shudder through Aphrodite.

'What was that?' Rika asked, frightened.

'Wait here,' she said, running to the bathroom door, knocking, screaming out his name, but there was no response. She tried to open the door, but it was jammed. Pushing with all her strength, she managed to squeeze through the gap. Angelo lay sprawled across the floor, his head between the toilet and bathtub. Slapping his cheek, Aphrodite shouted his name, but she noticed he wasn't breathing. Her heart raced and her mind spiralled. The neighbours would suspect witchcraft—she could almost hear Polixeni's voice already. Hossein was already at work. But her mother should know. 'Rika, call Yiayia!' Aphrodite cried out frantically. 'Tell her there's been an accident with Thio Angelo and to come to the villa as quickly as possible.'

Fearing it was his heart and aware of his long history of health issues, Aphrodite commenced CPR. The bathroom was cramped, and with Angelo's weight, it was hard for her to move him. She wanted to scream but didn't want to frighten Rika, who was on the phone talking to her grandparents. Angelo was starting to turn grey. Aphrodite began thumping his chest from whatever angle she could. Suddenly, she heard Rika cry out: 'Thio, Thio!' Rika cried. 'It's Thio Angelo!'

'What the hell is going on?' he yelled.

'Aphrodite!' Emilio called out from the corridor.

'In the bathroom!' she screamed back.

With some pushing and shoving, Emilio managed to squeeze in as Aphrodite lifted Angelo's feet against the door. Opening the door completely, he and Aphrodite took hold of each of Angelo's feet and pulled him into the corridor. A streak of blood marked the tiles behind them. Aphrodite looked down at her sticky hands, noticing the blood from when she lifted Angelo's head. A gash, probably caused by the corner of the bathtub when he collapsed, had gone unnoticed.

'Thank God you're here. I was trying to do CPR.'

Emilio immediately took over, thumping down on Angelo's chest.

'I came up to get some more things from Auntie's house,' he voiced between counts. Salome had moved into Margarita's overnight. 'I was just speaking to Hossein, and he asked me to check on you.'

Aphrodite was crying as she washed her hands in the bathroom sink. Rika, also in tears, approached her, wanting to hug her.

'Yiayia said they're coming.'

Taking her mobile from Rika, Aphrodite called the ambulance. Angelo's skin was turning a deeper blue, and Emilio, in business attire, relentlessly pounded down on his chest as sweat dripped from his forehead. The island's only ambulance was attending to a car accident on the other side of the island. It wouldn't arrive for hours needing to navigate narrow roads winding around cliffs. Aphrodite then called Peris and told him not to come in. On

Emilio's instructions, she rang the resort's concierge to cancel today's tour of her studio and café.

Emilio paused, pressed his ear to Angelo's chest, but there was no sign of life. Falling onto his side, Emilio tried to catch his breath before leaning over and gently closing his cousin's eyelids. In a soft tone, Aphrodite heard him say, 'I'm sorry, cousin. I'm sorry for what I said. You're not ugly. You're a beautiful man.'

***

Within thirty minutes, Margarita, Mihalis and Dimitri arrived. Seeing her son dead in the corridor, Margarita let out a yelp before collapsing onto him, sobbing so loudly that it startled everyone. Aphrodite and their father shared a silent understanding while Emilio looked confused, glancing at his sister, mother and father, trying to understand what was happening. Dimitri, dressed in his museum uniform, knelt beside his mother, trying to comfort her. Mihalis gently lifted Rika, whimpering, into his arms.

The front door suddenly slammed shut, as if the wind wanted to contain the privacy within the walls of the villa. Inside, an eerie silence reverberated through the long corridor. Outside, rain had commenced.

'Mummy! Mummy, I'm scared!' Rika cried, clutching her grandfather's checked collar, trying to climb down. Mihalis held her tightly, reassuring her not to worry; his tired, unshaven face showed a vacant expression. Rika loved her grandfather and could always be comforted by him. Mihalis gestured that he would take her outside.

'It's alright, my darling. Go with Pappou. If it's too wet, take Pappou to the studio. I'll be there soon.'

Mihalis carried her out, her sobs muffled into his shoulder. By this point, neighbours had already gathered in the courtyard, drawn by the commotion. Her father's yelling for everyone to clear out echoed through the villa.

Emilio approached Aphrodite, his eyes fixed on his mother. 'She never cried like that at her brother's funeral, nor her mother's,' he muttered under his breath. 'She didn't react at all during Christopher's. What the hell is going on?'

Aphrodite didn't know what to say and shrugged. He pulled away and leaned against the wall of the corridor, nestled between two of Aphrodite's paintings from her 'Ghost' series. These were part of her personal collection displayed throughout the house. In this pair, bold colours and thick brushstrokes depicted the faces of Irini Vlahos, Doctor Kaligeros, Mary and their three daughters. The paintings blended into a kaleidoscope of abstract motion and vibrant colours. There was nothing ominous about them—the life and energy of the ghosts framed Emilio as he stood between them.

Seeing her mother so utterly devastated sent Aphrodite into a panic. The woman who had always been so stoic and impenetrable now howled like a wounded animal. Aphrodite hurried to her side, wrapped her arm around her and felt the tremor coursing through her grieving body. Recognising her daughter's touch, Margarita immediately turned around, her shoulder-length grey hair now draped over her wet eyes. Aphrodite barely recognised her. Then, at last, Margarita spoke in a hoarse, barely audible yet deliberate tone: 'Tell them.'

Silence settled over the room as those two words sank in. The brothers exchanged glances, searching for a sign that perhaps the other knew something.

'Tell us what?' Dimitri asked.

Emilio detached himself from the wall and moved towards them, his eyes ablaze. For the first time, Aphrodite felt afraid of him. He wanted answers. Slowly regaining her composure, she stood up, walked down the hall, then turned around and beckoned them to follow her upstairs to her bedroom.

'We can't leave her like this,' Dimitri called out.

'Go with her! Please!' Margarita commanded.

***

It felt like a magnetic pull guiding her towards the sanctuary of her bedroom. Behind her, the old wooden stairs creaked as her brothers' heavy footsteps followed. Then, as if with the flick of a light, she recalled the moment her mother had summoned her years ago to unveil the truth about Angelo. It was a mix of déjà vu and renewal, as if the two time periods and emotional upheavals were finally merging.

Halfway up, Dimitri answered a call. She turned to see him murmuring into his phone, his voice hushed. He was speaking to Hossein, explaining that he wouldn't make it to work because his cousin Angelo had died. Aphrodite gestured that she'd call Hossein soon. She wanted to hear his voice too. Emilio trailed behind his younger brother, anxiously stroking his beard. He was sweating, and she could sense his heart pounding in his chest.

Entering her bedroom, she felt a sudden wave of calm. Morning light spilled across the bed where she and Hossein had made love overnight. She pulled the doona over the crumpled sheets and signalled to her brothers to sit. Above the bedhead hung another painting from her 'ghost' series. This large canvas showed a vast cyan sea, where tufts of waves bloomed into wildflowers, dissolving upwards into white clouds hinting at faces and figures.

Outside, rain lashed the windowpane; it was the first fall in six months. She shut it, wiped the deep sill with a handful of tissues and pulled up a chair to face her brothers, the Kleenex box cradled in her lap. Her mouth was dry yet her words poured out. When the rush slowed to a trickle, her own sorrow emerged, her voice hoarse and wavering, caught between confession and defence. The secret she had kept about Angelo's origins was finally laid bare.

They sat stunned into silence. She couldn't read their thoughts, only hear their laboured breaths and the dry swallow of unease. They had questions she couldn't answer, knowing that her inter- pretation of why they weren't told earlier would only betray their mother. Whatever she had endured, and the decisions she had made, were hers alone to tell.

Emilio slid down the bed and slumped onto the floor, sobbing. Dimitri sat down beside him and held him. Aphrodite placed the box of tissues at their feet and quietly slipped out of the room to check on her mother, father and daughter.

****

Once the ambulance had left with Angelo's body, Margarita sat with her sons in Aphrodite's kitchen, confirming all that Aphrodite had told them. Meanwhile, Mihalis had taken Rika back down to the resort for ice cream, away from the implosion. The rain had settled to a drizzle and the chill in the air had lifted.

After flipping the 'Closed' sign on the café door, Aphrodite retreated to her studio and called Hossein. He urged her to go to the museum, but she didn't want to leave the house. She didn't even want company. All she needed was a blank canvas, her palette, paints and brushes to purge the confusion and entangled emotions that had taken root within her. No elixirs. No chants. Only the raw essence of her being.

CHAPTER 29
Kamiros school hall, a week later

The mayor, tan suit clinging to his damp back, hid behind the red stage curtains, peering out now and then to gauge the crowd. Sweat beaded his forehead, his cheeks mottled crimson. He signalled five minutes with a raised hand. Onstage, Pandelis and Emilio nodded. As the audience settled into their seats, Pandelis took a call, leaving Emilio to study the students' large map of Phaedros hanging on the back wall.

The resort stood out as three white cotton cubes with silky-blue shapes for the infinity pools. Yellow twist ties formed the Temple of Artemis Ismene; tufts of green wool evoked the Forest of the Nymphs at the island's base. At the centre, a metallic cross marked Saint Constantine, and a brown button marked each village. The sea, fashioned from blue cellophane, teemed with pinned drawings of mermaids, birds and dolphins. Poseidon's furious face loomed over the Metopos Strait, while to the south, Artemis bathed in Butterfly Cove's lagoon.

The school hall seated around 220 people. Facing the town square, it stood out as one of the port town's most striking landmarks. Though still used for school parades, its main function had become a reception venue for weddings and christenings. During the resort's construction, Emilio funded an interior facelift, recognising its potential to host resort events, such as the antiquity conference and the recent expo.

'You feeling okay?' Emilio asked Pandelis after he'd ended his call, noting the editor's flustered face.

'I'm fine. Another media enquiry about the murder. And you?'

'Nothing like a room full of Phaedrians to get the adrenaline racing.'

Unlike the mayor, Pandelis was dressed more casually. His hair was stylishly cut, his sunken blue eyes radiating a mix of concern and curiosity.

The mayor had called the town hall meeting in response to the mounting hysteria following Kurush's murder. A news crew from Mytilene asked for an invitation. Pandelis and Emilio refused, warning they'd drop out if outside media were involved. After all, this was a community event and their only chance to speak before Pandelis left the island to cover Vasilis's murder trial in Mytilene.

Father Efthimios was invited to join the panel but declined. Days earlier, he led a moving service at Angelo's funeral, describing him as a lost soul uplifted by the strength of community. For the first time in years, the family gathered as a whole at Saint Constantine Church. Seated beside his brother, it struck him that it could have easily been Dimitri in that coffin. He glanced sideways at him—head bowed, curls slowly growing back. Slowly, he reached across, clasped Dimitri's hand, squeezed once, then let go. Dimitri flinched but kept his head lowered. Aphrodite, seated on the other side of Dimitri, leaned forward and smiled at him.

Emilio still wrestled with his mother's revelation about Angelo. He understood her need to shield them, but the sting of betrayal cut deep—a significant secret withheld by the very woman who raised him to value honesty. He reminded himself of all she had endured. She had survived and succeeded in a life that could easily have destroyed her. Now they were all together, all thanks to her.

***

Emilio initially refused the mayor's invitation. With elections just months away, he believed that a town hall meeting about the murder would be nothing more than a political stunt. But after his momentary meltdown to Aphrodite about threatening to sell the resort, she set him straight.

'Turn it around instead of turning away!' she yelled at him during a private moment at Angelo's wake.

'How do I turn this fucking mess around? Should I advertise: "Come to Paradisos, and I'll find you a cougar to fuck up your life?" And how am I supposed to turn up to Brussels as finalist? I need to contact them and withdraw. The only award I would be worthy of is Murder Associate of the Year. Better still, I could launch an immersive Mystery Murder Experience as part of the resort's entertainment program. That would be fun.'

'Don't be ridiculous! Use the media spotlight as an opportunity for marketing. You have a whole new audience—turn it around!'

'We've already had a twenty per cent reduction in bookings and six cancellations.'

'Well, get to fucking work, then! I've updated my website and traffic has tripled, and I may have two new commissions. People are curious—there's a new school of fish around. Cast your net wide, brother. I know this is all very sad and opportunistic, but do we really want the souls of the dead to take the guilt for this island's downfall?'

He knew she was right but couldn't accept it. Later that night he swallowed her elixirs, read the corresponding chants and journalled his achievements over the last twelve months. By the next morning, the noise in his head had dulled, but had not disappeared.

Emilio replied to the mayor's request and agreed to participate on the condition that Pandelis Milopitakis act as the main speaker. His news coverage of the murder had given him national exposure—Pandelis had become the new face of Phaedros.

***

Vasilis Kapakis had surrendered to police in Athens and was transferred back to Lesbos the previous day. Pandelis had been there for the proceedings and returned that morning. He shared the information with the Politis family, while Salome prepared to disappear for a while to a friend's holiday home in Crete.

Vasilis's suspicions were confirmed the night he followed Salome on his motorbike to the village of Kremasti. Instead of visiting her sick friend, she met Kurush at a secluded scenic lookout. Having seen enough, Vasilis returned home in disbelief and drank himself to sleep.

The next afternoon, Vasilis waited for Kurush to finish his shift at the museum. As Kurush rounded the bend on his moped, Vasilis rammed him with such force that he was thrown headlong into a tree. He had meant to make it look like an accident, but when he saw the extent of Kurush's injuries, he grabbed a rock and put him out of his misery. Hiding the moped off the road, he went home, washed, gathered a few belongings and told Salome he would be leaving for Lesbos the next morning to visit his sister. The trial was due to commence in a week's time.

The family was understandably shaken by the account. Even so, Emilio valued the clarity and sincerity with which Pandelis relayed the information. It was clear he had the family's interests at heart. His quiet love for Dimitri had also begun to soften Emilio's guard.

A week before Kurush's murder, Pandelis attended Rika's tenth birthday party where he spoke passionately about the island's ecological importance and its rich ancient past. Boldly, he outlined his vision of transforming the island into an eco-friendly holistic wellness centre, even citing Irini Vlahos's traditional remedies.

'It's gold. Imagine what you can do with the recipes: create your own brand of therapies and attach them to a wellness facility. I realise that topics on heritage and alternative healing will fall on deaf ears in the current economic climate, but we must plant the seed.'

Pandelis's impassioned plea moved Emilio. It was rare to find someone outside his family who shared his vision for revitalising the island, not that he had ever paid much attention to his ancestors' remedies. The recent expo had given him a new insight that perfectly echoed Pandelis's thinking. Like Hossein, this outsider was bringing some much-needed inspiration. Without hesitation, Emilio arranged for Pandelis to meet his marketing manager, determined to enlist him in drafting a new marketing strategy for the resort.

***

The evening meeting was due to start at seven. The hall was packed, with only a few empty seats. Policeman Harry sat at the front with his mother, Kyra Katina, beside him. She wore black and looked intimidating, her hand clasped around her walking stick as if ready to strike. Harry was in uniform and appeared agitated.

Mihalis Politis, dressed in a beige zip-up jacket, sat close to the front. He came alone as Margarita hadn't been feeling well. Angelo's passing had hit her hard, as if years of denied grief had finally burst open. Maryam was keeping her company while Dimitri had taken it upon himself to look after Rika up at the villa.

At twenty past seven, Mayor Poulos finally stepped out from the wings of the stage and tapped on the microphone. 'Kalispera sas. Thank you for attending this evening's emergency community meeting,' he announced as he dabbed his forehead with a handkerchief. 'This is an extraordinary turnout. We are here to come together as a community. The events of the past week have unfairly thrust Phaedros into the global spotlight. We are a community of hardworking, good Christian people who deserve to be truthfully represented.

'I have invited Pandelis Milopitakis, whom most of you know as our resident journalist and editor for *Island News*. He also hosts a weekly radio program on Radio Aegean, focusing on the culturally significant aspects of our region, which I encourage you all to listen to. We are incredibly fortunate to have him as a member of our community. He will be followed by Emilio Politis, who, of course, needs no introduction.'

Amid the applause there was booing, which Emilio anticipated.

A man shouted, 'You're our mayor. What are you going to do about what's happened?' It was Georgios Alexiou, the recently retired school principal and one of the more outspoken members of the Melissani community.

'Thank you for your question, George. As your mayor, my duty is to represent you, listen and understand your views.'

A cacophony of laughter and booing erupted across the auditorium. The mayor had recently lost favour because of his own public infidelities and allegations of corruption. Many suspected this was his last chance to redeem himself before the election.

'Please put your hands together for Pandelis Milopitakis,' the mayor yelled, causing the PA system to reverberate and then screech. He pulled his mouth away from the microphone and the feedback stopped.

Pandelis stood up, unplugged his fingers from his ears, and moved towards the microphone, careful not to get too close. He received a warm reception. For many islanders, it was their first time seeing the journalist in person.

'Good evening, ladies and gentlemen. The murder of Kurush Bassem was a shocking and unprecedented tragedy for our community. The previous murder on Phaedros happened before the War of Independence, when Panayiotis Sideris killed his seventeen-year-old daughter for eloping with one of the pasha's servants. Even during the Second World War, when the island was full of Italian soldiers, there was no reported violence. Phaedros has a long history of peace and calm.

'In the face of the economic crisis that has plagued our country in recent years, Phaedros has avoided the devastation that others have endured. I am sure you are sick and tired of the hostile and humiliating rhetoric that has seeped into the Greek psyche—the referendum, the bailouts, the austerity measures. We must look inward to this island, to ourselves, rekindle our motivation, rebuild our aspirations and, above all, instil hope in our children.'

'Our children know there's no future here!' someone shouted.

'They want to get out of here as soon as they can!' came another heckle.

Pandelis raised his voice over the growing rumble in the audience. 'What we have in Phaedros is something truly special. I say this without any local bias. As you all know, I wasn't born here. I don't have family ties. I'm an outsider, but I see the incredible potential of this beautiful, unique island, and that's why I've chosen to live here.

'The murder of a young refugee was a horrible, tragic incident. It was immoral and inhumane, and that's not who we are.

'Almost six months have passed since that small dinghy capsized in our harbour. What do you recall of that day, other than the cruel fate of those desperate people?

'Let's not forget, however, that Greeks are a population of refugees, whether it was the Anatolian Greeks arriving in 1923 or the Aegean Greeks seeking refuge in Syria during the Second World War. Yes, not so long ago, Syria provided refuge to our great-grandparents.'

There was murmuring in the audience; some looked surprised as they turned to their neighbours.

'As we did back then, we all came together. That's because we have philotimo—love of honour, or, as I understand it, doing something for someone without expecting a reward; doing something because it feels right. The philosopher Thales of Miletus once said: "Philotimo, to the Greek, is like breathing. A Greek is not a Greek without it. He might as well not be alive."

'The capsizing brought our community together to show the world our philotimo. It's time to do it again now that we are present on people's screens and in newspapers.

'We must unite and collectively restore our island's reputation with compassion, not hate and prejudice. Thank you.'

Pandelis sat down. Cheers and whistling filled the room. Emilio could see Aphrodite and Hossein standing at the back, smiling.

The mayor moved towards the microphone again, but before he could say anything, a woman screamed, 'Get rid of her!'

Another voice joined in, repeating the same line: 'Get rid of her!'

The woman called out again, 'Get rid of the Syrian!'

A few people booed while others clapped.

The woman continued, 'See what happens when you open your arms to Muslims? They stab you in the back, take your wives and humiliate you in front of the world!'

Emilio recognised the voice. It was Fotini Panagoulas, and she was back with a vengeance. He scanned the room to locate Eva. Andrew had texted earlier to say they were coming. Emilio spotted them in the back row near the exit, Andrew's posture tense, as if poised to lash out. Eva sat beside him with her head bowed. She had recently been providing pro bono advice on Lesbos, helping Syrian migrants with their legal entitlements. Her mother's Islamophobia had destroyed their relationship.

'Everyone, please! There is no reason for rudeness,' the mayor said tersely.

'Silence!' shouted Harry, standing on his chair, his bulky figure struggling to keep his balance. 'Silence. We are here to listen. Sit down, shut up and listen!'

The mayor acknowledged Harry with a grateful nod and moved his sweaty face towards the microphone. 'If you want to say something, raise your hand at the end, but please be respectful of our guests who have made the effort to talk to you.'

Emilio's blood was boiling. Pandelis leaned in and whispered, 'Stay calm and remain objective.'

'I'm okay. I just need a moment to refocus.'

'Ladies and gentlemen, please welcome Emilio Politis, recently nominated as a finalist for the 2016 European Boutique Hotelier of the Year and the mastermind behind the recent, and very successful, Beauty and Wellness Expo.'

Emilio looked up, smiled and walked to the microphone. The fanfare commenced—this time, the booing was louder. A scuffle broke out in the audience causing Harry to jump out of his seat threatening arrests. Kyra Katina also got up and waved her walking stick in the air. Silence fell.

The mayor immediately ran back to the microphone. 'Please! If this behaviour continues, I will have no choice but to end this meeting. Please be quiet and let Mr Politis speak.'

Emilio moved back into position and the mayor remained by his side, anticipating that he would need to intervene again. 'Thank you, mayor, Harry and Kyra Katina.'

The ripple of soft laughter filled the hall. Kyra Katina had momentarily broken the tension.

'I don't expect you to agree with everything I say or with Mr Milopitakis. However, it's important to think beyond personal biases. Phaedros must come first as a community. We need to work together towards economic stability for our children's future. I want to follow on from something Mr Milopitakis mentioned. Our generosity and concern for the victims of the tragic event demonstrated how rewarding it is to be humane together. Our spirits were lifted—we had done something good, together. We displayed our philotimo, *together*. We cared for the survivors and honoured the deceased. Let's not lose the pride we've gained, our sense of humanity.

'The mayor asked me to talk to you tonight to announce that we have a blueprint to sustain our beautiful island—its reputation and economy. We must ensure our visitors continue to leave this island feeling they have experienced something life-changing. We have so much: our history, incredible artefacts, extraordinary landscapes and forests, beaches, culture and cuisine. Where else in the world do you have so many wonders in one location? We live in a paradise most people would envy. It's all on our doorstep.'

'But we don't have the money!' somebody called out.

'How can we prosper when you give our jobs to foreigners?' shouted Fotini. The animosity in the audience was starting to brew again.

'We need the best people to create work,' Emilio replied sternly but calmly.

'Bullshit!' Fotini screamed. 'You rob our neighbours and children of the opportunity to work.'

From the corner of his eye he noticed Eva, her body half-raised in anger, trying to decide whether to lash out or not. Andrew sat beside her, trying to hold her back. The last thing either of them wanted was to steer the arguments towards something more personal.

But Fotini wasn't finished. 'Your Syrian bitch needs to leave. No more migrants! What's wrong with our own people?'

Some locals turned around to silence her, but others cheered her on.

'Is that why you're growing your beard? To look more Muslim? To win the heart of your domestic slave?' she hollered.

'Shame on you!' shouted the mayor as he grabbed the microphone to try to shut down the ruckus. 'Can I remind you that we have the esteemed Doctor Hossein Basra in the audience, who has done so much for our island, its history and our community. Please show some respect!'

Hossein looked very uncomfortable but felt compelled to acknowledge the mayor with a wave.

By now, Harry had stormed onto the stage and snatched the microphone from the mayor. 'Unless you all sit down, I won't hesitate to arrest you. I'll also ask Pandelis to expose your ugly faces in the next edition of the paper. Mark my words!'

With that threat, everyone sat down.

Mihalis then suddenly shot up. 'Can I speak, please?'

Emilio was taken aback. Allowing his father to speak would either calm the room or blow it apart. If he cut him off, it would look like fear, not authority. The room fell silent as everyone held their breath; the tension between father and son was well known. He recalled his breathing exercises and slowed his breath. *Let him speak. Grant him this moment. Don't confront him. Be supportive.* Aphrodite hurried to the left side of the room, likely trying to silence him.

'That's fine with me,' Emilio forced himself to say, looking to the mayor and Pandelis, who both nodded in agreement. Aphrodite stopped in her tracks.

'Thank you,' Mihalis replied. A council clerk, roving microphone in hand, quickly moved towards him as he stepped aside from the aisle to face everyone. Fotini's voice cut through sharply: 'You Australians and your money and your arrogance—that's what is killing this island.'

'*Us Australians?*' Mihalis said, his tone steady but fierce. 'Let me tell you about *us* Australians. But first, let's talk about us Greeks. For decades, we've lived with a sense of entitlement, perched on Mount Olympus like pampered gods, revelling in ancient glories beneath the Mediterranean sun. We're snobbish and arrogant. It's beneath us to do the menial work that others around the world shoulder—working long hours, paying taxes, building a country. As long as we can enjoy our souvlakia, ouzo and dance away our troubles, that's all that matters: a life of irresponsibility.'

He paused, eyes locking with Fotini's.

'Don't lecture me on arrogance. I could boast about my family's achievements, but you already know them. The effort my family has poured into this island demonstrates our dedication. Greece needs migrants—people willing to work, who have sacrificed loved ones for a better life. Why shouldn't Greece welcome such people? Look at Australia today. Where would it be without migrants?'

'You're all brainwashed!' Fotini shouted, her voice trembling with rage. 'You've been blinded by the Vlahos curse! Listen to his words, neighbours, and tell me they are not insults. What are we, ants? Are you just going to let yourselves be trodden on?'

The mayor lunged for the microphone, but Emilio gripped it firmly. 'I'm okay, let me handle this. Fotini Panagoulas, you are a danger to this island. Your views threaten the prosperity and wellbeing of this community.' He turned, gesturing towards the tapestry map behind him. 'Beautiful, isn't it? Made by the children. Imagine the pride they poured into it. But all you want to do is torch it, because that's the only outcome of your bigotry. You hide in isolation, festering in bitterness and propagate hatred from the safety of your reclusive existence. I'm sorry about your husband—'

'Murdered by a refugee,' she shrieked. 'Slain like an animal!'

'In self-defence, Mother!' Eva yelled, wrenching herself forward as Andrew grabbed her arm. 'When will you face the truth?' Eva tore free and ran out, Andrew racing after her.

'Your bitterness has destroyed your family,' Emilio shouted at her. 'Have you no decency or respect for your own daughter? Or the good work that she does? I will not sit back and let you and your toxic views turn this island to ashes, because that's what will become of us if we listen to such hatred.'

But Fotini was beyond restraint, her fury ablaze. 'May you, your father and all Politis and Vlahos fools be cursed! She spat. 'Ehete tin katara mou! I would rather see the Turks seize this island than have your family feed off the misfortune of its people!'

The audience erupted in shouts and boos. Emilio felt blood rushing to his face. Clenching his fists, he resisted the urge to stage-dive on top of her. Instead, he thought of Brussels, imagining himself drafting the withdrawal email. Europe's view of the island would be farcical after this gets out. He was well and truly over trying to sanitise the island. For what? European accolade? The way they had shat on them only to turn around and award them in some patronising gesture.

Most of the audience were on their feet, howling for her to get out. The reference to a Turkish invasion was the last straw. Emilio willingly handed over the microphone to the mayor.

'Enough! Quiet, please. What are we? Animals?'

Harry Drivas was moving between the seats, heading for Fotini. But she had already sensed the crowd turning against her and ran out, ranting, 'The Australians want to control all of you. They want the island for themselves so they can convert you all to Islam. The Quran will soon replace the Bible, and mosques will replace our churches. Beware, people, protect your Hellenism!'

The booing grew until Harry screamed at the top of his voice for everyone to shut up. His fury silenced the room.

Emilio seized on Harry's outburst as an opportunity to bring the assembly to a close. 'I apologise for what has happened. I want to make it clear: I run a professional, international business, and I employ the best people I can get my hands on—always with this island's reputation, prosperity and future in mind. And before we finish, I want to recognise my father—until now a silent hero. What we did out there, and what many others did that morning, was put our lives at risk to save those people. My father held a dead child as its mother came back to life. He comforted her—a stranger—with the compassion he would give to his own child. Those people were victims, not the enemy!'

The audience clapped half-heartedly for Mihalis, many, no doubt, insulted by his criticisms, but he didn't seem to care.

Aphrodite stood tall in the aisle, applauding with pride for both her father on the floor and her brother on stage.

For the last segment of the evening, Emilio outlined his intention to unveil the resort's marketing strategy in the months ahead. Though deflated and hurt, he knew this wasn't a moment to collapse. Looking around, he saw his father, eagerly waiting to listen, his hands clasped in anticipation and pride. Emilio promised to present the plan, co-authored by Pandelis Milopitakis, to the council. It was a vision for them all.

Harry and Kyra Katina took the lead by clapping and cheering, and soon others followed. Even Father Efthimios, ever measured, crossed the aisles to shake Mihalis's hand.

PART 7
PARADISE

CHAPTER 30
Paradisos II resort, January 2016

The 11 a.m. ferry from Lesbos was scheduled to bring Mr Vladimir Karatsigiannis, an immigration official, to Phaedros. His call the week before had taken her by surprise. He sounded very young and very nice, not the tone she was expecting. She initially thought someone had dialled her by mistake, but when he repeated her name, 'Mrs Maryam Hamoud', it took her a moment to acknowledge that he had the right person.

She doubted the renewed interest in her case was coincidental. The media frenzy surrounding Kurush's murder had likely reminded authorities that another refugee quietly existed on the island. Even though three months had passed since then, the recent call indicated she was no longer invisible. A meeting to address her status had been arranged and she was invited to bring a support person. Emilio reassured her that she had no reason to worry; he would be at her side.

It was a day of sporadic rain and roaring winds. Winter had gripped the island. The low tourist season had brought with it a subdued, almost sombre air. Though still fully booked, the resort seemed empty. She was still working her usual hours but had been granted the day off to meet with Mr Karatsigiannis.

Rising at her usual hour, she brewed chamomile tea, adding a few drops of the amber elixir Aphrodite had gifted her. Long conversations with Aphrodite about the remedies had rekindled her interest in pharmacology. With Aphrodite's blessing, she pored over Irini Vlahos's manuscript, analysing each elixir, intrigued by the choice of herbs and their precise proportions. She tried to imagine the women, centuries ago, using crude means to compound natural ingredients into something therapeutic. Not that it mattered anymore. Just as she believed she'd never marry and be a mother again, Maryam had accepted her career as a pharmacist was over. Nevertheless, it was a pleasant detour, a reminder of what it felt like to use her mind with purpose.

Over the past month, she had finally eased herself off the antidepressant, guided by the doctor and the cocktail of elixirs Aphrodite had prepared for her. The fog that had drained all motivation was beginning to lift. Her appetite had returned, her energy no longer felt rationed and sleep came more willingly. Yet her mood swung unpredictably, and anxiety surfaced in sudden, unwelcome spikes. Even so, she was starting to feel more in command of her thoughts and actions—a fragile step towards herself again.

While waiting to be called by reception to meet her visitor, Maryam spent the morning cleaning. Cleaning usually eased her nerves, and though everything was already spotless, this time she went deeper—pulling everything out from the kitchen and bathroom cabinets, scrubbing the hidden corners and cavities with bleach.

She had tried to make her studio apartment as homely as possible, but there was only so much one could do when arriving with nothing. No family photos, no trinkets, no heirlooms or embroidered doilies and tablecloths lovingly made by the women in her past. All the hours spent crafting those items wasted. For the first time since the tragedy, she longed for something of her past to hold onto or look at. At least she had Bassel's oud, thanks to Kurush. Though it was water-damaged and swollen along the neck, she cherished it, polishing it each day and occasionally letting her fingers strum across its rusty, out-of-tune strings.

***

The landline rang just after midday; it was reception, announcing Mr Karatsigiannis's arrival. The ferry had been delayed because of the weather, and rain still fell heavily against her window. She reached for her mobile, hands trembling slightly, and called Emilio to update him. Hearing his voice calmed her as he told her to breathe, assuring her that everything would be alright.

Standing before the mirror, Maryam draped Anna's soft emerald-green scarf around her shoulders. She gifted it to Maryam before returning to Albania. Maryam hoped her friend's scent might channel her feisty energy. But the longer she stared at her reflection, the more disenchanted she became. Frustrated, she tugged the scarf free and replaced it with her hijab. She needed to remind herself of where she came from and that she was still Mrs Hamoud.

Moving quickly through the grounds towards reception, she waved at Lorenzo who was chatting to some of the gardeners. They were huddled under a veranda having a smoke while waiting for the rain to pass. He gave her a smile, then a wink with a thumbs up, wishing her luck. The cold snap had hit hard, yet he refused to wear a cap. Anna always went on about how he loved his bald head.

'Hello. Mr Karatsigiannis?' Maryam asked the man sitting in the reception area.

'Mrs Hamoud. Nice to meet you.'

He got up and they shook hands. The young man was clean-cut and sprightly for someone of his profession. Wearing a padded vest over a checked shirt and khaki trousers and carrying a backpack, he looked more like a tourist than a government official.

'I am so sorry about the delay. There was a possibility they would cancel because of the seas today.'

'Are you alright?'

'Yes, luckily I took my travel calm lollies. Helps somewhat. Those poor people didn't do so well,' he said, referring to a group of

American tourists at the reception desk. One woman complained of seasickness and how her luxury getaway had been ruined.

'Is there somewhere we could talk privately?' he asked.

'Yes. In my office,' Emilio interrupted as he approached them. 'Emilio Politis. I'm the owner of the resort. Maryam has asked me to be her support person for this meeting.'

'Pleased to meet you, Mr Politis. Vladimir Karatsigiannis.'

The men shook hands.

'Please follow me,' Emilio said.

Vladimir and Maryam trailed behind Emilio as he sped through the back of the reception to the building next door.

'This is a beautiful resort. I've heard so much about it.'

'Thank you. I understand you have accommodation arranged?'

'At the Poseidon.'

'It's a decent hotel. Desar is a good man. He once worked here many years ago. An Albanian migrant. Vladimir? It's Russian?'

'Yes, my mother is Russian. She was a migrant and a cleaner in a resort on Crete for many years.'

Maryam studied the young man. She liked him; there was a gentle and polite nature about him that put her at ease. She tried to imagine his mother and the life she was leading, unable to help thinking of the similarities. 'Where is your mother now? Is she back in Rus—' She stopped herself, surprised at her inquisition. 'I'm sorry. That's none of my business.'

'No, no. She is still here, married to my father and living in Crete.'

'She married a Greek man?'

'She certainly did,' he chuckled. 'They run a taverna in Chania.'

Entering Emilio's office, Maryam noticed it was clean and orderly. The cushions were neatly arranged on the settee and the usual smell of cigarettes was absent, replaced instead by a subtle hint of citrus from the diffuser on top of the filing cabinet.

'Do you prefer we speak in English or Arabic?' Vladimir asked Maryam.

'You speak Arabic?, she asked.

'French too, but my English is far better.'

'English is good for me,' Maryam answered.

'A drink? Coffee? Soft drink?' Emilio offered as they sat at the round glass table in the middle of the room.

'A metrio coffee would be perfect, thank you,' Vladimir replied.

Maryam shook her head.

'I'll be back soon,' said Emilio, getting up. 'Give you both a few minutes alone.'

Once the office door clicked shut, Vladimir offered a gentle nod. 'Your boss seems like a nice man.'

'He is. He's the one who saved me.'

'Oh, I see. I'm so sorry for your loss. I have studied your case, and unfortunately, it's a tragedy I see far too often.'

'There are many like me?' Maryam asked.

'Sadly, yes.'

Maryam shuffled in her seat, feeling pity for the young man, wondering how he could do such a job.

'Well, I'm happy to hear that the locals have been hospitable and that you have found work—that's very rare.'

'Emilio and his family have been very good to me. Without them…I honestly can't imagine where I'd be.'

Vladimir reached into his backpack and pulled out a small notebook along with a set of coloured plastic sleeves. From the inside pocket of his jacket, he retrieved a pen and clicked it open. With Emilio out of the room, he gently proceeded to ask about the nature of her employment. Was she happy? Was she being paid appropriately? Did she feel pressured to work beyond what was expected?

Maryam answered his questions carefully as he took detailed notes. As she described her situation, her experiences and the family's generosity, she sensed a swell of emotions – sadness, acceptance, grief, gratitude, anger and hurt. Emilio had already placed a box of tissues on the table (he knew her too well), and she grabbed a few and wiped her eyes.

'Take your time, Mrs Hamoud.'

To change the mood, Vladimir quizzed her with trivial questions about her cleaning style, sharing a story about his mother's annoying quirks.

'She was obsessed with cleaning vinegar. Every lunchtime when I got home from school, I could never tell if she had made a salad or cleaned the kitchen. Now, I can't even have vinegar in my salad without feeling like something's been scrubbed spotless.'

Maryam laughed, conscious that she herself may still smell of bleach from the morning's clean.

Emilio gently knocked on the door. Maryam jumped up to open it. In his hands was a tray with two coffees, three glasses of water and a plate of baklava and dried biscuits.

They all paused to eat, drink and engage in small talk. Emilio shared stories from his postgraduate studies in Milan and snippets of his childhood in Australia. Vladimir recounted his time in Paris. The focus remained firmly on the men, and Maryam felt a sense of relief—a welcome respite from the probing questions. At the same time, she enjoyed the new insights into Emilio's life. She knew of his studies but had heard little about his childhood in Australia, a subject he seldom discussed, unlike his father, who often talked about it. But before long, the attention shifted back to Maryam.

'Tell me about your grandparents.'

'My grandparents?' she repeated, somewhat surprised. 'Of course. So, my grandparents, Saib and Hanna Chehab, were lawyers. As Maronite Christians, they escaped from Lebanon to Aleppo in 1975, where they established a successful legal practice serving Maronite immigrants. My father, George, was sixteen at the time.'

Emilio leaned forward to listen. She had spoken little to him about her extended family, and he never pressured her. But now, she wanted to share.

'My father studied medicine at Damascus where he met and fell in love with my mother, Yara, a neighbour and teacher who taught history at a local school. Her family were Alawite Syrians and opposed the relationship. My mother, being stubborn and strong-willed, resigned from her school and went to Aleppo and married my father.'

Maryam's voice softened. 'There were two of us: my brother, Elias, and me. He was destined to become a heart surgeon like our father but died young in a road accident.' Maryam drew a deep breath and shut her eyes as she tried to block out the memory. 'My father didn't survive that loss. His heart failed not long after.'

She took another breath then opened her eyes, the whites of her eyes tinted red.

'My mother found her way back to Islam after that, rediscovering the beauty and comfort in the words of the Quran. She would read passages to me, and together we immersed ourselves in the scriptures on grief and loss. She passed away some months after my wedding.'

Maryam wept as she recounted the story. Losing Bassel and Maya had temporarily overshadowed the grief of losing the other members of her family. She felt guilty for allowing herself to forget them.

'And your husband? Where did you meet?' Vladimir asked.

'At the University of Aleppo. We were studying pharmacy.'

'Was he also from Aleppo?'

'Bassel was from the Sheikh Maqsood neighbourhood in Aleppo. His family were Kurdish and did not welcome our marriage either, even after I converted. Bassel kept saying they needed time…but time ran out.'

Her voice began to break.

'Maybe we should stop?' Emilio suggested.

'Of course,' Vladimir agreed.

'No, no, I'm okay, truly.' Maryam surprised herself with her willingness to keep talking. She took a sip of water to clear her throat.

'When did you and Bassel marry?' Vladimir asked.

'On 28 July 2012,' she said, her eyes fixed on some far-off point outside the window. 'We moved into an apartment my father had left me. Bassel and I took over the management of a pharmacy in Al-Jdayde.'

'And how did that go?'

Her gaze returned to the men, her face softened.

'A dream come true,' she said. 'We loved it there…its lively streets, the warmth of our customers. When I became pregnant, it felt as if everything in my life had finally found its place. But within a year, it all fell apart.'

Tears now fell from her eyes. She reached for more tissues, then drew in slow, deliberate breaths, fighting to hold it together. Emilio pulled his chair closer and placed his arm around her. He didn't care how it came across. Vladimir kept his eyes on his notepad, flicking back through the pages.

After a few moments, he checked in on her. Maryam was happy to continue.

'Mrs Hamoud,' he said at last, 'we have located some distant relatives from your father's side in Norway and a second cousin in Beirut. If you wish, we can contact them on your behalf. The International Refugee Assistance Service has also secured funding to help you migrate under the refugee repatriation plan.'

Maryam looked at Emilio, confused.

'Migrate? Sorry, I don't understand,' Emilio said. 'I—we— assumed that she would be granted asylum in Greece.'

'I need to provide Maryam with all the available options.'

'Of course. Sorry,' Emilio replied.

'Another option available to you is resettlement in Australia.'

'Australia?' Emilio exclaimed.

'Yes, that's correct. Mrs Hamoud, I can organise a visa for the Australian option immediately should you wish. Australia has allocated an additional 1200 humanitarian visas for Syrians.'

'But my family is buried here. No, no, no. I don't want to go.'

'It's a good option for you, Mrs Hamoud,' said Vladimir.

'Does she need to leave?' Emilio interjected. 'Why can't she stay here? Australia is on the other side of the world. She has a job here! Friends!'

'Is this something you also wish to consider, Mrs Hamoud?' Vladimir asked. 'Staying in Greece?'

Maryam didn't know what to say. She could feel Emilio's hand squeezing hers, his heartbeat racing against her shoulder.

'Your situation, here on a small island such as Phaedros, is unusual, Mrs Hamoud. Almost all support services are based in Mytilene or on the mainland. It's difficult for us to give you the help you need if you stay here. I recognise that this is a very big decision for you, and I don't expect an answer right now. Just know that you have options. However, I will need to know within the week so I can make the necessary arrangements.'

'I can provide employment and housing for Maryam,' Emilio added. 'She is a good employee and we want her to stay. Phaedros can be her home.'

'That's very honourable of you, Mr Politis. And, of course, this is an option for you as well, Mrs Hamoud. I just need to ensure you understand *all* the options available. The International Refugee Assistance Service will stand behind whatever choice you make. Again, I apologise it's taken us so long to get back to you, but I must stress this is a once-only offer. Borders in Europe are tightening, and our resources are stretched thin. Soon, those who can't be resettled in northern Europe will be moved from the islands to the mainland. Last winter, many refugees perished due to the bitter cold and inadequate housing.'

Maryam remained silent, stunned by the unexpected offer. She already knew Emilio's proposition, having spoken of it often since Kurush's murder. His kindness and security had kept her from another breakdown; his emotional support unyielding like a pillar of steel. He had saved her again. How could she now disappoint him? She returned her gaze to the window, unwilling to face the hurt she'd find in his eyes.

Vladimir gathered the plastic sleeves, laying them carefully on the table. Each sleeve represented one of the three options— Norway, Lebanon and Australia—clearly marked on a yellow sticky label. Maryam listened to the pros and cons of each, his voice monotone and professional, avoiding any intonations. When she asked about her distant relatives, he offered little beyond what he had already told her. She was curious but not interested; all those she cared about were dead. Besides, there was no certainty these strangers by blood would welcome her let alone sponsor her. The idea of Australia seemed absurd at first, yet Vladimir brought it up again, this time his tone more upbeat.

'Now, the Australian visa will give you residency and enrolment at an English school for three months. I understand you are a qualified pharmacist. You can also take a bridging course to get your qualifications recognised. Financial support is also available for this course.'

'What about a fourth option?' Emilio interrupted. 'Staying here? I'm sure we could try to get Maryam a job at the pharmacy in Kamiros. It's small, but I know the owner. We could come to some arrangement.' Emilio nervously stroked his beard.

'Unfortunately, Greece won't recognise foreign qualifications unless they originate from the European Union. For Maryam to work as a pharmacist here, she would have to restart her degree. Something she'd have to self-fund.'

'What if someone else funded her studies?' Emilio quizzed.

'You mean someone like yourself?'

'Of course. I've sponsored many migrants; some are still here managing various departments at the resort. Desar! He now runs his own hotel—the one you're staying at. We supported him. I was even the best man at his wedding!'

'Of course, that is also an option,' Vladimir replied cautiously.

Emilio looked at his watch and said he had to attend a meeting. Maryam knew that wasn't the case. She sensed he wanted to leave to avoid appearing too imposing. He was stressing; she could tell by his rushed sentences and incessant stroking of his beard.

'I will be fine, Mr Politis. Thank you,' Maryam said, giving him permission to leave.

'I won't take up too much more of your time, Mrs Hamoud,' Vladimir said.

'Nice to meet you, Mr Karatsigiannis.' Emilio shook his hand.

'Likewise, Mr Politis.'

Emilio closed the door behind him. Maryam knew he was upset and wished she could run after him.

'Mrs Hamoud, here is my card with my mobile number. Please don't hesitate to call if anything is unclear. I'm taking the ferry back to Mytilene tomorrow, so you can reach me with any questions before then. Alternatively, we could meet again—perhaps at the port, whatever suits you best. I understand you may be working, but this decision is urgent. You'll need to decide within seven days. Should you choose to remain here, I must notify immigration, and a different process will begin. It's best to scan and email the signed document with your preferred option; I'm sure Mr Politis can help with that.'

Vladimir glanced at his watch, his posture shifting uneasily. 'I hate to ask this, and I promise everything you say will remain confidential, but I need to know—are you being forced to stay here?'

Maryam recoiled, sinking back into her chair, shocked by the question. 'No, of course not!'

Vladimir's voice softened, apologetic but firm. 'Again, I'm sorry for asking, but you must understand—some refugees end up being exploited, forced to work with no pay, trapped living in terrible conditions and blackmailed into demeaning work. I am not suggesting that's your situation, but I need to ask. If it is, I can help you. You just need to be truthful with me.'

'No! It's nothing like that,' Maryam's voice rose, sharp and trembling, as though the suspicion was an affront. 'These people saved me; they housed and fed me. It's nothing like that. Nothing!'

'I'm pleased to hear it, Mrs Hamoud, and again, I apologise for having to ask, but it was necessary.'

She drew in a deep breath before pulling her chair closer.

'Are you okay?' he asked.

'Yes, yes, I'm fine, thank you.'

He got up from his seat, offering a slight, encouraging nod. 'Goodbye for now. Don't hesitate to call me if you need anything… unless you have a question for me now?'

Maryam's eyes traced the colours of the plastic sleeves before her. Part of her wanted to say no, to end this ordeal quickly, to retreat to the solitude of her room, crawl under her warm doona and fall into a deep sleep. But her mind felt unusually alert—as if the neurons, long dormant since the tragedy, had suddenly ignited. She drank from her glass of water and then stared at the folder labelled 'Australia'. For the first time in months, her heart no longer ruled her thoughts. A thousand questions exploded.

'Australia? It just seems so far away. I don't know anything about it.'

Vladimir looked at her thoughtfully. 'I haven't been there, but I understand it's incredibly beautiful and vast, and home to millions of people from all over the world. You have an amazing opportunity waiting for you. Some call it the "lucky country"—even paradise.'

'Paradise? Does such a place really exist?'

He shrugged, offering a hopeful smile as he left the office. Maryam closed the door behind him. In the heavy silence that followed, she could hear the gurgling of hunger squishing in her stomach. She hadn't eaten anything since the night before. Reaching for a biscuit, she savoured its sweetness, then drank the last of her water. She owed these people so much. The beautiful Aphrodite and generous Margarita, whose care and counsel had been lifelines in those fragile early months; Mihalis, whose daily smile and warmth assured her that she was welcomed. Then there was Emilio, who gave her hope of a new life and distracted her from the old one. But those distractions were reprieves from an unrelenting grief. If anything, Emilio's attention deepened her guilt. Accepting his kindness felt like a betrayal. And what about the perception Vladimir alluded to? Do people think she was coerced? That she was Emilio's captive?

Living in Phaedros had saved her physically, but emotionally, it was slowly killing her. The resort had become a bubble—safe yet unreal—shielding her from the outside world, one she never dared enter alone. Since Kurush's murder, the prospect of independence on the island seemed remote if not impossible.

Hearing herself recount the tragedies in her life made her feel small, even a little pathetic. Surely she had suffered enough misery for one lifetime. As she sat alone with the rain tapping at the window, she ran her finger along each of the plastic sleeves then stopped. A new distraction stirred—the faint possibility of returning to her profession and perhaps finding that elusive luckier country.

CHAPTER 31

Ancient Tallos Archaeological Museum, six weeks later

It had been years since Emilio set foot in the museum. His previous visit—to confess his love for Maryam to Hossein—had been nothing more than a hurried blur: no leisurely stroll through the exhibits, not even a glance at the new gallery he had sponsored. The ancients were mere shadows in his muddled vision.

That morning, he woke longing to lose himself in a world outside his own—anything to escape the tiresome merry-go-round of small talk with guests and the endless stream of instructions to his managers.

If Andrew had been around, he'd have jumped at the chance of a cruise toward a new sunset, a wish upon a shooting star. But Andrew, Eva and the *Grand Duchess* had moved to Naxos. Eva could no longer bear to live on the same island as her mother. After her visit to announce their departure, Emilio sensed she couldn't bear to live on the same island as him either. Though they had made their peace, Phaedros remained steeped in memories she needed to escape. Losing Andrew made his loneliness even harsher.

The museum felt safe. Easy.

Welcome to Ancient Tallos—a city of dreams. Once a jewel of Hellenistic splendour, its grandeur was tragically cut short by envy and ambition. What finally wiped it from the earth?

*A natural disaster? War? A curse? Pause for a moment. Close
your eyes. Let that world rise again.*

A close-up of Artemis stared from the pamphlet, her fierce
glare unsettling yet magnetic. Inside, a folded map promised an
adventure he was willing to follow. An encounter with the gods
seemed appealing. *Today, I am a passenger, and I am at your will.*

As he lifted his eyes from the map, 'Artemis in Chase' rose before
him, commanding the centre of the expansive, minimalist room.
The weathered marble breathed centuries of dishonour and revenge,
something his resort's replica could never emulate. Aurelius had
captured her in the moment after Orion's assault: calves taut, head
thrown back in defiance, one arm flung forward to summon her
animals, the other clutching her bow and arrow at her side.

Emilio leaned back, taking her in before walking around her
with trepidation. Tourists entered the gallery, whispering. A young
woman in white sat sketching on a small stool, framed by the
projected fresco of woodlands and rushing creeks that spanned
behind her. She seemed like an apparition, an accomplice to the
deity who had stepped from the painted world into this one. He
felt compelled to speak to her, curious to see her interpretation. But
how would he introduce himself? The gallery's sponsor? Brother
of the artist Aphrodite Politis? A rescuer of refugees? Victim of
unrequited love?

A tap on the shoulder startled him. He turned to find Hossein
dressed in a navy blazer and tortoiseshell glasses, wearing that
familiar, astute smile. Taller somehow, more assured, he looked at
home among the ancients.

'Hossein! I thought you were someone else.'

'You look deep in thought. I wasn't sure it was you without the
beard and in your Sunday best.'

Emilio felt weirdly proud. The once-shy archaeologist had
become wittier, more assertive.

'Time for a fresh look,' Emilio said, returning his gaze to Artemis. He had shaved his beard off that morning. His casual clothes—a black-and-white hoodie, faded blue jeans, white sneakers—completed the reinvention. 'She's incredible.'

'They say she was most beautiful when she had blood in her eyes.'

Emilio winced. 'I'm so sorry I missed the fundraiser…and the gallery's opening. That was so fucking rude of me.'

'I'm sure the gods have forgiven you.'

'Maybe so, but my sister hasn't.'

Emilio remembered the fundraiser clearly. It was when he'd taken off to Milan after the argument with Eva over the wedding date.

'Aphrodite's speech was a revelation,' Hossein said.

'I'm so glad I convinced her. She deserved the spotlight.'

'You did me a great service. We spoke for hours afterwards. I was so overwhelmed, I gave her the keys to the museum. "Come whenever you need the ancients to inspire you!" I told her.'

'And does she?'

'Yes. She and Artemis seemed to have bonded. Now that we're together, it doesn't feel quite so awkward watching her wander the ruins on CCTV.'

'That sounds eerie.'

'An artist's quest mustn't be interrupted.'

'All this talk about my sister and Artemis is making me edgy. I need fresh air.'

'We can walk the city if you like.'

'Don't let me hold you up.'

'A visit from a major sponsor is reason enough. Besides, the next coach isn't due for two hours.'

Relieved, Emilio followed him. His last visit had been a compulsory school excursion, remembered only for his prank on Pelagoula, a fellow student. Hiding behind a column, Emilio had bellowed, 'Artemis has chosen Pelagoula for sacrifice!' Her squeals sent classmates into hysterics and archaeologists rushing from the trenches. His furious teacher ordered him back to the bus. On the slippery paths, he fell and scraped his knee, leaving blood on the ancient pavement. It was an injury he often recalled with fondness.

***

Outside, the morning sun cast a golden haze over the ruins. White marble columns gleamed amid collapsed limestone walls. Emilio tried to image the sounds and colour of the ancient city, but the spell broke as a group of tourists crossed their paths. As they disappeared around a corner, a sudden gust of cold air brushed the back of his neck—sharp, intimate, like breath. He froze then turned. The narrow, shadowed alley behind him lay empty. Hossein was already several steps ahead.

'Are you sure there's no ghosts around?' Emilio called out.

'Why do you say that?'

'I just feel a little weird.'

'This is a city of possibilities. Be open to it.'

'That's not reassuring.'

'What are you afraid of, Emilio?'

'Pelagoula's ghost, perhaps.'

'Who?'

'Never mind.'

'Have you ever seen the tablet?'

'I never got that far during my school excursion. I saw the replica inside, though.'

'Let's go then. It's just up the hill.'

After passing the agora and following a dirt path covered in thistles and dandelions, Hossein pointed to a towering stone arch. Set into its wall was the Katara Tablet, far larger than Emilio had expected, nearly a metre wide and twice as high. Its weathered surface bore an inscription so sharp it might have been carved yesterday. Hossein stepped closer and began to read:

ΚΑΤΗΡΑΜΕΝΟΙ ΥΜΕΙΣ ΟΙ ΒΡΟΤΟΙ. ΑΓΞΕΙΕ ΔΗ ΤΟ ΔΑΣΟΣ ΟΥΣ ΤΗΝ ΦΥΣΙΝ ΑΛΛΥΑΣΙ ΤΑ ΔΕ ΖΩΑ ΤΑ ΟΣΤΑ ΤΟΥΤΩΝ ΛΕΙΧΟΜΕΙΝ. ΕΜΗ ΝΗΣΟΣ ΤΟΥΣ ΥΠΟΜΕΝΟΝΤΑΣ ΤΗΝ ΘΛΙΨΙΝ ΔΕΧΕΤΑΙ ΜΟΝΟΝ ΚΑΙ ΤΟΙΣ ΓΕΓΕΥΜΕΝΟΙΣ ΤΗΣ ΠΙΚΡΑΣ ΕΛΠΙΔΑ ΠΑΡΕΧΕΙ. ΟΙ ΑΠΙΣΤΟΙ ΚΑΙ ΟΙ ΤΑΙΣ ΓΥΝΑΙΞΙ ΚΑΚΩΣ ΧΡΩΜΕΝΟΙ ΑΝΔΡΕΣ ΕΣ ΑΕΙ ΕΙΗΤΕ ΚΑΤΗΡΑΜΕΝΟΙ

'She sounds quite angry. What does it mean?'

'Cursed are you mortals. May the forest strangle those who destroy nature, and the beasts lick clean their bones. My island only welcomes those who endure sorrow and offers hope only to those who have tasted bitterness. To the faithless and to men who pervert women, may you be cursed for all eternity.'

'It has a nice flow to it,' Emilio said dryly.

'As you come to understand Artemis, you realise her words were weapons,' Hossein replied. 'When we excavated the buried temple in 1995, we uncovered artefacts revealing the many rituals once performed to appease her. Nicephorus left us with an incredible library of information.'

'Who?'

'Tsk. You really must spend more time here. Nicephorus was a slave who sought refuge in the temple when the city was besieged. The earthquake of 306 BC entombed him, the chamber sealed so tightly that moisture and air could barely penetrate, slowing decay. When we excavated, we found his skeleton beside an extraordinary collection of artefacts. In his final days, he inscribed lead tablets with lyrical accounts of Artemis, this city, and of the royal household he served as both slave and healer. One tablet records his shame at staining the temple's marble stairs with the blood from his wounds.'

'His blood?' Emilio asked, feeling a shiver run through him.

'Yes, he was injured in the crossfire of the advancing enemy and took refuge in the temple, offering Artemis his services as a scribe in exchange.'

'Where are his bones now?'

'Inside the museum, carefully preserved. Once my paper is published next month, they'll be displayed at the entrance of the Artemis Gallery. Years of translation and analysis will finally be made public in a forthcoming book. It's a discovery of real significance.'

'Could I see this temple?'

'Of course. It's just a short walk beyond these gates.'

***

As the two men approached the temple, Emilio's thoughts drifted to Maryam. He wished she were with him to discover this place together, along with the other places he planned to show her— Butterfly Cove and Artemis's Bath.

Three weeks had passed since she left. Maryam had severed the tightrope he'd been balancing on and he felt as if he were falling— slowly, painfully—towards an inevitable end. He could see it, but it was taking forever to reach. Christopher and Dimitri came to mind. Was this what it had been like for them? The foggy dread of simply existing? A lethargy that not only shackled his legs but blackened thought itself.

He had wanted to talk to his mother but couldn't bring himself to burden her. Margarita's cancer had returned. In the past week, surgeons had removed her remaining breast. It all happened so quickly, so matter-of-factly. She had gone to Athens for her five-year check-up, and within two days, they were operating. Now in recovery, she was expected home by the end of the week.

The news had dragged Emilio deeper into himself. A gnawing guilt clung to him that his arrogance and failed relationships had somehow contributed. For the first time since the resort opened, he took leave from work. Days passed in bed, eating poorly, drinking, smoking, and long nights were lost to idle scrolling and fleeting online encounters. He even tried contacting Sabine only to learn that she was in New York with her new husband inspecting properties. Another person taking off to a new destination while he squandered in self-pity.

His father came to the rescue, stepping in as interim leader. Dimitri stayed with Margarita in Athens, calm and reassuring, bringing word that the cancer had been contained. During those dark days, Emilio returned to journalling.

He focused on Maryam, concluding that their relationship was chronically parasitic. They had been feeding off each other's emptiness, mistaking survival for love. What bound them, eventually, was intimacy born of damage rather than desire. And like any deep wound, it never completely heals; it leaves a scar, a permanent reminder of what caused so much pain.

Maryam had emailed him the day before—brief, almost clinical. She was living in Brunswick in a small studio near a shopping centre. She had just submitted her application for a pharmacy bridging course. She asked about the family, and he replied they were all fine. The last thing he wanted was her pity. He was truly happy for her. She deserved everything. That glimpse of her survival—her moving forward—had been enough to prompt him to shave, shower, dress and step out of his self-made prison.

Now among the ancients, the words of the stone tablet circled his mind. Perhaps he was cursed, Artemis furious over a childhood prank. *To the faithless and to men who pervert women, may you be cursed for all eternity.* Or perhaps she saw his adoration for Maryam as a form of perversion. That he trapped her for his own selfish needs. His blood on the pavement? Was this retribution? Had the cold breath been the goddess herself?

'How do I apologise to her?' Emilio asked.

'What do you mean?' asked Hossein, puzzled.

'To Artemis. I think I'm cursed. Surely, with your knowledge and passion for the ancients, you must believe there's some credibility to their ideas.'

'Well, yes, it was woven into their very psyche, mapped in their cognitive development. But I'm afraid my personal and academic interpretation will always be grounded in the objective, the scientific.'

'Cut the bullshit, Hossein. Just tell me if you believe that this thing, this tablet, has the power to curse.'

'I cannot answer that, Emilio. I do know that you are a good man, and what you've done for this island would be looked upon most favourably by the gods. You owe no apology. Remember the words: *My island only welcomes those who endure sorrow and offers hope only to those who have tasted bitterness.*'

Emilio took a moment to savour the sentence. Hossein's emphasis on 'sorrow' and 'bitterness' offered some consolation.

'We're here,' Hossein announced.

Emilio looked around. A large, rectangular metal platform lay flush on the ground, fenced off by a flimsy plastic balustrade. Hossein unhooked the chain around the small gate and entered.

'It's not yet open to the public,' he explained. 'We're hoping to install a clear resin walkway so visitors can see straight down without entering the chamber. But until funding becomes available, this waterproof decking is all we have.'

Hossein took off his shoes, swung open the manhole cover inside the gate, and slowly climbed down into the darkness. 'Are you coming?' he shouted.

'Are we going down?'

'Of course. Leave your shoes. We want to limit any foreign matter where possible.'

Removing his sneakers, Emilio climbed down the ladder and felt the temperature suddenly drop, carrying the smell of wet clay. When Hossein reached the bottom, he flicked a switch, transforming the darkness into an amber glow. Pausing, Emilio peered across the dimly lit chamber. An eerie feeling washed over him, as if he had descended into the Nekromanteion itself.

'My God! This place is incredible!'

'I've been here countless times,' Hossein said, a thrill in his voice. 'And yet each visit gives me a chill.'

Emilio imagined Hossein as Indiana Jones, waving around a torch, its intense white beam cutting through the amber haze, revealing murals and pottery. When his feet touched the ancient mosaic floor, Emilio froze, captivated by the vivid and intricate symmetrical shapes in deep blue, burnt orange and white, culminating in the fierce head of a bear.

Hossein's dignified voice guided him through the frescoes, the lifecycle of women rendered in pigment and stone. He told him about Nicephorus's painstaking inscriptions and pointed out where his remains were found. Taking Emilio by the arm, he led him to the chamber's centre where the empty podium of *Artemis in Chase* originally stood. Hossein sounded like an ancient priest chanting an incantation, his voice reverberating through the chamber, creating the effect of entering another realm.

A tingling struck Emilio's fingers followed by sporadic twitching of his toes, as if they were taking root into the ground, anchoring him to this underworld tomb. His head spun and vision blurred as he gripped the podium, knuckles whitening as his nails dug into the marble.

'I think I'm going to faint, Hossein!'

'It might be the air pressure. Sit down.'

'I can't move my legs!'

Hossein quickly grabbed a chair from the corner of the chamber and steadied Emilio into it.

'What the hell is wrong with me? Are you sure there's nothing… else going on in here? I've never fainted, and now I feel as if my head is about to float away, and my feet—like they're sprouting roots into the mosaic.'

He desperately wanted to stand up and get out of there but was struggling to regulate his breathing.

'Take deep breaths, slowly,' Hossein said, kneeling beside him and rubbing his back.

Hossein's calm voice barely cut through the white noise that filled his head. Emilio knew what was happening—it was a panic attack. Maryam's screaming and the howling wind now entered his soundscape. The lighting in the chamber morphed into the dawn light of that morning, followed by the sensation of currents pulling him under.

The present slid away. Another chamber. The water turned to cold air, knifing at his bones. He was in the underground cavity of Citizens Corner Shop. Spiders skittered over his skin, forehead throbbing after a knock on a beam. Fear and anger from a seven-year-old surged through him. How could his parents do this to him? Take him away from all that was good and drag him to the other side of the world where nothing felt familiar. How could they ruin his life like that!

Emilio squeezed his eyelids tight and blocked his ears with the balls of his hands. Beads of sweat formed on his forehead. A wave of nausea gripped him, his stomach churned until a surge of vomit spewed onto the ancient marble ground, splattering against the side of his jeans. Horrified and embarrassed, he fumbled for a handkerchief in his pocket, his head reeling as he wiped his mouth. He gasped for air, feeling the acid burning the back of his throat.

When the dizziness eased and his head felt reconnected to his body, he glanced down at his feet, half-expecting roots to have entrenched him into the floor. Instead, all that was there was vomit.

'You don't by chance have any air freshener down here, do you? Something to wipe away this spew?' But Hossein had disappeared. Emilio panicked. 'Hossein! Where are you?' he yelled.

'I am in the inner chamber! Coming,' he replied, storming out of a back room carrying rags and plastic bags. 'No air freshener, but paper towels and plenty of cloths. We use these to clean away dirt and grit from the artefacts. I am sure they will do the trick.'

Emilio wiped his mouth with his hankie, spitting the last bitter remains of sick into it. 'I guess there's no water back there in your inner chamber?'

'I'm afraid not, just tools. But I do have a flask of red wine, or... something like it.'

'Wine? Why the hell have you got wine down here?'

'Your sister was down here recently. I snuck her in one evening. She wanted to make an offering.'

'You serious?'

Hossein reached behind the podium and rummaged through a box. He drew out a tangle of necklaces and bracelets. 'Gifts from Aphrodite to Artemis...sister to sister. And here's one for her brother.' He handed Emilio a silver flask.

Emilio hesitated before taking a sip. He jerked back. 'That's not wine!'

'I believe it's something she cooked up...from the book.'

'Oh God, a magic potion. Are you kidding me? So my sister's down here serving ancestral brews to a goddess now?'

'She came a few times last week.'

'Last week?'

'She's been worried sick about you, your mother.'

Emilio forced a humourless laugh. 'Maybe she can convince Artemis to lift her curse.'

'Maybe Artemis lured you here intentionally?'

Emilio swirled another gulp of the solution in his mouth and swallowed. 'So should I be grateful to Artemis and Aphrodite for their intervention?'

Hossein shrugged.

Emilio bent down, scooping up the sick with the cloths, some of it on the remains of Artemis's left foot. He was utterly embarrassed and felt so stupid. 'Fuck! I just vomited on Artemis's foot. The last time I was here I left my blood, this time my sick.' He peeled off his dirty socks and threw them in the plastic bag. 'If she didn't curse me then she fucking will now. And on top of that, I'm drinking from an offering meant for her. Shit! I'm so sorry, Hossein. I hope she doesn't take it out on you too.'

'I'll be fine. But if I'd known this place was going to make you ill, I wouldn't have brought you here. I didn't think you were claustrophobic.'

'It's not that. It was just a panic attack. I get them sometimes, depending on the environment. Certain things trigger them. They usually happen at night when I'm trying to sleep. I've never had one during the day or in front of someone else. And of all places, a sacred chamber taboo to men. I've really fucked up.'

'Don't worry about it. Look, I understand things have been difficult. Aphrodite is worried. I hope you don't mind me asking but have you considered seeing a doctor?'

'You mean a psychologist?'

'Yes.'

'You realise we live on a small island.'

'Yes, but there are plenty on Lesbos or Rhodes.'

'I don't really have time for it, Hossein. Besides, I have been reading a few books, and there is so much stuff online these days.'

'It's not enough, Emilio. You've been through a very traumatic incident, and it will get worse unless you deal with it.'

'What about you? You were there. Don't you get awful feelings about it? Nightmares?'

Hossein's voice was steady. 'I won't deny it's affected me. But… other events in my life might have…I suppose, made me more resilient.'

'Like what?'

'A car bombing when I was nine. My father taken away and murdered. Fleeing Iran in the back of a truck, crammed in like cattle.'

Emilio fell silent. 'Gosh, I didn't realise. I'm so sorry.'

'But I'm okay now. I found distractions along the way. And pharmaceuticals. Did you never discuss medication with Maryam? Her being a pharmacist, I would have thought it came up in conversation.'

'Maryam had enough of her own issues to deal with. Besides, she was the reason I could keep mine at bay.'

'Having someone to occupy your thoughts certainly helps.'

'Like you falling in love with my sister?'

'Well, yes, you could put it like that.'

'I tried falling in love but failed.'

'You can't *try* to fall in love with someone. It's got to take you by surprise, not something you work towards. Do you think I tried to fall in love with your sister? She's the last person I'd ever imagine being in love with. I tried to fall in love with my first wife and failed miserably.'

'So you're saying that's the case with me and Maryam?'

'Only you can answer that. But you need help. Proper, clinical help. I saw a psychologist for years. Trauma isn't something you can lock away. It clings to you like a second skin. You've got to always care for it. You may think you're strong enough to contain it, but that's often an illusion. Look at Artemis—she was immortalised as someone who buried her trauma, and it twisted her into a life of vengeance. Yes, she was adored, but I wouldn't say she was ever happy.'

Emilio felt his chest tighten and a flush to his face. Was it the drink? He didn't feel sick this time, just an overwhelming need to spew words—a barrage of sentences soaked in self-pity. Not even with past girlfriends had he shown such vulnerability. But he didn't care. He was teetering on the edge, and an archaeologist was on hand to unearth what he had buried for so long.

Emilio recounted the rescue—the adrenaline, the dives back into the sea, the refusal to leave anyone behind. Even though he nearly drowned, he felt compelled to return. This was his home, and such devastation couldn't happen in paradise. The endless bravos that followed and the flood of media acclaim had made him feel invincible. And then came the silence. As more bodies washed up on the shores of Samos, Chios and Mytilene, the accolades for the hero of Phaedros disappeared. But what he couldn't extinguish were the images and sounds of that tragic event, etched forever into his mind.

With Maryam nearby, she was both anchor and lifeline. But with her gone, the scaffold to his pretend castle had crumbled. The confusion and sadness that had consumed him as a little boy under the family shop returned uninvited to claim him.

***

Back inside the museum, Emilio felt an urge to visit the gift shop, wanting a souvenir to remember his visit. After freshening up and rinsing his throat in the bathroom, Hossein gladly escorted him down the long corridor towards it.

'What are your plans for the rest of the day?' Hossein asked.

'I might head to Butterfly Cove,' Emilio said, the words daring him. 'It's been a long time since I've been in the water. I'll see if Dimitri wants to join me. Take him out on my new boat.'

'A new boat?'

'Yes. A reckless spend during one of my darker moments. The old one couldn't be repaired. Andrew organised it through his contact in Lesbos. It arrived last week, but I haven't set foot on it yet. Dimitri's never been to Artemis's Bath. Thought it would be a nice thing to do together.'

'It's good the two of you have reconnected. He seems so much happier these days.'

'Just needed to put things into perspective.'

'It's lucky you have a brother.'

Emilio rubbed his chin out of habit, forgetting the beard was gone. 'And a sister, a father and a mother. I'm very lucky indeed.'

'Maybe one day you can take us all to your little oasis.'

'Why not? Though it's not mine, is it? I just use that term to market my own self-importance.'

Hossein chuckled. 'Well, I hope I get to see it before it's too late.'

'Too late?'

'If Brexit becomes a reality in June, my tenure here may not last. Without EU citizenship, I'd lose this post.'

'Can't you get naturalised or something? Marry my sister— surely that would do it.'

Hossein grinned wryly. 'Strange times ahead, my friend. You're lucky you don't have to worry about such things.'

A sudden burst of voices echoed down the corridor. Hossein sighed. 'The first tour bus has arrived. I need to go. Our new security officer is on duty alone until Manos arrives. If you're considering a career change, I could use a few more security officers. Your brother came in the nick of time, but now he has bigger adventures ahead—Crete, I hear?'

'Yes. He and Pandelis leave once Mum gets back.'

'It will be good for Pandelis to have a change of scenery.'

'His cousin teaches history at the University of Crete.'

'Yes, Aphrodite mentioned it. Hopefully Dimitri will gain some inspiration. She said that he's considering starting his degree there?'

'What do you think?'

'I think it's a great option for him. It's a fine university.'

'They'll stay with Salome for a few days.'

'That will be good for her. She could use family around.'

'Thank you for pulling a few strings to get her that job at the museum.'

'It's not what she's used to—selling tickets—but I'm sure she'll step back into the limelight somewhere soon. Perhaps even back here?' Hossein said lightly as they reached the gift shop.

'I think she's well and truly done with Phaedros,' Emilio said under his breath.

Entering the small gift shop, Emilio was amazed at the range of souvenirs: large posters of Artemis, jigsaw puzzles of temples and ceramic mugs stamped with the Katara Tablet. A young woman peered out from the storeroom door.

'Oh, hello. I was just checking stock.'

'Iliana Venizelou,' Hossein said. 'This is Emilio Politis, Aphrodite's brother. Would you mind showing him our range?'

'Of course,' she replied shyly.

Emilio recognised her instantly. It was the young woman he'd seen sketching in the Artemis Gallery. Still dressed in a loose white shirt and baggy pants, she was striking in her simplicity: olive skin, jet-black hair pulled into a tight bun, gold-hooped earrings and a small stud in her nose. He guessed she was in her mid-twenties.

'Hi,' Emilio said. 'I noticed you in the Artemis Gallery. I didn't realise you worked here.'

'Iliana only just arrived from Volos,' Hossein explained. 'She's an archaeology graduate, and I'll be supervising her PhD. In the meantime, she'll be working at the shop. Emilio, as you know, is the sponsor of the Artemis Gallery.'

'Yes, of course.' Then, almost apologetically: 'I hope you don't mind but I added you to my sketch. I liked the way you were looking at Artemis. It felt as if you knew her.'

Emilio laughed softly. 'That's fine. My sister often sneaks family members into her paintings—some not so flattering.'

'Your sister's work is incredible.'

Her voice was deep, resonant—almost musical. For a moment he imagined her breaking into a bluesy rasp.

Hossein excused himself, disappearing down the corridor, leaving them alone.

'I feel rather stupid showing you around,' Iliana said.

'Please, the stupidity is all mine. I should know far more about this ancient city's treasures than I do.'

'Is there anything in particular you were after?'

'A catalogue might be a good start.'

'Of course. Our bestseller, apparently.' She reached beneath the counter and placed the heavy volume between them.

'Really?'

'All because of you.'

'Me?'

'Doctor Basra told me the story of your generous donation when you first met.'

Emilio flushed. He hadn't realised his donation had gone towards this edition. Or perhaps he had and made nothing of it. He felt so embarrassed having never looked at it.

'And congratulations,' she added. 'Doctor Basra mentioned your nomination for a travel award.'

'Thank you. Yes, that coming up in a few weeks.'

'That must be exciting.'

'Mostly for my father. He's never been to an award ceremony before.'

'That's so sweet. Correct me if I'm wrong but your father ran the original Paradisos Hotel?'

'With my mother. But unfortunately I can only take one person, and her health hasn't been great lately.'

'So sorry to hear that.'

'It's all good. She's a fighter. The strongest woman I know.'

'Well, I hope you win.'

'If I don't, I hope you'll still think highly of me. Assuming you already do.'

'Of course I do.'

'That's a relief. At times I wonder myself.'

As he flipped through the pages, Emilio couldn't shake his disappointment at how little he'd ever engaged with the collection. His sponsorships and donations had never been acts of devotion, only marketing. The aesthetic vision of weaving archaeological motifs into his resort now felt superficial. He lacked any deep-rooted connection to the island's past.

Iliana guided him through the catalogue, her voice illuminating each page. As he listened, it felt as though the story of Phaedros was being returned to him. And in that moment, Emilio understood that it took the devotion of outsiders to steer him back to the heart of his own paradise.

ACKNOWLEDGEMENTS

Thank you to all the people I met while writing *Paradisos*. Looking back, I feel deeply fortunate for all the generosity and encouragement I received along the way.

My thanks to Professor Reza Gholami, Doctor Andrew J. Bayliss, Doctor Archondia Thanos and Eleni Faltaka, whose time, research and insights during the early drafts encouraged me to pursue writing this story. I am also grateful to Tomas Watson and Cindy Camatsos for introducing me to beautiful Sigri and their art retreat on the island of Lesbos; I'm especially grateful to Cindy for her constructive feedback and editorial assistance.

My sincere thanks to my editors, James Bean and Craig Hillsley, whose craftsmanship proved transformative. I am also indebted to Fotis Panagou, whom I met in Greece by chance—or perhaps by godly intent—and who generously shared his professional expertise in contemporary Greek resort design and construction. My gratitude also goes to Panayiotis Ladias for his Ancient Greek translation. Thank you as well to Simone Ford for proofreading and Evan Shapiro for his design work and for bringing *Paradisos* into print.

I am greatly indebted to friends and family who provided feedback on drafts and pushed me to keep going: Doctor Sudeep Apana, Eleftheria Prodromou, Joanna Mantziaris, Elfa Moraitakis, Maria Lomis, Artemi Kokkaris, Elena Kokkaris, Seth van Mechelen, Alexandra Mills and Christiane Bradshaw. I am especially grateful to Michael Nest for his ongoing editorial assistance, heartening support and guidance throughout the writing and production of this book.

Finally, my deepest thanks go to my family, whose patience and encouragement carried me through the long and often uncertain process of writing this book. To my wife, Joanna, and daughters, Artemi and Elena, your belief in me never wavered even when mine did.

ABOUT THE AUTHOR

Bill Kokkaris is a Greek-Australian visual artist and playwright. His plays *Baraki*, *Night Journeys* and *A Lifetime of Summers* were produced by Take Away Theatre. Bill has also written one-act plays for Carnivale and Sidetrack Theatre.

In addition to his creative work, Bill has held roles across several New South Wales government agencies as an editor, communications manager and corruption prevention practitioner. He has had a longstanding interest in immigration studies and has collaborated professionally and creatively with migrant communities throughout his career.

In 2020, Bill received an Invited Residency at Varuna, The National Writers' House in Katoomba, where he completed the first draft of his novel *Paradisos*. In 2023, *Paradisos* was a finalist in the Eyelands Book Awards (Unpublished Novel category). When not writing, Bill paints and draws from his studio in the Blue Mountains.